WHEN IMMOR... [barcode] they cast their enchar... the mortal lands, be... own realm forevermore ... working mischief or wreaking vengeance on those foolish enough to challenge their powers. Now, thanks to the talents of those gifted with the imagination to see into the heart of magic, you, too, can make the acquaintance of elves high and low in such memorable tales as:

"A Midsummer Night's Dream Team"—It was the strangest Olympic competition Samantha had ever seen ... with a Dream Team that was spellbindingly great. . . .

"Home Key"—He'd been sent to the mortal lands to learn from those he considered beneath his notice, and though he'd indeed learned some surprising things in his years of exile, he was afraid he'd never discover the one thing he most wanted to know—how to get home again. . . .

"Elfarama"—Brian didn't think even magic could change his life, at least not until he met those fast-talking elves at the mall. . . .

Elf Fantastic

More Spellbinding Anthologies
Brought to You by DAW:

TAROT FANTASTIC *Edited by Martin H. Greenberg and Lawrence Schimel.* Some of today's most imaginative writers—such as Charles de Lint, Tanya Huff, Rosemary Edghill, Nancy Springer, Kate Elliott, Teresa Edgerton, and Michelle West—cast fortunes for the unsuspecting in sixteen unforgettable tales ranging from chilling to whimsical, from provocative to ominous.

CASTLE FANTASTIC *Edited by John DeChancie and Martin H. Greenberg.* Here are sixteen original stories created especially for this volume, from the final tale set in Roger Zelazny's unforgettable *Amber,* to the adventure of a floating castle in search of a kingdom, to the legendary citadel of King Arthur. Join such master architects of enchantment as Roger Zelazny, George Zebrowski, Jane Yolen, David Bischoff, and Nancy Springer on a series of castle adventures that will have fantasy lovers and D&D players begging for the keys to the next keep on the tour.

WITCH FANTASTIC *Edited by Mike Resnick and Martin H. Greenberg.* From a timeless coven gathering on All Hallow's Eve, to an old woman brewing up the promise of love requited, to a witch and her cat with the power to rewrite history, let such masterful magic-makers as Jane Yolen, Judith Tarr, Katharine Kerr, Roland Green, and David Gerrold lead you to the secret glens, the inner sanctums, the small-town eateries, isolated farms, and city parks where the true practitioners of magic claim vengeance for ancient wrongs, free innocents from evil enchantments, and play their own private games of power to transform our world.

Elf Fantastic

Edited by
Martin H. Greenberg

DAW BOOKS, INC.
DONALD A. WOLLHEIM, FOUNDER
375 Hudson Street. New York. NY 10014

ELIZABETH R. WOLLHEIM
SHEILA E. GILBERT
PUBLISHERS

First Printing, April 1997

1 2 3 4 5 6 7 8 9

DAW TRADEMARK REGISTERED
U.S. PAT. OFF. AND FOREIGN COUNTRIES
—MARCA REGISTRADA
HECHO EN U.S.A.

PRINTED IN THE U.S.A.

ACKNOWLEDGMENTS

Introduction © 1997 by Martin H. Greenberg.
Bard's Crown © 1997 by Andre Norton.
The Law of Man © 1997 by Michelle West.
I Sing the Dark Riders © 1997 by Dennis L. McKiernan.
A Midsummer Night's Dream Team © 1997 by Tanya Huff.
Home Key © 1997 by Barbara Delaplace.
Elfarama © 1997 by Craig Shaw Gardner.
Jerlayne © 1997 by Lynn Abbey.
Spinning Webs and Telling Lies © 1997 David Niall Wilson.
The Dancing Ring © 1997 by Jody Lynn Nye.
Sun and Hawk © 1997 by Jane M. Lindskold.
Eine Kleine Elfmusik © 1997 by Karen Haber.
By the Oaks © 1997 by Janni Lee Simner.
All That Glitters © 1997 by C.J. Henderson.
Jingles the Elf © 1997 by Richard Gilliam.
Images of Smoke © 1997 by John Goodnow.
Mercenary of Dreams © 1997 by Lawrence C. Connolly.
The Legend of Slewfoot © 1997 by Mark A. Garland
    and Lawrence Schimel.
The Girl Who Was Taken Into the Hill © 1997
    by Diana L. Paxson.
Changeling © 1997 by Mickey Zucker Reichert.

CONTENTS

INTRODUCTION

Among all of the faerie folk, the elves have long been recognized as reigning supreme over all others. Of course, it took them a while to achieve this status, having to endure such slights as the German folktales translated and published by the Brothers Grimm.

Most people will recognize the title of "The Shoemaker and the Elves," in which the elves mentioned are industrious and helpful in assisting a shoemaker out of poverty. Actually, there are two other tales of the elves in the translations of the Grimm brothers, one which tells the classic story of elves swapping changelings for human babies, and the other where a young maid is summoned by the elves to be a godmother to one of their children. She leaves for three nights, and returns home only to find that seven years have passed.

Then, of course, who can forget Santa's elves? Those happy-go-lucky little men with nothing better to do than slave away making toys at the North Pole until Christmas. Ruled by Santa Claus, a human, no less.

Is this what the elves of legend have been reduced to? Baby-stealing, shoe- and toy-making, and, when they actually do have children they want to keep, hiring human babysitters. Oh, how the mighty have fallen.

To really understand the majesty of the elves, one must look back to the 2nd through the 5th centuries, when the Celts ruled most of the European peninsula and the British Isles. Before the Roman conquest of the British lowlands, the Celts ruled from what is now Spain to Czechoslovakia. At the height of their power, they traded with the Greeks, and even sacked Rome in 390 B.C. Eventually, the Romans decided enough was enough, and gradually forced the Celts back to the Britain where they began. The Celts finally died out around A.D. 850, leaving a profoundly different world behind them.

Which is not to say that they died forgotten, however. The Celts shaped the European continent in many ways, including laying the foundation for the Middle Ages version of the faerie folk.

To the Celts, fairies appeared in many forms, such as brownies, korrigan, korred, and lamignac. Of them all, the most powerful and mysterious were the near-humans known as the *sidhe*. Regal, beautiful, proud yet mischievous, the *sidhe* were, or so the legends say, the rulers of all the faeries, and held their court in the magical lands in another dimension.

It is the honor-loving Celts that attribute the *sidhe* with their otherworldly beauty, aristocratic manner and playful sense of humor. It was said that if a *sidhe* ever decided to capture a man, he was as good as hers. Even the legendary hero Cu Chulainn was not safe from their charms. Ordinary men, however, would occasionally find a more dire fate in store for them, as tales of the *sidhe* also include tricks and betrayals played on their human lovers.

The elf is one of the few legendary races that is at once both very similar and yet very unlike humans. In many tales, they share our love of life, our curiosity, and appreciation of honor, manners, and sport. Yet at the same time their eternal life spans and the difference that brings to their culture make them forever apart, truly from another world. We aspire to emulate them, yet at the same time, at least in the Middle Ages, feared them for the powers they controlled.

In the stories that follow, elves are brought to life in a variety of stories. From the folklore-inspired "Bard's Crown," by Andre Norton, to a group of elves determined to prove once and for all who the real "dream team" is, the grandest of the faerie folk are waiting to dazzle, delight, and detain you . . . in the myriad worlds of the elves.

BARD'S CROWN
by Andre Norton

Andre Norton has written and collaborated on over 100
novels in her sixty years as a writer, working with such
authors as Robert Bloch, Marian Zimmer Bradley, Mercedes Lackey and Julian May. Her best known creation is
the Witch World, which has been the subject of a number
of novels and anthologies. She has received the Nebula
Grand Master award, The Fritz Leiber award, and the
Daedalus award, and lives in Winter Park, Florida.

Catlin shivered and pleated her shawl nervously between
her fingers. She noted that the two serving maids had
crept into the corner of the small bower as closely as they
could, away from the door into the great hall.

Another burst of raucous laughter reached her. There
was no way she could deal with this. Kathal, like any son
of Clan Dongannan, had gone to the High King for a
year's service in the Guard near a year ago. Now he was
back because he was the o'Dongannan, their uncle having
died of a rheum. But the boy who had gone away, as reckless and thoughtless concerning others as he had been,
was lost. That mead-swigging brute at rough play with his
cronies out there—brother or not, she could say nothing
to which he would listen.

In the meantime the whole of the valley was in disorder. There was no master to guide, advise, praise, or
deal justice. And the people had learned to keep as far
from the Great Hall as they could.

She raised a hand and pushed back a wandering curl of
hair, anchoring it again under her hair coif. So far—so far
she had largely escaped Kathal's notice, but she could not
creep around forever looking over her shoulder. Being of

the High Blood she could not be caught by one of those
turbulent roisters out there and unceremoniously used (as
two of the maids had already suffered) but there was
nothing to prevent Kathal arbitrarily handfasting her to
one of his drinking mates.

Even Kathal would have to learn soon that the supplies
from last harvest were not inexhaustible and any yield
from the new planted field was months away. Yet he had
done nothing but order stored seed grains to be drawn
upon. And she could feel the stir of black hate rising
whenever she dared venture out to do the little she could
to aid.

That high-pitched voice carried above all the clamor
from the other room, somehow stifled much of it.

"Treasure, look you. 'Tis well known that Lugh's
Mound holds it. The old stories are that every king who
went into the Shadows took much of his treasure with
him—though how much that could comfort his bones who
can say."

There was utter silence now, and Catlin clasped her
hands so tightly together that the bones seemed to lock on
each other. Treasure—Lugh's Mound—surely Kathal
would not be so utterly lost as to try for what might lie
there!

"Wager! Wager!" one of the other voices rang out. "Let
us see true treasure by the next moontide, and we'll shield
raise you!"

Catlin's hands now sped to cover her ears. Somehow
she knew Kathal's mood. He'd take up this challenge as
eagerly as he would raise a sword on the practice field.
There was no longer any priest to aid. Brother Victus had
been ignominiously bundled out two months ago and told
he was lucky he still kept his head on his shoulders.

She knew well the legend of Lugh's Mound which was
raised on the tallest peak of the surrounding hills. No one
went near it, but there had been those who had seen at a
distance a company of riders on mounts like gray mist
who circled it as guardians. Brother Victus had said they
were Those of the Hills, outside human laws and duties.
But the country people would leave at times a fine fleece
or a bowl of honey out on the flat stone by the faint path

which perhaps those mist horses had worn through the years, and were sure that luck for their households followed such gifts.

Her uncle had said it had naught to do with the People but was rather the resting place of one of those raiding lords from overseas who had been ceremoniously buried with a goodly portion of his loot when a last foray went against him. Catlin sucked in a breath. When they were children, she and Kathal, her brother had often spoken of that treasure, and now he shared the tale with those in there.

For him to venture to Lugh's Mound might cost him the rest of the ragged loyalty of their people. She could bear no more of their drunken swaggering. They were now taunting Kathal to his deed, and she knew well that her brother would take up such a challenge.

Catlin arose from the stool where she had been sitting and stepped past the two cowering maids. Closing the door to the great hall firmly, she shot the bar across it though she knew that if Kathal discovered such an act, he would have that door hacked from its hinges as being shut against his authority.

Then, turning, she went to the window and drew aside the heavy draft-defeating curtain to look out. There were no lights to be seen in the village—why would there be? Honest men and women had been long abed. But she searched through the gloom of the night—to Lugh's Mound. The moon was only a new crescent now and gave little light. All she could see was a darker shadow against the star-studded sky. She folded her hands and repeated the ward-off words Brother Victus had used.

Then she turned and signaled to the maids who saw her to her bed before they sought their own pallets.

There are dreams and dreams. Some vanish when one opens eyes in the morning, parts of others either linger on in sharp memory or shadowy uneasiness. Catlin brought out from slumber with the morning light what might be a vision—of land she knew well, having ridden and walked over it since childhood. But this carried no trim of growth—it was black and seared as if fire had claimed it. The houses were tumbled and deserted, there were no beasts in the fields. No one showing in farmyards—even the smoke of family hearths did not wreath from any chimney. A dead land!

She forced herself to wash and dress—to unbar that door and look into the foul disorder of the hall. Two men lay snoring on the floor, one was sprawled across the table—a puddle of spilled mead ruffled from his breath where his head rested.

But there was no sign of Kathal, nor the two of his companions he held the closest. There was the sound of a step and she turned swiftly. The newcomer was old Timous, once her uncle's steward, now a broken man with a new bruise on his forehead. His eyes as they met Catlin's were as empty as those of a dead man. Then there came a flicker of recognition, and he said between broken teeth, "This be black days, Lady. Himself has gone to Lugh's Mound with those to stand aside and watch that he does what he wagered to do."

"What will be the ending of this, Timous?"

"Death—and for more than those who dared this night."

His back was straightening now, and he was more the man who had been right hand for her uncle. "Lady," he protested now, "this place it not fit for your eyes. Let us cleanse it before you come within—"

"Not so, Timous. This be the Hall of my Blood and Kin. Who better should set it in order?" She knew well that the old man had few to serve with him. Some shambling farm hands and kitchen boys.

With the aid of such unhandy helpers, plus her maids, they did bring order. The comatose drinkers were blanketed and stowed away, Catlin hoping, with a viciousness she had never felt before, that they would suffer the worst pangs of a morning after this drink-filled night.

It was the second of her uncle's old trusted retainers who came in before they were done and sought her out.

"Lady—the people of the valley—they have come in fear and need."

"Hew, why—" But she did not try to guess what other happening from the sottish debauch of the night before might have occurred. The knowledge that Kathal had gone treasure hunting in Lugh's Mound was enough to raise most of the villagers.

So the girl followed Hew out into a gray drizzle of a day, a day which somehow threatened that a full sun would never shine here again. The villagers were gathered waiting, from children in arms, to the elders, some of whom hobbled painfully on two sticks—with the hale and hearty in between.

Each face was pale, and frightened eyes darted from her at her coming to the gate of the courtyard and back as if they had been pursued to this haven and looked now upon her to defend them from some danger they could not meet themselves.

"Lady—" It was again Hew who was the spokesman beckoning her forward so that the throng there parted and let her through, past the outer gate into the open.

Here also hung mist, but her eyes were drawn to the ground. Down the crooked lane which was the center of the hall village, out and around, circles, arcs, lines as straight as a spear shaft, marked the ground. They were silvery and yet she was sure that they had no substance and were only prints. And they were the tracks of some mounted troop which had encircled again and again each cottage, crossed and recrossed every field within her range of sight.

"The Riders—of the People." Hew pointed to the tracks.

Already the sharpness of that sign was fading. She did not want to believe in what she had seen and yet she could not put it from her.

"Ill—ill" somewhere in the crowd behind her a woman raised that wail. "Ill be this day and that which follows."

Catlin could feel the cold rise of fear. They might well panic and what answer did she have? She was not the Dongannan—where was Kathal?

Her silent question was answered then by other riders, substantial enough that the blowing of their horses and their own mumbling voices could be readily heard. Kathal at their head, his face flushed, his jerkin and shirt gone, and the stains of earth on his bare arms and what was left of his clothing.

"A wager!" his voice rang out. "A wager you said, Clough and Dongal. Well, have I not won it and fairly?"

He held up something, which in spite of the dullness of the morning, flashed as if for a moment he held a brand aloft. That it must be some gem Catlin was sure. His eyes held steady on it and on nothing else around.

"And there be more!" he crowed. "Richer than the hall of the Great King will be Dongannan—and all just for some delving in the dirt."

Then, for the first time, he appeared to note Catlin and he grinned at her. For a moment she thought she saw some evil mask instead of her brother's face. He leaned from his saddle, urging his mount closer, and dangled what he held over her head.

It seemed to be a spray of flowers, and yet not possessing the quick passing beauty of true flowers but fashioned from the cold hardness of colored stones. Treasure indeed—the richest ornament she had ever seen.

Kathal raised it up to his face now and nuzzled at it as if it were the first mouthful of some feast. "Ah, the taste of treasure!" Again he crowed.

Catlin and the others behind her opened a way for him and his two companions. They bore no signs of toil she saw, but neither were they in such glee as her brother showed. Instead now and then they glanced over their shoulders as if they felt other and perhaps threatening eyes upon them.

Then Catlin saw that they did have a follower. A donkey, its head hanging, plodded well to their rear, and on the spirit-broken creature hunched a misshapen lump which, as he advanced, she could make out as a man. But such a man, as gnarled and time twisted as some ancient tree. Though his back was hunched, he bent over a hand harp of some dull black wood and the strings of it appeared to be the same color as the mist about.

As Kathal's mount trotted into the courtyard, that strange rider halted. Three times his crooked fingers plucked those harp strings. However, the notes which arose from them were not of any music as mankind wanted to hear, rather gusty sighs, the last dwindling into a wail.

The harper grinned, showing yellowish teeth and eyes near buried in the wrinkles which seamed his face. Then he urged his donkey around and the animal plodded away, out of the village. Yet that which the harper left behind him moved the villagers to shrink, until some of the women and children broke and ran for their homes.

So did all peace and sanity leave Dongannan—its fields and homes, its great hall, and its peoples. The two who had ridden forth with Kathal for that ominous wager sickened and within a fortnight were dead. Their three drunken fellows rode at a wild gallop out of the holding after they witnessed those deaths.

But nothing seemed meaningful to Kathal. He sat in his high chair at the table for hours, pushing aside any food or drink offered him, playing with his treasure and talking mainly to himself, for it finally came that only Catlin would approach him, of the even greater riches to be gained when he was in a mind to do so.

The fields which had been hoof-printed were now bare of even a blade of dying grass, as were the gardens of the cottages. On the hills lay the bodies of sheep along with their tenders. The few cattle seemed to go wild, two of them horning their owners before they disappeared into the wild lands beyond.

Catlin pulled herself wearily from one sickbed to another in the ailing village. Each day she saw more of the still hale burdened with pitiful bundles of their most needful possessions going out and away from this cursed place.

It was a toll of days later that she once more saw the harper. And because she had come from the deathbed of the miller's last child, she dared to walk as quickly as she could to face him, nor did he withdraw at her coming.

"I know not who or what you are," she said in the voice of one so wearied she found it hard to hunt for the proper words. "It is plain we are cursed—Dongannan dies—and all for the wildness of a man deep in drink. If there is anything of good within you, light some hope that we can survive."

Even as she spoke, Arran, the miller's wife, came into the

street. She had loosed her hair to hang in a wild tangle and she went to her knees before the entrance to the great hall.

"The curse of a mother, may it lie heavy on you for your greed and black heart. No lord of ours are you and may you die unforgiven, lie in our cursed fields, and meet with the Black Master who sent you to torment us."

Then she keened forth the wail for the dead and other pale women tottered to stand behind her, adding their voices to hers.

Catlin, however, after a first glance, kept her attention for the hunchbacker harper. And now a spark of anger rose within her and she burst forth, "For the sin of one man do you doom a village? If aught is to be done, tell me now!"

Those cavern-set eyes met hers and she held the glance between them with a fierce tightness. Dongannan she was and Dongannan she would fight for.

"What is taken can be returned. There is no promise— you have only hope." In spite of his age his voice was certainly that of a bard.

Once more he turned the donkey and went from her. But what he had said gave her purpose now.

"Return what is taken." She thought of Kathal who had retreated to his inner chamber and barred the door against all comers, as if he feared the very thing she now knew she must do.

Hardly able to keep her feet because of hunger weakness (for she had seen supplies from the hold divided in the village) and weariness, Catlin turned back.

The keening of the women was a sobbing in the air and she saw the sullen, angry looks of the men, slowly gathering behind them before the great gate. They did not deter her from entering. In fact, they shrank away from her as if she now carried the burden of the curse on her bowed shoulders.

Catlin came into the silent great hall, now a cave of dusk in spite of the wan daylight without. She knew well where Kathal was. No food or water had passed his barred door for more than—she tried to count time dizzily—two days now. She had gone each morning to call out to him but had heard nothing in return except movement and a low muttering as if he carried on long debates with that which only he could see. Now, as she summoned up strength to pound on that surface, there was no answer at all.

The door had been readied, from the day it was hung, for a place to make a final stand in hours of peril. She certainly could not beat down such a defense.

With one hand she brushed aside her lopsided limp coif and its draggled veil which somehow had stayed with her during the past days, for she could not remember now when she had bathed, worn clean body linen, and a fresh overrobe. The door remained a barrier, but there was the window.

Dongannan had not stood a siege since long before her own birth. The single window was barred, of course, but it was her only choice. Now she made herself look around for weapons against those bars.

At length she picked up a spit still in place above a long-dead fire. So armed, she went resolutely out into the open once more. The crowd at the gate had split apart. She thought she could see a dim and ominous blot, the hunched bard, far back, though none of the villagers looked upon him.

So wearied that she saved what strength she still had to drag the spit by one end rather than lift it, Catlin rounded the corner of the inner keep until she at last faced that window.

Yes, the bars were still there. It now remained to be seen how securely they were still set. She steadied the spit, raised it, and aimed one end spearwise at the base of the nearest bar.

"Lady—" That was a ghost of a voice, but she turned her head slowly, looked at Hew. His body was gaunt, his face thinned down to mere flesh over bone.

She had not time for explanations, there was that to be done—swiftly—and she was the only one left to do it.

"In," she panted. "Must get in."

She was too wearied to know triumph as a fall of long-decayed mortar followed her first jab. Then the spit was twisted from her hands and Hew was aiming with twice the force she was able to summon and to good purpose.

There came no sound from within to answer the noise their efforts produced. And a weather-stained curtain clouded what lay beyond. But Hew kept to his pounding and prying and at last two of the bars came free.

"Leave it—I shall be able to get through," Catlin told him. She dragged off her coif. Luckily she wore the less-confining skirt of a riding dress. But the opening looked small and she feared the attempt she would make, though she said strongly to Hew, "Give me that to stand upon—"

Wobbling the man went to his knees. "My strength here and now, Lady."

Somehow she made it, clawing her way through the curtain into the darkness of the room before. The smell of death had been with her for days, but here was another more subtle stench—that which was of madness and evil.

Though the room was dark, there was a single spot of light coming from something lying on the bed. She could hear snuffling as from a beast and a hand appeared within the limits of that dim light. A hand holding a drawn dagger.

"Out—away—thief—" the three words came as three separate shouts. The knife swung viciously through the light into dark and back again, weaving a pattern over that spot of light.

Catlin swung out her own arm in a need for a weapon to defend herself. She caught at the edge of the curtain and found strength to rip it from the hangers.

Now she could see better. Kathal—no, that thing crouched on the bed, filthy, ragged, bearded, twisted of face bore no resemblance to even the drunken youth she had last seen twirling his treasure as he rode home. It was the treasure piece which had given off that spot of light and now what it emitted was growing even brighter.

Like a giant spider Kathal sprang for her and only a half-instinctive swirl of the length of heavy cloth in her hands kept that dagger from her flesh. He was screaming raggedly such oaths as perhaps even most armsmen would not know. But the cloth fell over him and brought him down.

Before he could rise, she seized from a side shelf a tankard—empty but heavy enough to pull down her weak-ened arm. Catlin swung it awkwardly until the wallowing thing at her feet gave a gasping cry and was still.

She lurched across to the bed, and her hand closed upon the jeweled spray. It was like grasping a coal from the fire's heat, but she held on. Backing, her eyes ever on that mound of Kathal and curtain, she reached the window and dared enough to turn around and struggle out. The jewel she had put in her bodice for safekeeping, and there also she felt its fire.

As she slipped through, there was no one to steady her to the ground. There was only the body of Hew, still grasping the spit. Shaking herself after her tumble, she was at his side quickly. But she had seen death too many times within the past days not to be unable to detect it now.

With the spit as a staff to keep her on her feet, she went on to the open gates. Those who had been there were gone. She might indeed be in a deserted village. She was kept on her feet only by the need to do what she must do.

Catlin was not surprised when she came to the opening of the faint trace which led to Lugh's Mound to see there the hunchbacked bard. But she had no strength to gasp out any words—only the climb before her.

In the end it was the staff-spit which drew her up one painful step at a time. Until she did at last reach the heights and see the disturbed earth where Kathal must have delved.

Only it was filled in. With a broken sigh Catlin fell to her knees, and, using the spit, and then her own bruised and torn hands, she worked doggedly to scoop away the earth. To her surprise what she uncovered first was undoubtedly a shield, the metal of it half rust-eaten away.

"Iron, cold iron, Lady, and as a taunt years ago."

Even turning her head had become an almost impossible task, but she looked up and over her shoulder. Yes, it was the hunchback who sat there on his donkey, and, as she sighted him, he once more swept a hand over the ancient harp and notes of sorrow, such sorrow as even the last few days had not brought her, sent tears channeling down her grimy face.

She caught the shield with both hands and put all her

strength to pulling. Since it must have been moved by Kathal earlier, it yielded to her now.

Light blazed forth and she was looking into what might be the end of a stone-walled chamber. There was a raised block in its middle and on that lay— she could not be sure what it was since the blaze was so bright. But unconsciously she brought her hands to the thing which had been searing her breast. When that was in the open, it twisted and turned and moved from her hold like a living thing until it joined with that other on the stone.

Then came such sound as entered into every part of her bone and flesh. What words beat in that refrain she could not tell, but strength was flowing back into her. It was almost as if she had become some other, apart from the earth she knew. She could remember with pity, but even that emotion was fading.

Catlin was on her feet, but she did not try to enter that chamber. Instead she was startled by a whinny and turned to see the harper. That was no donkey on which he was ungainly crouched, but a fine stallion of cloudy gray whose hooves shone like burnished silver.

And mounted in the saddle, his fingers lovingly caressing the strings of a silver harp, was no hunchback. This was a youth, and yet there was age in his eyes as if the years had no hold on him. Black his hair, held by a silver band, and his clothing was green, the green of first spring leaves—his cloak flung back a warm scarlet.

She knew him then for one out of the ancient tales—he was one of the People—those who had their own dwelling place which was not her world, though they might journey through that at their will.

His harping fell to a muted thread of sound. "No longer is the High Crown held from us by the menace of our old enemy," he was speaking and yet every word was a note of song. "Lady, of your courtesy, bring hither that which is rightfully that of my Queen."

Now Catlin did enter the chamber and her hands went out to what lay on the block. She indeed held a circlet of bright stones, pale gold and brilliant silver, formed as might be a wreath of flowers. It no longer burned, rather from it flowed such peace as filled one even as had his song.

Slowly she turned, reluctant to give to another this marvel which renewed life. But take it she did, passing the spit, then pushed aside the shield—both of the iron which legend said were deadly to what she believed him to be.

She held up to him the crown. He had swung aside his harp and brought forth what seemed a veil of mist in which he wrapped her find.

"You have held our power in truth," he said, "for this is one key to our own place. Lady, I have watched you fight that which the great cursing brought about and fight it valiantly. Come to us in all honor for already you bear within you something of that which is our birthright."

Catlin looked up into his eyes—green—or were they gold? They were pools which beckoned her to dive within. He had dismounted and now came to her, his hands empty and outstretched. Catlin took a deep breath. She was filled again, not by mist, but by a sheltering warmth of one coming home after a long sorrowful journey. She laid her palms on his. It was as if they were now one and always would be.

THE LAW OF MAN

by *Michelle West*

Michelle West has written two novels for DAW, *Hunter's Oath* and *Hunter's Death*, and with any luck is finishing her third, *The Broken Crown*, by now. Her short fiction has appeared in *Tarot Fantastic*, *Sword of Ice* and *Other Tales of Valdemar*, and *Phantoms of the Night*. She lives in Ontario, Canada with her husband and son.

It is twilight. The light of day is fading, and the night's fall is imminent. With the passing of the day, many things change; the shadows hide much from eyes that are not meant for the dark. Mortal eyes.

But our eyes see well the nuance and the subtlety.

There are circles beneath my feet, ill-traveled these many years, but there nonetheless for those with eyes to see them. In such circles, we once gathered our mortals, and took with them an evening's pleasure, be they unwary enough to heed the strains of our music. In such a circle, we will gather again; my kin are waiting my return. But these circles, these circles we will not dance in again while I live.

And I will live, I fear, forever.

It is cool. The coming evening will rim the forest trees in frost, will curl the fallen leaves with a white, hoary edge that will sharpen and crispen their tiny deaths.

Leaves, like mortals, die so quickly.

And what is death to one of our kind?

In the dawn of our time we gathered our mortals with impunity undreamed of now. Where in the spring and high summer we danced in glades such as these, we walk now in winter, for in winter, there are few indeed of the priests whose travels have almost destroyed these lands.

Ah. Archeraon calls me. He is cruel. I believe that he chose these circles because he, as I, remember what started within them. Her story.

He knows it, and he does not know it, and he hopes to catch it, pull it from me in the wilds of the dance itself. I will tell it, I think, but not for Archeraon. Never for he. I call out to him. I tell him to wait—merely to wait—I have set my snares, and when a human trips them, I will draw him in and then we may begin.

Yet the circles have done Archeraon's work.

The story is upon me, and I must tell it, or the memories that are too sharp and too clear will cut me enough that he'll see the pain. I would not expose that pain to him to save the eternity before me.

Let me begin this story within these circles, before the ghosts of old dances, ancient offerings, making of the words that tell it a tighter binding than I have yet known; speaking the truth, finally, because in our lands truth is something that no one expects, and to speak it is to make of it a lie.

And if it is a lie, perhaps the telling will ease me, and I might be free to turn once again to the pleasures of a court that ruled the world in dawn and rules it still in twilight.

Innocence has always fascinated our people, because it has been so long since we have known that state, that we have forgotten the knowledge of it. Human children, especially the very young, are a source of amusement that the most jaded of us—even the Queen herself—have never been proof against. They know nothing; they are easily twisted; they are easily lied to, if the will is strong and the heart is steady.

Mortality has a feel and a texture that is unique. In the beasts of the forests and the birds of the air, there is a taint that speaks of growth, of age, of *change*. We surround ourselves, always, with them; they are beautiful to us, more so than mortals will ever understand.

It is change that fascinates us: change, decay, the impulse toward death that every life knows. It is as if knowledge, once gleaned, cannot be contained by mortal frailty, eroding the spirit and the body until they are at last severed.

We study this erosion with fascination, as I have said—but much less so now that the Law of Man has come to the lands of mortals. For the mortals are not without will, not without fire; death does not prevent them from attaining a greatness that echoes throughout the lives of their descendants. They have dreamed their bloody dreams, and out of the sleep that we do not—can never—know, they have fashioned their law. They call this law God, and they worship it with the full force of their brief and petty lives. They burn for it, kill for it, die for it—just as they do for gold and jewels, magic and beauty.

We take no law but Hers; we obey no force but She. But we know that this Law of Man is a force made real, and made potent.

Where once we walked without caution, we must now display a cunning that we reserved for the games of the Court. Where once we walked in splendor, in raiment dazzling to the mortal eye—where once we chose to wear a glamour bright and bold and so beautiful the remainder of their lives would seem tawdry and dull by comparison—we must walk in secrecy, or in the isolated places the Law of Man has not yet touched.

It is harder to catch mortals; they must stumble into our wild hunts, our places of secrecy, the dells at the night hour of the moon dance. We catch them by a whisper of midnight wind, a hint of the perfume of flowers so fragrant they have never graced a mortal forest, a glimpse of light that glitters more brightly than anything but the sun, but more delicately, more darkly.

And we ensnare by the song of the dance, by a music so wild no words will ever contain it or force it to even the law of the Queen itself.

And this is a story begun by such a dance, and the life that it brought us when the circle was, at last, broken.

An infant, taken almost direct from its mother's womb, is a creature beyond price—or beyond any price that would fit such a short and meager telling as this. We have our songs and our lays to remind us of the value and the lure of a babe; whole courts have fallen when the siren cry of a child's hunger has proved too much of a temptation to the listeners. The songs would take years to sing, for our songs are our history, and reflect much.

Even this will become part of it, but it will not be told as I will tell it now while I have this short space of private time before the dance.

Suffice it to say that, at the time of evereve in the slender crescent of the pale moon, such a creature was brought over human field and enclosure, to me. It was a work of daring, and a work of fear; no one of our kin was responsible for the gift.

No, it was an old mortal woman, with a servant's worn clothing and bent back, who came to the circle in which we dance. She sat in its center for but a human hour, holding to her chest a bundle that her arms—and her heart—found heavy. She was lovely to behold, and we stopped our preparations for the dance itself to watch her in the thin light.

Her skin was pale and spotted, and hung over her bones like a fine, heavy silk, with folds and creases that spoke of a texture uniquely human. The harper began to tease her shadows into the weave of the circle's ground to hold her there while we watched. But her ears were keen, and she heard his notes and his whispered song.

"Aye," she said, gazing into the darkness, "I know you're there. And I've come with a boon to ask, and I'll pay the price of its asking." Her voice was a creak and a rustle, like dry leaves to a tree making ready for winter.

It was I who answered her as she stood at the circle's heart. "We cannot decide the price before we hear the boon you would have us grant. Tell us, mortal."

She looked up, and up again, for we are a tall people, and I among the tallest of our number. Her eyes teared, a trail of liquid glinting along the folds and creases around her dark irises.

She has seen us before, I thought, for there is a look of recognition across a human face that is unmistakable: wonder, awe, and a curious sense of relief. There are always tears.

"This is the boon I crave of you." She held the bundle

high, and then unwrapped it carefully. There, at the center of the rough cloth, a child slept. It was frail, tiny, and silent. "There's a new law taking the land, and there are new men and a god of a type that has never entered our villages before.

"They've words and a magic like iron—cold and hard, for all that they speak of their lord's love—and they've come to take our children into the waters of their baptism, and steal their souls."

I nodded gravely. "It is the Law of Man," I whispered to my brethren. "It has come to reach out to us, even here." I stepped forward, hands outstretched, and she bundled the babe away from my sight. Almost, I reacted with anger, but not quite; even if she showed insolence, she had brought the rarest and most precious of gifts into my presence. I was willing to let her speak. "Your boon?"

"I'm a child of the old ways," the woman said roughly. "And my daughter, the child's mother, was as well, before this night." Her tears fell again, but they were all of anger; the wonder was lost. "But she's dead, and gone to what we were promised. I remain, and this, her only daughter." She held the child high. "I would have this child kept from the new god and his soldiers. Raise her in the old ways—or even in your own—for our mark is on her, and when she dies, she'll come to us." She wiped the tears from her eyes with a dirty, sweaty hand. "She'll come to us, and we'll have peace then."

"It is a rare task that you ask of us."

"Yes," the old woman whispered. "It is. In the old days we would have warded and guarded her against you. She might see you—as I have seen you—in the morn of her womanhood, but no more than a glimpse.

"Now, we would give her to you; you're part of the old ways, and no matter what her life may be with you, and no matter how you shape it, her spirit will still come to us, mother and grandmother." She started her tears again, and they fell almost hypnotically. "A mother takes care of her children in this world or the next. A mother does all that she can to protect 'em."

"I see," I looked down at her, standing beside the harper. I lifted one hand slowly, and he began to play.

Breeze lifted the hem of my robes and sent them, like shadow, scuttling over the tops of the grass. "Then I will ask of you only this price: Dance with us."

She lifted her head and met my eyes, and I saw that she knew what the end of the dance would be. We had her anyway. The strains of the harp had already touched her aged blood with the wildness. But she did not deny it, or even make the attempt. Human dignity is, in itself, a thing of grave beauty. It does not always last, of course—but sometimes it outlives the life that clings to it, and when it does, it is a rare gift indeed—a thing of beauty. Human dignity does not come at the expense of fear, after all; the fear lies beneath it, held at bay like the dogs of the wild hunt. And it is always a curiosity to us, a part of a larger game, to see whether the fear will win out, ere the end.

"I'm old," she said as she rose stiffly, "and I'll dance very slowly and very poorly."

"You will be a thing of beauty," the harpist replied, before I could. "I am Kallaran, and I would be honored if you would partner me."

The old woman curtsied, a clumsy, artless motion that was made lovely by its lack of artifice. Then she bent her wizened face over the bundle she held, and brushed her lips across the infant's forehead.

I held out my arms, and she placed her granddaughter in them. Almost, she spoke—but the music started, and carried her words away; it carried all words away.

For the first time in millennia, I did not join the circle. Instead, I held the small child, and fashioned for her a song of sleep. I built it strong, and made of it a quiet place, for she was too young to join in the dance, but mortal enough to be affected by it should she hear the strains of its calling.

After the dance, I saw to the old woman's body. It lay as if in slumber, artfully arranged, but death had visited her, and left us with the shell. One or two of my kin were already watching her; if left there, they would stay to see time's march across features that no longer lived in the days and weeks to follow.

But she brought me the babe, and I was conscious of

some small debt to her. I ordered her buried in the manner of her people, although it grieved Archeraon much to see it done, and then I left the circle for the season, carrying the child close and binding it to me with my inner vision.

"The child is mine," I told the Court. As I said, it is rare indeed that one so young and so unformed comes to us— and over such a temptation have wars been fought, although they are not the wars of human kin and nature.

"If you keep the child, it is indeed yours," Archeraon said, for he was still angry at the loss of the body to the earth and the worms of the upper soil. "But there is much in our lands to entrance one merely human, and we will deny her none of that should she express an interest and a will to follow it. Of course," he added, as he bowed so deliberately, "what of interest could attract her when she has the attention and the gifts of one of the greatest of our number?"

Oh, he was clever; he was always clever. Were we to be ruled by a King, in the mortal fashion, and not a Queen, it would be Archeraon for eternity, and we his handmaidens and courtiers.

"What, indeed," I said, for he had left me little room in which to say anything else.

"Then we abide by the mortal gifting," he replied, and he maintained his bow. In time, I rose, and he with me. But it was in my arms that the child left the clearing and began its life in our lands, and he did not forget.

Nor did I; our memories are longer than our lives, and it is said that our lives are without end.

The blush of infancy had left her before we returned to our lands. Time's passing, in these lands, was at its swiftest, and I made haste to repair to the court of the Queen. Mortality could not, of course, be removed from the mortal; what was born, died. It was the law of the living. Even so, in the court of the Queen such passage of time might be slowed, even as the rivers were that passed through the Queen's demesne; for if the law of the living prevailed, so, too, did the law of the Queen.

Did we tarry? I believe so, now. Because she grew so wondrously quickly, and we were each of us afraid of missing the moment in which her wrinkled flesh became smooth and soft and perfect, of missing the first tooth, the changing color of her baby's eyes, the ability to sit, to grip. It passed so quickly we had to bear witness, for few enough of our number had seen a babe grow, and few would; we could not waste the opportunity.

The child was unnamed; the naming of a mortal held power, and I wished that binding performed in the Court, not in these lands in which life ebbed so quickly. But named or no, she grew; before we had reached the true road, she learned to speak our tongue because our tongue was the only tongue which had touched her ears. Her voice was a strange lilt, a squeaking song, a tortured attempt at speech; the world was new, to her, and as we gathered to watch, as we made of her a window through which the world might yet be viewed, it became new to us as well. Dangerous. Beautiful.

She listened to the voices of the animals that we rode, speaking as we spoke. But more than the voice binds our creatures to us, and try as she might, she could not understand the words they framed in reply—which is just as well, for they were words of warning, a caution meant to spoil my child by adding to her life a darkness and fear of captivity.

For she was, of course, a captive; it was mine, all of her too-short life, and I had laid my wards around her and upon her that others of my kind might understand that my claim was made and my wrath invoked to he who would dare to taint it. I would have struck the animals dumb, but Archeraon would not allow it. In the matter of the child, there would never be peace between us.

The Law of Man was a swift and ugly blossom, but it did not flower and die; it grew roots so long and deep they were like the glittering mines—cold and hard and dark. We did not fight it well, for it grew, it seemed, in a season, and by the time we were prepared, so, too, were the men who built it.

It was Nimradel who came to the Court to tell us of the bells; Nimradel who dared to whisper about the song of man in the Court of the Queen. He came to her, wind-touched and haste-sped, his raiment a sorry spill of fabric without so much as a spoken glamour to sooth it into perfection.

"What is this?" she said, for she took poorly to the interruption.

He was brave enough, and foolish in his way, but he was no mortal, to be punished and humiliated for daring her wrath; none of the Court dared her wrath without reason, especially not so cunning a one as Nimradel. He fell to his knees before her, and he spoke his words to the ground without once lifting his face.

Had we not been able to hear, we would have known the word was bad indeed.

"The Law of Man," he said softly, "has taken the Brighten Grove. The trees have been felled and taken to burn; their leaves are scattered across the land."

The Brighten Grove was the Queen's grove. Built into the hillocks and the glittering, cold stream were passages between her Court and the dying lands. The living lands.

"The road?" she said, in command.

"We could not close the ways," Nimradel replied. "Mordenel fell in the attempt." His voice was as harsh as any mortal's that had graced the Queen's Court. "They are building, there, in the land beside the river. The Law of Man. And in the tower that rides the shoulders of their ugly dwelling, there is a bell."

"A bell?"

"It peals," he said softly, "with the voice of iron, cold and hard. It takes no glamour, and accepts no silence. The music that comes from that bell would break the dance itself." He shuddered. "We cannot see this new castle that they have built; not clearly. The bells protect it, and we cannot approach.

"The beasts that we ensnare fly out as far as the edifice itself. The bell frees them. They do not return to us word of what they've seen."

"But *nothing* can break the dance."

All eyes turned then, even Hers, as my child spoke. Out of turn, out of place, her words far sweeter to my ears than Nimradel's, she stepped onto the green, and the flowers there parted, shying away from the weight of the ball of her heel. She had learned much from us of grace and movement, but she was still mortal, and would remain so; she walked with weight, whether she willed it or no, and when her thoughts "wandered," she was not careful.

She was not cautious, my child.

"Anna," the Queen said, enchanted, I think, in spite of her inclination. "If Nimradel believed that these . . . bells . . . can break the dance, he believes so with reason. Mordenel fell, and he rode with the host."

A reminder, to Anna, that she never would. She was younger than any of us had ever been, younger than we knew how to be. Younger, I think, than most of us could even comprehend. But I who watched her knew.

I touched her shoulder, quickly, and pulled her back to me; I did not trust her exposed before my kin. She came, but not gladly. The Queen was her law, and the rule that governed her life, and although she knew herself for a mortal, she felt little enough for their passing or their deaths when she happened upon them; she was *ours,* of us, in a way that those who came late in their lives could not be. And yet.

I should have known then.

But although I cautioned her to silence, she was willful, astonishingly willful, beautiful in her unbroken pride. "The touch of iron does not touch me."

"No, little Anna, it does not," Archeraon said; her voice had stolen mine for a moment, but he was ever watchful.

"And these bells—how would they hurt me if I heard their song?"

"They would not."

"The bells would not," I said, perhaps a little too sharply, "but the men most certainly would. Think, child. Iron affects us, yes—but if that iron were made into a sword, it would affect you no differently. You would perish, as your mother did, at the hands of these Men of God."

"I know the hidden ways," she replied, defiant, eager as ever to help. "I would not need to come within the reach of their swords. The bells, I might see at a distance; I could tell you of them."

Archeraon said softly, "You are brave, to offer us such a gift."

He understood her well.

But the Queen understood, as well. Turning, to me, Archeraon and Nimradel forgotten, she asked, "Will your bindings hold her?"

And I lied. I lied, not knowing how to tell her the truth. "Yes," I said.

She had no reason to distrust my word—for who among us would eagerly risk the mortal that Anna was?

"Anna," she said. "If you would do this in Our name, and in Our service, we would be grateful."

But perhaps it was not so much a lie as that.

Not all bindings are magical in nature, although few of my kin remember that singular truth, if we ever knew it at all. It is a mortal truth, and Anna was a mortal child, for all that she lived in the court, the hidden court, with no mortal parent to teach her the weaknesses that plague her kind. She knew me as her mother, as her only parent; I placed no binding on her but my presence in the spate of her dwindling years; I laid no spells upon her but those that might keep her within our lands, for otherwise she would age and pass more quickly than I—than any of us—desired.

She could not speak of love, of course; there was no word for it in the Court if it were not the name of the Queen, and her name we did not speak, not even I. But she was, like all mortal creatures, a thing of flesh and substance. More than once I woke to the feel of her arms around my neck, to the breeze of her breath, the sighing passage of air between half-opened lips. More than once she would seat herself at my feet and ask, plaintively, if I would not brush and bind her hair in the fashion of our kin. Her hair was not our hair—it was too thick and too prone to damage—but more often than not I would accede, and we would sit thus, whiling away the hours.

She did not understand that she was beautiful to us.

But she understood how important she was to me.

I knew she would not leave me.

And was that not, after all, what the Queen asked?
And yet.

"Why are you so angry at me?"

"I am not," I told Anna, "angry."

"I thought you'd be happy with me. Or at least proud.
Isn't it time I proved myself to the Queen and the Court?"
She shrugged herself into her common dress, a thing of
rough, stiff linen. She looked and she sounded so mortal
the Court of the Queen might never have touched her at
all; the fey peace was gone from her face.

"You sound so . . . human," I said, and I recall my
voice perfectly.

Because she did sound human, suddenly. Her cheeks
adopted that shade of purple red that was both fascinating
and ugly; she looked down at her feet, her jaws com-
pressing the lower line of her face.

"You all do it," she said, accusation in her tone.

"We all do what?" I turned from her, to the forest, to
the dark shadows that were the daylight haunt of the
Queen's Court between seasons.

"You all prove yourselves to *her*."

She could be so sullen when she chose it. "We do
not prove ourselves to her for any reason other than our
survival."

"You're lying."

"Perhaps. Truth shifts so much between decades, a lie
serves just as well with the passing of time."

"I never do anything right for you, do I?"

Had there been the slightest contrition in her words, I
might have answered differently; there was only anger's
edge. "You do as you please, Anna."

"You *are* angry."

"Anna, I am of the Court. I do not feel pride in the
sense that you mean the word. I have pride, yes—but you
want me to feel pride *in* you—and that, that is not the way
of my kind. You are Anna. If you are proud, that is a
matter of yourself.

"What you want from me—this pride *in,* these feelings
for—I cannot give you. Not a single one of us can."

"Archeraon can."

She said it to wound. That was her way, in anger. She was of us, and yet she could never be of us. She did not understand that her words took no root, found no purchase. "And if you choose to believe him, you will prove yourself, ultimately, human."

She flushed, darkening to the shade of red that I had grown to dislike. 'Why do you say things like that? Why don't you ever just tell me the truth?"

"Anna, child, the one thing that I have never done to you is lie." And that was true, but she heard truth so rarely she could not separate it from her desire. "If you wish to play games with Archeraon, you may."

"I don't need your permission."

"No."

She stormed around the room like an angry girl. Which, raised by me or no, she was. At last, she said, "Don't you care at all?"

Of course, I thought. *You were given to me. Your life has been mine since the moment the old woman's responsibility ended. If I choose to shelter you, or to indulge you, or to hunt you when it is the season, all of these are my right by the Queen's law. Archeraon seeks to steal something, from me, from one of his kin. He has sought you, and your life, since the day that I answered the old woman's call before the spring circles. And I grow weary of his games.*

He will pay.

But I did not speak. We had had this argument before, and no words were the right words in which to cloak it. She did not, she *would not* understand.

"Come," I told her. "You made your offer, and the Queen accepted it. You will give her what she desires."

Archeraon was there to greet us. I half-expected it, but although I snared my path with magical traps, none of them caught his scent. And why would they? He rode, and no part of his shadow touched ground; he left not even that hint of his presence to warn me.

He played his game, and he played it well.

"Archeraon," I said, before he could speak. "You

would do well to remember whose quest this is, and at whose request it was undertaken."

"Ah, but I do remember. I have come to offer safe passage across the ford to the lovely Anna, the hope for our salvation." His smile was sharp as a dagger's edge.

"Archeraon, if this is a game—"

"It is, of course," he said, bowing slightly upon the back of his light-footed mount, "but inelegantly timed. The cursed bells of the Law of Man have eroded some part of our Lady's enchantments; the ford, held back from its natural course these many years is attempting to right itself in a moment or a day. You, of course, will have no difficulty forging your path; it is only water, after all." He turned to Anna, to my child. "I know that, given time, you would have no difficult crossing either, little Anna. But we do not have time. Will you accept my offer and ride with me?"

She turned to look at me, and then took his hand in silence; I do not think a word could have escaped the tight press of her lips. He lifted her effortlessly. She seemed a small thing as her feet left ground, fragile for all that she was of heavier build than any of my kin.

They rode into the roaring water then.

And the water swept them away.

I heard Archeraon's cry, and to this day I do not know if it was genuine. And if I knew, if I knew for certain that it was not, Archeraon would be a stone in the standing ring—and aware for every immortal minute, trapped there, of all that he might never know again: the glory of the sun's rise and fall, the growth and the death of seasons, the music of the dance.

And does it matter?

She was swept away that day, still cloaked in her youthful anger. Away from the grip of Archeraon and into the land of man.

I knew it before he returned to me bearing the signs of the water's anger, the river's welter glistening off the tangled length of his hair, his clothing rent and damaged, and his mount, in which he placed a particular pride, nowhere to be seen.

He could have smoothed away the water's damage, spoken a word or two to conceal it beneath an artful seeming; he chose not to, and indeed, chose wisely. To display weakness before his kin was almost never done—and when it was done, it was done after the risks had been weighed and measured.

He came to me, almost humble, and because of it I stayed my hand.

"It is not to me you will have to answer," I told him, as the water rolled up the bank, lapping at the enchanted ground as if it were a beach.

"I know it. Is Anna dead?"

He thought as the Queen thought, that the ties between the child and I were formalized by magic and ritual. "Who can say?" I answered quietly. "The Queen's own magic was no proof against the Law of Man, or the river would never have returned to its natural course. I do not feel her, if that is what you ask—but if you ask me what I believe, then, no, I do not think her dead."

He straightened as I spoke. "Then if she is not dead, I believe that she will return to us of her own accord. We are," he added, his gaze veiled, "all that she has ever known."

"Of course." I turned to him then, forcing myself to lay hand upon his shoulder. "Her mother would have run to us as well."

And to that, there was little enough he could say.

The tolling of the bell was an evil that could not be tolerated save at this, our twilight hour. The Queen took no council and kept none save her own, but among ourselves, the matter of man's encroachment was keenly discussed. I think, now, that we were watching the sun set without understanding the glory and the beauty of what we saw; there will be no others.

"Let us," Nimradel said, for Mordenel's loss rode him hard, "call the hunt. The wild ways are not yet dead, not here; the ground remembers the passage of the hunter."

He was not the only man to speak thus. For he spoke a measure of truth; the ground did indeed still bear the marks of the hunt's last passage.

"The Law of Man is strong," I replied, "for all that it is newly proclaimed. Call the hunt, and the priests will come, with their chants and their iron and their god."

"And would you have us flee this, the heart of our dominion? Would you have us give way for fear of—of *men?*"

I forbore to mention that we had done just that over the centuries, coming, each of us, from the wilds of forests which no longer contained the shadows by which we lived, the hidden recesses, the moon's wild music. Because Anna was there, somewhere, and her time was passing quickly.

I took to the still waters, to gaze upon them, to find in them an answer to my dilemma. Water is a deep magic, a steady magic, one that requires patience. Although we live a longer span of years than any of us yet know, patience is not a skill that we develop without cost and struggle; the measure of our time is still precious to us, no matter how long it might extend. There are always deaths that wait, and if time is not one of them, it does not change the fact: We are only immortal. We are not invulnerable.

I knew the truth of this better than any of our kin, and because I accepted it, I learned to be patient, to offer to the task at hand—to any task I chose—my time, my dedication, my effort, over and over again, until the task was done.

The water's stillness was a mirror, and in it I saw many things: first, myself, skin white as snow, eyes of changing color, hair a pale, long skein that caught light like a spiderweb. Beneath this face, this seamless mask long since perfected by art and glamour to resemble all of our faces, I saw time, time's tracks, a horrible intimation of something that the kin of the Court did not know: Age.

Almost, I recoiled, pulling my hands from the water's surface. Almost. But the truth that I desired lay beyond that image, that vision; I had to know it, and its horror, to find what I sought—for the water plays its tricks, and it demand its price, before it surrenders the knowledge that it holds at its heart.

It named me: Fallen. The price that I paid for a sight of my Anna was high. I accepted the truth of its name.

All the things that I could not, by rearing, take out of my Anna she had given to me, and she owed me in the giving. Such a dangerous creature, my child.

Although the Law of Man was strong, the truth of the waters was stronger still, and so it was, standing among the eternal lilies of the Queen's Court, that I saw her.

She was greatly battered; her skin was gray and purple and tinged by a bright yellow the like of which I had never seen. I thought her teeth might be broken until she spoke, and when she spoke, when the waters finally lifted their curtains enough that I might hear her words, her teeth no longer mattered.

For she spoke in a voice as ugly as I had ever heard from the lips.

And she spoke, halting and broken, in the tongue of Man.

I did not discover more that day, but the next, when the dawn's light made the horizon a blaze of pretty color, I made my way to the waters. Archeraon watched me, and I stood, torn between my pride and his pleasure, and this second day, I did not call upon the water's gift.

But the third day, the third day I left him and found a well of still water in my own domain, and there, with greater effort, I sought my child out.

I found her, although the way was hard and difficult.

The bruises were gone from her face, the swelling from her lips. She had aged, and quickly, but not so much that the members of the Court who had not made her life their study would recognize the loss of time in her features. Her hair had been cut. Sheared from her shoulders as if she were no more than a mortal's daughter, a thing of man. The clothing she wore must have chafed at her skin, as the life she led chafed at her spirit.

Or perhaps, like any human, she had settled into the life that was forced upon her; she had grown to think that it was the life that she desired. A mortal mind is a danger-ously weak place, a thing of seasons and time.

I had thought that the Law of Man had trapped her, and it had, but it became clear that the cage was not entirely unpleasant. She stood at the side of an older woman, a plump one with a gap-toothed grin and sun-stains across the breadth of her broad face.

"We'll not be asking questions today," this woman told my Anna. "Today, the father'll be off with the bishop. But you mind what I told you—it was an act of God hisself that brought the father to your side when the river flooded—and you should offer your thanks to the lord and his blessed Mother." She wiped her brow with the back of her sleeve, washing her face in her sweat. Setting aside her hoe—her iron-tipped, terrible reaver of dirt—she looked at my child with a softening expression.

"You still don't remember your parents."

"No."

"Aye, well. Don't you worry. They weren't like me," the old woman said. "Look at your hands. You've made a mess of 'em just doing an honest day's work. No, you're highly born, and the father knows it. He's looking, lamb. And he won't stop till he finds your family. I think he's hoping the bishop might help."

By afternoon of that day, weeks had fled her face, and the sun's touch was darker where it fell across her skin. She was put to work, but the work that she did was always too fine and too slow a work for her mortal companions; they marveled at her, and about her, while they waited on word.

By evening—ah, by evening, the worst of my fears came true. Wandering in the light forests that survived the clear-cutting that the Law of Man demanded, my child met a man. And he, a young man, a robed boy with a grave and serious face. They stumbled into each other unaware, and then stood a moment, blushing and stammering; it was my child who took the lead in the end, by lowering her face and backing away as if she were a suddenly wild creature.

And he said, "Wait—I've heard of you. You're Father Ingbrook's lost girl."

I pulled away from the waters then.

But although I traveled to the Queen's Court, I received no audience; she took none. In the matter of the tolling bells, she had not yet made her decision. And I could not wait much longer.

The earth remembered us.

It remembered the blood we had shed, and although the Law of Man shed blood in its time, it was tied to a master that did not recognize, did not desire, the hollows of earth, the wild heaviness of the ground.

Iron and earth are tied, and it is earth magic that is hardest to work, hardest of all magics to wield. And how is that difficulty measured? In time, of course.

Time. I had all of eternity, and less than a short mortal life, and the loss of the one would echo through the length of the other. Yet there was no hunt, not yet; and the waters had given me warning, but they would not carry me past the tolling bells of man, of men.

I, who had made the study of water my specialty now turned my will in a different direction: the ways of earth. Those passages were the darkest, but they were simplest to reach, for the price that the earth demanded was a part of the hunt itself. The forests became my home for one week, and for that week I took bow and spear and snare, forsaking the garments of the Twilight Court for those of the host.

I took deer, and fish, and great flying bird, cloaking myself all the while in the colors of the trees, the turning leaves, in the scent of the forest-heavy breeze. I could have called them to their deaths, were their deaths for any other sport but this. But the earth demanded blood, and the blood of the fallen could not be willingly granted—unless it were my own.

I felt young again, a moment, arrow nocked and bow drawn, waiting for the whisper of the breeze to turn against me, to carry me, and the sounds I might make, away from my prey, proud hawk seeking, as I sought, sustenance. I felt wild as I paced the proud stag, antlered in his season, king of his herd and willing, with young at his feet, to stand defiant against the forest's hunters.

Last, of course, a creature from the deep element, a fish, multihued and gasping, silent, for the breath I would deny it. Another time, and each of these hunts would have

had a resonance that would have satisfied an urge to restlessness for a decade. But I did not have a decade. I did
not have a month.

To the earth, I brought these kills, and to the earth, I
gave them. Then I planted roots, of a sort; I waited,
moved by breeze and sun and the rising of the dew, but by
little else. A three-day later, the ground opened at my
behest and swallowed me whole.

When it released me, I could see the shadows cast by
the light of the torches that illuminated the edifice built to
proclaim the Law of Man where all might see it and obey.

The bell hung like shadow in the belfry high above the
earth's floor. In the evening it was silent; the night was
our dominion, but palely. If I stood upon this tainted
ground when the bells broke dawn, I would suffer Mordenel's fate.

And I had not come all this way, through the tunnels
beneath the water and the cold, cold iron, to suffer that
fate. My Anna was here. Beneath the ford, the earth
waited, satiated; it would wait until the voice of the bells
told it to sleep.

There were huts of pressed mud and reed, cabins dark
and gloomy from which light struggled for escape as the
fires burned low and lower still. The time for repast had
past; they slept, these wary creatures, these ugly, fascinating, dying mortals.

And I cared for the fate of only one of them.

I knew where she was, of course. I knew it, as we all
know the location of things that we possess. But as I
approached the small house, I knew more, and I froze on
the other side of the wooden walls. Had it been so long?
The hunts, surely, hadn't taken more than a seven-day. Or
had they? In the Queen's forest it was hard to remember
time as a fact without—without a mortal by which to
measure its passing.

I stood outside the house as the moon's passing length-
ened shadows cast by things with deep roots; the trees.
Myself. Stood, listening, for we can hear much, and what
we hear, we seldom forget.

Her voice came through the open cracks of shutters that

possessed not even the thinnest of glass, came against the breeze and the sound of crickets and the whisper of night creatures slinking from one hole to another. She was singing.

And the song was a song that she had not learned in the realm of our kind—yet it caught at me, pulled me, twisted me. The greatest of our harpers might have ensnared a mere mortal and forced them into the circles, to dance their lives away at our behest with more difficulty.

"Anna," I said, speaking while I *could* speak. "Anna, child, come."

But the song continued unabated, soft and warm and full of a mortal clinging. I had arrived late, too late.

No. Was she not my child? Had I not taken her, from her granddam's arms, had I not raised her, protected her, taught her, had I not schooled her in the wonders of the Court itself? She was *mine,* and the land itself bore witness to my claim, for I stood here, upon these shores, with the tower of man's God a mute and silent witness.

I gestured, and the door came; it flew open, given wings by the words that I whispered to its wooden timber. And there, in the moonlight of the midnight hour, she stood. And she was not the daughter of my dreams or of my memory, for the years had been leached from her life as I hunted and struggled to open the road I might travel to reach her.

Her brow creased; she gazed at me as if I—as if I were a stranger. "Hello?" she said, and I recognized her voice, even given to man's ugly language as it was.

"Anna," I said, in our own sweet tongue, "it is I, Sioban. The Law of Man holds these lands fast; it is only at night that I might come to you at all—and it is only for this one night. The earth waits us; the ways are open briefly, briefly. Come, child," I said.

She took a step forward, and in her arms I saw the thing for whom she sang: a swaddled bundle, an infant younger, even, than she had been when she had been given to my care and keeping.

"Sioban?" she said, and she spoke my name as only she could speak it, although time had robbed her voice of its heights. She stepped forward again, a step, another—and then she stopped, wrapping her arms more tightly around her infant child. I saw it all, in her eyes, the passing of an age; I saw our Court, I saw her wonder, I saw the yearning—all clear, as if I gazed at the still waters, the lips of a spell bringing to their surface the depths I desired.

I lifted my hand, and she, one of hers, and I knew, then, that she would not come.

"Leave it," I told her. "Leave this. This is not the life that you knew—this is not the life you were meant for. The waters—"

"It is the only life I know," she answered tiredly. The lines in her face caught the shadows and held them, and the shadows there were not mine to work. "I have a husband, Sioban, and two children."

"What of them? You belong with—"

"I never belonged with you. You were all so beautiful, so perfect, so distant, so cruel. These men, these women—they're not what you were, but they've given me the kindness that they can, all of it. They—" she hesitated, and then she said, softly, "they love me. If you had ever loved me, Sioban—if you understood what it was, what the need for it meant—I would never have climbed up on Archeraon's mount." There was a momentary anger in her voice, and then, worse than anger or defiance, a terrible, terrible pity.

"This is my daughter," she said, holding the babe, "and my son is sleeping inside." She did not tell me their names, and I knew that she would not; she knew us too well. "My husband is a difficult man, but he tries to be a good one."

"What is this? Good? Anna, you cannot have forgotten everything that we taught you."

"No. And it hurts me, to see you standing there as perfect as you were when I left you years ago. But I—" She stopped speaking then, her arms tightening reflexively around her babe.

No mortal could have heard what she heard. I take pride in that, for she heard it, although its sound was faint. Her skin paled, paled almost to the white that it had been when she had lived by my side in her youth.

"You cannot—you cannot call the hunt—"

"I did not call it," I told her softly.

"But you knew."

"I knew only that the Queen considered. We, none of us, have the ear of the Queen, as you well know."

The moon was round and full and silver. The wild dogs were howling beneath its august light. They had power; we both knew it. We stayed thus, listening. And then she heard them, as I did: the hooves of the host. The host was riding.

"Anna," I told her softly, "leave this place. Now. There will be nothing left for you in it. Come with me, and you might save your life."

"No," she said softly. "These are my children, and these my people, and I will not leave them."

"Anna, please—" but I knew from the set of her lips that the only choice I had was beguilement, and such a spell against one who knew my name was not a spell easily cast. Or quickly. And she had so little time.

"Help me," she said softly.

"I do not know how. I can no more turn back the hunt than you."

"Hold her," she told me. "Hold my child. Keep her from harm."

She turned from me, then, and ran into her little dwelling. I heard her voice, her human voice; I heard the fear in the words that she used to wake her husband and her child from their sleep. And as her voice grew hoarser, I heard her slipping away from me, as if the past were a dream that she had finally broken by waking, as if she were a river finally caught by the sea.

She ran past me, and after a moment her husband followed, lamp bobbling wildly in the darkness of the moonlit night. He returned for his children, seeing me as a shadow the trees cast against the ground. I set the bundle upon the ground and stepped back, that he might see it in time; he caught it up, shouting to the young boy who could barely understand the words he spoke, *Follow, follow.*

And I watched as they struggled to wake their distant neighbors; as they struggled and gave up their struggle.

What had the water named me?

Fallen.

"Anna! Anna, child, Anna."

She came to me, came to me at a run, her skirts snapping the thin dry branches that skirted the ground beneath the rounder girth of wild bushes.

"You cannot outrun the hunt. There is only one place that has any safety for you and your own, and while you might reach it in time, they will not." Her husband and her son and the bundle that he carried. "Run, child. Run to the tower of the Law of Man. Peal the bell, peal it for all that you are worth. Only you will reach those grounds in time, but I will give you one last gift: a glamour. They will listen to you when you speak of the hunt. They will aid you when you call down the Law of Man upon the host."

Her eyes grew round, as round as they often had when, as a child, she discovered something wondrous and new and unknown. "Sioban," she said, softly.

"*Hurry,*" I told her.

And then, I bid farewell to my child. And I returned to the earth, to its safety, in haste. For if the bells of the tower were not certain protection against the wild hunt— and they were not, could not be, if the Queen herself rode—they were more than enough, at this small distance, to sunder my ties with the earth.

The host did not fail in the hunt, but it did not succeed; three men, it brought back, and three strong men at that— but not one of them the men who spread the Law of Man across our dwindling lands.

I did not choose to visit the Court when these three prizes were brought before the Queen, for although she was splendid in her wrath, and glorious, I had other concerns; concerns of my own making.

For I had promised, on the eve of a dance not long past, that I would keep a child from the Law of Man, and I failed. Failure is the one thing that we cannot abide in ourselves.

And yet, and yet. If I have failed with the granddaughter, let me consign, instead, the great-granddaughter.

Yes.

Anna was too frightened to think, and too determined; she accepted the gift I offered without once pausing to ask the cost of it.

And you, my child, my babe, you are the price that she paid. I do not know what she felt when the hunt retreated and her husband gave her her swaddling clothes, empty of life and warmth.

I do not know if she hated me, or if she was angered, or if she went to the lords of the Law of Man and began to plot her vengeance. Plot as she might, she made her choice; she accepted the glamour I placed upon her.

I hope she is happy.

I made my mistakes with my Anna, and I will not make them with you, for I know what I am now. I know why the water named me.

And I will keep you, little child, for as long as your life lasts, hidden from the Court and the Queen and Archeraon. I will age, although they will see no signs of it across the perfect lines of my face, and as you grow, I will grow.

Fallen.

I will love you, as your mother would have loved you, as no one of my kin but I might ever do.

I SING THE DARK RIDERS

by *Dennis L. McKiernan*

Dennis McKiernan is the best-selling fantasy author of *The Voyage of the Fox Rider, Eye of the Hunter,* and *Caverns of Socrates.* His latest novel, *The Dragonstone,* was published in November 1996. His short fantasy fiction has been collected in *Tales of Mithgar,* with other fiction of his appearing in *Weird Tales from Shakespeare* and *Dragon Fantastic.*

*There are times when on the wings of night
the Dark Riders come riding by*

Cor', Elodan, but I don't like this. Not one bit, I don't."

Striding onward, Elodan cast a glance down at the halfling scurrying at his side. "Don't like what, Brink."

"This, this . . . *place!* That's what." Brinkton gestured out ahead, where long tendrils of wraithlike fog curled low across the moonlit moor, drifting over bog and heath alike. "I mean, *look* at it, just lurking in the dark, waiting for the unwary to take a wrong step and sink down forever in a quag. And this fog, it's utterly sinister, the way it slides about the grassy hummocks as if hunting poor souls who may have stumbled."

"And what would it do to them, Brink?"

"Do to them? Do to them? Throttle them, that's what. Strangle the life from them."

"Ah, my friend, 'tis merely a low fog."

Scuttling across a flat stretch of peat, Brinkton looked up at his tall companion, the elf at six feet nearly twice his own height. "Low to you, perhaps—no higher than your knee, as it were—but look down here: It's up to my chest!"

Elodan laughed, but kept striding on.

"Why is it we have to cross in the dark?" grumbled Brink, veering around a hummock. "Can't we just make camp? The peat will make a nice fire, that which is dried out, I mean. We could have a nice cup of tea and cross the rest after the day comes."

Elodan glanced up at the sky, where the crescent moon sailed silently among ragged clouds. "Nay, my friend, not this darktide. I would be quit of this heath ere the belling of mid of night."

"Why? Is there something about these moors? They're bad, aren't they? —I knew it! You can just look at them and tell that they're—"

" 'Tis not only the mire, Brink, but the entire realm. Though I do admit that heaths and bogs and moors are more perilous than aught else."

"Perilous?" blurted Brink. "Oh, my. I knew it. I just knew it. And the land, too?"

Elodan nodded and hitched his lute higher on his back and said, "Hast thou not noted on our travels in this realm that with each sundown, we've been well ensconced within an inn?"

"Yes, but I just thought that we were there early simply to make more money."

"Nay. We were there for safety's sake."

"Safety? Why didn't you tell me this before?"

"I did not wish to cause thee worry."

"Well, I'm plenty worried now. But tell me, this peril, just what is—?"

Suddenly, Elodan stopped in his tracks, and Brink trotted on a few paces ere halting. He turned and frowned and ambled back. "What—?"

The elf threw up a hand to stop Brink's words, and he cocked his head this way and that, as if listening.

Brink listened as well and heard nothing but the soft susurration of drifting air.

Finally Elodan lowered his hand and looked at Brink and sighed. "They are early."

"Early? Who?"

But before Elodan answered, Brink heard a ghostly baying, as from a hunt far off. "The dogs?"

"Aye," said Elodan, sadness in his eyes. "Whatever thou dost, my friend, do not run."

"Run? From what? Why would I run from a simple pack of foxhou—?" Brink's words juddered to a halt, and his tilted gemlike eyes widened. "Oh, lor', Elodan, look."

He pointed upward at a shallow angle into the sky.

And in the distance among the ragged clouds they came running through the air, a vast boiling pack of ghostly dogs baying—two hundred, three hundred, four hundred, or more—trailing long tendrils of shadow behind.

And beyond the pack came galloping horses, coils of darkness flying in their wake, black sparks showering from hard-driven hooves, though there was no stone for steelshoes to strike, high in the air as they were. And on the backs of the ghastly steeds were tenuous riders, twisting shadows streaming in their wake as well.

And in the fore rode the fell leader, his ebon cloak flying out after him, and he lifted a black horn and pealed a dreadful call, and Brink shrieked in terror and turned to flee, yet Elodan wrenched him back and shouted, "Do not run, Brink, else thou art doomed."

Now spying their quarry, down came the hounds, baying their ghastly yawls, deadly jet fire gleaming in their eyes. And they rushed toward the standing pair— five hundred savage, raven-dark hounds slavering blackness—Elodan holding Brink fast. The shrilling halfling could not bolt.

On came the hounds, leaping o'er one another to be the first to the kill, the vast pack a boiling inky mass, mad with the lust to rend the quarry asunder.

Yet Elodan did not move, and Brink could not escape his grasp.

And the crescent moon looked down in silence, indifferent to those below.

Dark fangs gleaming, onward they came, tendrils of black trailing away. And galloping after came the riders, streaming shadows vanishing behind.

"Eeeee. Eeeee," screeched Brink, wrenching against Elodan's iron grip, to no effect whatsoever.

One hundred, seventy, fifty-thirty-twenty feet vanished

the gap and hurtled the hounds, black fire in their jet eyes. . . .

And then they hurled themselves at the pair . . .

. . . the two to be lost in the boiling pack . . .

. . . the hounds . . .

. . . the dogs . . .

. . . the frightful dogs . . .

. . . brushing by, rushing past, their fangs bared but not striking.

And then the pack was away and gone . . .

. . . but now came the riders.

Galloping, galloping toward the two, wraiths upon steeds streaming black.

All but the leader, who seemed substantial enough, ghastly though he was.

And he reined his steed to a halt, the other riders stopping as well.

And from nowhere, somewhere, everywhere, there sounded groans of a thousand faint voices, like the wailing of the wind, yet the air itself did not stir a single blade of grass.

Dressed in an ebon black and wearing a darkling crown, the leader on his huge dark horse gazed down at the pair, with his grim cold eyes of jet.

And his voice came as an icy whisper, freezing the very marrow of bones. "Ye are brave," he hissed, "and I would have ye ride with me."

"Gladly, my lord," replied Elodan.

"*What?*" shrilled Brink. "Elodan, are you mad?"

Elodan looked down at the halfling. "We must, my wee friend," he said as he squeezed hard upon Brink's shoulder, a desperate but certain warning.

The rider turned and gestured behind, and a wraithlike figure ahorse led two riderless mounts to the fore.

Brink looked up at the great animal. "I need a pony, not a monster like this."

"This is your mount," came the bitter whisper.

"But I can't ride a great horse. I'll fall off."

"I would advise against it," the icy voice said.

"Here, Brink, I will shorten the stirrups," said Elodan, reaching for the straps.

"Leave them," coldly hissed the rider.

"As thou wilt, my Lord," replied Elodan. And he swept Brink up and set him in the saddle ere the halfling could object.

Adjusting the lute on his back, Elodan mounted his own steed, and then the dark rider raised his terrible horn to his lips and belled its dreadful call, and Brink shrilled in fear at the sound of it as all the horses sprang forward in pursuit of the hounds.

His feet flopping loose and his hands clutching the cantle in a white-knuckled grip, Brink managed to hang on but just barely as the wraithsteeds rose into the sky, writhing shadowstuff streaming behind and boiling off and away. And Brink closed his eyes in fear as the ground below receded, for he was up in the sky, in the sky, and if he fell, if he fell . . .

Finally Brink gained a bare enough courage to open one eye and after a while the other.

With their cloaks flying out behind, Elodan rode at Brink's side, ghastly riders all about, the ghostly horses plunging through shredded clouds across a moonlit sky, while far ahead dark hounds bayed.

"Elodan, Elodan, what are we doing?" called Brink above the rush of the wind. "Why are we riding with these, these . . . ?"

"We have no choice, my friend, for this is the wild hunt."

"Wild hunt?" cried Brink. "What are they hunting?"

"Cowards, Brink," called Elodan back. "Those who bolt in fear. These, their souls, they rend to shreds."

"And these riders about us, Elodan: who are they?"

"The brave, my friend. They are those who did not run, but stood fast instead."

"But they're ghosts, Elodan. Wraiths. Apparitions."

"Aye."

"But we ride with them. Does it mean we, too, will become as they are? I don't want to be a ghostly figure riding forever through the night, hunting down any innocents who flee from this ghastly band, ripping their spirits to shreds."

"Neither do I, Brink. Neither do I. Yet we may escape

that fate in the end, for if we can stay ahorse until dawn, then we have a chance to be set free."

"A chance?" cried Brink. "Merely a chance?"

"Aye, for Lord Death, as some call him, though he has many names—Lord Terror, Lord Fear, Lord Dread, and Lord Grim among them—has been known to have mercy on those who are brave and ride well in the hunt. Yet if he shows no mercy, we will ride the night forever and never see daylight again."

"Couldn't we simply ride down at first opportunity and jump off?"

Elodan threw out a hand in negation. "Nay, Brink, nay, for thou and I must remain ahorse until dawn cracks the sky." He gestured at the wraiths on the shadowsteeds. "Should we dismount we become as they, and should we fall, we are fair game for the hounds, and they will rend us asunder."

"Oh, my. Oh, my. We are lost, Elodan. We are totally and utterly lost."

Elodan did not reply.

And across the sky they plunged, trailing tendrils of black, dark sparks flying from under hoof.

And of a sudden, the black horn sounded, and Brink shrieked in fear and lost his grip and began to slide from the saddle, as following the hounds the horses spiraled down like ebon leaves on the wind. With his dark steed turning under him, and with his hands scrabbling at the smooth leather of the seat, Brink shrilled, slipping to his death, yet in the very moment he was lost, Elodan managed to master the swirl of the wind and the turn of horses and spur alongside and reach a strong hand across and steady the halfling long enough for him to grab the forecantle and pull himself back upright.

And down and down swirled the spectral horses, the dark hounds ahead and baying. And out before the hounds and across a plowed field ran a shrieking man, and then the pack caught him, and as each of the helldogs flashed by, one by one they slashed at the fleeing mortal and then raced on beyond, black fangs not drawing blood but another essence instead.

One by one they slashed at him . . .

. . . and the man fell down, and still the dogs slashed and ran on . . .

. . . five hundred one by one.

And now the horses thundered by, if a shade can be said to thunder, and Brink wept to see the slain man, his pale face white and staring, his dead eyes filled with fright.

And on through the night sky the wild hunt ran, ghastly hounds baying, ghostly horses racing, spectral riders astride . . . all but three: a halfling, an elf, and the lord of the hunt in the lead.

The crescent moon set and still horse and hound ran on, flying through a cloud-shredded sky and trailing ebon black behind.

Yet at last the dreadful horn sounded once again—Brink shrieking in response—and down and down through the midnight sky swirled the deadly band, spiraling down as would black raven feathers fall. And lo! they came to ground before a splendid inn, four stories high in all, with peaked roof and weathercocks above, though it seemed quite dark.

And the lord of the wild hunt came striding back to where Brink and Elodan sat.

"Come inside and sip the black ale," came the cold whisper.

And even as Brink leaped down, Elodan shouted, "No!" and dark Lord Death looked up at the elf and smiled a heart-freezing grin.

Brink looked up to see the horror in Elodan's eyes, and then he knew. And he reached up and grabbed the stirrup strap and attempted to regain his horse, but he was too small, and as he flailed away trying to find purchase, an icy whisper came to his ear, "Too late, my wee friend." And a chill hand reached down and touched him on the shoulder.

And Brink fell to the cold ground and wept, for now he was truly lost, for he had dismounted ere dawn.

Yet he felt warm hands take him by the shoulders and raise him, and Brink looked up through swimming eyes to see Elodan smiling down at him.

"Oh, Elodan, Elodan, what have you done? Now you are lost, too."

But Elodan merely said, "Come, my friend, let us enter the inn and taste of this fine brew."

Yet weeping, his eyes filled with blinding tears, Brink let Elodan lead him across the sward and up the broad shallow steps, where the door sprang open of its own volition, and they entered a great common room, and lanterns within sprang to light.

And all of the riders followed.

The chamber itself held dark mahogany tables and chairs and a great long ashwood bar, and splendid tapestries decorated the walls—hunters ahorse with dogs—and scarlet velvet drapes hung with gold piping matched the scarlet and gold of the chairs.

The ale itself was delicious, a strange and darkling brew, and Brink quaffed one flagon and then another, and then another still.

Elodan unslung his lute from his shoulder and extracted it from the leather bag and the silken one within, and then he limbered his fingers, and set to a silvery tune.

And he sang as only an elvin bard can sing, and he sang of life and living, and all the riders crowded 'round closely, as if by hearing the very words sung they could recapture the dear essence of that which they had lost.

All crowded 'round but Lord Terror, that is; he sat in a corner alone.

Now Elodan sang of children, and the shades of the riders groaned, sounding as would a cold winter's wind swirling among the stones.

And Elodan sang of love, and the spectral riders hid their faces in their hands.

And still Lord Fear sat unmoved and unmoving in his corner alone.

And the elvin bard sang of women and joy and of ships sailing on the sea, and of rivers and trees and of farming the land, and of buying horses and going to market, and of things and things more.

His songs were happy and sad and short and long, ballads and ditties and long spoken poems, and Brinkton, quite drunk, fell asleep.

And just as Lord Dread pushed away his mug, Elodan called out, "The Wild Hunt."

He struck a chord and began a chant, and Lord Grim settled back to hear:

> *The sky was dark,*
> *The storm clouds blew,*
> *A chill was on the land*
> *Yet, Molly dear,*
> *The message read,*
> *I need your healing hand.*

> *Across the moor*
> *She started out*
> *To reach her father dear.*
> *For he was ill,*
> *And she would aid,*
> *Yet Lord Death she did fear.* . . . .

Elodan sang as he had never sung, his words telling of the wild hunt and of its reaping of souls, whether cowards or heroes, it mattered not, for the leader of the hunt was cold. And as Elodan sang he moved among the shades, and they sobbed as would a frail wind, and still Elodan sang and sang, verse after verse pouring golden words from his silver throat. And his lute seemed enchanted, the notes pure and clear, the concordant strings voicing precious sounds.

Yet at last the song, the very song, came to the end.

And as Elodan's voice and the silver strings finally fell silent, a quietness settled over all . . . only to be broken by a far off cock's crow.

Elodan threw back a drape, allowing in light from the rising rim of the sun just now broaching the edge of the world. The elf turned to find the chamber empty of all but Brink who was asleep.

And the fine inn, the splendid inn, it was naught but a ramshackle ruin.

Elodan packed his lute away, and shook Brink by the shoulder. "Awaken, my friend, my timid small friend, and see the glorious new day."

A MIDSUMMER NIGHT'S DREAM TEAM

by Tanya Huff

Born in the Maritimes, Tanya Huff now lives and writes in
rural Ontario. On her way there, she spent three years in
the Canadian Naval Reserve and got a degree in Radio
and Television Arts which the cat threw up on. Her last
book out was *No Quarter* (March 1996), the direct sequel
to *Fifth Quarter* (August 1995) and her next book will be
Blood Debt (April 1997), a fifth Vicki/Henry/Celluci novel.

Long years ago, when lesser were the shadow veils
That hang 'tween this world
And the courts of proud Oberon,
Who rules the spirits with fair Titania by his side,
Men oft times saw the elven folk.
Saw them in the waters,
And riding beasts of bone or horned head,
Saw them duel each other and more than saw;
Battles there were in those days, great battles.
Blood did spill red and hot upon the ground
As immortal warriors challenged mortals of renown.

But Gentles, times do change,
Though slow within the Faerie court,
And battles now must be a different sort.

"One hundred and ninety-seven countries; ten thousand,
seven hundred athletes; we've been at this for two hours
and we're only at Belize!" Sam Gilburne squinted
through the viewfinder on her camera, saw that the
entrance to the stadium was still perfectly framed and
leaned back. "We're going to be here for-fucking-ever."
The camera went live as the director cut to her wide shot,

but the red light blinked off again almost immediately when they went in for a close-up on one of a multitude of mobile units. "Mobile. Yeah right. If you're a steroid-carrying member of the weight lifting team." Fixed positions might be boring—all right, fixed positions were inevitably boring—but boredom never produced a hernia.

She checked her shot again, made a miniscule adjustment in focus just for something to do, and wiped at the sweat dribbling down her neck. Years of practice blocked out the steady chatter in her headphones; when they wanted her, she'd hear them.

A number of the European countries were using computer-controlled units in their fixed positions, but the Canadian Broadcasting Corporation, while as fascinated by high tech as anyone in the industry, recognized two very important things. The first; even the best computer couldn't respond to the unexpected the way a trained operator could. And the second; since, this time, they had lots of room on the trucks, people were cheaper.

Although she swore to deny it later if anyone asked, Sam found herself caught up in the excitement as the Canadian team entered.

"Camera one, when they all get down into the bowl of the stadium, I want you to give me a long, sweeping shot. Start at the flag and move back. I want to see happy faces."

"I thought three was doing the happy faces."

"Just give me the shot, Sam."

As the last of the Canadian team stepped off the ramp, Sam unlocked her camera.

"Just keep it moving. Ready one . . ."

By the time she got to the end of the team, she'd grown heartily sick of all that smiling. There were those around the CBC, those who'd worked with her for almost twenty years, who believed Sam herself never smiled. That wasn't entirely true, although it was highly possible that they'd never seen her actually do it.

When she finally managed to reframe her establishing shot, the Ethiopian team had almost reached the bottom of the ramp. Behind them, heat shimmered up off the concrete.

Shimmered in the gap between Ethiopia and Fiji.

"Camera one, what are you doing?"

"There's something wrong with my focus."

"There's nothing wrong with your focus, lock it and leave it."

Sam locked the camera in place and squinted around it toward the stadium entrance. Ethiopia. One of the irritatingly frequent empty spaces. Fiji.

She took another look through the viewfinder.

The heat shimmer maintained a careful distance behind the Ethiopian team. Within it, under a gossamer flag, shapes with flowing edges took form for a heartbeat then faded, replaced by others, who were replaced by others in their turn. Some bordered on the grotesque. Some on the beautiful. But they were all tall.

Real tall.

"Swimming?" Sam glared up at the assignment board. "Why swimming?"

One of the technical directors handed her a cardboard cup of coffee. "Why not swimming?"

"Chlorine makes me itch."

"You're not going to be in the pool, Sam." He nodded at the board. "You're up by the booth."

"Great. Announcers make me itch."

"Camera one, what are you doing?"

Sam frowned and flipped her microphone back around in front of her mouth. "I'm establishing the venue. What does it look like I'm doing?"

"If I knew, I wouldn't have asked. I want the pool framed, one. You've got way too much deck at the bottom of the shot. There's only eight lanes."

In the ninth lane, naked women, with flowing hair the color of a sun-lit sea, swam lazy circles and waited.

Many of the men, irrespective of country, swam a personal best that day. Personally, Sam was amazed that none of them drowned.

"Horse Park?" When she got an affirmative, Sam climbed onto the bus and collapsed into the first empty seat. Because daily temperatures were expected to climb into and then out of the nineties, equestrian events started at seven a.m. In order to have everything ready in time, crews were pulled out of bed at five. Sam didn't do so well at five. "What the hell is a three-day event," she muttered darkly.

Her seat mate stared at her in astonishment. "You don't know horses?"

"Not biblically, no. I'm just filling in for Burbadge; he's down with heat exhaustion. Don't look so worried, I can fake it if I have to."

She didn't have to fake it; she had to remember not to follow the horned horses, the skeletal horses, or the horses who left flaming hoofprints on the course.

"Do you hear dogs baying?" one of the Irish sound techs asked, fiddling with the bass gain.

"I don't think they're dogs," Sam said.

"So, how'd your day at fencing go, Sam?"

Sam shook her head as she swallowed a mouthful of beer. "Can't say as I'm surprised we only had one camera there. It's either so complicated it's beyond me, or it's just plain old fucking dull."

One of the gaffers laughed. "Got that in one."

"What do you think it needs to jazz it up, Sam?"

"How about two guys, six-and-a-half, seven feet tall, with hair down to their butts, wearing thigh-high boots, skin-tight pants, no shirts, and lotsa jewelry, hacking at each other with great bloody swords until one of them falls to his knees and begs for mercy."

The din in the bar dropped by about two decibels as everyone in earshot fell into a thoughtful silence.

"I'd watch that," a video editor muttered at last.

Sam finished her beer. "Damn right."

On the second to last day of the games, the crowd around the assignment board seemed more animated than usual. As Sam approached, one of the younger cameramen exploded out of the group and grabbed her arm. "We've got the two CBC spots at the basketball finals,

Sam! You and me! Gold medal round! Do you know what that means?"

"It's almost over?"

"It's the U.S. against Yugoslavia! It's *the* game to see! You'll be able to tell everyone back home you were there!" He paused, actually focused on her, and released her arm. "Okay, maybe not."

"You're John Lowine, right?"

"The very lucky John Lowine, that's me. I don't believe I'm going to be shooting this game!"

Sam studied his face for a moment, wondered how much of these Olympics he'd been aware of, and had no chance to ask as the rest of the team descended.

Assignments were nonnegotiable. Those were the rules. In spite of the rules, Sam could've retired on what she was offered for her spot. Another time, other games, she might've been tempted.

"You've been at this a long time, haven't you?" John asked as they started their equipment check.

"Long enough," Sam agreed.

"I bet you've seen pretty much everything."

"I used to think so."

Tucked into the bottom third of an enormous stadium packed with over 35,000 screaming fans, the game turned out to be unexpectedly exciting basketball. The Yugoslavian team stubbornly refused to fold and stayed within two points until the U.S. center finally kicked it into high gear in the last thirteen minutes.

Not all the sweat dripping off the U.S. team had to do with exertion. Losing would be an embarrassment none of them would ever live down. In the end, they managed to fulfill expectations—if not as easily as they'd all believed they would.

"Camera one, what are you doing?"

Sam zoomed back until she had the whole court in focus. "Waiting."

"For what?"

"Something's going to happen." All the hair on the back of her neck was standing on end. The static electricity was so high she wouldn't have been surprised to see lightening jump from rafter to rafter, run down the bleachers, off the backboard, and hit nothing but net.

"It's already happened, one. Get in close and let's get some shots of those idiots sniffing the sho . . ."

Then another team appeared at center court.

Their bodies were too perfectly in proportion, their movements too sensuous, their faces too eerily similar for them to be human. And, if all that wasn't proof enough, beneath meters of multicolored hair clubbed back with gold and silver bands, their ears came to graceful and prominent points.

The audience, the players, the officials, who had all one short moment before been hooting and hollering and just generally carrying on, stared in silence. Even Sam, who'd expected an appearance of some kind, found herself at a loss for words.

"What are you guys, Vulcans?" one of the U.S. players demanded at last.

"This isn't some freakin' *Star Trek* episode," the man beside him added.

And pandemonium broke loose as people discovered they couldn't leave their seats.

"I find it absolutely appalling how no one seems to get a classical education anymore."

Sam, not at all surprised that her headphones were dead, turned to see a curly haired young man dressed all in brown—shorts, T-shirt, running shoes—perched on the light standard beside her.

He grinned and leaped down. "Robin Goodfellow. And you must be Sam, no one calls you Samantha, Gilburne. How've you been enjoying the games?"

"They've been . . . interesting."

"Haven't they just."

"My gentle Puck! Come hither!"

Sighing, he turned to go. "Our Faerie captain calls and when fell Oberon doth summon, I must move my butt." He tossed a grin back over his shoulder. "I'll be back."

Oberon wore a gold circlet around silver hair and a golden "C" on a leaf green jersey. His voice carried. "This fool pretends to understand me not." A long, pale finger poked a trembling games official in the chest. "Explain, good Puck, the terms on which we play."

Sam couldn't hear the explanation, but it involved a great deal of arm waving, consulting of clipboards, and ended with the young man in brown turning the official to face a glowering Oberon.

The crack of thunder shut everyone up again. Hysterics screeched to a halt all over the stadium. As the official was carried off the court, Puck turned to face the U.S. bench. "My lord challenges those proven best in the world to play for the gold. What say you?"

Arms folded and eyes narrowed to disapproving slits, the coach shook his head. "I say that you can all just go back where you came from. My boys don't have to prove anything."

Puck favored him with an extraordinarily rude gesture. "Who asked you?" All at once, the stadium lights seemed to shine brighter over and around the twelve members of the U.S. team. "I was talking to them."

The team milled about for a moment as a single unit then spit out a spokesman.

"He's challenging us?"

Oberon answered for himself. "I am."

"Then we say, let's play ball!"

"They might as well play," Puck said a moment later, back by Sam's side. "He wasn't going to let anyone leave until he got his game. Me, I blame television."

"For what?" The two men—*Well, two males,* Sam amended—stood eye to eye at center court.

"The shorter attention span of children, the sudden popularity of orange bathing suits, the inexplicable interest in Snack Masters . . ."

Oberon won the jump off.

"You watch our television?"

"Sure. Everything but Fox scrys in beautifully."

"What about the CBC?"

Puck shrugged. "It comes in, but no one watches it. All *this* started when His Majesty discovered the symbolic warfare channel."

One of the elves took a three point shot. It hit the rim, rolled, and dropped through.

3 - 0, Faerie.

"Discovered the what?"

"Oh, sorry. Sports. This specifically . . ." He waved at hand at the action on the court. ". . . I blame myself for. His Majesty asked if I thought he should take up the game; I said, why not; you're tall, you're arrogant. The rest, as they say, is mythology."

3 - 4, U.S.A.

Oberon went down with an elbow in the throat and made both foul shots.

5 - 4, Faerie.

Thirty-one seconds later, it happened again.

7 - 6, Faerie.

"That's a man who likes to live dangerously," Puck observed with glee. "Oberon is not going to take kindly to a third foul."

Twelve seconds later, a terrified rooster raced under the U.S.A. bench.

After that, the game settled down. Sam, who'd never much cared for basketball and had not been thrilled at the prospect of having to watch a second competition, found herself enjoying the show. The elves made no sound as they ran, their feet only barely touched the floor, and more than one U.S. player lost the ball when he turned suddenly and came face to face with an unexpected feral grin.

Sam had a strong suspicion that no one on the court was named Mustard Seed.

38 - 35, Faerie at half time.

Early in the second half, an elf took a rebound and immediately stepped to the other end of the court. During the time-out, the officials huddled by the scorekeeper and after a moment declared seven league boots to be illegal. The U.S. made both their shots.

38 - 37, Faerie.

Finally realizing that the opposition wasn't going to give them this game either, the U.S. team started to play the basketball the way only they could, matching Faerie's ruthless calm with a near telepathic sense of precision teamwork.

65 - 68, U.S.A. with three minutes to go.

"Up and down! Up and down!" Puck screamed, balancing

on the back of two chairs. "You've got to chase them up and down! This is no time to play defensively!"

He wasn't the only one rooting for the elves, Sam noticed. The Yugoslavian team and their fans seemed solidly on Oberon's side—considering how close they'd come only to lose to a stacked deck, she couldn't blame them.

Impossibly graceful, eyes glittering with an emerald light, Oberon swept past the U.S. defense and took a shot from just outside the line.

Tie game.

Twelve seconds to play.

"What happens if he loses?" Sam wondered.

Puck shrugged. "Ass-heads all around, I'm afraid. He doesn't like losing."

The U.S. got the ball on the turnover. At the elven net, a guard with raven hair and ice blue eyes blocked the shot.

Five seconds. Four.

A green-haired elf took the pass at center court, ducked under the long, sweaty arm of a U.S. player, and on a single bounce got the ball back to Oberon.

Three. Two.

He leaped. Higher. Higher. His arm rose over his head, the ball held balanced on fingertips, and, at the apex of his flight . . .

. . . slam dunk.

The buzzer sounded.

70 - 68, Faerie.

Astonished to find herself on her feet, stamping and cheering, Sam fell silent as Oberon walked slowly toward the exhausted U.S. team. By the time the elven lord stood an arms-length away, his court behind him, an eerie quiet had settled over the entire stadium.

For a heartbeat, great branching antlers rose above a golden crown and robes, in colors almost painful to mortal eyes, swept the floor.

"Good game," he said.

And they were gone.

"Could someone please tell me *why* I am under this bench!?"

Frowning, Sam watched and listened and realized . . .

"They remember nothing; not the challenge nor how the challenge ended," Puck told her.

"I do."

"Someone must. What point our being here if no one makes a story of it?"

"Why me?"

"Why not you? You had the eyes to see." He held out his hand. "I must be off, Night's swift dragons cut the clouds full fast and my lord will want his Puck to share the revels."

Half expecting a joy-buzzer, Sam was relieved to note that a firm grip contained nothing more than calluses.

Stepping back, Puck spread his arms and grinned. "Time to party!"

"Camera one? You sleeping up there, Sam? I told you to get me the reactions to that shoe!"

She swung the camera around and panned the strangely subdued crowds. "What shoe?" The shoe had been tossed back for the Faerie game and now covered the foot it belonged on. While the control room argued over just where the alleged shoe should be, Sam turned back to Puck, saying, as she turned, "Still, it's a pity you won't get your medals."

"What was that, one?"

Robin Goodfellow had disappeared.

"Nothing."

Later that evening, as they played the anthem they'd had cued up and ready before the final game began, Sam peered through her camera at the athletes on the podium.

And she smiled.

> On the morrow, many voices were in rage and
> wonder raised
> As the twelve who met the challenge
> Of proud Oberon and his court
> Did find a leaf against their breasts
> Instead of that which they believed they'd won.
> Silently, were medals struck again
> And those who witnessed never told
> How sunlight acts on Faerie gold.

Home Key

by Barbara Delaplace

Some of Barbara Delaplace's more than thirty short fiction pieces appear in *Deals with the Devil*, *Christmas Bestiary*, and *Horse Fantastic*. She has been nominated twice for the John W. Campbell award, and lives in Florida.

"Goddam tourists! They're a menace on the streets. Breaking all the laws." The heavyset man's voice carried all the way across the patio. "If I was still a cop, I'd ticket them six ways to breakfast."

"Please, not again," groaned Noel quietly. He'd come to Mimi's to enjoy a little congenial human company, not listen to Pete the ex-cop from New Jersey complain yet again about moped-riding tourists disobeying traffic regulations.

"Amen to that, brother," replied Jerry equally quietly. Noel watched the bartender's congenial face close up behind his wire-framed glasses as he turned to the sink to rinse beer mugs. "Bet he'd like it better if tourists drove cars around instead of mopeds. *Then* they'd obey traffic regulations. Of course, then all those extra cars would clog up Old Town even worse than it is now."

"Jerry, if Pete had his way, there'd be no tourists at all roaming the streets," replied Noel. And Key West would be much poorer, in many ways. Tourists were the island's life blood.

It would be a lot less interesting, too. Lost souls of every sort washed up on Key West, carried by the tides of humanity. *Even the occasional* very *lost soul*, thought Noel with a wry inner smile. Yet they all blended into the easygoing polyglot that made up the Rock's social fabric.

"Oughta be wearing helmets. And seat belts." Pete's

tirade showed no sign of abating. Mimi's regulars—the bar was a favorite with locals—tended to a group philosophy of live and let live. And they generously extended that view to the occasional tourist perceptive or adventurous enough to look past the barely-readable sign outside, and step into the cool, wood-paneled interior. The tasty food and expertly-run bar did the rest, along with the tree-shaded patio, concealed from the street by a tall, sun-bleached fence. Many a chance visitor had become part of the Mimi "family," returning again and again.

Alas, Pete, too, appreciated a fine bar, and showed no sign of wanting to quit what was becoming his regular hangout. The regulars were growing restive, and Jerry's expression darkened again. "Man, he just *can't* keep coming back. He brings the tone of the whole place down."

Noel could feel it, too. The warmth that had drawn him inside on his very first visit, the reason he returned several times a week, now was subdued by Pete's hostile aura. "Maybe he'll decide he likes it better somewhere else, Jerry."

"Yeah, and maybe I'll win the Florida Lotto. I hear it's up to $27 million this week," replied the bartender gloomily. "I could use $27 million. I'd buy him his own bar. On Little Duck Key."

"Better yet, make it Homestead," said Noel. Jerry laughed at that, his face brightening, and he moved away to serve a new couple that had seated themselves at the bar.

Pete's monologue at last wound down, and he demanded his tab, then swung heavily off the barstool. As he walked out the door, Noel's eyes narrowed. Jerry probably wouldn't win the lottery, but *he* could arrange to ensure Pete would decide he liked it better somewhere else. All it would take is a light—well, humans would use the word "spell," which only showed how little they understood the subtler interactions of energy and matter. A little reprogramming of memory by rerouting the electron flow along the neurons just *there* and . . . yes, that would do the trick. Pete wouldn't even remember Mimi's existed; he'd find some other bar to frequent. All it would

take was a brief laying on of hands, and that was mostly
to enable him to focus his attention properly.

"Jerry," he called down the bar, "keep it cold for me.
I'll be back in a few minutes." Jerry nodded, and floated a
new plastic cup containing ice in his beer. Noel unobtrusively followed Pete out the door.

He returned ten minutes later. His eyes shimmered in
satisfaction as he discarded the cup floating in his mug
and took a long refreshing swallow of ice-cold brew.
There were times when being an elf among humans had
distinct advantages.

Pete, he knew, wouldn't be back.

He hadn't wanted to come here. But he had no choice in
the matter. Elvenkind had traveled the world of man for
centuries, nearly always concealing their true nature so as
not to attract unwelcome attention. And for good reason:
Humans had no extended senses at all; their understanding of the world around them was limited to the very
coarsest, most obvious phenomena. The interplay
between energy and matter that elves perceived so readily
escaped them so utterly they labeled such phenomena
"magic." And those who attempted to understand had
only the most childish notions of how such interactions
occurred. It was laughable.

But the Council—those mysterious elders of elvenkind—said it was good training for a young elf to come
through the Gate and learn to deal with other races. So he
came. After all, it wouldn't be for long. Just until the
Council decided he had learned . . . well, whatever it was
he was supposed to learn. His own instructor had been
conveniently vague about that. "You'll know when it's
time, Alassar. The Gate will come, and you can step
through and be home in an instant."

That had been a long time ago. So long that he'd become used to thinking of himself by the human name he'd
chosen. He didn't think he'd ever hear himself referred to
by his elven name again. He didn't think the Gate would
come for him, not any more. Not after what he'd done.

Noel smiled sadly to himself as he walked the dark,
quiet streets back to the dock where his boat was moored.

He'd been so arrogant at first, so sure he'd had nothing to learn from man.

He hadn't realized it, naturally. For a long time, he was scornful of humans, and interacted with them only when necessity compelled him. For an elf who preferred living as simply as possible, necessity didn't compel very often. Black Jack Key, the island he chosen to settle, was so small no one else lived there, and it was easy to ensure his isolation with the aid of a fractional shift in dimensional phase, just enough to make the tiny island unnoticeable, nothing more. Boaters simply overlooked it as they passed by.

His physical needs were few enough. He salvaged a small sailboat, anchorless and drifting after a storm. A cistern to trap rain water, a small cabin for protection from thunderstorms, an easily woven casting net for fish, driftwood for the occasional cheer of a fire—he required little more. (He later discovered, rather sheepishly, that he was not the only one to prefer simplicity: many humans scattered about the Keys lived lives as unencumbered as his.)

And he found unexpected beauty in this world. There were no craggy purple mountains as in his homeland, but there were spectacular clouds, fleeting ranges of them towering into the sky, building, then vanishing, daily. When the sunset turned them into canyons and pillars of fire, it matched any display of light manipulation by entertainers of his own people.

There were dolphins, cavorting in the glittering water. He learned to swim with them, dancing among the waves far from the sight of humans. Their interactions with each other and with him were continually fascinating. And they led him to yet another delight: coral reefs, swarming with a staggering array of sea life in colors and shapes almost beyond imagining.

And there were thunderstorms. He gloried in the rumble and crash of the thunder, feeling it shake his bones when the storm raged overhead. He loved watching the vicious white bolts of lightning leap from cloud to cloud or cloud to ground, feeling the waves of electrical potential wash over his skin like water as they rippled through the air. And he could *see* those waves, vast shifting curtains of charged particles, like rivers in the sky. He found himself pitying humans unable, because of their narrower visual spectrum, to see the fullness of such a commonplace spectacle in their own skies.

But man does not live by bread alone, and neither, he learned—if slowly—does elf. The Gate did not come, and he grew lonely for the sound of voices, even the unmelodious voices of humans.

So he ventured cautiously to explore Key West, a short sail due south of Black Jack Key. He wandered Mallory Square at sunset, listening to the performers give their spiels over and over, and watched the reactions of their audiences to learn what were considered appropriate responses. He roamed the streets of Old Town and browsed in the stores, further absorbing English and Spanish from overheard conversations. After a couple of weeks, he felt ready to tackle those bastions of free speech and open discourse, the bars.

The problem of money was easier to solve than he'd first expected. He had brought gold with him into this world. And collectors of gold scavenged from the many shipwrecks around the Keys could be found at nearly any bar. Intent on enriching their own personal hoards, they asked no awkward questions. It was a simple matter to alter the shape of the gold he carried to something they expected to see.

Thus supplied with local currency, he was able to sit in a quiet corner with a slowly-sipped beer, eavesdropping on others' conversations. As he learned, he found himself unwillingly intrigued. Humans were not as subtle as elvenkind, but that didn't mean they weren't complex in their own ways.

Or as simple as Pete the Ex-Cop, Noel reflected as he untied his boat. Sometimes things were as shallow as they seemed at first glance. *Ah, well, variety is the spice of life, as humans say.* He rowed away from the dock, then set his sail to catch the night breeze. Much as he enjoyed Mimi's, his cabin on Black Jack would be a welcome refuge tonight.

He sailed home under the star-studded velvet sky.

* * *

The next day was market day. He'd learned in his solitary sojourn on Black Jack that a diet of foraged food eventually becomes monotonous. To his surprise he found that humans were as devoted to good eating as his own people. He hadn't expected them to appreciate the nuances of taste—one didn't expect such things from creatures just barely above the brute. And yet. . . .

Key West was full of little shops selling unique sauces, spices, and other condiments; even Mimi's sold its own brand of hot sauce. And there were stores offering a wide array of fresh vegetables and fruit. He became an adventurer in gastronomy, and found that his biweekly grocery runs were an important part of his life, not only for the new tastes but also the discussions he had with the merchants about ways to use this or that foodstuff. Cooking, he discovered, was as good a way to make new friendships as was drinking.

The storm warning was out as he sailed into the harbor, and he noted the line of clouds in the distance. Tropical Storm Frieda had been bumbling its way across the Atlantic for some days now, never building up to hurricane strength, but never quite withering away either. And last night at Mimi's, the weather reports warned Frieda had finally turned toward Key West. He had time to shop, but if he wanted to return home before the storm broke, he'd have to forgo a leisurely beer at the Bottle Cap— another small bar catering almost entirely to residents— with the Bird Lady. He moored quickly and headed toward the market.

That was too bad because he always enjoyed hearing about her latest rescue effort; she was forever having to run some egret with a broken wing or pelican with a fishhook-torn pouch across the Seven Mile Bridge to the nearest wildlife clinic. Noel had long ago decided her husband possessed the patience of a saint. Good-humored about her causes, he was the one stuck with the miles of driving, since she had to restrain the feathered victim by hand to prevent further injury to the bird—or to its rescuer: Several species had an alarming habit of aiming their daggerlike beaks for the eyes. He was also the one stuck with the clean-up duties while the Bird Lady and the vets were dealing with their patient: Seabirds, he assured Noel, did not grasp the idea of paper training.

He was so lost in thought that he didn't notice the gaunt figure weaving toward him. " 'Scuse me, Mr. Hemingway . . ." said a rusty voice. "Couldja spare a little change for another writer who's down on his luck?"

Noel refocused his attention and recognized Shrimper Tom, one of the regulars on the street. He smiled at him. "And when did you start hitting up your old pals, Tommy?"

Tommy looked at him blearily. "Oh, hiya, Noel." He tipped his salt-stained cap."Sorry 'bout that—I didn't recognize you for a moment. Got a lot on m' mind, you know."

Such as where to find your next drink, thought Noel. Tommy hadn't been fully sober since Captain Tony had declared the island the Independant Conch Republic, nearly fifteen years ago. Noel was startled. Had it been that long? *Time passes so quickly,* he thought.

"So howzit goin'? World treatin' you right?" the old man asked. He may have been one of the Rock's legendary drunks—no small distinction in a town crammed with both transient and permanent devotees of the bottle—but he always took a genuine, if somewhat blurry, interest in those he considered his friends. Who were a select group, because Tommy had an unerring nose for phonies, whom he loathed.

"I'm doing fine, thank you, Tommy. How about you?"

"Never better."

Not quite true. Noel's perception, attuned to those around him in a way human senses were not, told him Tommy needed food. Of course, he'd never admit it; Tommy's pride wouldn't let him hustle his own friends. The situation called for a little manipulation. Noel glanced around; a passing tourist with a wallet carelessly stuffed in the rear pocket of his Bermuda shorts provided the opportunity. A very slight mental tug on a protruding bill and the creation of a swift little breeze and . . .

"What's that by your foot, Tommy?"

Tommy bent down to pick up the five-dollar bill

whirled by the tiny gust to his feet. His face brightened when he realized what it was. "Well, wouldja lookit that?"

Good luck for sure," said Noel. "Better spend it before the wind blows it away again." He winked at Tommy. "I think Cactus Carrie's having a two-dollar special on Cuban sandwiches today."

"Say, thatsa great idea. S'long, Noel." Tommy tipped his battered Navy cap as he wove his unsteady way around Noel and on down the street toward the sandwich vendor's cart.

Noel smiled to himself as he recalled an all-candidates' rally he'd attended some years ago—he found humans' politics almost as fascinating as their bars—where a speech was being given by a notoriously self-righteous prospective member running on a county reform ticket. She'd been in full-throated flight about her concern for the less fortunate, particularly street people, "life's unfortunates," whom she felt should be "treated humanely, treated so they can lead normal, useful lives once again."

Perhaps it was the word "unfortunates" that caught Tommy's attention. "Or—knowing Tommy—maybe it was the term "normal." At any rate, he decided to take issue with her remarks, and before more level heads could restrain him, he'd pushed to the front of the crowd and bellowed "Where ya gonna treat 'em?"

She was a little startled, although as a long-time resident of Key West, she shouldn't have been—political emotions ran high in the Keys, and the security staff at the door was not there for merely decorative purposes. However, she replied smoothly, "They should be treated by the best medical personnel available, sir. Nobody knows better than I just how tragic the loss—"

"Yeah? Where ya gonna get 'em? There ain't nobody on Key West lookin' after us old soaks. I oughta know. I've looked everywhere, and I sure's hell can't find anyone." The crowd chuckled. Most of them knew Tommy.

She replied, a little less smoothly this time. "You are, unfortunately, all too correct, sir. Key West *doesn't*, alas, have the resources. We're just too small. A larger com-

munity like Marathon—or better still, Miami—does have
the resources, and that's where I propose—"

"Gonna ship us out, eh? Don't like us cluttering up the
streets, I betcha is more like it." The audience stirred
slightly at that.

Her smile was becoming a little forced, but she kept it
firmly in place. "Not 'ship out,' sir. Just temporarily relo-
cate people like yourself, temporarily down on their
luck—"

"Temporarily? Lady, I ain't had a job in fifteen years."

Her smile suddenly became sharklike. "Indeed? Then
perhaps you don't belong in a decent, hard-working, God-
fearing community like ours. Welfare bums have no place
in our town." By now the crowd was becoming restless.
Many of them knew Tommy's service record, one of the
reasons he was gently tolerated.

"Bum?" Tommy roared. He stepped up to the foot of the
stage. " 'Least *I'm* an honest panhandler. How much're
you gettin' paid for showin' up here tonight, huh?"

She went scarlet, for—as the *Key West Citizen* later
printed in its prize-winning investigative series on her
financial activities—she had indeed pocketed a hefty, and
highly irregular, appearance fee from the party bagman
just before appearing on stage.

Nobody could later recall just how Tommy had managed to get his contraband past the security staff. The
guard at the door had sworn a mighty oath he'd patted
Tommy down and that the old man hadn't been carrying
anything other than his usual battered cap and worn
wallet. But somehow he'd smuggled the can through, and
at the moment of the candidate's maximum discomfiture,
he let fly.

The results were the topic of conversation in bars all
over Old Town, and the consensus was that Shrimper
Tom had outdone himself: spraying a candidate with fluo-
rescent green plastic string made a real political statement. Of course he'd been tossed out of the meeting, but
he'd hung onto the edge of the stage like grim death and
emptied the entire can before allowing himself to be carried away. The security men had been careful as they
hauled his fragile carcass up the aisle, so he was able to

complete his triumphant, evening by sneering at their efforts. "Call yerselves bouncers? Dribblers is more like it. I bin thrown outta the best bars on the Rock, and this sure's hell ain't the best bar. Fact is, it ain't even the worst."

"Gotta agree with you there, Tom," said one of the guards, as they reached the door of the hall. "Take care of yourself."

"Can't. Madame Candidate back there's gonna make sure I get looked after. Vote early 'n' often, guys." He shook off their hands and had swaggered, slightly unsteadily, off into the night.

Noel, lurking unobtrusively at the back of the auditorium, had enjoyed the whole affair immensely, and made a point of making Tommy's acquaintance the next time he went bar-hopping. They'd been friends ever since.

And perhaps the friendship helped make up for another man, he thought. One he hadn't treated with as much respect.

As he loaded his purchases on his boat, he saw the gale warning flags flying at the harbor entrance. A glance at sky and water showed why: the clouds he'd noted earlier were piled even higher, and there was a strong chop on the water. He finished stowing the bags and cast off.

He made it back to Black Jack ahead of the storm. As he tied up the boat, a tiger-striped orange tabby emerged onto his tiny dock to supervise operations.

"Hello, Castaway," he said. "Come to help unload?" Castaway didn't answer, and didn't help unload either, so he had to work single-handedly to get his gear and groceries ashore, and the boat safely hauled well up the beach. And all the time he was working, the clouds milled across the sky, a blanket of roiled gray to human eyes, vast columns of shifting electronic potentials to his eyes. The storm would break soon.

When it did, it was every bit as violent as he'd expected. The rain fell in torrents, with thunder and lightning constant companions. The wind lashed up the surf to almost tidal wave levels, so that he was glad to be snug within his cabin, well protected from the ocean by the bulwark of the mangroves which broke the force of the wind and water. He glanced at Castaway, a true cat of the Keys and never bothered by mere storms; she was curled up asleep on his bed, every line of her body radiating contentment. He joined her on the bed, although not to sleep—sleeping through a storm like this would be a wasted opportunity. Instead, he assumed a meditative posture that would keep his body secure, and began a series of deep, cleansing breaths. After a short time, relaxed yet focused, he knew he was ready. One final breath, and his spirit soared out of his body and into the splendor of the storm.

He saw it while he was skimming over the white-foamed waves. A fourteen-foot Larson, floundering in the huge swells, lost and helpless and taking on water, in danger of sinking at any minute. And aboard, equally helpless, a human. Noel knew there was no help to be found nearby—every vessel was anchored, riding out the storm in some harbor or lee of an island. Black Jack was the closest land. Mentally he sighed, unwilling to leave the exhilaration of the storm to return to his body. But of course he had to return—there was no one else who could rescue the crewman.

Spirit and body reunited, Noel hurried out into the storm down the sturdy walkway through the mangroves to the dock. Yes, there was the motorboat, just barely visible through the downpour. But how would he get out to it? His small sailboat was totally unsuited to rescue work—it would be tossed about like a cockleshell in the gale and the swells.

You knew it would come to this the instant you decided to save the humans, he chided himself. *There is no other solution.* He could only hope the human wouldn't notice, in all the commotion of the storm. *Small chance of that,* he thought. Not with what he intended to do.

Reaching out with his mind, he felt for the shapes of the air, the swirls of high and low pressure that made up the storm in this immediate area. Ah now, if he slowed the movement of that mass of air over there, and speeded up this mass here, the resulting changes in wind dynamics ought to . . .

There.

The wind stilled.

Like the eye at the center of a hurricane, Black Jack Key became, literally, an island of calm. Noel ran to his boat, pushed it into the water and scrambled aboard, then carefully—for the dynamics were dangerously unstable—raised enough wind to sail toward the now tranquilly floating boat. *At last I appreciate the benefits of an outboard motor,* he thought with a wry smile. *Never again will I sneer at human technology.*

As the wind and water stilled, the human emerged from the cabin onto the deck of his craft. He saw Noel approaching and moved to the railing. "I don't have to tell you how relieved I am to see you, do I?" he shouted as the sailboat drew closer.

"Not at all," Noel replied as he tossed him a line. He didn't need extended perception to see the paleness of the man's skin, or how strained with worry his face was. "Is there anyone else with you?" Though he knew there was no other living creature aboard, his long sojourn in this world had made concealment of his abilities an unthinking habit.

"No—I'm alone," the man replied as he pulled the two boats together. Noel grabbed the railing of the motorboat, holding their position. "Then jump aboard—I'm not sure how long this calm will last." Indeed, he could sense wisps of wind nibbling at the edges of the stillness he'd created. The man scrambled onto the sailboat, ungracefully but quickly, and Noel immediately pushed off from the other boat.

Another cautious mental command and again a puff of wind filled the sail. They headed back toward the island, Noel concentrating hard to keep the air masses under control for a just a few minutes longer. Thankfully, the human was silent, allowing him to focus his whole attention on getting them safely to shore.

One last gust of wind drove the boat up into the shallows, and both elf and human jumped out. Together they drew the craft up the beach, until Noel said, "This will be far enough." The man stumbled to his knees, but the elf took his arm and lifted him to his feet again. He'd relaxed his control of the air the moment they'd reached the shallows, and the wind was picking up rapidly. "We'll have to keep moving—the storm is coming back."

Gamely, the man steadied himself. "I'm all for getting out of the storm, but just where are we going?"

Noel chuckled. "I've got a small cabin on this island. It's not far, I promise." He led the way to the boardwalk. "Just follow the walkway." They trotted through the walls of mangroves as the wind rose higher and higher, and rain began to pelt down. *Storms abhor the vacuum of stillness, I guess,* Noel thought to himself as he opened the cabin door. "Welcome to my home." The man entered, and Noel followed, closing the door just as a crash of thunder echoed over head. The rain began pounding on the roof in torrents.

"You have the best sense of timing I've ever seen," his new guest told him. "Showing up when you did, and now getting us inside just before the storm starts up again."

"Just a lucky break," Noel smiled.

"You must have horseshoes hanging all over you," the man said, looking at him soberly. "My name is Matthew Stewart. Thank you for saving my life." His hand reached out.

"I'm Noel Paxson. And believe me, I'm very glad I was able to help." There was a pause as they shook hands, and Noel raised a mental eyebrow in surprise. The physical contact enabled him to assess the nature of the man before him more fully than was possible in casual day-to-day interactions. This man was deeply spiritual and unusually perceptive. *I'll have to be very careful around this one,* he thought. *He'll pick up right away on any manipulation I attempt.*

There was a meow at their feet. Noel glanced down and laughed. "Why, Castaway, how rude of me." He picked her up and looked up at the man. "Matthew, I'd like to introduce you to an orphan of another storm, one from a couple of years ago. Castaway washed up on shore clinging to a broken-off dock section. I'd never owned a cat before, and I thought I'd never seen such a lovely creature." Castaway arched against his hand, purring. "She agreed with me, and it was the start of a beautiful friendship."

Matthew grinned and offered his hand to the cat, which she sniffed with dignity. Then she leaped out of Noel's arms and returned to her perch on the bed.

"I'll get some towels, so we can dry off. And some dry clothes, though I don't think my shorts will fit you." Like all his kind, Noel was tall and slim in comparison with humans, whereas Matthew was broad and stocky. He rummaged about a shelf, and tossed Matthew a towel. "No, wait, I've got some drawstring shorts here. And here's a T-shirt that's pretty baggy on me; I think it'll probably fit you just fine. He handed the man the clothes, then dried off himself and changed clothes.

Matthew spoke as he pulled on the fresh shirt. "Boy, that feels wonderful. I didn't think I'd ever feel dry again."

"I'll bet you never thought you'd feel hungry again either."

Matthew grinned at him. "How did you know? I'm starved."

"Me, too. I'll rustle up some sandwiches. Sliced jerk chicken okay?"

"Great."

Noel made sandwiches, and they ate and chatted casually while the storm continued to rage about them. It turned out that Matthew was a minster. *Which explains what I sensed from him,* Noel thought. He'd been vacationing in the Keys on the cruiser, borrowed from a friend—"I'm going to have to come up with a heckuva an apology when we salvage her"—when he'd been caught by Frieda, thanks to unfamiliarity with the waters and the weather. "Talk about going from the valley to the pinnacle. I'd given up any hope of being rescued when you came along. Two miracles in one day is rather a lot, even for a man in my profession."

"Two?"

"The calming of the storm, and then you and your boat appearing. The former wouldn't have done me much good without the latter."

"You've been a very fortunate man, then." Noel smiled at him.

"For which I give thanks to the Lord," Matthew replied. He yawned, then apologized.

"No need to apologize. It's been a pretty full day for both of us. Why don't we turn in?" Noel insisted Matthew take the bed, over the man's protests. "I'll spread a quilt on the floor and be perfectly comfortable. You need the rest more than I do—you were the one who went through the storm. I just sailed out to get you."

Matthew gave in gracefully, and laid down on the bed. Noel blew out the lantern. The storm still raged outside, but inside the little cabin, the atmosphere was full of peace.

Noel didn't need sleep, of course. He glanced over at the man sleeping in the bed across the room. *Perhaps this will help balance the scales slightly for what I did to Miguel.* He sighed. *I've learned—oh, yes—I've learned, lords of my people. I wish the cost of my learning hadn't been paid by a simple, harmless man.*

Frieda still thundered outside the cabin; perhaps he could ease his restlessness roaming the storm again. He arranged himself in meditative posture, then began breathing slowly. . . .

It was dawn when his spirit returned to his body, but he was not calmed. Restless, Noel got up and went over to the window. The storm had finally died down, and the temperature had dropped with it, enough that a fire would feel good. And the dancing flames would be soothing to watch.

Preoccupied with his thoughts, he laid the kindling and spoke the Word that awoke fire from the air. It wasn't until he heard a movement from the bed that he remembered he had a guest. And one every bit as perceptive as he'd feared.

"H—how did you do that?" stammered Matthew. Then, as full realization hit him, "What *are* you?"

So much for finessing my way out of this one, Noel thought. Aloud he said, "I'm nothing that will harm you, I promise." As Matthew looked fearfully at him, he tried to reassure him further. "Why would I rescue you if I had some evil purpose in mind?"

The minute the words were out of his mouth he knew they were the wrong words. Matthew immediately recalled just how timely Noel's appearance had been. "Come to think of it, how is it you happened to know my boat was drifting and that I needed help?"

"I saw you, of course."

"Of course. The only window in this cabin looks out on all those mangroves. You've got X-ray vision to see through them to to the sea, right?"

"No, I don't. I was out in the storm." Which was the strict truth, though not in the way Matthew was going to take it, Noel knew.

"Taking a little stroll in the midst of a hurricane. Of course."

If he only knew the half of it. Aloud, Noel said, "Truly, I *did* see you because I was out in the storm." As Matthew continued to stare at him in edgy disbelief, Noel considered. He couldn't simply erase the memory of what had happened, as he had with the ex-cop—that had been a minor part of Pete's life. The cop spent many evenings in many bars, and losing the memory of a few evenings in a single bar was nothing significant.

But he'd saved Matthew's life, in a way that Matthew—too sensitive for Noel's own good—now realized was extraordinary. There was no way Noel could alter memories connected with major life events like this; he simply didn't have the skills or knowledge needed. Meddling with Pete's memory was the equivalent of stitching up a simple cut; this was comparable to extremely delicate surgery. *To say nothing of the fact that I'd be doing it purely for my own convenience and privacy. I've paid* that *price already.*

No, there was nothing for it but to admit the truth about himself and hope that this man was able to accept the fantastic. He took a deep breath.

"Matthew, I *was* out in the storm. My spirit wandering over the ocean, while my body was back here in the safety of the cabin. That's why I was able to spot you." *And here's hoping you don't think to ask how the eye of the storm appeared so very conveniently.*

"Out of body travel?"

"Yes, I suppose that's how you could describe it, although I've never heard that term used before."

Matthew looked skeptical. "I'd never really believed in it. I suppose I'll have to now." He paused, considering. "But that doesn't explain how you started the fire. I've only read that sort of thing in fantasy novels. Magic spells and all that. You're not going to tell me you can cast magic spells, are you?"

Noel looked at him steadily. "No, I'm not. What humans label 'magic' or 'spells' is, in fact, merely possession of a better understanding of the interrelationship between energy and matter, and knowing how to manipulate it."

" 'What *humans* label magic'? Do you mean to tell me you're not human?" Matthew was looking more skeptical by the moment.

"That's correct. I'm not human, and I wasn't born in this place. But my people have roamed your world for so long that we've become part of your legends. We're scattered all through your folklore, called by man names. But in English, the world 'elf' is probably the most commonly used name."

"An elf," said Matthew. "This is crazy. Next thing you'll be telling me, that you calmed the storm." He saw the expression that appeared fleetingly across Noel's face. "Wait—you did *that*, too?"

I've got to learn to school my expressions better. Noel looked slightly abashed. "It's a case of knowing how to handle the dynamics of high and low pressure air masses. Not difficult in theory, but tricky in practice."

Matthew shook his head. "He calms a storm and calls it 'tricky.' This is too much for me. I can't believe it."

At that, Noel smiled ruefully at him. "It'd certainly give me great peace of mind if you *didn't* believe me. My kind has not always fared well at the hands of your people."

At that, Matthew's face went from skeptical to saddened. "No, mankind is far from perfect. We need God's help for that." He was silent for a long time, looking at the elf. At last he asked, "Why on earth is an elf . . . on Earth?"

At that, Noel breathed a sigh of relief. By some miracle of faith or open mind or the experience of the last few hours, Matthew believed him. "You might call it part of my training. My . . . well, supervisors I guess you'd call them, decided that there were things I needed to learn by traveling this world."

"What sort of things?"

Noel shook his head. "The pupil is never told, because it might affect his experience. Looking back now, I suspect it had to do with my immaturity—I was arrogant and had no patience. I was sure I knew it all. Such traits are considered unbecoming, to put it mildly, among my people."

"That doesn't sound much different from the teenagers I've dealt with. I'd say our two kinds have a lot in common," said Matthew.

"From what I've seen, I'd agree with you."

"So how did you get here? Where's your world? Another galaxy?"

"Oh, no. Our two worlds are very close—only a narrow dimensional gap separates us. And I came through a Gate, what you might call a doorway between our two worlds." He smiled. "From my reading, it appears the Gates have also become part of your mythology. There are stories of humans simply vanishing without a trace, in situations where there seemed no way for them to vanish. With lots of witnesses present and so on."

"How long have you been here? You speak English perfectly. And when will you be returning home?"

"I'd thank you for the compliment, but really, I don't deserve it. Languages are easy to learn. It only took me a few weeks to pick up English." He smiled bitterly at Matthew's expression. "As for returning home . . . I don't think I'll be going back." Noel's long, green eyes became ancient and his finely chiseled features suddenly appeared carved from granite. "I've been here a very long time, and the Gate hasn't come back. I've failed my teacher, and the Council won't let me return."

Matthew had never befriended an elf before, but he knew the sound of a being in emotional distress. He looked at Noel with compassion. "You know, in my profession there's a common saying: 'Confession is good for the soul.' It sounds to me like you've been carrying this burden on your conscience for a long while. If you'd like to tell me the story, I'll listen. I'm a good listener."

Noel looked back at him in some wonder. *I see I still have much to learn about humans. I never expected understanding from them.* The thought humbled him; after all these years, he still hadn't freed himself of that sense of superiority. "Yes, I can see that you are." *Perhaps it would help to talk about it.* His mind roamed back along the years. . . .

It was just after he'd started exploring Key West. He was younger and contemptuous then, still convinced that humans were insignificant creatures. He had no idea what the man in the alley wanted; his grasp of Spanish wasn't very good at that point, and the slurred speech made it even more difficult to understand him—had he cared to. He didn't. All he saw was a human with glazed eyes and trembling hands who wasn't even able to speak clearly. He couldn't even be bothered to focus on him enough to learn anything about him. All he was, was a moment's nuisance. He could have just walked away. He didn't.

But he *could* be bothered enough to swat the man away with a mental blow—a defensive gesture normally used by elves only when under telepathic attack.

The blow's effect on a mind totally unprepared for it was devastating. The human staggered blindly for a few steps, until he caromed into the wall, then collapsed like a puppet with the strings suddenly cut. He lay twitching in the alley, drooling and whimpering.

Noel walked away without a backward glance.

Ah, but I was cruel then. And I didn't realize one had to live with the consequences of one's actions. It was only later, once he'd begun making friends among the humans, that he learned the full results of what he'd done.

For the man, Miguel Escobar, hadn't been drunk. He'd been ill—a diabetic in insulin shock. A *marielito,* he'd settled down in Key West, married, and begun practicing his trade as a fisherman. By the time of his meeting with Noel, he'd bought his own fishing boat, and was the proud father of three small children. His future had looked bright—the American dream playing out once again.

Noel had snatched that from him with a single careless gesture. No doctor could determine what had caused it, of course, but they explained to his distraught wife that her husband now had the mental age of one of his own children—whom he no longer recognized. Nor did he recognize his wife. Unable to ply his former trade, he drifted from mental health unit to social worker to home shelter to, eventually, the street. His wife was unable to cope with both a childlike husband and three young children, and returned to Cuba to live with relatives, her hopes for a better future for her children shattered. *By me. No wonder the Gate has stayed closed.*

Noel saw Miguel on the street from time to time, and always made a point of buying him a meal or giving him extra money. Using his elvish skills, he healed Miguels' cuts and bruises, inevitable wounds caused by living on the street, But he couldn't heal the damage he'd done to his mind. And Miguel's body was running down, faster than it should have if life had continued unaltered on its course. There was nothing he could do to heal that, either. Actions have consequences.

"I've tried to repay for what I did," said Noel. Tears were coursing down his cheeks. "But of course, it will never be enough."

Matthew's eyes were also full of tears. He reached out and put a hand on Noel's shoulder. "None of us can repay the hurts we've done to others. We make amends as best we can, and try to learn from the mistakes we made. Final restitution lies with God, I believe."

Noel brushed the tears from his face. "Perhaps you are right, my friend. I've learned much from my sojourn here—more than I'd have dreamed possible when I first came. And there's much more to learn." He looked soberly at Matthew. "Do you know, you're the first human who knows what I truly am? Another new experience." He gripped the hand on his shoulder. "Thank you for listening. *For listening and not condemning. I would never have expected* that *of a human either. Ah, Noel, the Council is wiser than you. You still have much to learn.*

Matthew smiled warmly at him. "I'm very glad I was able to help. After all, I can't repay you for saving my life."

Noel looked at him in some surprise. "You know, I hadn't looked at it quite that way."

"I think perhaps we all owe one another debts that can't be repaid, you know. Maybe that makes us all a family, in a way one that shares a Creator."

"Perhaps so," replied Noel. "I no longer think there's quite such a huge gap between elvenkind and humankind."

Matthew smiled at him. "Surely that's the beginning of wisdom!" He glanced at the sunlight checkering the wooden floor—the sun was high in the sky. "Why, look at the time!"

Noel laughed. "May I offer you a berth in my sailboat to Key West?"

"Sold!"

Their voyage to Key West was smooth, the air fresh and clear as crystal after the storm. They tied up at the dock, and Noel guided Matthew down the quiet waterfront to the nearest phone, since they were off the beaten track frequented by tourists.

It was while Matthew was dialing his friend that they were jumped. One moment the little street was empty and sleepy in the early afternoon heat; the next, there were three tough-looking young men around them.

"Hey, man, wanna share some of the wealth?" asked one. Matthew dropped the receiver in shock.

"C'mon amigo, hand it over." The second speaker was the meanest-looking one. He was casually flipping a heavy knife from one hand to the other.

Noel glanced around. There was no one else on the street.

"Whatcha lookin' for, pal? Ain't no U.S. Cavalry down here," said the third, grabbing Noel's arm. "Now gimme the—hey, guys, we hit the jackpot. This guy, I seen him before, in Jocko's. He's always selling gold coins from shipwrecks." The others closed in on Noel, Matthew secured by the first mugger in a hammerlock to keep him quiet. Matthew looked at Noel in mute appeal. Plainly, he was hoping for some exercise of elvish powers to save them both.

He's in for a shock there, thought Noel. Too much was happening all at once. *I might be able to take two of them, but I can't handle three.*

"Yeah, I remember Jocko talking about him," continued the tough. "No one can figger out where the hell he finds 'em all. Now maybe we'll find the mother lode, eh, pal? Our very own *Atocha.* We'll all be millionaires, just like Mel Fisher."

Oh, brother, thought Noel. Treasure hunter Mel Fisher had indeed made a fortune from finding the Spanish ship *Atocha,* but Noel was no Fisher. Stalling for time, he said, "Take it easy, guys. You don't think I carry gold coins around all the time, do you?"

"Nah, I guess not. But we could take care of your friend here, while you go get 'em, couldn't you?"

I don't like the way this is headed. Neither, from the look in his eyes, did Matthew. Noel could sense him gathering himself to make a break for it. *Maybe if I can create a distraction—*

His plans were interrupted by a hoarse shout and a dull thunk. The man holding Matthew went down like a sack of potatoes, and Matthew took advantage of the confusion to lunge forward at the second hoodlum. A powerful roundhouse right put the second man out for the count. Noel kicked the knife-wielder in the crotch as hard as he could. That finished him—and the fight was over.

"What did you do to him, Noel?" asked Matthew. "He just collapsed, and I was able to get loose."

Noel shook his head. "I didn't do a thing."

"That's 'cause *I* did." Shrimper Tom stood there, wobbly but triumphant. An empty wine bottle in his hand explained the thunk they'd heard.

Noel burst into laughter. "Tommy! Talk about the nick of time. You're a hero." He gave the old man a bear hug, then turned to Matthew, and said with great sincerity, "Matthew, may I have the honor of introducing you to our rescuer, Shrimper Tom."

Matthew rose to the moment. "Tom, you wield a mean wine bottle. I admire that in a man."

Tommy actually blushed. "Shucks, guys. Who the hell can you count on if you can't count on your friends? Folks here on the Rock are a family."

Matthew and Noel exchanged glances. "Indeed they are," replied Noel.

One of the thugs gave a groan. Matthew said, "Gentlemen, may I suggest we leave the scene of the crime before these guys become fully functional again?"

"Good idea. Let's go—I know the man who runs the bar just up the street. We can phone the police from there," replied Noel. "Come on, Tommy—I'm buying you a beer. I'd say it was the least I can do for a gen-u-ine hero."

Tommy's face lit up. "That's a great idea." They headed up the street.

It was while they were awaiting the arrival of the sheriff in the cool darkness of the bar that Noel felt the subtle vibration. His head went up like a hunting dog's. Yes, there it was! The telltale glow was easily visible to his ultraviolet sensitive eyes. The Gate! He saw it clearly, through the open back door of the bar. All he had to do was walk across to the other side of the alley, and he'd be home.

Home.

Family and friends.

His own kind.

Then he looked at Tommy and Matthew, an old friend and a new friend. Both of whom had shown how much humans were capable of to a skeptical, disdainful elf.

"Yep, folks on the Rock is a family," said Tommy once again.

I think I have more to learn, thought Noel.

He watched the glow fade, then turned and ordered another beer.

ELFARAMA

by *Craig Shaw Gardner*

Craig Shaw Gardner is the author over twenty novels,
including various movie and computer game noveliza-
tions. His latest book is *Dragon Burning,* the third in the
Dragon Circle series. His short fiction appears in *Sherlock Holmes in Orbit, A Dragon-Lover's Treasury of the
Fantastic,* and *Phantoms of the Night.*

Brian slammed down the phone. Why did he bother to
even talk to his parents? The conversations were always
the same. Raves about their retirement community, point-
less news about relatives Brian barely remembered, and
then the inquisition.

"Why aren't you doing more with your life?" "Compared to you, your brother Carl is a rocket scientist!"
"When are you going to invite us up to meet Gail?"
"Shouldn't you two be married by now?" "Any children
in your future?" And on and on and on. They may have
sounded like questions, but Brian knew they were
demands. His parents had his life all planned for him, and
he had no say in the matter.

Brian sighed. He hadn't even had the nerve to tell his
mother and father that he and Gail had broken up. It was
easier to listen to his parents badger him for half an hour
than it was to actually interject any real information. His
parents' version of the world was so much more active
than his own. How wonderful and full their life was. And
he was left feeling empty and exhausted.

The phone rang.

Oh, no. His parents had forgotten some important bit of
information or other about Aunt Agatha or second-cousin
Lucille or maybe some neighbor Brian couldn't remember

from his childhood. Or they hadn't reminded him enough
how much they were looking forward to being grandparents. If it was important to his parents, they'd go on
about it forever.

Brian sighed and picked up the phone.

"Brian?"

It wasn't his parents after all.

"Gail?"

"I'm glad you still recognize my voice," she laughed
self-consciously "at least when I'm not shouting." She
paused for a minute, and Brian listened to the sound of
her breathing. He thought about the way she bit her lip
when she was unsure of what she wanted to say. It had
been a little over two weeks since they had had the fight.
To Brian, it had felt like forever.

"Brian?" Gail started again. "Now that we've had a
little time away from each other, and—well—I've had
a little time to calm down, I've been thinking. Maybe I
was too hasty. Could we get together and talk?"

Somehow, Brian found his voice in time to answer her.
Gail suggested they meet at Sweeny's. Brian thought Gail
hated Sweeny's. But then, after the night of the fight,
Brian was sure Gail hated him. But now? Her entire tone
had changed.

He hung up the phone. Maybe he could actually feel
happy for a while, even after talking to his parents.

The phone rang again.

He shivered. This would be his parents for sure, as if
even thinking of them would conjure a call. Or maybe it
was Gail, having second thoughts. Sweeny's? Talking to
Brian? What was she thinking of?

He picked up the receiver anyway.

"Satisfied?" a man's voice said on the other end of
the line.

Brian felt as if he had come in on the middle of the conversation. "What? Who is this?"

"Your friends from the mall. I told you we delivered."

"Delivered? Delivered what?"

"Hey," the voice drawled, as if the speaker was only
repeating the obvious. "The girl friend?"

Brian frowned. This guy was talking about the phone

call? When he thought delivery, he thought more in the line of pizza.

"*You* got Gail to call?"

"Only the tip of the iceberg," the voice on the phone enthused. "The first rain drop of the hurricane. The first spark of the meteor shower. And you owe it all to Elfarama! Service is our business!" He paused for an instant, then added: "We'll be talking soon."

Brian listened for a long moment to the dial tone. The man had hung up. For the few moments of his call with Gail, and for the few seconds since she had hung up, he had thought of a hundred reasons why Gail might really want to talk. But *Elfarama?*

Somehow, this all came from yesterday, and the trip Brian had taken to the Tri-State Mall.

He remembered seeing the sign as he walked in the entranceway. The mall was always trying some gimmick or other to drag people in, and this one sounded sort of lame, nowhere near as good as "Santa's Magic Village" or "Eegah! The Deadly World of Dinosaurs."

But there it was, sitting in that great center space between the mall's magnet stores, a hastily constructed booth with large red letters:

ELFARAMA!
Your Every Dream Fulfilled

It wasn't quite as obvious as the usual display. The booth itself was a muted forest green; the half-dozen people running the place were all dressed in earth tones. There were no little guys in pointy-toed shoes (Unless, Brian thought, pointy-toed shoes weren't worn by elves. Maybe that was brownies), no evident pots of gold (Come to think of it, Brian realized that was more a leprechaun thing) or obvious promises of great wealth (Then again, Brian realized, that would be Republicans.)

The guys behind the booth were wearing suits (they had that in common with Republicans) and sporting big smiles. And, somehow, as he walked from Suits R Us toward Hobby World, one of them was standing right in front of Brian. The suit was made of some vaguely shiny green material, some new synthetic, no doubt. Brian found the way it caught the light in swirling patterns unsettling, but he couldn't take his eyes off it. The man's voice boomed in his ear. Would Brian mind walking over to the booth? Brian walked. Why not take a seat? Brian sat.

Someone on a seat nearby was complaining about how people on talk shows had such interesting lives; certainly more interesting than his. "Don't worry," another Elfarama rep said behind his big grin. "We'll fix everything."

The representative looked away for a moment to shuffle through a stack of papers before him. The talk show man looked over at Brian, his face an odd mix of relief and confusion.

He stuck out a hand in Brian's direction.

"Nate. Nate Sampson."

Brian shook Nate's hand. He wanted to ask what either one of them was doing here.

"This is bound to help, right?" Nate did not sound convinced. "I mean, remember last August, when the mall brought in the medical van? That did a lot for my blood pressure."

This other man's ambivalence fed Brian's own feelings. Why was he sitting here? He had things to do. He didn't have time to wait around.

"Sorry about the delay," a voice boomed from behind Brian. The rep had returned.

The man sat down. Brian glanced at the elf rep's suit. Light danced before Brian's eyes.

"Now," the rep continued behind his perpetual grin, "this Personality Test will only take a minute."

Personality test? He didn't remember agreeing—

But the questions the elf rep asked were easy. The so-called "test" allowed Brian to talk, to let out some of the things that had been bothering him. How much he missed Gail. And, somewhere in there, he talked about his parents. Something like: "I don't want to hear them complain about anything—ever again."

"Wow!" the rep said when Brian was done. He turned

to one of his coworkers. "Sid! This guy jumps right off the scale!"

"What?" Brian asked, alarmed that they were going to share his information. Some of this stuff was pretty private! "What do you—"

The rep turned back to him. "Brian, you have come to the right place! An elf will be assigned to you shortly, and, after that, your troubles will be a thing of the past."

Another elf rep, this one in a suit of shiny brown, stepped over next to them. Brian guessed this was Sid. He glanced over the first rep's shoulder at a computer screen Brian couldn't see.

Sid whistled and looked at Brian. "Everything's going to be great, fella! And all you've got to do is—believe!"

An elf will be assigned to you shortly? All you've got to do is believe? This had gone far enough. "What are you guys?" Brian demanded. "Some sort of religious organization?"

His rep looked horrified. "Oh, no! We are certainly not a religion—"

"—except possibly for tax purposes," his friend Sid added.

Brian still wanted to get to the bottom of this. "But elves? I always thought they were like—"

"You can say it," his rep broke in. "Like a fairy story. Hey, we've been away for a while. But we're back, and ready for action." He glanced up at Sid. Both of them nodded.

Alarm bells were going off in Brian's skull. "Wait a moment. You guys are elves? I know these stories. You'll give me all this stuff, right? But don't I have to sell my soul or my firstborn or something?"

"Propaganda!" Sid's smile wavered for an instant. "Human authorities could never cope with elf magic."

"No, Sid," the other rep interjected. "We were responsible for it, too. You know all the stories, Brian. We do, too. Bargains involving gold and firstborn sons. Singing merfolk who would drive you mad. Bloodthirsty demon horses hiding in the swamp. All variations on a theme."

Brian still didn't understand. "A theme?"

The rep shrugged. "Elves just want to have a little fun."

Sid glanced at his co-worker. "Should we?"

The other rep pointed to the computer screen. "He's a star candidate!"

Sid nodded. "He deserves to be told."

"Okay, Brian." His rep's smile became slightly more confidential. "We went away for a reason. Elves and humans used to get along just fine, you know, way back when. But then the Renaissance showed up, you know, the enlightenment and all. People started asking too many questions."

"And we made our big mistake," Sid interjected.

The other rep nodded. "We retreated to the world under the hill; the perfect world of Elfland." He sighed. "Do you know how boring it gets, what with all the endless parties, the fabulous clothing, the indescribably beautiful elven women?"

"Lithe and lovely. Everyday, lithe and lovely," Sid added in a husky whisper. "It makes you long for humans! Somebody who's actually short! With a few extra pounds to go around!"

Sid's mouth froze back into a smile as the other rep glared at him. The rep looked back to Brian. "But things changed all over again. Look at this modern world!"

"Technology has made life so confusing, no one's going to know we're even here. The very thing that drove us away has allowed us to come back!"

"Yes! Now we can experience it all! The short! The fat! The really interesting little moles with hair growing—" Sid stopped, withering under the heat of another glare.

"Look at it this way, Brian," the rep continued smoothly. "You get your heart's desire. We relieve the boredom; although maybe not in the way Sid mentioned. By helping you with your heart's desire, we get to see a whole new world!"

"It's a win-win situation!" Sid added, his grin fully back in place.

Brian couldn't remember anymore. He guessed that was the end of the interview. Things were a little hazy. He didn't even remember driving home.

And he hadn't thought about the whole incident until now.

The phone was silent now. He stared at it for a long moment, daring it to ring again. He glanced at his watch. Whoa! It was time to get ready to meet Gail, and maybe regain his heart's desire.

He had said yes.

It had all happened so quickly. He had walked into Sweeny's and, as soon as his eyes got used to the smoke and lack of light, he spotted Gail, smiling at him from where she sat at a corner table. He had kissed her before he sat down; the best kiss they had had in months. They were still waiting for their drinks to arrive when Gail had confessed she was lost without him, and asked him to marry her. He had gone home, deliriously happy.

The phone had rung.

"Another successful delivery!"

He didn't have to ask who it was. The elves were working overtime. He was so happy he didn't even mind a few minutes later when the his parents called.

"Married?" they cried as soon as he'd told them the news. "It's about time! We'd just love to be grandparents!"

Gail had moved in the next day. They were married with a simple civil ceremony as soon as it could be arranged. Their love life had never been better.

And after each triumph, there would be another phone call from the elves, each one more cheerful than the one before. The elves seemed to be having the time of their lives, but then, so did Brian.

And then Gail announced she was pregnant.

Brian's parents called as soon as the elves got off the phone. He didn't even have to tell his parents the news. They just knew.

Brian frowned. He wasn't so sure he wanted to be quite so happy quite so quickly. Still, when his parents insisted on a visit, he couldn't say no, could he?

He hung up the phone. For once, the elves didn't call back.

The ringing doorbell woke the baby.

Brian glanced at his watch. Who would be at the door at six o'clock in the morning?

He opened the front door. There, surrounded by luggage, stood his parents.

"Hi, honey!" his mother waved.

"Where's the little wife?" his father chipped in.

"And the bundle of joy?" his mother added cheerfully.

"We just love being grandparents!" they cried together.

Brian frowned again as his parents bustled past him into the house. They weren't supposed to be here for weeks, were they? His time with Gail had started as one happy blur. Now he didn't seem able to even keep track of things.

When had the baby been born? Recently, he was sure of that. There was that infant crying in the other room, after all. He vaguely remembered the congratulatory phone call from the elves. Why couldn't he remember anything else? Like the baby's name? Or whether it was a boy or a girl?

"Brian?" his mother called from the other room. "You're keeping secrets from us?"

"Yes, son!" his father added. "Why didn't you tell us you had twins?"

Twins?

Brian would have remembered twins.

"Oh, we just love being grandparents!"

"Triplets!" Brian's mother and father screamed in delight.

Triplets? What was going on here?

The phone started to ring.

Brian decided he didn't want to talk to anybody; not even elves.

His mother bustled past him. "Oh, why don't you get that? It's probably your brother!"

"Yes!" his father called proudly from the other room. "He's promised to take off a couple days from rocket science to come to see his nieces and nephews!"

What? Brian thought. His parents only called his brother a rocket scientist, to compare him to how dumb Brian was. He wasn't really—unless—

There were three new babies in the other room that Brian didn't quite remember. Reality seemed to be slipping, slipping—

"I just love being a grandfather! Madge! Guess what Gail just told me!"

"What's that, Hyram?"

"There's four of the little sprouts!"

The phone rang again.

Elves.

How could this have gone so wrong?

He thought back to that first day, to that interview at Elfarama. How he had talked about wanting Gail. And then he had complained about his parents. He had wanted them off his back. He had wanted them happy.

Well, they sure were happy now.

"I just love being a grandmother! Five? Five of them?"

"Elves just want to have a little fun." That's what one of them had said. He had never asked what they wanted to have fun with.

"I was born to be a grandfather! Six? It's a medical miracle!"

He had to put an end to this, and he had to put an end to this now.

Maybe he could gag his parents. Or maybe he could just shoot them. No, no, there had to be a better way.

He had to get in touch with the elves. But how? They always called him.

Except for that time at the mall.

Brian drove and tried to think about how things had become so complicated. It was the elves after all, twisting and turning his life to relieve their boredom. His life had gone from wonderful to odd to impossible in what seemed like no time at all.

One way or another, he had to put an end to it.

He pulled up in front of the Tri-State Mall and ran inside.

The Elfarama exhibit was gone, replaced by "Tulip Wonderland; Bring Holland to Your Own Back Yard!" Well, what did he expect? These exhibits never lasted for long; certainly not long enough for him to have a family. But the mall must have some records of who was behind the elf exhibit.

"Brian?"

He turned around at the mention of his name. A harried, but oddly familiar man hurried toward him across the mall.

"We met before?" the man called as he approached. "Nate! Nate Sampson. I was sitting next to you at your Elfarama interview."

"You know, then!" Brian cried in relief. "My life's out of control! I have to get the elves to stop this!"

"You're telling me?" Sampson laughed. "I don't blame you for not knowing me. I hardly recognized you either. We've changed a lot these past three weeks."

Three weeks? "What are you talking about!" Brian demanded. It couldn't have only been three weeks!

Sampson shrugged. "I think that's when we met. That's what the calendar says at least. Elves can mess up everything, including time." He shook his head ruefully. "My life is so much fuller now. Too full really. I find myself on a different talk show every morning. This is one of my better days. Last Tuesday, when I was a lesbian nun, I just hid inside the house."

Brian decided this wasn't helping him. He had to find some answers!

"Then there was 'Can a transsexual save my marriage?' " Sampson continued. "Actually, that one was sort of interesting. The one I really hated was that three-parter on body-piercing."

Brian grabbed the other man's shirt and shook him. "We have to find the office for this place! They'll have to have some records of Elfarama!"

But Sampson just shook his head. "I already tried that. They have no records of the exhibit. They claim they never heard of it."

"So what can we do?"

"Wait for the elves to contact us. They're not done with us yet." He smiled sadly. "Today I'm a man who loves too much." He pulled his hand from behind his back. He was holding a bouquet. "These flowers are for you."

"There he is!"

Brian whirled around to see his parents, his wife, and his brother, all wheeling very large strollers.

"How dare you desert your wife and fourteen children?" His father called. "We should have known someone as worthless as you was hiding down at the mall!"

No! Brian couldn't let this go on! He's have to do something—even if it was something desperate.

He turned and ran. Maybe someplace as large as the Tri-State Mall would have some solution to his problem.

He had never noticed a gun store in the mall before, but there it was, right between Knives R Us and Explosive City. It would be so easy—

"Don't you run away from us, young man!" his father called.

No, Brian told himself, no. The elves wanted it interesting? There was more than one way to do that.

He whirled and glared at his family.

"If I'm so worthless, why are you following me?" he called.

"I ask myself that question day after day—" his father started.

"There's no way I can take care of fourteen children!" Brian continued.

"At least he admits—" his mother added.

"Besides, you have a much better candidate for fatherhood with you now!"

"What?" Gail said. "What do you—"

But Brian was on a roll. "I understand rocket science pays rather well."

The others stared at him for an instant in stunned silence.

"Well, yes," his brother said after a moment. "It pays very well."

"And you'd be so much better as a father!" their mother enthused.

"You're so much better at everything than Brian!" their father agreed.

"Well," Gail mused. "I do have fourteen mouths to feed—"

Brian decided to get out of there while the getting was good. Nobody ran to follow.

His parents were happy. Gail was taken care of. Maybe the elves would be satisfied.

He ran around a bend to the left and a bend to the right,

up a flight of stairs and down a long corridor, with nothing at the end but a men's room, a utility closet, and a pair of pay phones.

It seemed cool and quite here. How much he had missed quiet! How much he had missed being alone! He took a deep breath.

The elves had given him all the things other people had wanted. And he had wanted to make the other people happy.

Maybe now he could figure out a way to be happy for himself.

The phone rang.

JERLAYNE
by Lynn Abbey

Lynn Abbey was the co-editor of the successful *Thieves'
World* anthology series with Robert Lynn Asprin. She has
also written several well-received fantasy novels, the
most recent being *Siege of Shadows*.

Amber sunlight settled on the smooth surface of the
blessing bowl. With her breath caught in her throat, Jerlayne waited for the brass chimes to sound their second
note before swirling her hand through the water.
Aulaudin, beside her, waited for the fourth. Then two
chimes struck together produced a fifth. Before the harmony faded, man and woman brought their dripping
hands together, fingertips against fingertips.

Aulaudin smiled as the joining began. Jerlayne's breath
escaped with a sigh. She meant to return her new husband's smile, but looked away instead. Elves weren't supposed to blush. Elves were supposed to dwell in
unshakable serenity with smiles instead of laughter or
embarrassment, frowns or furrowed brows. Most times
Jerlayne lived comfortably within the traditions of her
kind. Aulaudin certainly did; she'd never seen him falter.

He was older, a bit more than twice her age. His auburn
hair and mischief-blue eyes were, like her parents' faces,
a constant in Jerlayne's memory. A decade ago, when
she'd realized that marriage was more than a wedding
celebration, she'd surprised her father in the trove room—

"Aulaudin," she'd announced. "I want Aulaudin for my
husband."

Jereige had set aside his counting. He'd folded his
hands and closed his eyes in the elven way before
speaking important words. "If he'll have you, child, when

your time comes. If no other father's daughter catches his eye and no other father comes to terms with Maun."

Someday Jerlayne might know if any other father or daughter had tried. If they had, they'd been rejected, because Aulaudin was still living beneath his parents' roof when Jerlayne's time came last autumn. The fathers had negotiated, of course; Jerlayne didn't eat or sleep for a week. And an auspicious place for their homestead had to be found; that had taken forever.

But a place had been found and the land had been cleared. Wedding gifts waited there, protected by a shimmering rainbow of wards. Jerlayne hadn't seen the clearing yet—bad luck, the sages said, and elves were never careless about luck. Her mother had visited it, though, and pronounced it perfect, and Elmeene was rarely wrong about the land of fairie.

"Peace grows there," Elmeene had assured Jerlayne this morning while they gathered roses for the bridal wreath. "Your happiness will bloom."

Joining swirled around the crook in Jerlayne's upraised arm. She felt the strength in Aulaudin's muscles, his tension and anticipation, as if it were her own. Elmeene, on whose smiling face her absentminded gaze rested, dipped her chin a finger's breadth; Jerlayne turned back to her husband. Joining touched her shoulder. She shivered, her fingertips slid away from Aulaudin's: an ill omen, if ever one had been imagined, until Aulaudin caught her. He held her tight and safe, and the joining progressed more swiftly. Jerlayne closed her eyes when it reached her heart, and carried an image of Aulaudin into the darkness.

Elmeene had cautioned that there would come a moment when her entire world would turn bleak. Jerlayne needed no reminding that, on occasion, elven weddings ended in disaster, as bride or groom failed to complete the joining. Her moment lasted longer than any moment should, but with Aulaudin in her memory, Jerlayne mastered her despair. The moment passed, and when it did, their joining was complete.

«I will love you forever.»

Aulaudin's voice, not as his tongue shaped it but perfect as it formed in his mind. Elmeene had warned her, too, that joining progressed faster in men. Jerlayne had been angry—she didn't like to finish second in any race—but she rejoiced now that the first words her mind heard came from her husband.

She was a woman now, part of the adult elven world where she discovered—and much to her astonishment—palpable affection surrounded her. Opening her eyes, Jerlayne found that Aulaudin's hand still clutched hers, no more, no less. The warmth she felt, the musk intoxicating her senses, came from joining.

For a wracking heartbeat Jerlayne knew neither what to say nor how to say it with her mind alone. Then both the words and the knowledge were with her, as natural as squeezing her fingers against Aulaudin's.

«And I've always loved you.»

An elven wedding lasted three nights, three days. The first night and day was marked with ancient ritual. The second was the time for family and joining. Jerlayne's kinfolk were around her: her parents, of course, her brothers and sisters—she was neither the first nor the last of her parent's elven children. Her aunts and uncles by blood and by marriage arrived before noon, her nieces, nephews and cousins of varying degrees, some of whom were more closely related to Aulaudin, whose family was, if anything, more far-flung than her own. There were elves she knew by reputation only and elves she knew not at all. The oldest was Gudwal, Jeriege's thrice-great grandfather, Aulaudin's twice-great uncle, who blessed them both with a steady hand.

The sprites, dwarves, nymphs, brownies, nixies and other fairie-folk came after sunset. The last to appear was a goblin, shrouded in twilight mist.

He went to the bridal table where two iron ingots waited and stood in watchful silence as Jerlayne took the deadly metal in her long-fingered hands. She shaped the first ingot easily into a slender knife, then she closed her eyes and took up the second. Her hands disappeared in a sphere of yellow light from which fell smoking links of chain that she gave directly to the black-cloaked goblin.

The sound of iron sliding past iron was the loudest

sound in earshot as the goblin passed the chain from one hand to the other. His thick, black braid swayed in a breeze no other fairie-folk could feel. Aulaudin settled his arm around Jerlayne's shoulders, as if to protect her or share her fate in goblin judgment. He needn't have feared. Jerlayne was Elmeene's daughter and each link was flawless.

Another goblin emerged from the mist. The first gave the measured chain to the second, then bared jet-black, pointed teeth. "The same on midwinter's eve, dear lady, and again at midsummer. The shadows will never deepen across your gates, and your name will be well-spoken on the plains."

It was a good bargain, though not as good as the one Elmeene had for StoneWell homestead. But no goblin bargain was engraved on stone—or iron. Jerlayne could hope for better as her skills and homestead grew. She turned to her husband, reaching for his thoughts, as was her married right. But Aulaudin gave nothing away; a man's trade lay beyond the veil, foraging among mortal human. Women shaped fairie and bargained with goblins; the decision was hers and her alone. Jerlayne held out her hand.

"Goro," the goblin said, giving her the public syllables of his name.

"Jerlayne," she replied. Elves had no secret names. With joining, they had no secrets at all.

Their hands touched, as Jerlayne's had touched Aulaudin's two sunsets earlier. There was a joining between them, not an elven joining of husband and wife, but honorable and binding.

It was a signal to other goblins who waited in the mist with pole-slung hides, each filled to bursting with wine. Hides were pierced and goblets filled. The dignified melodies of elven harps gave way to the wild rhythms of goblin pipes and drums.

In the hours that followed, as the moon slipped across the sky, Jerlayne danced with Goro and the other goblins. She danced with her father, with her brothers, her mother and her sisters. She danced with her kin and with Aulaudin's kin, with everyone except her husband. She saw him often enough, always on the far side of a wall of fairie folk. Not so long ago, when she was a maiden, not the bride, she'd have been the first among the pranksters. Then, it had been great fun to whirl the couple close together and apart again. Now, she tried to laugh as Aulaudin vanished, but the sound was shrill.

By dawn, she wanted only to escape—with or without her husband—but elven weddings lasted until the third sunset, anything less was unthinkable, ill-omened, or worse. She drained another goblet of goblin wine in quick, breathless gulps and gave herself back to wild music with an unvoiced prayer that this day be shorter than all the rest.

For all she knew, her prayer was answered. Elves admitted countless gods without worshiping any, and Jerlayne never remembered much of her third wedding day until, suddenly, the sky was golden and she stood at the gate in traveling clothes of heavy cloth and soft leather. Her hands were between Elmeene's and there were tears—tears!—glistening in her mother's eyes.

"You're so young," Elmeene whispered. "There are so many questions you never asked—"

Jerlayne tried to free herself from the awkward embrace. Elven tears were so unseemly, so unexpected, so ill omened. She was younger, yes, than her sisters had been on their wedding days, but she'd known what she'd wanted. There'd been no reason to wait.

Elmeene clutched Jerlayne's wrists tighter. "When questions cloud your mind, come home. You can always come home to me; the answers are here."

What questions? Jerlayne thought. What answers?

But Elmeene's eyes had dried between one blink and the next. Concern and confession both vanished as if they'd never existed, leaving Jerlayne—already exhausted and wobbling on her feet—convinced that she'd imagined the whispered words. Then Maun was coming toward the gate with Aulaudin beside him. The sight of her husband in traveling clothes banished all thoughts save two from Jerlayne's mind—the wedding was over and it was time to leave.

Hostlers led four horses behind Aulaudin: her own gray

mare, Aulaudin's chestnut stallion and two bays, both
with bulging packs of gifts and food. The bays were
mares, too. In fairie, what magic could not provide was
left to nature. With Jerlayne's shaping and whatever
Aulaudin foraged beyond the veil, the couple could rea-
sonably expect a long, comfortable life, but here in the
beginning the four horses, along with cows, pigs,
chickens, and sheep that would follow them, were worth
more than all their magic.

A gnome cupped his hands to boost Jerlayne into the
saddle. Any other time, Jerlayne could mount her mare
without help. But she was weary—wearier than she'd
imagined and accepted help. The mare shied as she landed
hard. Goro appeared in the mare's shadow, as goblins did,
and clamped a cautionary hand on the reins. He offered
Jerlayne a token.

The metal had been tempered in goblin magic. It blis-
tered Jerlayne's palm, but she gritted her teeth, closed her
fingers, and thanked him gratefully. Fairie was a more
peaceful land than the human lands beyond the veil, but
travel had its outlaws, most of whom would think twice
before attacking newlywed elves protected by goblin
magic.

And for any dangers that didn't emerge from a sharp-
eyed shadow, Gudwal had a blessing that he brushed over
them with wild herbs and sparkling powder. Their parents
blessed them, too—mothers first, then fathers. Maun
spoke last. He wished them health, happiness and then,
without warning, he smacked the stallion's rump and sent
his son on a headlong bolt into the future with the pack-
mares raising dust behind him.

Father and son were as different as two men could be.
With broad shoulders and thick torso, Maun could be mis-
taken for a dwarf. His skin, hair, and eyes all verged
toward gnomish silver. Yet one glimpse at Maun's grin
and only a fool would wonder from which side of his
family had Aulaudin inherited his mischief.

Maun had put a quick end to an otherwise interminable
leavetaking. Jerlayne drummed her heels against her
mare's flanks and galloped after Aulaudin. She caught
him easily, but not before StoneWell—her home—had

disappeared. The sound of goblin music was barely audible above the horses' breathing, then that, too, was gone and they were, at last, alone.

They rode in silence, stirrups nearly touching as the horses ambled along the cart-road. Taking the reins in her right hand, Jerlayne reached across to touch Aulaudin's arm. He contrived a one-handed grasp on three sets of reins to free a hand for her. As it had three sunsets past, joining seeped between their fingers. This time there were no relatives or rituals to pry them apart.

Jerlayne heard her nervous laugh in her own ears and in her husband's. She saw a moonlit stranger—a beautiful, dark-haired stranger—and watched that stranger blush as her own cheeks grew warm.

"Are you tired, my love?" Aulaudin asked. "Ready to fall asleep?"

She shook her head, not trusting her voice. At that moment, sleep with the farthest thought from her mind. She knew what lay ahead, and not entirely by rumor. Love and sex were natural parts of fairie. She'd had a tryst or two, nothing serious, but joining was the magic part, the part that could only be experienced, never quite described, because it sealed two immortal lives together for eternity.

"Who will know if we arrive a day late?" Aulaudin continued casually, though his hand was warm around hers. "I'd sooner dismount while I still can than fall off asleep."

It was difficult to imagine Aulaudin falling off his horse, but Jerlayne rose to the challenge. They shared a laugh; the horses came to a halt.

She kindled a fire and set cook-pots among the coals while he set up their camp. Fire-making was not her favorite magic, though Elmeene's lessons hadn't stopped until Jerlayne could lure a flame out of wet wood in the rain. Cooking was another of her less-renowned skills. She was scowling at the pots when Aulaudin knelt behind her. His hands were wonderfully gentle on her arms. His breath was warm and moist on her neck when he brushed her hair aside.

"Forget supper, my love," he advised.

"A wife—" Jerlayne began, and lost her thought as his mouth moved over her skin. "I should . . . *cook*—" Another distraction: Aulaudin's fingers were in her hair, another lost thought. "Aren't you—?"

"Not for *supper,*"

They had a tent, but Aulaudin hadn't raised it. The night, he said, was warm enough for lovers. The stars would protect them from storms, and with Gudwal's blessing fresh around them, no insect would dare disturb their rest. He spread their blankets under the cloudless sky.

Jerlayne caught his hand and pressed it against her lips—all the assent a husband needed to sweep his wife off to bed. His taste was sweeter than goblin wine and just as potent. She lost her way in joining and with no idea what was real or what was a dream, wrapped herself around him. When dawnlight opened her eyes again, Jerlayne could not be sure that her maiden days were over, only that there were a thousand new colors in the light and all of them were reflected in Aulaudin's hair.

If they could arrive at their homestead a day late, Aulaudin suggested, then they could be two days late—or a week, if they chose. Jerlayne agreed with a kiss and held him tight against her. This time she was sure.

It took a week to make a two-day journey. They were hungry and dirty and without a care when they reached the sage-chosen place. Their gifts were safe under oiled canvas. The cattle, chickens, sheep and pigs that had passed them on the road were equally safe under the dark, watchful eyes of a gnome couple. A dour folk, gnomes preferred funerals to weddings, but they offered ripe apples as a welcome gift. When the apples were eaten, the gnomes announced their intention to dwell on the bank of the nearby stream and to plant an orchard around them.

"We have seeds," the gnome-man declared, "but we need more, and hooks for pruning and harvesting. And a crank for the press, if you want cider any time soon."

Aulaudin bit his lower lip before nodding. Jerlayne shared her husband's thoughts easily and shared his sober realization: They were elves and they were married.

Fairie folk would come to their homestead, offering their life service, and they, in turn, would provide whatever was scarce or difficult.

"A crank," Aulaudin repeated.

"Aye, and a metal one." The gnome-man met Aulaudin's eyes. "Wood's best for the plates and the staves and leather'll hold it together, but iron's best for the crank. There's a good press where we come from, if you're not familiar."

"I know a cider press." Aulaudin's voice took on the sharp edge of pride. "When there's a roof over *our* heads, you'll have your crank, your seeds and whatever else you need."

"Petrin," the gnome-man said, extending his hand. "Banda." He cocked his head toward his wife. "From Dawn stead in the east."

"I know it." Aulaudin took Petrin's hand. He gave the gnomes their names.

"I will care for your children." Banda's bright eyes pierced Jerlayne's soul as she seized Jerlayne's hand and squeezed it painfully. "However they grow, I'll care for them as if they were my own."

Banda could bear her own children, but she wouldn't. She'd be Jerlayne's midwife and she'd wait for Jerlayne's gnomish sons and daughters. Her own children, if she'd borne them, would be mortal. Except for the goblins, only elves and their children—all their fairie children—were immortal. Jerlayne had six sisters, six brothers—twelve *elven* siblings. She had no idea how many other siblings she might have had; Elmeene swore she didn't know.

They worked together marking the homestead lines in the earth, digging trenches and post-holes, laying in foundation stones. It was harder work than any Jerlayne had done at StoneWell. Though Elmeene had rough-shaped the beams and stones that formed the larger part of her dowry, Jerlayne's hands ached each night form the finishing: This was *her* homestead, hers and Aulaudin's. Every sill had to be level. Each corner had to be precisely square.

Frost rimed the last thatch sheaves they tied to the roof. A threat of snow hung in the mottled sky when Aulaudin gathered the tools of men's trade for the first time since they were married. The human realm beyond fairie's veil was a dangerous place, but not so dangerous that a quick-witted elf couldn't provide his homestead with all it needed and many of the luxuries besides, or so Jeriege said each time he left. Jerlayne had watched her father come and go countless times. She'd waited anxiously beside her mother as, one by one, her brothers mastered their father's trade. They'd never come to any harm, none of them, and didn't Gudwal still go foraging now and again? Hadn't he foraged the glittery cloth for her wedding dress?

And would her father have allowed her to join with a man who couldn't forage, as every man had foraged since the beginning of time?

They stood at their own gate.

"I'll be gone two days, less if I can find that crank quickly."

Aulaudin took her hand. Joined, she saw the sharp shadows beyond the veil. She saw things for which she had no names and felt Aulaudin's confidence as he named them *car, skyscraper, train,* and *washing machine.*

"Do they climb inside to wash?"

"No, they have *showers* for washing themselves, *machines* for their linen. It will be all right, my love."

Jerlayne sought courage, but the subtleties of deception within joining were not yet in her control.

"It is less dangerous that shaping iron," Aulaudin chided.

He didn't add that he would never interfere with her shaping and Jerlayne didn't counter that shaping iron was different. She could drop the iron if it grew too hot or threatened to steal her soul. What could he do if he were injured or, worse, if the humans trapped him? It happened. Men didn't always return. Sometimes their mangled bodies were brought back to fairie, but more often they were lost . . . forever. She'd lost an uncle, several cousins; the memories still ached.

"I will be back in two days," Aulaudin said sharply, releasing her hand. He put an empty arm's length between them. "It is what I *do*, what we do—me, your father, my father, your brothers and mine."

Aulaudin turned away, slow as ice. The words to restore peace and trust hovered just beyond Jerlayne's grasp. In mute horror, she watched him walk away from her. Petrin waited with the bay mares—one saddled for riding, the other for forage—beside him. In her heart, Jerlayne wanted to banish the gnome and the horses to the farthest corner of fairie and keep Aulaudin safe beside her; in her mind, she knew her heart was wrong.

"May luck and shadows surround you," she called: Her mother's last words each and every time her father left.

Jerlayne feared Aulaudin hadn't heard, then he stopped, turned, grinned. Without the catalyst of touch, joining raced through Jerlayne's body, grounding itself a handspan beneath her ribs.

"Less than two days. Tomorrow by sunset! I'll find you a present. What would you like?"

"You—only you—safe, again, beside me, that was what Jerlayne wanted but she asked for a rose, a blooming rose because there'd be no flowers in fairie until spring. Aulaudin swore he'd find a rose as beautiful as her. Joining burned so hot within her that Jerlayne stood like a sightless statue until he was gone.

"How does a woman endure this?" she asked herself, pressing her hands against her belly where, not ten days ago, she'd felt the first stirring of a new life. "Elmeene laughs when father goes hunting. How? How does she endure this?"

When questions cloud your mind come home . . . the answers are here.

Jerlayne could go to StoneWell, but she couldn't return before tomorrow's sunset and, afraid as she was, she had to be at the gate to greet Aulaudin. Unseemly tears ran down her face as she sought a dark corner beneath the thatched roof and, sinking to the floor, wrapped her arms around her knees in misery.

Aulaudin returned the next day, just as he promised. His clothes were dirty and torn. He was torn as well: a nasty gouge on his left arm. He wouldn't admit how he'd gotten it, even when they joined.

«You've seen worse, my love.»

She had, of course, countless times on her father and brothers. Elven men were resilient; they had to be. Those who came home alive, healed swiftly, without scars—and went off again. She hugged Aulaudin tight enough to crack ribs and wrung his shirt with helpless fury.

"You'll break me in two," he chided, but made no attempt to free himself.

"Next time—take me with you."

"Beyond the veil's not for women, my love."

Men didn't shape metal. Women didn't forage. Women couldn't pierce the veil. Women couldn't even sense the veil through fairie's forests.

"Let me show you what I found—"

Aulaudin pulled treasures from the bulging packs: iron for the cider press, iron already formed into a bar with holes at either end and tempered to a hardness no elf, not even Elmeene, could match; shards of jewel-colored glass and a coil of lead ribbon to bind it in a window's shape; a copper bowl for cooking; a silver mirror for vanity; a box of nails to spare her the tedium of making them; a score of useful items the fairie folk could not—or would not—fabricate for themselves.

Jerlayne's spirits lifted—they could hardly do otherwise—but there were shadows across the thoughts she shared until Aulaudin brought forth his final treasure.

"For you, my love."

The gift was two handspans high, half that in width and depth. It was hard and heavy and wrapped in a piece of emerald silk that would have been gift enough. Within the silk Jerlayne found a polished wood box.

"Open it, my love."

The box was lined with velvet and cunningly padded to protect a clear glass dome, a wooden base, and a single rose in sunrise colors. The rose wasn't real—human magic was mostly artifice—yet it was beautiful. Jerlayne's fingers lingered above the glass, as if touching it might break the flower's spell. Aulaudin laid his hand on hers, pressing it down until she felt the unnatural perfection of human shaping. At his urging, not her own, Jerlayne lifted the domed rose from its cradle.

«Porcelain,» Aulaudin told her, in joining, as the painted, fired clay shimmered in the golden light.

Then his hand slid around hers. She heard a click and, from somewhere within the wooden base, music began to flow. It was strange music, metal music—though nothing like the purse notes of elven chimes—but beautiful, like the rose itself. Together, they carried the gift inside and set it carefully on a shelf, then forgot about it as their reunion continued.

The rhythm of Jerlayne's life changed, from the idyll of newly wedded bliss to the bustle of a growing homestead. More gnomes appeared at the gate—disgruntled that they weren't the first to arrive, but content to establish themselves with Petrin and Banda. A trio of stoneworking dwarves arrived. They dug themselves a cellar before the hard freezes came and chiseled foundation stones throughout the winter.

Aulaudin spent more nights beyond the veil than he did in his own bed. Even so, the homestead they named Sunrise, for the rose, needed more than he could provide. He turned to Maun and his brothers, collecting debts, incurring obligations as he led countless expeditions for lumber, bricks and lengths of pipe.

For her part, Jerlayne scrambled to keep them all fed, warm, and dressed in dry clothes. A steady stream of messages and supplies flowed between her and Elmeene. She mentioned her pregnancy; Elmeene replied that she'd make the journey—if Jerlayne needed her, if Jerlayne had *questions*. But elven pregnancies were rarely difficult and Jerlayne had Banda waiting.

And as for questions, her life was too busy. Each night, when Aulaudin foraged and she was alone, she listened to the music of her sunrise rose as she pulled the blankets tight in the half-empty bed. She'd fall asleep before the strange melody ended and awoke with another full day in front of her.

Her first child was born when snow still crusted the ground and the tree buds had swelled but not burst. Aulaudin was beside her—foraging could be set aside for a day, or a week or a month, if needed. Banda was there, too, with boiled water, piles of cloth and—just in case—sharp, silvery knives. They needed the water and cloth.

"A daughter," the gnome-woman said, displaying the swaddled bundle in her arms.

The infant's eyes were gray, her skin shone with a healthy blush and the tiny hand she waved in the air showed the proper number of fingers, each in its proper place.

"An elf—" Jerlayne sighed. "What name shall we give her?"

Aulaudin's smile, before he kissed her, was more awkward than proud. "We'll see."

"I'm sure she is— Look at her!"

But Aulaudin didn't look and later in the day, when Jerlayne was thinking clearly again, she was ashamed of herself. It was too soon to think about elven names for elven children. Twenty years, maybe thirty, could come and go before parents could be sure their daughter was an elf. So many of fairie's rare folk sprang from daughters. It was easier with sons. If a son hadn't changed by his sixth birthday, it was safe to take him into their hearts, to give him a name.

Jerlayne's daughter did change. Her head, hands, and feet outgrew the rest of her. By her third birthday it was clear to anyone with open eyes that she was a dwarf. The stone-working brothers came to the gate to claim her.

It was the first adoption Sunrise hosted. Almost as many fairie folk came as had come to their wedding, including the goblins with their potent wine. The only sad face was Banda's. Tears slipped down the woman's pale cheeks whenever she saw Frunzit—the little girl had a dwarven name now—in the arms of her adoring aunts and uncles.

Jerlayne drew Banda inside, away from the laughter and celebration. She held her close, as she had never held her daughter, but as Banda had held her for three years. Her own eyes were dry.

"How do you survive?" Banda asked between sobs, then answered her question: "Elves are strong. Elves are the trees of our forest."

Jerlayne said nothing. She wasn't strong, not as strong

as Banda who would endure this anguish many times, at least until a child changed into a pale, bright-eyed gnome. One of *her* children, Jerlayne reminded herself, expecting the thought to spark a twinge of loss or regret. But Frunzit wasn't her child. That was how elves survived; they gave infants away, then adopted elves back—no different than the dwarves.

Then Jerlayne thought of her mother and how she remembered no arms but Elmeene's around her nor a time when she hadn't known her elven name.

When questions cloud your mind—she heard her mother's voice as clearly as if Elmeene were in the next room—which she was, along with everyone else. A storm had blown up while Jerlayne comforted Banda, and the celebration had moved indoors. Sunrise was five rooms larger than it had been when Frunzit was born—more than enough space for two elves—but nowhere near enough for the crowd it suddenly contained.

There was no time for private conversation; Jerlayne needed Elmeene's help keeping her homestead intact. The celebration ended quietly after the goblins—and their wine—departed with the mist. Aulaudin departed, too, leading all the elven men on a grand foraging beyond the veil: The homestead needed another room, he said.

Elmeene caught her daughter's eye. Jerlayne shook her head. She was exhausted; questions and answers could all wait until morning. But when morning came, it brought the men with it, and great piles of lumber, brick, and glass as well. Every question in Jerlayne's mind regarded breakfast or the room her husband seemed determined to build before noon.

Four days passed before Jerlayne remembered the conversation she hadn't had with her mother. By then Elmeene had been gone for two days. She and Aulaudin were alone in Sunrise and the discrepancies between what she remembered of her childhood and the elven traditions that defined her adulthood seemed quite unimportant.

Sunrise grew as the years passed. Aulaudin was a good forager and a generous one, too. Jerlayne was Elmeene's daughter, skilled from childhood in the shaping of iron and, on her own, slowly mastering the secrets of the light-weight, silvery metal humans named *aluminum*. Their reputations spread beyond the circle of their kin. The goblin, Goro, offered better terms—for a few bits of the new metal, everything they'd had before, plus a goblin camp nearby. One never knew, Goro grinned, when the neighbors might whelp something unpleasant. Jerlayne swallowed her anger and shook the goblin's hand: One *didn't* know.

She and Aulaudin had had other children. A son was born in the middle of a bitterly cold winter. By summer, he'd grown all he'd ever grow, turned nut-brown, and vanished into the forest. Sunrise hoped he'd found his brownie kin, but he'd come and gone too fast for even Banda to mourn his passing. After him, another daughter, the image of Aulaudin, until her eighth summer when her hair and eyes bleached pale in the sun and she became Banda's yearned-for child.

Jerlayne mourned the loss of her third not-elf child with a bitterness that frightened her and Aulaudin alike. Aulaudin was about to send to StoneWell when a messenger arrived with fairie's grimmest tidings: Elmeene had gone into seclusion with a daughter-by-marriage whose husband—her son, Jerlayne's brother—was ten days missing. Aulaudin joined the frantic search. Jerlayne roused herself and hastened to the paralyzed homestead.

A month of searching passed, and another, then Gudwal came to the gate with all the men of his lineage behind him. Dirty and weary, they'd each aged a thousand years since the man had vanished. Gudwal crossed the threshold alone. His hands shook as he spoke to the women.

"I have seen my grandson's shadow among the trees. I have heard his voice in the morning air. He—" The old man covered his eyes. His words—the desolation and despair—passed directly into each joined mind. "He does not know. He is at peace."

Elves were immortal, but elves could die in many ways, including a simple decision to live no longer. Gudwal stood before the young widow, waiting for her to speak. In her mind, joined as it was to all the other elves present, Jerlayne understood that he would do what her brother's widow did. After an endless moment, the widow elected to live. There had been children—elven children. She owed them more, not less, now that her husband was gone.

But there was no son old enough to forage for the homestead and, anyhow, that wasn't the elven way. The widow set fire to what she and her husband had built, then, with a black veil between herself and fairie, she followed her eldest daughter to a new, empty life.

Another month passed before Aulaudin saddled a horse—the grandson of his old stallion and Jerlayne's gray mare—for a trek beyond the veil. The parting was worse then their first had been: Aulaudin kept his fears to himself, but Jerlayne could taste them as they kissed. And as it had been that first time, there was new life within her.

An elf, she prayed to the nameless gods of fairie. *Let my child—*

The prayer died. Her brother was with the nameless gods. At peace, Gudwal said, and alone because his wife chose to live for their children rather than die with him. Jerlayne wanted an elf-child, but not at any price, not if she might have to choose between her husband and her child.

Aulaudin returned early with everything he'd wanted and another rose besides—a living rose, a sunrise rose with flowers identical to the porcelain rose in the trove room, he swore, though the thing was thorn canes and bare roots.

"We will grow old together, my love," he promised her when they planted it in bright autumn light, then added a confession. "I'm not so bold beyond the veil as your father and brothers. I forage the midden fields and bring back what's already discarded."

Joined with him, Jerlayne saw the dank, human places in his mind. Such places could truly be the source of their lumber and bricks, and of the stench that clung to his foraging until she, with her shaping magic, removed it. But such places could not be the source of either sunrise rose. There had to be more and, as if to confirm her suspicion, Aulaudin appeared suddenly between her and his memories.

«I love you, my love, and you alone.»

His passions swept over her with peculiar intensity. He had something hidden; that annoyed her, but not enough to raise a complaint. In front of their children—which was to say in front of everyone in fairie—elven couples were reserved, aloof, even cold with each other. It was different when they were alone, joined in body and mind to the exclusion of all else. They ignored the dinner bell and were not sated of each other until dawn fingers stole through the bedroom draperies.

Winter came. The time of cold days, long nights, and the deepest snows Jerlayne had seen since leaving StoneWell. Aulaudin was home for days on end. The veil that separated fairie from the human realm did not block out the stars—or so the men said—nor, certainly, the weather. Magic and midden fields might lessen the risks Aulaudin took, but only a foolish elf left tracks when he foraged and Aulaudin—though he proved inept at any domestic task he undertook, nursing Jerlayne through the early months of an uncommonly uncomfortable pregnancy—was not a fool.

Frunzit left in the spring, an expected loss—man or women, dwarves were a restless folk who needed to experience the length and breadth of fairie before settling down—but a loss nonetheless to the homestead she left behind. Jerlayne became aware, as she had never been before, of the yearning that grew apace with her unborn child—another daughter born after a hard labor in the hazy days of summer.

"Elves are strong," Banda said as she swaddled the infant. "Their strength makes them fight, that's what I've learned. This one fought all the way; she'll stay. Mark my words, Jerlayne: This daughter stays with you."

Jerlayne gave this daughter a name, Evoni, and made a place for her in Sunrise with Aulaudin and herself. When Aulaudin quietly advised caution, distance, Jerlayne replied with anger.

"Did your parents send you to live with gnomes until you came of elven age?"

Aulaudin shook his head. "No," he admitted and worried his lip between his teeth. "My mother said she knew—"

"And *I* know. Evoni is *ours!*"

"But—?"

"Our daughter, my love," Jerlayne snarled with very little love in her voice. "Let there be no more discussion."

After a few months of numbing variations, discussion, regardless of its subject, retreated from Sunrise. For ten years peace lay fragile between Jerlayne and her husband. The lovingly planted rose bloomed and was ignored.

Throughout the strained silences, Aulaudin minded his duties as provider for his homestead. He spent this time beyond the veil, and when he did return, he dwelt among the gnomes and dwarves, among the folk who needed what he brought from the human realm and quickly learned not to ask questions or speak of Jerlayne or Evoni.

They could not always avoid each other. The rhythms of homestead life required elven magic, the magic of men and women alike. When duty drew them together, Jerlayne and Aulaudin tried to bridge the chasm between them—the magic of joining was too powerful to be resisted or denied. But their wounds were as deep as their love and the longer the reconciliation lasted, the bitterer the explosion and parting that followed it.

Jerlayne folded her life around her daughter. Evoni was the moon bathed in the sunlight of a mother's devotion. She learned to shape simple things soon after she learned to walk. By her twelfth summer, Evoni could bend cold iron without burning her hands. Goro was awed when he came to Sunrise for the midsummer trading. Jerlayne foresaw the moment when her husband would, at last, concede what she had known from the very beginning.

Then came an autumn day, little different from any other. Aulaudin was beyond the veil. He'd been gone a day, or three and might be back tomorrow, the day after, or the day after that; he made no promises. Jerlayne spent the morning teaching her daughter the intricacies of metal-magic, then they'd eaten, rested.

"Come swimming with me?" Evoni asked, braiding her auburn hair.

Jerlayne shook her head. She didn't share her daughter's love of water. Swimming was pleasant enough in high summer, but come autumn, she'd rather sit at a tapestry loom. She was already sitting there with an array of muted fairie wools and bright, human-dyed silks. Aulaudin had never stopped bringing her gifts, their estrangement hadn't widened that far, though—predictably—he said nothing about the pictures she wove of her life with their daughter.

Evoni persisted with a mischievous smile. "You've got all winter to weave!" She was her father's daughter, if only he would open his eyes—and heart—to her.

Jerlayne returned the many-colored threads to their basket. Evoni was well ahead of her, laughing as she ran toward the water, braids and hems flared out behind her. It was a scene Jerlayne had watched uncounted times— ever since the dwarves dammed the stream to make a pond for winter fishing and her water-loving daughter. Today, her heart skipped a beat. Premonition and prophecy were as rare in fairie as ordinary magic was beyond the veil; they were nothing to ignore. Jerlayne shouted her daughter's name as loudly as she could.

But not loud enough.

Evoni heard nothing—or didn't want to. Running a race with herself, the girl kicked off her sandals without missing a stride, stretched her arms above her head and dove gracefully from the grassy bank.

"No—" Jerlayne's voice was a whisper. Her body, at last, began to move. "Come back. Evoni! *Evo*—"

The pond was calm, smooth as the glass Aulaudin foraged. Evoni could—did—swim beneath the water like a fish. This was different; Jerlayne knew that. She thrust her fists beneath the surface. Ripples spread.

"Evoni!"

Nothing.

Banda came out of her cottage with the daughter they shared, full grown now, close behind her. And behind them, roused by Jerlayne's cries and the heavy magic squalling suddenly out of the quiet, afternoon air, came the rest of the homestead.

"Evoni!" Jerlayne slid off the bank and stumbled

toward the center of the pond where a wind-whipped froth broke the surface.

As the bards recounted fairie's legends, what the squall and froth foretold was inevitable, but Jerlayne would not release Evoni without a fight. Using magic meant to shape and transform, she strove to keep her daughter unchanged. Striving wasn't enough. The squall trapped Jerlayne's magic within her and pushed her deep beneath the water. Defeated—drowning—Jerlayne surrendered, only to be snatched to safety by goblin hands.

The froth became a dark-water pillar swirling upward. The pillar swelled, put forth arms and eyes. It began to sing.

Someone shouted "Siren!" others added, "Break the dam!" and "Open the weir!" but Jerlayne said nothing. She'd looked into the watery eyes and, finding nothing there that recognized her, collapsed with one hand over her heart, the other around her neck.

Echoes of Evoni's transformation reached far beyond Sunrise homestead, far beyond fairie. They touched Aulaudin as he foraged: a cold hand over his heart, another around his neck. He cast aside the swag he'd collected and begun to run, bursting the veil not in the forest, as was his custom, where his horse waited, but at the foot of Petrin's orchard.

The thunderclap that accompanied his arrival caused most of the 'steaders to blink, but those few who kept their eyes open witnessed a second nightmare in a single day: the bizarre angles, colors, noises, and smells of the human realm momentarily shimmered around Aulaudin, then were gone.

He ran from the orchard to the pond. The 'steaders parted silently, letting him see for himself the disaster that had drawn him back to fairie. His wife lay senseless in the damp grass. Evoni—her discarded body—lay facedown in the mud of the now-vanished pond.

"A siren—" a goblin began, and was silenced by an elven scowl.

Aulaudin looked out across the mud. "Bury her," he said as he knelt beside Jerlayne.

Later the 'steaders would all agree that the elf's face
was inscrutable when he lifted his wife from the grass,
darkly inscrutable and too intimidating for any of them to
move a muscle. Later still they would speculate on
Aulaudin's thoughts: the rage that surely lurked beneath
his stony exterior.

Their speculations, though, would be entirely wrong.
Aulaudin's face was inscrutable as he strode heavy-footed
from the pond because his mind was empty. Nothing
more profound than the habit of moving one foot after the
other stirred his thoughts. Habit, too, guided him through
the rooms, past Jerlayne's unfinished tapestry and
Evoni's adolescent disorder. He laid her on the bed they'd
seldom shared these last several years, loosened her
clothes, removed her shoes, and whispered her name.

The rage came later. Aulaudin slashed the tapestry from
the frame, tore it warp from weft, and cursed everything
and everyone with language seldom heard on fairie's side
of the veil. Then, in the dark and quiet hours after midnight, he called on the magic he'd learned from Maun and
with thought alone disturbed his distant father's sleep
with images of muddy corpses and Jerlayne.

«I cannot rouse her. Tell mother I'm coming home with
my wife. We'll leave after sunrise. Tell her I don't know
what to do.»

He was packing bundles before dawn when Maun burst
into his mind like a clanging gong.

«She says No!» Maun proclaimed with a finality that
flattened his son against the nearest wall. «If Jerlayne
had—» Images of death and despair filled Aulaudin's
mind as his father contemplated life without his mother.
«You could return, but your mother doesn't know Jerlayne—not well enough for this. She says you must take
her to Elmeene and you must—» Another gap as Maun's
words dissolved into Maun's confusion. «You must join
with her . . . with Jerlayne . . . now, before you depart.»

"Join with her!" Aulaudin sputtered aloud in the empty
room. He loved Jerlayne, loved her still, but to join with
her as she was— «Father, I cannot.»

«She says you must, completely—for yourself and for

her.» Maun passed along a sense of inevitability, of men's magic, which included the mysteries of the veil and the aspects of joining which involved thought and images, contrasted with women's magic: the physical mysteries of shaping and joining's sensual pleasures.

There could be no sensual pleasure between Aulaudin and his scarcely conscious wife, but he respected his mother's judgment more than he respected his own. The experience was worse than unpleasant. Despite his best efforts to bathe her, scents of pond-scum and mud still clung to Jerlayne's hair; and her wispy thoughts were bleak with death. He couldn't escape the notion that he'd joined with a corpse.

But join with her he did and, confirming his mother's wisdom, felt the first resurgence of Jerlayne's consciousness: she wrapped a pall of shame around herself to shut him out completely. Jerlayne rose from the bed. She washed and dressed herself. She ate enough to live. She heard, she listened, but said nothing and when she looked at Aulaudin, her eyes went wide, as if she'd discovered herself beside a frightening stranger—until Aulaudin, after two grim days, returned to his mother's advice.

"We could—if you're well enough—leave Sunrise for a while. We could visit your parents. Perhaps Elmeene—"

Jerlayne quivered head to toe. For a heartbeat, Aulaudin's thoughts were fear for her and rage at fate—at Evoni, the siren-daughter who had confounded their lives. Then Jerlayne steadied herself.

"Yes. Yes, I have questions now. It's *time* for answers."

Aulaudin became the elf in a stranger's company, hovering nearby as Jerlayne prepared for a journey. He followed her silently, repacking her haphazard bundles, tending the mare she saddled too soon, then left standing in the sun. He assured the 'steaders, who could scarcely be assured, that Sunrise would endure, that all would be well again . . . soon. And when the right moment finally came, Aulaudin boosted his wife into her saddle—receiving neither thanks nor notice for his efforts—and followed her west, to StoneWell.

* * *

She couldn't bear to look at him, at Aulaudin, her husband, and so Jerlayne chose not to see him, even knowing that her decision was a step along the path to madness. Her husband was not a ghost, as Evoni had become a ghost, flitting at the corners of her consciousness, singing a song that was madness in all its terrible glory. Better, she thought, to pretend that she was alone and had always been alone, to retreat from the truth, to embrace a lesser madness until she was with Elmeene. She could endure the chaos she had created for herself that long without shattering entirely.

At least, Jerlayne hoped she could, and quickly closed her eyes lest she see the man who'd urged his horse abreast of hers.

"Jerlayne! Daughter!"

A stinging blow to her cheek brought Jerlayne back. She was in Elmeene's sitting room, where she learned to spin and to weave and the mysteries of magic. A shaping lesson had gone badly; she'd lost herself in some other substance—lost herself badly: afternoon light slanted through the windows and mornings were for lessons. She was embarrassed, ashamed; she looked down at her hands, and failed to recognize them.

"Jerlayne! Look at me! Talk to me!"

Another slap.

"Mother . . ." Her voice was wrong: not a girl's voice, as her hands weren't a young girl's hands.

Jerlayne raised her head. She was in Elmeene's sitting room, that was true enough, but it wasn't a shaping lesson that had gone awry. There was another face in her mind. Evoni—And when Jerlayne recalled her siren-daughter's name, she recalled everything.

"Tell me everything," Elmeene suggested as she took Jerlayne into her arms.

The sitting room was silver with moonlight before Jerlayne finished her tale. "I was so certain. How could I have been so wrong as well?".

Elmeene rose from the upholstered bench where they'd sat side by side. She lit a lamp and set it beside an iron-sealed chest. "I'm to blame," she said as shaping magic flared between her hands and the metal. "When you didn't come home, I thought you'd guessed for yourself. Some women do: two of your sisters didn't need me to tell them—"

"Tell them what?" Jerlayne complained, bitterness overcoming despair. "A siren mother. I gave my husband a daughter, a *siren!* Could I have known—*Should* I have known what she'd become and strangled her before she opened her eyes?"

No answer. Jerlayne heard a strap of iron clatter to the floor, nothing more as Elmeene rummaged through the now-opened chest.

"Tell me, Mother! Tell me what Aulaudin and I did and what we could have done to prevent it!"

Elmeene returned to the bench with an armload of flat, silk-wrapped parcels. "Nothing," she said, heaping the parcels between them. "There is no curse, no failure, no shame. Sirens must be born. Sirens, ogres, and all the rest—even dragons; fairie must have its guardians. When I was a girl, a dragon was born. He took flight three days later, scouring everything in his path. Twenty elves died, including his parents, before he reached the mountains, but he was elven-born and even now he dwells in the mountains, guarding them and us. We shape more than metal, my daughter, I *thought* you understood: we shape fairie itself through our children. The goblins help, but we're strong. We could do it all ourselves."

Jerlayne stared at the incongruously bright parcels. "I'm not strong. Sometimes I want to run away from Sunrise. I can't face saying good-bye again. I want my own children, Aulaudin's children." Tears made their way unhindered down her cheeks; they stained the silks. "You knew, Mother. You and Father must have known, you never sent me away. I always knew my own name. I grew up under this roof. How?"

"Your father didn't know, not at first, though he believed me by the time you were born." The edge was gone from Elmeene's voice as she selected a red-wrapped parcel from the middle of the heap. Unknotted, the cloth revealed a wooden plaque.

"How did you know? How do you know which child
will change and which one won't."

"It's very simple." Elmeene placed the plaque in Jerlayne's hands. "I know your father. Turn it over . . ."

Jerlayne refused. She had questions, lots of them: the
answers weren't written on a plaque. "I—"

"Turn it over. Then I'll tell you everything my mother
told me and everything I've learned since."

It was portrait, a man's portrait, painted on the wood,
but the man was not her father, not an elf at all, nor a
gnome or dwarf, nor a goblin or any other man of fairie,
which left only the men beyond the veil, the men whose
faces she'd never seen.

"Jerlayne, there is only one way to secure yourself an
elven child: pierce the veil and join with the mortal men
you find beyond it."

Beyond words, Jerlayne could only shake her head as
her mother unwrapped the other parcels. This had to be a
nightmare, but Jerlayne wasn't asleep; it had to be a de-
ceitful jest, but there was no mockery in Elmeene's voice
or in her hands as she exposed portrait after portrait, one
for every elven child she'd born until the last, which was
only a charcoal sketch on raw wood.

"You have a brother coming, Jerlayne."

"No." She poured her soul into the denial. There was
magic in her hands. She had the power to shape the wood,
to change the portrait into a face she knew and cherished;
she lacked the will. The stranger in her hands—the
mortal, human man—was her father. "Why?" she asked, a
world of questions in a single word.

"No reason, only the truth. When elves join, all the
other fairie-folk are possible. If you want an elven child,
you must find a mortal man."

Jerlayne traced the portrait's outline with her finger
tips. "Father—" Her voice caught. She cleared her throat
and went on: "Father knows." Jeriege would always be
her father, her immortal father. The other one would
never be more than a painted image. She could never
know him, even if she'd wanted to. Jerlayne was young,
still, for an elf, but far older than any man. "Father
pierced the veil; he took you with him, you foraged for a

man to be my father." She was babbling; it was easier to
speak each thought as it came to her than to consider its
implications. "I asked Aulaudin once—he said *no*. I'll ask
again. I didn't know; maybe he didn't, either. When are
men told . . . ?"

Elmeene seized Jerlayne's wrist and shook it hard.
"You will say nothing! No man has ever known this! You
must *never* speak of it to them. The truth of our elven
children has been a women's secret for too long to ever be
shared. I didn't learn . . . I couldn't tell you until you were
old enough to understand the risk *and* experienced
enough to keep a secret from your husband."

There was an awful symmetry to her mother's revela-
tions that, combined with the plaques and Jerlayne's own
failure to conceive a fully elven child, shaped a single
truth. "Is there no other way? Must I deceive Aulaudin?"
She shivered and dropped the plaque. "I won't—I've
done too much wrong already. I can't—" Her spirts lifted.
"I don't even know where the veil is." The whole notion
was impossible—

"It's everywhere, Jerlayne. In the forest, where the men
find it. In this very room. You need only to think about it.
Our shaping magic must be taught, and the subtleties of
thought are passed from father to son, but anyone born in
fairie can find and pierce the veil—a gnome, a sprite, a
brownie—anyone." To prove her point, Elmeene opened
her arms. A mist not unlike the goblin mist bloomed suddenly and, through the mist came the shapes and sounds
of the mortal realm. "Come with me. I'll show you the
rest."

Jerlayne balked and the mist vanished. She had a thousand questions, twice that many objections, but Elmeene
countered each one with an explanation and an invitation
until, in despair, Jerlayne confessed her darkest, most
shameful secret:

"Aulaudin and I are estranged. We haven't joined in
months—"

Elmeene's eyebrows arched.

"You understand, then, Mother. What you propose—
He'll *know*. It's unthinkable, if men are not to guess the

truth. It will take time to heal the breach between us. Years, perhaps. We'll return to Sunrise—"

Elmeene scowled. "Nonsense. Aulaudin says you two joined soon after the siren left. He apologized, of course, but his mother had guessed correctly and told him exactly what to do. No excuses: You want an elven child: What better way to heal any breach between you?"

The mist reappeared in the middle of the room and with it, the smells and sounds of mortality. Elmeene took Jerlayne's hand.

"They're not so bad. Not like joining with your husband, of course, but not without their charms. You shouldn't think of it as a betrayal. Remember, we're strong—"

SPINNING WEBS AND TELLING LIES

by David Niall Wilson

David Niall Wilson's work has appeared in *100 Vicious Little Vampire Stories*, *Werewolves*, *Murder Most Delicious*, and *Robert Bloch's Psychos*. He lives in Norfolk, Virginia.

Spinning Webs scuttled beneath a tree as the sound of horses announced the warriors' return. Dust flew in whorls up to meet the heat of the sky. Their faces were grim—sweat and dirt blending with the painted symbols of the hunt. There were no kills slung over the horse's flanks.

Spinning Webs felt the hunger spirits piercing her abdomen gleefully, poking and prodding with tiny spears of ice. She remained in the shadows, waiting. Telling Lies would come to her with the story of the hunt soon enough, what story there was. There would be no singing at the fires.

Slipping off through the camp as unobtrusively as possible, she made her way to her tent. There would be charms to blend; songs to sing. She wondered how many times the spirits would laugh at her, bending her vision and steering the warriors from the herds. Before long, it would be she who was called Telling Lies.

The corners of her tent were littered with pouches, bowls, gourds, and containers of all shapes and sizes. Spinning Webs gathered a small pile of leaves and bark, herbs and feathers, working carefully, but quickly. As she worked, she sang softly to the spirit of each item she brought forth before tucking it into a leather pouch. This was not the time for small magic. She needed to prove her vision to the tribe once more, to renew their strength and their faith in her—to bring them to the herds. She needed to spin webs that would capture spirits, webs that would bring her the vision.

Telling Lies parted the tent's flap and entered quickly, glaring at her. She could see the questions warring with the anger in his eyes. She said nothing, continuing to mix the herbs and leaves, bark and dust, accompanied by the sound of her voice, forming the ancient words—calling to the spirits.

Telling Lies wanted to speak—the desire seeped from his skin and blazed from his eyes. He wanted to scream at her—to grab her and claw at her eyes—her skin. He wanted to vent the rage of another frustrated hunt. He said nothing. He saw her hands moving quickly and surely, heard the musical lilt of her voice. The spirits hovered about her—the eyes of the ancients watched him—waiting. He moved to the far corner of the tent and sat, his back to her, staring at nothing.

Spinning Webs drew forth every ounce of power she possessed. She called to her spirit guide, eight-legged and clever, vicious, and yet necessary to the pattern of life. She climbed the web of smoky vision, eyes wide, alert. She sought a vision of direction—of prophecy. She focused on the dry, barren land—on the clouds far above. She sought the rain spirits and the soul of the herd.

She saw the eagles floating high across the desert sand. She saw coyote slinking behind a rocky outcropping, sly eyes watching her, but tongue and mind silent. The herd was nowhere to be seen. Nothing but spirit—nothing that could feed her people. Dust swirled and mocked her. She sought to climb higher—to reach the places beyond thought where all answers lay in wait, but the web began to unravel. Failing, dropping from the network of spirits and vision, she opened her eyes to her tent—to Telling Lies and his accusations. She had nothing to offer, and, falling to her knees, she lowered her head and wept.

Telling Lies rose from his crouch, making his way to Spinning Webs' side. He grabbed her by the hair—not violently—but with authority. He lifted her eyes to meet his own. She fought him, at first, but his strength was greater than hers. She met his eyes.

"You must find an answer. To cower against the Earth Mother is beneath you. You are the one with the spirits—there is no other to take your place."

"I have called to the spirits," she whispered. "I have called, and none have answered that can help me. Coyote slinks about the desert, and the eagles soar, but the herd eludes me."

"Then you must seek a new vision," he asserted, the arrogance of his certainty challenging her. So simple to say it. So simple to assume the spirits would be there, would lead them to food and water and peace. Spinning Webs knew the truth of spirits. She knew the darkness in the light. She knew the balance. Still, Telling Lies spoke the truth. The burden was hers. There was none to pass it on to. She would have to find a new way—a new vision.

"I must go among the trees," she said softly. "I must find a thread that will bind me to the spirits—a thread they cannot unravel and escape me. I must go, and I will not return until I have an answer."

Telling Lies nodded, as though it had been his idea—as though he understood. He would go to the fires, and he would tell her tale. He would embellish it—making her the greatest of the spirit-talkers. He would dance and howl with what energy was left to him—he would tell the lie of the truth, would speak of clouds heavy with rain and a plain dark with buffalo, and the others would nod sagely—agreeing with his wisdom, admiring her courage.

Ducking away, Spinning Webs grabbed the pouch she'd been preparing. She took also a small gourd of water, and a robe of buffalo hide. Telling Lies watched her in silence, already confident of her success. He visualized the world in absolutes; Spinning Webs dreamed of such freedom.

As shadows nipped at her heels and stole her courage, she slipped away from the tent and through the camp, being careful to alert no one. She sensed the presence of the sentries at the perimeter as she passed, but they did not see her. She was one with the shadow, a wisp of fog. Nothing to their eyes. All they saw was hunger. All they sought was release. Behind her the fire blazed suddenly, and she hurried her steps, blending into the night.

Dust flew each time her feet struck the earth, and she knew the truth behind the disappearance of the herds. The water was drying up. The rain spirits had been silent for too long. She could direct the tribe toward the distant river—though the water there would be low as well, but that would serve only to bring them too close to other tribes. Many would die.

Ahead she saw a small stand of trees. She hurried her steps. The weight of unseen eyes was heavy on her shoulders. Perhaps it would be a night for the spirits—a night for power.

Entering beneath the low-hanging branches, she pushed her way through to the center, where there was a small, rounded clearing. Spinning Webs stopped short, staring. It was, perhaps, too round. It seemed as though someone had prepared this spot for something—for her arrival? She could hardly believe that. If the spirits wouldn't hear her songs or the hunger-cries of her people, would they go to such trouble for her now?

She stepped into the clearing and took a seat near the center, dropping the small leather bag on the ground before her and closing her eyes. She had no time to waste on fear, or self-pity. Reaching deep within herself, she began to pull the darkness about her—to drive out the thoughts and sounds of the world and to make room for the spirits. It was a soft, cleansing sensation. Even the hunger faded as she drifted deeper and deeper into the vision.

She called out to the spider. She formed the strands of his web easily, calling them from memory, calling them from her own spirit. They hung from the fabric of her vision, glistening silver with captured moonlight. She could feel his presence, could see the web shaking and vibrating as he scuttled closer, and her heart quickened. So many years, so many visions, and still her totem thrilled her—frightened her—vitalized her mind and her spirit.

Without opening her eyes, she sought the leather bag and brought it into her lap. Quickly she untied the leather thong and reached inside. Allowing the spirits to guide her fingers, she rummaged about, latched onto a small object, and brought it forth, bringing her hand in a small arc upward toward her forehead.

With a gasp, she felt the wind lift the charm from her fingers, blowing it away. Trembling, she tried to regain her composure, to banish the tremors that had taken hold of her flesh. Then she felt it. Softly, almost too softly to be detected, something brushed against her forehead. Her mind conjured images instantly, but her spirit knew. It was a leaf—it was the charm from the bag. She brought her hand up slowly, thinking to press the leaf more tightly into place.

Her hand did not meet the leaf, but soft, supple skin. Jerking back, her eyelids snapping open and her mind shocked alert, she scuttled backward. In the center of the clearing, a slender man stood—no warrior, for he was without paint or ornament—pale and beautiful against the backdrop of trees and washed in the light of the moon. His hair was a fountain of silk—like the web of Spider. He held the leaf in his hand, and he was smiling at her.

The wind picked up suddenly. It wasn't the wind, it was laughter—soft, musical laughter that reminded her of breezes slipping through tall grass, or a stream dancing over smooth stones. Whipping her head to the side, she saw that she was surrounded. They sat in a large ring about her, pale and smooth—like spirits.

Turning back quickly, she glared up at the intruder who held her charm.

"Who are you? What do you want?"

"I came to your call," he replied softly. He spoke her tongue fluently, but with an accent that breathed new magic into ancient words. "It is you who wants, is it not, little sister?"

"I am Spinning Webs," she stated defiantly. "I did not call to you, but to my spirit-brother, Spider."

"And yet, you have called, and I have come," he replied, his smile infuriating. "It has been long years since I've heard the call of one of your people so strongly—perhaps too long."

"Who are you?" she repeated her question.

"I am Alanis," he answered. "These are my brothers, my sisters—we have always been here."

"I have never seen you," Spinning Webs spat. "You are pale and thin—weak. I have never heard of your tribe."

"We are not a tribe," Alanis said, still smiling, though the lines around his eyes hardened. "We are a part of the trees—of the wind. We are one with the voice of the clouds and the soul of the herd. I have spoken with your "Spider" spirit, shared songs with the buffalo. The world as we have known it is fading—we fade with it, but sometimes there is one such as yourself who can call us back."

"Why have you come?" Spinning Webs asked, softening her voice. "My people are starving—the ground thirsts and I cannot reach the spirit of the herd."

"We understand." Alanis replied. "I have little to offer the world these days—little enough to offer my own people. I will offer you this. I will offer you a dance, little sister. You do not believe it, but you are a part of us, as well. Your vision, your 'spider spirit' are gifts from one of our ancestors. In the ancient days, our peoples lived side by side."

"I cannot *dance!*" she cried, rising to her feet. "I must do what I can for my people—did you not understand?"

Alanis did not respond, but he moved closer, holding out his hands. All around them, the others rose, their limbs brushing against one another and whispering like silk, long white hair whipping about in the breeze and luminous eyes glittering with captured moonlight.

From somewhere the soft strains of a flute rose—music such as she had never heard. It snaked about her limbs, working its way through her thoughts and wiping away her resolve as if it were nothing. She moved forward and took Alanis' hand wonderingly. Then he was moving, and she was following, and the small clearing became a blaze of color and sound, light and magic.

She felt the wisping touch of Spider—felt as though she were clothed in nothing but his silken webs. Alanis laughed and pulled her close, his flesh warm and soft against hers—his eyes filling her sight and his voice capturing her mind. She danced, following his lead, and visions replaced the clearing that surrounded them. They whirled and leaped through a field of silver flowers, soared across the sky like bolts of lightning to lightly come to rest on billowing gray clouds that dampened her calves and swirled about her. Her clothing grew damp with the moisture of the storms and clung to her as she danced.

The others danced with them, sometimes pressing close, sometimes whirling her away from Alanis and around the circle, only to come around once again and be flung into the center—into his arms. They were on the ground again—suddenly, but not jarringly. The trees stood as silent sentinels—and Alanis held her close, moving slowly in time to music that seemed to be fading.

"You are special to us, my sister," he said softly, and even his voice seemed more substantial—Spider's voice—her spirit soared.

He drew her gently down onto the grass, kissed her cheek, and pulled her to him. She felt him gently removing her clothing and pressing her back into the soft earth. She let her mind wash clear of everything but his scent—his caress. She drifted with him—the breeze tickling her flesh—the magic of the moment sliding her away from the dusty world once more—away from the tribe, from responsibility.

Sometime later, he left her. Her memory was unclear—unfocused. She opened her eyes to find herself lying in the clearing, alone and fully clothed. Small droplets of rain trickled through the trees to run down her cheeks, bringing her up quickly from the soft embrace of her dreams. She stood, gathering her pouch to herself and looking about.

She was partially protected by the trees, but she could hear the rain beating against the ground, could hear the thunder and the lightning dancing through the skies. For just a moment, she felt those clouds beneath her feet—felt the power of the lightning—then she was moving, leaving the clearing and pushing her way through the trees toward home—toward Telling Lies and the others.

Something was different, though. She sensed it within herself—a glow. Softly, so softly she couldn't be certain she'd heard the words—his voice returned to her.

"Raise her well, little sister. She will be as you are, beautiful and full of the spirits. Look for me in the leaves of the trees and the dance of the wind. Feel me close to you as the rain runs over you and brings the herds. Take time to dance, always—teach your people. The dance will set you free."

As she made her way into the camp, Spinning Webs touched her belly in wonderment. She didn't know how she could be certain, but she was. She would bear a child—his child—and she would raise her to the secrets of herb and spirit. Her steps quick, and her heart light, she made her way to her tent and inside, sliding beneath the blanket where Telling Lies awaited her.

As if he could sense the magic, he pulled her close.

"The herds will come," she said simply.

He nodded, not speaking, but brushing the hair from her eyes to see her more clearly. There was another hour before the dawn, and she felt the chill of the rain on her skin melting in the heat of his embrace. His spirit would join that of Spider—Alanis—spinning into a web that would produce her child.

In the distance, thunder rumbled, and she imagined the sound as the hooves of buffalo as the herds returned. In her mind, the flutes played intricate melodies and tall, slender bodies leaped and whirled among the buffalo, keeping time to the rhythm of the storm. It was a good night to be alive.

THE DANCING RING

by Jody Lynn Nye

Jody Lynn Nye lists her main career activity as "spoiling cats." She lives near Chicago with two of the above and her husband, SF author Bill Fawcett. Among Jody's novels are the *Mythology 101* series, *Taylor's Ark*, *Medicine Show*, and four collaborations with Anne McCaffrey: *Crisis on Doona*, *The Death of Sleep*, *The Ship Who Won*, and *Treaty at Doona*. Upcoming works include a new contemporary fantasy, *The Magic Touch*, *The Ship Errant*, and an anthology, *Don't Forget Your Spacesuit, Dear!*

Dark was coming soon. The last thin, golden rays of the sun fell around Grainne as she searched the forest floor for mushrooms. Just a few more, she thought, pulling the fleshy stems lose from the rich, acidy humus underneath the oaks. Mam would be pleased. These were nice and plump. They would go well in the stew.

Only a few feet away were fat, top-heavy fungi that looked tempting, but Grainne knew the difference between the mushrooms that grew freely and those in a fairy ring.

"Don't dare take away any of these," her old gran had warned, showing her the pure white gills underneath the lip of a fairy mushroom. "They're poison to humans. Only the High Ones can eat them." And, of course Grainne knew better than to step into the fairy ring. Those who did were either swept away to Tir-na'n-Og, or left mad and lamenting.

The trick was that fairy circles moved and changed, and sometimes white-gilled mushrooms would be left behind for the unwary to pick. The headman's own daughter had died of eating them, a terrible tragedy. Grainne wondered how she herself would want to be remembered when she was gone. "Died of eating mushrooms," she thought, not without sympathy for Maire. Oh, no. For her, let it be something more interesting, pray Gods! "Ripped by wild boars . . . no, died of her wounds defending the village . . . no, died surrounded by her twenty sons and twenty daughters, all as fair as the children of Lir." Not with her in-between-colored hair, neither blonde nor brown, or her almost-gray eyes, or her undeniably round face. No, the most likely thing would be that Grainne would dance herself to death, and the village would talk about it until no one was left who had known her.

The sun was gone, and the moon, a huge white ball, was rising in the east. On her hands and knees she reached for one last, tempting puffball, then flinched back as if the innocent mushroom had burned her fingers. She had seen movement beyond it in the fairy ring. Was someone there? She almost cried out, and then her eyes focused upon him.

Framed by the light of the white moon, a man was dancing. Silently, to no music that she could hear, he leaped and cavorted, spun and bowed. The grass and leaves on the forest floor made no noise under his feet. He was slim and lithe as a hazel twig, and he had long hair that fell over his shoulders in a silky mass.

She thought that his profile was handsome, and wished she could see more of his face, and his costume. An occasional wink of colored light burst to show where jewels studded his tunic, and she saw where more gleamed in his hair as he whirled around in a circle. He was a wonderful dancer, grace itself for all his great height. Who was he? Where had he come from?

Grainne's curiosity nearly overcame her caution, but sense landed upon her with a hard thump. This beautiful, noble being was still a strange man, and she was alone with him in the forest on the darkening night. Better to withdraw quietly before he saw anyone had observed him. With deep regret, Grainne let go of her basket handle. She couldn't crawl and carry it, too. Mam would be cross, but she'd rather have the daughter back safely than the mushrooms.

She started to creep backward on hands and knees. Her skirt scooped along a litter of leaves that was cold and damp against her legs. It was distracting as an unreachable itch, but she must concentrate on being silent. She had to get away. A little at a time, she backed away from the dancer in the ring. A little more. Concentrate, she urged herself. Don't watch him, beautifully though he moved. The very moonlight wrapped itself around him. A little more. She was nearly to the big beech tree where she could stand up and tiptoe away. A little more. Soon she'd be away. She'd tell Mam and Da what she'd seen. A moonshine tale, they'd say, but she'd have the deep satisfaction of knowing it was the truth, allowing herself a private grin.

Grainne glanced up at the dancer, and gasped. He had stopped his gyrations. He was looking straight toward her, his eyes glowing pale green with their own inner light. He was an elf lord, one of the High Ones! Grainne almost bolted like a coney.

Standing straight and tall, he put one hand behind his back, and held out the other, palm up, to her. It was an invitation to the dance.

"Oh, no," Grainne thought. But the hand extended farther, the fingers arching more. It was an appeal and a command. Come!

Grainne rose slowly to her feet and brushed the oak leaves out of her skirt. Still, she hesitated.

"Come dance with me, maid," the man said. His voice was compelling, clear and resonant as a horn call. The moon had risen far enough to frame his shoulders and head like a halo. "This night is for dancing."

She moved toward him, one dreaming pace at a time. Grainne told herself later that it was the power of his voice that drew her to him, but her wish to know was the real overwhelming force. How would they dance together?

He awaited her, his hand still outstretched. At the edge of the circle, Grainne halted before stepping over it. Would she be struck mad? Or swept away? She thought of her mother, and how sorrowful Brigid would be if her only daughter vanished in the night. Then, his fingers reached out and closed gently about hers.

The touch of them was unexpectedly cool and soft. Grainne looked down at his hand. She felt a thrill of fear and excitement. In the strong moonlight filtering now through the thin tree branches overhead, his skin was pale blue-green. She gasped and looked up into his eyes. They were tilted up at the corners, like a cat's, and his ears were tall and pointed.

"Fear me not, maid," he said and took her other hand.

Grainne felt rather than heard the music as the elf lord swept her into his arms. Together they cavorted from one side of the bright ring to the other, skimmed lightly around its perimeter, and swirled in complicated steps and skips to the center again. There was a sensual pleasure in dancing with him. Though the top of her head came only to the middle of his chest, he measured his steps to suit hers. He made her feel as if they were one flesh, one will. She felt tingles of delight as he twirled her out, then brought her effortlessly in again, guiding her with his hands. He had a perfect sense of rhythm, so she found herself counting the beat of their steps without worrying that she couldn't hear a tune. Grainne was considered to be a good dancer among her folk, but she felt like a spavined cow by comparison. Yet, the green-eyed elf lord seemed pleased with her.

"What are you called, maid?" he asked, when they paused after a vigorous and satisfying reel.

Grainne looked up at him and bit her lip. To tell her true name to one of the High Ones was to give them power over her. Yet, for a moment, she thought that might be nice. If he tumbled her, surely he would be as gentle and as proficient at that as he was at dancing, and that would be no bad thing. His smooth skin smelled of lavender, unlike the men in the village, who reeked of cow pats and ill-cured hides. His lips looked soft. Would they feel blue on her skin?

Hold, girl, she told herself. The very seduction of the High Ones was what left broken minds behind them. Still, if she could remember this glorious dance and the ones before it, she could ask for no better price for her sanity.

He must have guessed her thoughts, for his glowing eyes were full of laughter, and she threw away caution in the delight of them.

"I'm Grainne," she said, suddenly shy. "My father is Anluan."

He bowed deeply, his arm folded at his middle. "Well met, Grainne, daughter of Anluan. I am Lorcan, son of Conor. And farewell."

As he straightened, he took a pace backward. Grainne started toward him, and felt an invisible barrier between them. The moonlight grew about him, thickening into a cocoon.

"Don't go," she begged. She could no longer see him clearly. "Please, what have I done?"

She heard his wonderful laughter from the heart of the ball of light.

"You'll see me again, Grainne!"

It was a promise. She hugged that to herself as the bright glow shrank until it was no more than a light silver wash on the ground of the fairy ring.

She looked up at the moon, and was stunned at how far it had moved in the sky. Gracious, it was late! Mam would be furious. Grainne snatched up the basket of mushrooms, and hurried toward home. On the way, she couldn't resist trying a few steps of the dance she and Lorcan had done together.

"His skin was blue-green, like a beryl," she told Brigid.

"As if you'd seen a beryl," her mother clucked. The hour was late, but dinner had been delayed because a king's messenger had arrived in the village to give them news. As she sliced mushrooms, Brigid listened with half an ear to the measured tones of his voice.

"His name is Lorcan, Mother," Grainne said, loudly, tossing a handful into the pot. She wiped her hands on a cloth and waved them about in the air. "He was so beautiful, and he . . ."

"Hush, girl," Brigid said, more sharply than she'd intended. All the men had turned to look at them. She waved her knife at her husband and went back to the task.

"Everyone's hungry, girl," she told Grainne. "Keep

your dream tales to yourself. You're lucky to be getting a bite to eat at all, you were so late in coming home."

"But it isn't a dream tale," Grainne insisted, now in a whisper. "He was real. We danced in the fairy ring."

Brigid was annoyed that Grainne couldn't simply be quiet. Now she'd have to ask Anluan to repeat the herald's news to her, and he had no head for detail at all. The men were nodding, now, and speaking in the low tones of serious conference. She sighed.

When she turned back to her daughter, Grainne looked sad. "You don't believe me, do you?"

Brigid clicked her tongue. Grainne was her youngest and most fanciful offspring. "Oh, child."

"It is true," Grainne insisted, her face earnest. "I swear it by God. Lorcan was there. We danced. He liked me, he did!"

"Oh, yes, a maid on a night with a full moon. I can see we'll have to think about getting you married off one of these days."

"But, Mother!" Grainne protested.

But then the conference was over, and the men were demanding their supper, with special hospitality for the guest, and there was no time for more foolishness.

Grainne couldn't persuade her father that she was telling the truth either. He didn't give her the chance to finish her tale, but waved her away to her tasks. Grainne wasn't one to sulk, though. If Lorcan appeared again, she'd ask him for a token of proof of his existence. If not, well, then she'd enjoy his company all to herself without the belief of her family. They couldn't disapprove of her dancing with him, if they didn't believe in him in the first place.

But it was a long time until she saw him again. Grainne made excuses any evening she could to visit the place in the forest where the fairy ring had been. She had hope that on the full moons of July and August he would appear, as he had in June, but the mystic light didn't come. Grainne began to wonder if perhaps she had imagined the elf lord.

A second full moon fell in late August. Grainne spent all her days in the field, following the reapers and

gathering the sheaves of grain, or picking bushels and pun-
nets of ripe fruit. Everything was golden and smelled
richly of yeast. Here and there a tree, freed of its summer's
burden, began to glow golden. In the evenings, she helped
her mother and the other village women to cook huge sup-
pers, and then sort and prepare fruit for preserves.

When at last the reaping was finished, and the wheat
had been winnowed, the village held a mighty harvest
feast. Everyone contributed the finest produce they had.
The carcass of a fat bullock roasted in a pit filled with
applewood charcoal. Special breads baked on the hearth
of every home. A cask of barley ale made from the first
grain gathered had been fermenting for a week. The heady
scent added to the other delicious aromas perfuming
the air.

Just at sunset, Fiochan the baker brought out his
wooden pipe and played a tune to call everyone to the
house of Grainne's uncle Donal, the headman. In no time,
Fiochan had gathered an impromptu band, with half a
dozen musicians of skills ranging from indifferent to
good, while more gathered around to enjoy the music.

Grainne and her family joined the merriment with glad
hearts. Tired as she was, the pipes called to her, and made
her pick up her feet. With a look over her shoulder at her
mother for permission, she left her tasks, and went to
dance in the middle of the torchlit floor.

Other young people joined her, and soon there were
dozens of feet tapping, kicking, and skipping. Grainne
shared the joy of her friends and cousins as the music
drained her weariness away. The pipers swung into a
cheerful reel. Her cousin Mihall began to clap, nodding
encouragingly to her in time with the music. Her friends
joined in. Brita called out, "Dance, Grainne, dance!"

Mihall took up the chant. "Dance, Grainne, dance!"

Grainne didn't need much persuasion. She hopped
into the middle of the floor, and stepped daintily back
and forth in the traditional jig. The musicians, encouraged, played faster and faster, but she kept pace with
them, loving every moment of it. The tune rose to its
crescendo, and Grainne whirled to a stop. Her family and
friends applauded her, and she curtsied to them.

"Again!" her mother called. "Go on, girl! Give us another." Grainne did. And another, until she was breathless and hot.

"Enough!" she said, laughing at one more call for an encore. "I'll dance more in a moment. Give me a chance to rest!" They let her go, and she went out into the night to cool off.

She wished she could share her joy with Lorcan. On an impulse, she ran down the hill and out of the compound gate to the place where the fairy circle had been. Nothing and no one. She sighed.

"You'd have enjoyed tonight, my lord," she said out loud. "Music and dancing, and everyone having a good time! Farewell until I see you again." If ever, she thought, walking back up the hill with a heavier step. Ah, well. She went back into the great hall, into the midst of the party. It was hotter than before with the heat of roasting food, and torches, and many bodies.

"Leave the door open to cool us off," Brigid said, going past with a pitcher of ale in each hand. "You can see miles by that moon, can't you?"

Not quite all the way to the Summerland, Grainne thought with regret.

She was passing from hand to hand in a skipping dance, when she saw him standing outside the door, smiling at her. The moonlight crowned him with silver. The music came to an end at that moment, and she ran outside.

"You came!" she said.

"You called me," Lorcan said, with a laugh. "A party, you said?"

"It's the harvest," Grainne said. "We've brought in the crops, and we're celebrating."

"Seasons," Lorcan said, with great satisfaction. "Ah, I want to see it all. May I enter? Will I be welcome?"

"I . . . certainly," Grainne said. She wondered why she hesitated. Here was the proof that the story she had told in the springtime was no false tale. She took his long, cool hand in her short, damp fingers, and was instantly ashamed of her ordinariness, but he did not seem to mind. He followed her inside. The musicians, tuning up for another reel, stopped silent when they saw her guest.

First, Grainne led Lorcan to the side of the room, where Brigid was having an earnest conversation with her brother Donal's wife, Caitlin.

"Mother, look who followed me home!" Grainne said.

"Eh?" Brigid said, without turning around. "Oh, not another pet, child. You've too many already."

"It isn't a pet, Mam," Grainne said, patiently.

Brigid noticed then that the whole room had fallen silent, including her near-sister. She turned around and her eyes traveled up the length of Lorcan's long body to his tall ears and his green eyes. "Oh. I guess you can keep this one. If you wanted to."

Lorcan laughed his deep chuckle. "I bid you greetings, lady," he said, offering her a courtly bow.

As quickly as the silence had fallen, it broke into a flurry of whispers. Grainne remembered her duty, and led her guest to her uncle Donal and her father.

"May I make you known to our headman. Donal Mac Donal, this is Lorcan. Also, my father, Anluan."

The elf lord made a deep bow to both of them. Anluan shot a sharp glance at his wife.

"The tale she brought home in the summer," Anluan said, aggrieved.

Brigid only shrugged her shoulders. "Who knew?" she said.

The chieftain's eyes narrowed. Donal was a great and handsome man, but Grainne thought he looked like a sheep next to Lorcan. He was afraid, she realized.

"These are my people," he said.

"And well met to them all," Lorcan said, setting his hand lightly on his belt.

"They and this land are under my governance. Are you here to challenge me?"

"I do not seek to rule your people," Lorcan said with his breezy laugh. "I know naught of your government. As for the land, you do not own it, nor do I. It was here before your many-times grandfathers came, and it will be here when your five-hundred-generations' grandsons are dead and dust. But may I not pass through here? I leave very light footprints."

In spite of herself, Grainne let out a giggle, which she smothered at once under her uncle's baleful eye.

"One of the Fair Ones," said old Lugh, starting up from his warm corner near the hearth. He was their storyteller, their ollave, and had had the history of the ages passed down to him from his father. His gaze devoured the visitor, committing every line, every trait, every gem to memory. "Why do you come, my lord?"

"Why, to dance with this maiden," Lorcan said, holding out his hand to Grainne. Shyly, knowing all eyes were upon her, she approached and took it. Lorcan swept her into a lively dance. Fiochan's pipe and Brendan's bodhran burst into an appropriate song and caught up with the dancers' speedy tempo, but the less proficient musicians dropped out, unable to keep up with the beat. Lorcan spun her faster and faster, until the great room and all the faces were a blur. Man, woman, song, rhythm all became one. Grainne had never been so happy in her life.

When the music stopped and they whirled to a halt in the middle of the room, she felt as if her heart had stopped, too. She clung to the elf lord's hand, trying to regain the glorious sensation.

"Ah, you feel the pulse of life as I do," Lorcan said, gazing into her eyes as if no one else was within miles of them. "I think that is why I noticed you at all. Again?"

She hadn't the breath to say yes, so she just nodded. This time, Fiochan was ready with his best jig tune, and Brendan's drum rolled as fast as a racing pulse. And this time, other couples joined them on the floor.

Grainne whirled past them, feeling the joy rekindled in her heart. She noticed the boys looking at her now, in ways they never had before. She was a hard worker, and considered to be goodhearted, but not comely or desirable, as were the weaver's daughter and the headman's daughters. Her talent for dance was admired, but not considered particularly useful. As Brigid always said, it fed no one, housed no one, and cleaned nothing, but in every pair of eyes, she saw just the least bit of envy that it was her gift that had brought the elf lord there.

When the music stopped, Grainne's heart was pounding so hard that she thought her death by dancing was truly

upon her. Lorcan seemed puzzled by the symptoms of a
red face and shortness of breath, but did seem to understand that she was in distress. He drew her to a chair near
the door and helped her to sit down in it.

"You mortals are so fragile," he said. "Forgive my
ignorance. I do not journey to your world very often."

Donal approached them, and addressed Lorcan as noble
to noble. "We dine now. We invite you to partake of the
best we have to offer."

The elf lord beamed at him, showing sharp white teeth.
"You are most kind to share your bounty with a stranger,"
he said.

Lorcan was shown to the guesting seat beside the
headman at the center table. Brigid gathered up Grainne
to help serve, and bustled her to the hearth along with the
other women. They were all whispering about the
stranger. Some were openly terrified of Lorcan. Others
were fascinated.

"Blue skin! He looks like something dead five days!"
Caitlin's daughter Eilidh muttered into the platter of meat
she was carrying.

"I don't think so," said Nela, the weaver's lovely
daughter. "He's handsome as can be. And his hands!"

"Did you let him . . . you know?"

"No," Grainne said, almost wishing she had a more
exciting tale to tell. Brigid handed her a steaming bowl of
spiced cabbage. "We were only dancing."

The girls carried their burdens to the head table, where
Donal presented each dish in turn to his guest. Lorcan
looked at every platter with the appearance of enjoyment,
but took nothing. Donal wrinkled his forehead. Here was
the best food in the village, at the finest time of year, and
the elf lord refused it all. He glanced at Grainne for
enlightenment, but she shook her head, equally puzzled.

"Does none of this suit you, High One?" the chieftain
asked.

Lorcan smiled. "I need none of your food. The very
gifting feeds me. I am well satisfied with your hospitality.
Accept my thanks. In return for your kindness. I offer you
my protection."

"Bless this harvest, lord," one of the women pleaded. "The signs say that it will be a hard winter."

"If it is in my power," Lorcan said. He put out his hands to either side as if feeling the air. Then he closed his eyes. Light came out through his fingertips and filled the room like water running into a pond. Grainne sensed, not an intelligence, but a sentience in the world around them. It came in through the open door, down into the ceiling, and up through the floor into her very bones, flooding her mind. How could she not have been aware of it before then? Could this be what the priests meant when they talked about being one with God? The villagers muttered in fear and astonishment to themselves. The elf lord lowered his hands and the light died. Lorcan opened his eyes.

"None shall ever starve here," he said. "The land is blessed."

"Need we swear you fealty?" Donal asked, foreseeing a conflict between his duty to his king and the High Oncs, as well as between the old gods and the new.

"That which you have offered freely, you have already done," Lorcan said. Grainne tried to work this out, but failed to understand it. Lugh was nodding to himself.

"It's as the priests tell us about the thought and the deed," the old ollave said. "It would seem the tradition is older than theirs."

"Older than I am," Lorcan said cheerfully. "But what do we sit here for? The night is just begun."

He pulled from his belt a wee silver pipe only the length of a hand. He struck up a tune with a lively beat that had the menfolk all tapping the rhythm with one hand while they ate with the other.

The music was merry, but at the same time indescribably sad. It carried Grainne into lands in her imagination full of people as beautiful as Lorcan, with long hands and glowing eyes, but they had all lost something that couldn't be retrieved, nor even named. The ache rose up in her chest, and she felt terribly sorry. She didn't know there was so much pain in the lives of the High Ones. The legends always told how powerful and happy they were in their Summerland beyond the world. It never spoke of

despair. When it was over, she turned tear-filled eyes to
Lorcan, who bowed his head over his small pipe.

"I'd grant you a harper's boon for that, good Lorcan,"
Donal said, into the long silence that followed, "but we
have nothing of sufficient value we could offer for such
playing."

"Your generosity abounds," Lorcan said, with a smile.
"I will dance with this maid, and watch you all in your
joy, if I may. That is all I require."

The festivities carried on until the early hours of the
morning. Every woman in the village vied to catch the
visitor's eye, but he stayed at Grainne's side. Even Eilidh
stopped pretending he did not fascinate her, and tried to
persuade him to partner her. He just laughed, and told
another story or played another lovely, poignant tune.
When he did dance, it was with Grainne alone. She knew
her friends and cousins were jealous, but she didn't care.
Could she compel the actions of a High One?

He departed late that night just before moonset. He bent
in a sweeping bow that took in the whole hall, and strode
out. The villagers scattered to get out of his way, and
stood watching silently as he trod down the path toward
the woods. The moment he was out of sight, every tongue
in the hall began to clatter.

Lorcan was the talk of the village for months afterward.
They wondered whether to tell the traveling priest when
he visited, and whether to inform the kind that the Fair
Ones really existed. Many wondered if Lorcan had really
given the Sidhe's blessing to the crops, or if the light he
had produced was just a conjuror's trick. They questioned
Grainne exhaustively about her tryst with him, and openly
speculated that it had been less than innocent. Grainne
enjoyed the controversy a little—it was something to
gossip about, and did her no harm—but she wondered if
she would ever see him again.

In the months that passed between harvest and winter,
the village was concerned with matters very much of their
own world. They heard news of battles going on along the
border between their kingdom and the next, but no armies
ever invaded their village. Grainne attributed their immu-
nity to Lorcan's blessing, but more skeptical folk sug-

gested that their village was too small and too poor to be attractive to the invader.

It had become her custom to visit the oak grove in the full of the moon to see if Lorcan had come through the fairy ring from his realm to visit. She was disappointed. The season of Christmas had come and gone without him. Their feast of the new year seemed to her to lack the magical spark that had made the harvest feast so special.

Wrapped in all her skirts, shawls, wool cloak, and the wool blanket off her bed, Grainne went out into the cold night of January as soon as the moon rose. Her feet crunched through a light crust on the snow as she followed the familiar path into the woods. She heard rustling in the bare branches as night creatures fled at the coming of a human being. In the distance, she heard one lonely owl.

The last fairy ring of the season had been at the far edge of the glade. She wondered how the gateway between the worlds would open when snow covered the mushroom border, or if the elf folk even noticed the change in weather.

No, they didn't, Grainne thought, with fond exasperation. Lorcan was here, all right.

The elf lord wore the same light tunic and leggings as he waded barefoot in the snow like a child paddling in a pond. He danced a few steps up and down on the ice crust, and looked surprised when it broke beneath his weight. She let out a snort of laughter, and he looked out at her, his glowing eyes spotting her at once even in the shadows.

"Greetings to you, Grainne! Only a few days since I saw you last, and what changes!"

"Days, my lord, it's been months!" Grainne said, tramping through the snow toward him. "Many things have happened since we last met." She wondered what to tell him first, how the smith's son had started coming by their cottage to see her in the evenings, or how her cousins had asked her to teach them to dance, or the news of the far away war.

"Indeed!" Lorcan shouted, whirling around with his

arms out. "Look at how bare the branches are without their leaves."

Grainne sighed. His leggings were unbound at the ankle and pushed up to his knees, showing fine calf muscles under the blue skin. Not a goosebump to be seen. "What are you doing out here like that?" she demanded. "It's cold!"

"What glory you humans have in your world. This is cold?" Lorcan tossed back his head and laughed. "I have never experienced cold like this. Cold is . . . fun!" He twirled in a circle, taking in gusty breaths of air.

"Jesus Christ, you may have it!" Grainne exclaimed, holding her arms around her as tightly as she could. "It must be nice to be a High One, and immune to the weather."

Lorcan turned from his contemplation of the snow to see Grainne shivering, her lips and fingers turning blue like his.

"Your pardon for my discourtesy, maid," he said, and took her hand to draw her to him. Grainne opened her mouth to tell him she was too cold to dance, when the light began to grow around them, and she felt warm wind on her skin.

The familiar winter night exploded into honey-colored light. Grainne gawked and gathered her wraps closer, as if clutching her sanity to her. The sun was shining all around them. Under her feet was green grass studded with yellow and pink flowers like stars. As far as she could see were smooth green meadows and trees with branches like bronze and leaves like satin. The landscape was perfect. The only jarring thread in the tapestry was her.

If there was a part of Grainne that hadn't believed in Lorcan before, it was as thoroughly convinced as the rest of her now. The men and women she saw sitting under the tree at the bottom of the hill by the brook. They were High Ones, too. The Sidhe. The Good Folk. The immortal ones who wielded swords or bright magic and against whom no mortal could stand. She looked at Lorcan, seeing him anew, as her friends and neighbors had seen him that night. The strange beauty of his ears and eyes and skin were no longer just the peculiarities of a man she knew and liked, but of a demigod. How beautiful he was, and how beautiful his homeland. She felt low, ugly and unworthy.

"What is it you want, my lord?" she asked in a voice that trembled. "Why do you come to my . . . my world when you have all this?"

"You have seasons," Lorcan said, gently, moving closer to her. She edged away. "You and your world pass through fascinating changes in your cycle of life. Spring, summer, autumn, winter, and round again. I saw them in the faces of your village, and the branches of your trees. My lady wife (oh! Grainne thought, as a dream she didn't even realized she had was shattered) was born in her springtime, and grew to a state of summer ripeness, where she is and will forever remain. As will our world. As will I," he finished, sounding wistful.

"Oh, I would love to live a in world where it is always summer," Grainne said, as her joints eased in the smooth sunshine. She took the blanket and shawls off her shoulders, and lifted her face to the sky. The air was perfumed with the scent of apricots and roses. "It's terrible to be cold. This is so beautiful!"

"You may see it any time you like," Lorcan promised. "But after centuries, it palls. When I discovered the door to your world it was like being given treasure."

"It's a lot of dirt and little gold," Grainne said, skeptically.

"Don't underestimate your gifts. You are just entering your summer season, are you not?" Lorcan said, his eyes scanning her critically. "Yes, fair Grainne. You'll be a grown woman soon. It will be a joy to see all those aspects in you."

"You'll like it when I grow old?" Grainne asked, disbelievingly, thinking of herself as a bent, gray-haired crone.

"Oh, yes, and all the stages in between," he assured her. "It will be like watching a work of art in progress, or a story being written. All the stories here end in the middle."

"I will not mind growing old, then," she said, trying to see the nobility in toothlessness and creaky joints, "because I will live on in your memory. That will give me a sort of immortality."

"I will try to remember you, but the day will surely come when I can't," the Sidhe said, his little laugh touched with sorrow as his flute song had been. "Memories fade. It is the difference between our races. We are not burdened with the clutter of the past, so we can face our eternal futures without dread."

"Memories are all we have," she said sadly.

"Then enjoy them for me!" he said. "I will be happy because you remember me. It is one thing to be immortal, but joyless when no one cares. We leave no footprints upon life, as mortals do. What we do we've done a thousand, thousand times, until what might be an adventure to a mortal is as uninspiring to us as taking the next breath. You strive so. We do not. Every experience means so much to you in your limited lifetimes. I . . . I feel the lack of urgency. I fear fading away. That is what happens to the Sidhe when we weary of life."

If someone had told her six months ago that she would feel sorry for an elf lord, Grainne would have called the priest to exorcise a madman. She reached out and took Lorcan's arm.

"I will never forget you," she assured him earnestly. "I will tell my children and my grandchildren, and they will be proud that I knew you. Why, everyone in the village has done nothing since the harvest feast but talk about you."

"Oh, maid," Lorcan said, seizing her under the arms and sweeping her in a circle as effortlessly as he might a kitten. "You give me joy, indeed."

He let her drop to her feet, and began a lively dance about her. Grainne realized to her surprise that she could hear music playing. It came from everywhere, and had been going on around them while they stood talking. This, then, was what Lorcan listened to while he danced in the fairy ring. It was bliss made audible. She would have to tell her mother and her cousins later.

"Are you warm enough now?" he asked, holding out his hand to her.

"Oh, yes," she said, dropping the blanket on the ground. "Warm and happy."

It took an act of will to resume her heavy clothes and follow Lorcan through the gate of light back into the winter cold. The moon had traveled a third of the way across the sky. As soon as she poked her nose outside the fairy ring, a sharp wind nipped at it.

"Come again soon," she begged, turning back for just a moment to the warmth of the Summerland. Lorcan laughed.

"Soon," he promised. "Look for me. I'll count on you to remind me."

"I will," Grainne said. She pulled the cloak closer around her face and set out across the open glade toward the path.

The cold stillness was a shock after the honey-colored bustle of the Summerland. If it hadn't been for the token of a shiny green leaf that Lorcan had put in her hand at the last moment she might well think she had dreamed the whole thing. She clutched the leaf in her palm, not wanting to crush it, but to keep it warm until she could get it home to show Mam.

In the distance, she heard a wolf howl. Best hurry home, she thought, forcing as much speed as she could from her tired feet. She didn't want to fall victim to a hungry beast, not after dancing all night with an elven prince. It would be an ignominious end, unworthy of the story Lorcan wanted her to write for him.

Another sound, of feet crunching through the snow, came from not far behind her.

"Lorcan?" she called, turning toward the sound. Instead of the resonant voice of the Sidhe, a harsh whisper rasped in her ear, and a rough hand clamped over her mouth.

"Be quiet, you!" The man's other hand felt at her waist. It found her small dagger and tossed it aside, and continued to grope, obviously seeking a purse. An outlaw! Da had said things had gone missing from the storerooms. Uncle Donal had even complained of chickens that vanished in the night from their roosts without a single fox track in sight. He must have followed her from the

compound and into the woods. The hand felt at her neck,
and yanked the small crucifix loose.

"All pink and pretty from your lover, eh?" the man
rasped, sticking a dirty, unshaven face in hers. "Give us a
kiss, girl."

"Let me alone! I have no money," Grainne said, struggling to get loose. "Please. I won't tell anyone I've seen
you!"

"You won't tell anyone," the man said, running a wet
tongue around his lips. "No, you won't."

He was thin, but strong. Grainne tried to push out of his
arms, and he just laughed, breathing the smell of rancid
onions in her face. She kicked out, scoring a hit on his
leg. He howled, and threw her down into the snow, scattering her woollens all about her.

"You've got to learn manners, girl," he snarled, dropping down on her with one hand pinioning her hands
above her head. Grainne was terrified. He couldn't leave
her alive. She'd tell Da and the men of the village that he
had been living in the compound, living off stolen food.
He probably should have starved to death, but he'd bene-
fited from the blessing Lorcan had laid upon the village.
Grainne almost laughed, but the situation was deadly
serious. This lawless man would rape and kill her, then
hide the body where beasts would find it and tear it apart,
so no one would know what had become of her until
spring—if ever. She turned her head to avoid his ugly
mouth trying to cover hers, and screamed. Then, the cold
lips covered hers, sucking the life out of her. She felt the
other hand tearing at her clothes, baring her to the biting
wind. She writhed and kicked, trying to get loose. He hit
her in the stomach, knocking all the fight out of her for a
moment, and pushed up her skirts.

A wave of unexpected warmth passed over her, scented
with roses, and suddenly, Lorcan was there, silhouetted in
the moon over the outlaw's shoulder. He was still barefoot and in his light clothes, his long hair wind-tossed as
if they had just finished one of their lively dances. But his
face was wild and fierce, showing green gums and sharp
white teeth, like a dragon.

He reached down and picked up the outlaw by the

scruff of his neck and held him in the air like a handful
of rags.

"This maiden is under my protection," he boomed, his
voice resonating through the empty forest like a hunting
horn. Grainne cowered on the ground, curling her legs up
into her skirts. She had never seen Lorcan angry. He had
always seemed so gentle. This was the warrior aspect of
the Sidhe. Lugh had told tales at the fireside, but no mere
words could capture the true sight. "No one shall harm
her, not while I live. No one!"

With every word, he shook the thief. The man looked
first defiant, then terrified. Then, Grainne heard a loud
pop. The outlaw's face blanked with sudden surprise, and
his body fell limp. Lorcan regarded him, puzzled, and
threw the corpse into the bushes. He reached down to help
Grainne to her feet.

"Are you all right, maid?" he asked.

Grainne started to speak, but she was so tired she
started to shake. She leaned against Lorcan's lavender-
scented shirt and cried. He put a gentle arm around her
shoulder.

"Will you tell them of this, too?" Lorcan asked, after a
moment. "Your children and grandchildren, I mean?"

"Oh, yes," Grainne said, with a sob that was halfway
between tears and laughter. How Lorcan could think of
absurd things at a moment like this! "And they'll know
you to be a great hero." She thought for a moment of mortality, and being sad that when she grew old she might be
too weak and bent to whirl about with him, and that he
would abandon her for another lithe young woman, perhaps even one of those children or grandchildren.

As before, Lorcan read her thoughts. He offered her a
smile as he helped her gather up her clothes and the green
leaf, crumpled but still shining.

"Forget the future! Let us have one more dance
together, and I'll escort you safely home. We have the
circle of life to discover, you and I."

SUN AND HAWK

by Jane M. Lindskold

Jane M. Lindskold resides in Albuquerque, New Mexico with six cats, all named after figures in British mythology. To support them (and her four guinea pigs and four fish) she writes full time. Her published works include the novels *Brother to Dragons, Companion to Owls, Marks of Our Brothers, The Pipes of Orpheus,* and *Smoke and Mirrors.* Her short fiction has appeared in a variety of collections, including *Heaven Sent, Return to Avalon,* and *Wheel of Fortune.* Currently, she is under contract to complete the two novels left unfinished by Roger Zelazny, as well as several novels of her own.

Sunlight dappled the forest path along which Solis Sunsong rode his steed. For anyone else, the mare might have rolled her eye or shown her more fiery nature, but for Solis she was tranquillity itself, contenting herself with an occasional flirting side-step around a blowing leaf.

The elf lord, his pale hair bound beneath a silver fillet, his slim form clad in a tunic of aquamarine silk, let his thoughts wander to a small problem in spell design that he had been working with this past decade. Yet, his abstraction was not so complete that he failed to notice the figure who stepped forth from the heart of a grove of hawthorn and holly. It was an elf woman, regally garbed in leaf-green and crystal, a high-peaked crown of impossibly delicate gold filigree set on her fair hair.

"Your Majesty," he said, smoothly dismounting and bowing. "Your servant."

"Do you mean those words, Solis?" The Elf Queen's voice was musical, but its sweetness could not disguise an underlying strength.

"How not?"

"Your duty to me requires you to perform one task of my choosing."

"So I recall."

He schooled his features, anticipating, remembering. At majority, each member of the Elflands swore personal loyalty to their Queen and sealed that loyalty with a promise to grant her a single boon, no matter how impossible.

"I have come to name your task, Solis Sunsong."

Despite his outward composure, Solis' heart raced. Others had been sent to defeat armies of orcs and dragons, to seek the elements to create magical talismans, to succor the weak. Still others had vanished for years at a time to realms of which they never spoke.

"I await your word, my queen."

"You speak bravely, Solis. The forms are right, but tell me—Have you ever considered how much we elven folk have been given?"

Solis cocked a pale brow in puzzlement as the Queen continued, "We are given from birth beauty, immortality, harmony with all that is of nature, innate magic—this last quite strong in you."

Solis bowed again. All she said was true.

"From those who have been given much, much will be expected. I am sending you to a land whose people are in dire need of the harmony with nature that is an elf's birthright. The task you have been given is great, so you will have a companion. She is called Kestrel Stormforce. . . ."

Kestrel stood looking out the plate-glass window at the insect swarm that was afternoon rush hour in Washington, D.C. In the year or so since she and Solis Sunsong had come to the place that its inhabitants blithely called "the" Earth, she had yet to learn any ease with the vast metropoli that infested the globe. She was more comfortable in the wild places—although that comfort was a relative thing compared to the harmony she had known in the Elflands.

Still, she was a warrior. Under others' command, she

had ventured into foul goblin warrens and kingdoms tainted by evil magic. If her queen wished her to deal with "the" Earth's urban jungles, she would. Even so, she was glad that her current campaign would take her far from Washington, D.C., and its ilk. She wondered how Solis managed to venture here day after day.

Then, through the closed door behind her, she heard the outer door of the office open and conversation.

"I think that was a successful meeting," a male voice said.

"Yes," another voice, Solis', replied. "I believe we can count on the support of the committee for this latest provision in the water control bill."

"A relief," the first voice said. "I was worried we wouldn't be able to swing the vote of the agricultural representatives. With the bad effects that the weather has had on farm production this year, I didn't think they'd agree to anything that would raise costs for the farmers."

"A short-term raise," Solis reminded him. "The long-term ramifications promise a drop in costs due to protection of the watershed."

"You don't need to sell me on it, Mr. Sunsong," the man chuckled. "I'm on your side. Can I buy you a drink?"

"Forgive me this time," Solis said. "I have a long commute home."

"That's right. You're out on the Bay, aren't you. Must be nice and tranquil. Well, have a good drive, then."

"Thanks."

The outer door closed. Kestrel heard Solis shuffling through some papers—presumably the heap of mail she had seen resting on the table in the foyer. Then the door opened.

"Kestrel!"

Solis' tone was surprised and not completely pleased.

"Solis Sunsong."

She bowed in the manner of their homeland. After a slight pause, he returned the gesture.

An observer, seeing them together, might have thought them siblings. Both were beautiful in a fine-boned fashion, above average in height and slimly built with high cheekbones and large eyes. Both wore their hair longer than was usual on the East Coast of the United

States of America and both had something indefinable in their body language that might have made the observer suspect foreign birth.

There the similarities ended. Solis Sunsong's hair was a blond so pale that it was almost white, though his brows and lashes were dark enough to give definition to his face. His eyes were a startling green even against skin tanned golden-brown.

Kestrel's hair was a dark-brown, bound into a ponytail that fell half-way down her spine. Her eyes were jetty. Although she was tanned as dark or darker than Solis, her skin seemed pale against the darkness of her hair and eyes.

Their clothing contrasted as sharply as their coloring. Solis wore a finely tailored suit of undyed, raw silk. His shoes were soft leather; his accoutrements understated and expensive.

Kestrel wore khaki trousers, a green silk blouse, and ankle-high hiking boots. She wore a watch—a concession to the human obsession with time—but no jewelry. Again as a concession to the humans, she had left her sword and her bow locked in the trunk of her car. (This another concession to humans—she would have preferred a horse, but at least both her car and Solis' were powered by means of enchantment, not by petrochemicals).

"May I offer you a drink?" Solis asked.

"I thought you were in a hurry to start for home," Kestrel said, almost but not quite mockingly.

"I was, I am, but you are here now and I suspect you have reason to be. Please accept my hospitality."

Kestrel did so, and when they were settled with iced drinks and some fresh fruit Solis had taken from a small refrigerator, Kestrel came to the point.

"I am going to South America. I have come to ask if you wish to join me."

"Is this another of your eco-terrorist ventures, Kestrel Stormforce?"

"Eco-terrorism is an ugly word. I prefer to think of it as an anticipatory move. Rather than waiting for the destruction to occur, my colleagues and I are seeking to prevent it."

"And creating ill-will in the world community as you do so."

"Shall I take this as meaning that you do not wish to come with us?"

"I do not."

Kestrel did not argue. She glanced at her watch.

"You were later than I had planned. I need to drive to Dulles to catch my plane. Of course, if you were coming with us, we could use your magic to travel in a less environmentally destructive fashion."

"Kestrel . . ."

"And I would not need to entrust the tools of my profession to the whims of the baggage handlers. Even on international flights, swords and bows are too large to qualify as carry-on luggage."

"Kestrel . . ."

"Farewell, Solis Sunsong. You need not see me out."

She left, ignoring his words. They could have the old argument another time. They had certainly had it frequently enough since their arrival on "the" Earth.

Paddle dripping a thin, silvery stream of water, Solis Sunsong paused to enjoy the gathering evening. As the canoe continued to drift from the combined influence of his last stroke and the faint pull of the current, he was left free to contemplate his surroundings.

The creek on which his lightweight craft floated was narrow and twisting, bordered with reeds and cattails that flourished in the mud along the shore. A Great Blue Heron cried from somewhere within the marsh; hidden spring peepers made the air vibrate with their chorus. Nearby a snail, its shell tighter twisted and more conical than those that he removed from his garden, made slow progress up the stem of a reed. The surface of the water rippled as a small blue crab skated at the surface of the water, claws folded complacently, back-fins moving so smoothly that it appeared to fly.

In imitation, Solis returned his paddle to the water and with a few deft strokes he was borne within sight of his home. The wooden house rested on relatively high ground beneath the shelter of a pair of towering oaks. It was a simple structure, two stories high, vaguely Victorian in its gingerbread fretwork, dormer windows, and wraparound porch, painted white with the shutters in green. A lawn interspersed with scattered patches of buttercups and dandelions came down to the creek.

A pear tree, the remnant of what had once been a much larger orchard before the creek eroded the ground and contaminated the soil, hung bent and twisted over the water. Its fruit was hard and woody, but Solis had made no attempt to change it. The tree had survived despite the creek's brackish water and nature's annual series of thunderstorms, hurricanes, and ice. He admired it for what it was and that was enough.

Solis had brought the canoe up to the pier and, having disembarked, was carrying it into its cradle when he heard a car crunch up his gravel driveway and stop. A door opened then slammed, momentarily silencing the peepers.

Chocolate, his Chesapeake Bay retriever, barked once in warning, once in greeting, and then fell silent—enough for Solis to know who his caller was.

Sighing, he ran his hands through his hair and bid peace farewell.

In the driveway a sleek forest-green Corvette was parked next to his own pale-blue Lexus. The Corvette's owner was crouched down rubbing Chocolate's ears. Hearing Solis' footsteps, she rose and bowed. Solis smiled greeting.

"Kestrel, you are returned."

"That I am." Kestrel hesitated, then smiled as if the expression was harder than usual for her. "I hope I have not interrupted any important plans for this evening."

"No. I was just returning from canoeing. It's a lovely evening. Come, take a chair on the porch and have a glass of iced tea."

"Actually, if your canoe is still available, I would prefer that we paddle about. I am weary of chairs."

About her the aura of tension and storm was so powerful that Solis inadvertently glanced out to the horizon. All was as calm as it had been before; the westering sun had dropped below the tree-line, but she made herself known in the reds and purples with which she tinted the sky.

They walked down to his pier and together removed the still dripping canoe from its cradle. Even when both elves and Chocolate were aboard, the well-balanced craft drew somewhat less than three inches of water.

Solis, in the stern, set pace and direction. Kestrel, in the bow, barely touched her paddle to the water, relaxing in the peace of creek. They went on this way for some time, listening to loon call, cricket song, watching the swoop of barn swallows after midges and mosquitoes.

Kestrel spoke at last. "I'm just back from South America."

Solis made a polite noise, vaguely indicative of inquiry.

"The rain forests. The deforestation is terrible. We did what we could—made example of a few logging camps, destroyed a lot of machinery. Nothing we can do can bring back what has been destroyed any faster."

She paused. Solis sat silently. Sensing her master's unease, Chocolate thumped her tail against the canoe bottom in an effort to soothe him.

"I said," Kestrel repeated. " 'Nothing *we* can do can bring back what has been destroyed any faster.' "

"I heard you."

For the first time, there was an edge to Solis' voice. Kestrel raised her paddle from the water and turned her head to look at him.

"Solis, how can you be so passive? So uncaring? You love the natural world." Kestrel gestured broadly at the creek, at the broader blue of the Chesapeake Bay just visible over the marsh, Kent Island thin and green at the water's farther side. "You love all of this as much as I do, but you do nothing to protect it."

Solis frowned. "I protest! I do a great deal! Day after day I drive into Washington, D.C., to meet with authorities. I lobby for protective legislation, for parks, for preserves, for clean air and water acts. I work with . . ."

"Lobbyist!" Kestrel's tone made the single word a curse. "You are a mage—you have the power to change much without resorting to such ridiculous channels. Why do you persist in this foolishness?"

Solis clenched one fist out of Kestrel's line of sight. Old as the argument was between them, it still had the power to make him furious.

"We have been in this world for a fraction of time, Kestrel. What has it been, two years? When we arrived, the horrors we confronted terrified me—forests clear cut for fields and pastures without regard for their role in maintaining and renewing soil; industries pouring their waste into waters, strip mines, the cities. . . ."

He shuddered. "And even those humans who claimed to love the natural world and its creatures often expressed that love through wanton destruction. Sometimes I think if I am offered another opportunity to support the Audubon Society I will be ill—the sheer numbers of birds that man decimated in order that he might dissect and draw them. And don't speak to me of Lewis and Clark!"

"I'm not," Kestrel said mildly.

"I realized then that if I employed my magic to mend the results of humanity's destructive actions, that all I would be doing is slightly slowing their progress down the road of destruction. They must see what their actions do. They must change. If they do not, nothing I do matters in the long run."

"Tell that to the orchids shriveling to extinction!" Kestrel responded fiercely. "Tell that to the birds whose habitats are ruined. Tell that to the snakes, the lizards, the insects, all the little mammals. Tell that to all the creatures too small, too unimportant, too 'unsexy' to be preserved in zoos and gardens. You could make a difference for *them*."

After her first sentence, Kestrel did not raise her voice, but her furious, level delivery possessed more violence than mere shouting could hold. Dexterously, she turned in the canoe to face him.

"Solis Sunsong," she pleaded, "you have magic to heal and preserve! How can you persistently refuse to use it?"

Solis refused to meet Kestrel's fierce, dark eyes. Instead he looked out over the marsh. Humans were only just coming to realize what a complexity of influences shaped it, what it harbored, what it gestated. An elf would *know*. A human must learn.

"I do what I do because I am Solis Sunsong, an elf. This is a world in the custody of humans. Humans must learn to desire the solutions to the problems they have created."

Kestrel's hand shook and the canoe shook in sympathy, but she kept her temper in check, her tone a parody of Solis' studied calm.

"I, Kestrel Stormforce, I, too, am an elf. I may hide my ears with glamour, hide my centuries of experience with lies, but I try to change things. Unlike you I do not have the power to do what I would. Warrior born, warrior trained, my elfin steel is little enough weapon against enemies who are corporate entities rather than orcs and goblins, but I do what I can. . . ."

Solis interrupted, an almost unspeakable rudeness for him. "Why are you troubling me again, Kestrel? We have had this talk before."

Kestrel tossed her dark hair from where it threatened to tumble into her eyes.

"Perhaps it is my innate 'humanity' as my mortal colleagues would call it. Time and again, I come to you, hoping to find that exposure to the horrors that cripple this globe has at last made you willing to alter your sluggish tactics."

" 'Humanity,' " Solis laughed, a hard sounding thing that caused Chocolate to whimper. " 'Humanitarianism.' 'Humane.' Don't you find the words ironic, bitter? Whenever humans make a sane and reasonable decision, a noble, altruistic action, then they say they are behaving in a 'humane' fashion. What are they the rest of the time? Animals? No animal would behave as the human race does."

Kestrel retorted, "They aspire to the best they can be—what they think of as 'human.' "

Solis nodded, pleased at the opening her words had given him.

"I try to believe in this 'humanity,' this striving for the best. This is why I work within their own political channels and organizations. The United States currently has more influence than any other single nation. If I can get this one nation to alter its behavior, then it can become a beacon for all the world! Even now the Virginia Coast

Reserve in this very bay has been recognized by the United Nations as an internationally important biosphere—an example for the future."

Kestrel shook her head angrily. "The United States is a wealthy nation. Its need for industrialization and its abuses is waning. Why should the people damage their own land when the poorer nations are clamoring for the opportunity to do so?"

Sighing, Solis continued paddling. "Kestrel, do you believe that destroying whaling boats and lumber yards will change this?"

"My actions are more visible—a true beacon. And whether or not anyone notices them, they are more immediately effective than any number of fat, complacent yuppies eating 'Rain Forest Crunch' ice cream and sanctimoniously recycling the containers!"

Solis squared his shoulders. "I will not clean up the humans' messes for them. They must become committed to do so themselves."

"And I cannot stand by and leave the innocent creatures of the natural world to become victims of human greed and your inaction!"

Jetty eyes met green and neither looked away. The uncomfortable silence was broken by Kestrel's whisper, "And we will never see the Elflands again. We have been exiled by your stubbornness."

Solis shook his head. "I cannot believe that. Either you or I am right. Either way, we have the solution in hand."

"The Queen sent a mage and a warrior," Kestrel said her voice husky. "Her warrior seeks battle, but the mage has transformed himself into a mere courtier."

"Kestrel . . ."

"I can do no more." The Stormforce's expression became enigmatic. "Here. Therefore, I propose a compromise. Come and see this world as I see it. You were right in noting that it has been two years since our arrival, nearly that long since we each chose our paths. Perhaps it is time we compared experience."

"And you will come and see the world as I see it?" Solis said guardedly.

"Yes. I will attend committee sessions, listen to lectures, bore myself with inaction. Whatever you ask."

Solis grinned. "I would not ask that of you. However, two days hence I am meeting with some people from the Nature Conservancy. These are the people who set up the Reserve I mentioned earlier. They are militant, in their own way, but they believe in using the tools of law and government to obtain their goals."

"That could be interesting," Kestrel agreed. "I am familiar with some of the Conservancy's work. And you will accompany me on one of my missions?"

"I will, but I will not take part in destruction, nor will I use my magic to do so."

"I would not ask that of you," Kestrel said, with a shadow of his smile. "We do not seek to destroy, only to draw attention to abuses."

"Then simply give me warning, and I will be with you.

Long after Kestrel's Corvette had vanished into the darkness and the spring peepers had fallen to sleep, Solis Sunsong sat on the porch, wishing that the stars would spell out a simple solution. Even as he shaped that idle thought, the susurrus of the marshland's breathing reminded him that solutions are rarely simple.

Solis and Kestrel sat at a round patio table at Phillips Crab House in Baltimore's Inner Harbor watching the ebb and flow of the human tide. Tourists gazed out over the wind-licked waters or hurried in and out of the Harbor Place mall.

The meeting had largely revolved around how to get certain commercial landowners in the vicinity of the Patapsco, Baltimore's harbor, to donate land for additional parks. It had been more an enumeration of problems, rather than a finding of solutions and Kestrel was clearly troubled.

"Come stroll along the water's edge with me," Solis suggested.

"I don't really care for crowds," Kestrel said.

"But you promised to come look from my view."

She wiped her hands on her napkin, took a final sip from her glass of ice water.

"That I did."

Ignoring the sign requesting that customers use the door, they slipped out between two large pots of petunias and walked down the shallow steps to the walkway near the water.

"Within living memory—living *human* memory," Solis said, aware that he was lecturing, "this area was so filthy, forsaken, and dangerous that only those who must come here to work did so . . . and those reluctantly."

"It certainly has changed," Kestrel said, "but is this any better? The walkways are more colorful than the usual concrete, but they still allow water to flow unchecked and unfiltered into the Bay. The automobiles pollute the air. The humans hide in air-conditioning, unwilling to face the humidity."

Solis decided to try another tactic. "You never asked me why I chose to live on the shores of the Chesapeake Bay."

"I assumed that it was a convenient commute to your job." Kestrel could not keep a certain negative inflection from the final word.

"There are other places as convenient," Solis retorted. "And many more wooded and more like the lands we left behind.

"No, I chose to live by the Bay because nowhere else in this region—perhaps in all the world—is there such a potent symbol of how humanity has intertwined itself with the natural world. The Bay and all its tributaries have shaped society in this area and, perhaps because its proximity to a place of power, when the problems of human habitation have become evident, steps have been taken to correct them."

"You consider shopping malls correction?"

"No, not in themselves, but in their expression of the human desire to be near nature—"

"Nature under plastic!" Kestrel spat.

"Somewhat, but still, a desire to feel the wind, watch the water. Kestrel, a generation or so ago humans were proudly filling in—'reclaiming'—wetlands. Today, under the highways, acres of new marsh are being planted. They are learning!"

"Slowly!" Kestrel almost shouted, lowered her voice when a few curious tourists turned to stare. "Solis, these people are not elves. They cannot take millennia to learn. I listened at the meeting today. Despite the best efforts of the last twenty years, the underwater grasses essential to the Chesapeake's ecology are still dying. Several species of fish are almost gone—including herring that were once so plentiful that their spawning runs took them into upper Pennsylvania and inner Maryland."

"But they have set the fishing restrictions," Solis realized that he was no longer proudly lecturing; he was pleading. "They are limiting new construction on the shoreline. They are recognizing the importance of a healthy watershed."

Kestrel took him gently by the shoulders. "And the local population continues to grow, attracted by easy access to this 'natural' beauty. Most of them don't see what they have already lost."

"I . . ."

"Solis, stop thinking like an elf. As you are fond of reminding me, we are dealing with humans."

The phone rang at eight in the evening. Solis Sunsong, one small spell keeping the mosquitos away, another providing just enough light to read by, sat on his back porch taking notes on an EPA report on aquifer contamination in the vicinity of landfills.

"Hello?"

"Solis, Kestrel. Something has happened. It's not precisely what I had intended, but I want to call in my turn to show you my view of this world."

"Can't it wait until another day? I must rise at six to make an early committee meeting."

"Sorry, lord. It cannot wait. That's often the way of such things"

"Very well, lady. I will heed your call."

On the morning news the media would be calling it a small spill and a fortunate one. The tanker's hold had been compartmentalized and only a fraction of its contents had escaped before repair crews had sealed the breach. The tanker had been outside of the usual navigation channels (thus the collision) and the tide had been going out so that the oil had not been carried into a coastal town with a burgeoning tourist trade but rather into nearby marshland.

A fortunate spill.

Solis had arrived to find the rescue and clean-up operation already underway. Cars were parked in every available space along the road. Volunteers worked alongside officials from the Coast Guard and various other specialists. Some set up holding tanks, others operated veterinary first-aid stations, most simply slogged back and forth between marshland and relatively solid shore carrying the victims of the disaster.

In the darkness, the effect was weirdly surreal. Spotlights and flashlights brought some light to the muggy night. Solis Sunsong stood ankle-deep in oily water, sinking into the mud. Although some miles south, this marshland could be the one that surrounded his home. The land had not yet been "reclaimed" for use. It remained a haven for water birds, blue crabs, toadfish, minnows, fingerlings, myriad shellfish, and all the creatures adapted to the Chesapeake's peculiar ecosystem—shallow water not fresh, but not as salt as the Atlantic.

Here might have begun the tiny clams he sometimes found on the beaches (if the miniature sandy crescents could be dignified with such a name)—their pastel pink, blue, or white shells rarely larger than a nickel and as thin as fine porcelain. Or the razor clams, long and narrow, edges bordered in dark brown. Or the oysters, nacreous interiors less valuable to some than those of their ocean cousins, the pearls irregular and mysterious in shape. Or the mussels, fanlike shells lined with an iridescent sheen of color.

He lifted a sea gull in his hands and tried to wipe the oil away from its white feathers. He knew with despair that the bleary-eyed bird was doomed. Too much of the thick oil had penetrated its skin. Who knew how much it had swallowed?

A few paces beyond him a tall, burly man with a neat, dark beard waded through the mess. A cane was hooked over his arm, not forgotten as much as discarded in the greater need to haul creatures from their deaths. He carried a pair of ducklings like gems in his broad hands, tears falling unnoticed as he sloshed to one of the rescue pens.

Professionals shouted orders, directing the placement of containment areas, skimmers, booms, pumps, and various chemicals that (hopefully) would do less damage than the oil they sought to neutralize.

Despite the best efforts of the volunteers, the dead and the dying lay contorted on the shore or twisted in the contaminated water. Yet stumbling through the darkness, old and young, stony-faced or openly weeping, the volunteers continued their work, hoping against all reason to make some small difference.

"It is all undone so quickly, isn't it? And by accident, not by malice."

Solis looked away from the destruction to find Kestrel approaching. The elf warrior was covered in mud and oil, her coverall matched those worn by the professionals. Unlike Solis, she seemed to know what she must do and Solis was sharply reminded that Kestrel had been at the site of more than one such disaster.

"Have you come to gloat," Solis began, "that at last disaster has come to my doorstep?" A more horrible alternative occurred to him. "Or did you *cause* this to change my mind . . . ?"

Kestrel stared at him, amazed almost as much as angered. Her voice grated as she replied:

"Were we in our homeland I would demand that your heart be placed at the feet of our queen to wipe those words from memory."

Solis saw the exhaustion and anguish that scored Kestrel's face beneath the veneer of oil and anger. He swallowed hard.

"If you so demanded, I would tear out my heart myself," he said, knowing that the words were in the way of a promise to do so. "I apologize, Kestrel Stormforce."

Some of the anger left Kestrel's face.

"I accept." Without another word, she took the sea gull from Solis' hands. "I'll take this to where the humans will do what they can for it."

"I . . ."

Kestrel interrupted. "Save your explanations for them."
A jerk of her shoulder indicated the dead and dying
creatures around them.

"Elf Mage." Kestrel turned away.

*"Have you ever considered how much we elven folk
have been given? We are given from birth beauty, immortality, harmony with all that is of nature, innate magic—
this last quite strong in you."*

The Elf Queen's words echoed from memory. Sloshing
through the water, lifting a ball of matted fur in his hands,
finding the muskrat quite dead, Solis remembered. He
was certain his solution was right.

His magic could not be the answer. Humans must
change their ways or all the healing his natural magic
could do was as vain a gesture as Kestrel's eco-
terrorism—and in the long term far more dangerous since
it would cultivate the belief that there were guardians who
would rescue humanity from the consequences of their
actions.

Yet.

Magic could *not* be the answer. As the ending of the
second millennium of the Christian era approached, the
superstitious belief that merely the passage of time would
be enough to heal the world had grown—that angels or
aliens or God Almighty would come and make the world
anew. Solis could not take actions that would cultivate
such futility.

Yet.

Almost mechanically, Solis continued with the rescue
effort. He helped because he must, because as an elf
he could feel the weeping of the tortured land. Yet why
did the humans help? Weren't they the destroyers?
Didn't their very dependence on such comparatively
cheap solutions as petroleum products rather than renew-
able resources make them the problem?

Conservationists, whether politically sophisticated or
violently radical, were in the minority. Most humans
cared more for the newest car, the most convenient meal,
the latest luxury.

Yet.

Hadn't the humans torn down forests to raise cities and then abandoned the cities as they grew old and sick to spread their asphalt tentacles farther and farther? They were the problem. They must be taught to be the solution.

Yet.

Solis passed a girl in her teens carrying a faintly stirring rat over to one of the cleaning areas. At another time, the same girl might have set poison to kill the rat. Now she tried to save him.

A woman, her hands gnarled, her hair dyed the same shade of blue as the paint on his car, laughed in triumph as a rockfish began to circulate fresh water through his gills. At another time, she would cheerfully gut it for dinner. Now, her time-worn face rejoiced at its recovery.

Kestrel paused at his side. Solis turned.

"I don't understand them."

"Neither do they."

"They are so contradictory."

"I know. So do many of them."

"What are we supposed to do?"

"The queen sent a warrior and a mage. I have been fighting. What can your magic do?"

"I . . ." Solis began the old protest, bit it back. "I . . . must be able to do something."

"What?"

"I see now that you are right, I have been trying to make them into elves . . . yet they are not. They are humans."

"That they are."

An idea came to Solis, faint and bright as the false dawn on the eastern horizon.

"What I must do is reinforce their humanity. The queen was right, elves are given so much that humans lack. We are born with a sense of our place as part of the natural world, not as its lord. We are also given such long lives that our goals may be more gradually and carefully cultivated."

Kestrel nodded. "Time. How often have I heard it said: They do not have enough time. Yet, bitterly, the same speed at which the humans live hastens the rate at which they plunder natural resources."

"But," Solis said, "they are prolific, versatile, and intelligent. They can learn and can teach their children. Already some seek to heal what their forebearers have done and to avoid creating new mistakes on the same lines. I am right in recognizing that there have been many changes. . . ."

The two elves had not paused in their rescue efforts while they spoke. Now Solis moved to join those who sought to treat the dying animals. Kestrel came with him.

"What will you do?"

"I cannot save all the creatures, nor would it be right to do so even if I could. But small magics can produce results so that the human's efforts do not seem futile."

"A reward?" Kestrel sounded dubious. "A sop."

"Humans must learn to cultivate their world," Solis insisted, "to balance their desires against the needs of the larger ecosystem. But while they do this, I will use my magic to cultivate the humans so that they may not lose hope in the task at hand."

Solis took a dying heron from the bearded man with the cane. Filthy, his tears dried in tracks on his round cheeks, the man was still working, though he now leaned heavily on his support.

"I'm afraid that it's too far gone," the man said, weariness and sorrow choking his voice.

"Maybe not as far gone as it seems," Solis said softly.

He took a cotton swab and touched it to the heron's eyes. Masking his spell-weaving with the motion of wiping away the oil and grit, he encouraged the oil to rise from the water, to separate itself from the delicate membranes. Next he forced apart the beak and swabbed out the mouth. The heron began to breath more easily.

"You've got the touch, sir," the bearded man said excitedly. "I think it's going to make it after all."

"I think you're right," Solis shared the smile. "Let me see what else I can do."

"That's why I'm here. To see what I can do," the bearded man said. "Can't change much, maybe can change a little. That's the way it is."

"Trying to do a little despite the impossibility of the

task," Solis agreed. "It's the humane thing to do—the human thing."

Under the aegis of Kestrel's approval, Solis walked back into the marshland.

EINE KLEINE ELFMUSIK
by Karen Haber

Karen Haber recently completed a science-fiction trilogy
for DAW books, ending with *Sister Blood*, which was
released in late 1996. Her short fiction appears in *Warriors
of Blood and Dream*, *Animal Brigade 3000*, and
Wheel of Fortune. She lives with her husband, author
Robert Silverberg, in California.

Suzanne Samuelson checked her list of clients, rang the
door bell of Apartment 6-G, and waited in the warm,
airless hallway. Sounds of a baby wailing, of children
fighting, sifted up through the dust. Rancid cooking odors
reached her nose from somewhere down the tired corridor.
She was accustomed to these sounds, these smells,
by now. A social worker, especially a family maintenance
worker, couldn't afford to be too particular about her
working environment.

Time passed. She rang again.

Waited.

Was that the sound of somebody inside, clearing her
throat? She imagined that she could hear the slow breathing
of somebody hiding, waiting for her to go away.

I know you're in there.

She leaned full-bore upon the buzzer. Didn't these
people understand that she was only here to help?

She was twenty-five but looked older, with a frazzled
air that was a hallmark of her profession. Her short
curling brown hair was never quite under control, her
gray eyes never looked as though she had gotten enough
sleep. Most days she wore a lumpy tweed blazer, white
shirt, dark pants, and sensible shoes. What was remarkable
about Suzanne Samuelson was her sensitivity: she

was filled with relentless compassion. Her supervisor, Dale, had twitted her about it. "Suzanne," he said, "you take a micro approach to social work. You want to save the world, case by case. I give you two more years before you burn out."

Privately, Suzanne thought that her approach was better than that of Dale or any other "macro" approach social workers who had grandiose theoretical ambitions of saving humankind but really had no use for people. They all seemed to disdain the nitty-gritty of casework. But she firmly believed that each and every person was precious and worthy of attention, not merely a statistic to be juggled in some year-end report.

Suzanne pressed on the buzzer once more, and this time she heard the sound of heavy footsteps. A voice muttered, hoarse and low, "Who the hell is it?"

She raised her voice. "Mrs. Mellison? Mrs. Arthur Mellison? I'm Suzanne Samuelson. I'm from Family Services."

"Doris comes from the agency."

"Doris is on maternity leave. I'm taking her place for a while."

"I like Doris."

"So do I. Please open your door, Mrs. Mellison. I have to see you before I leave."

"I'm not dressed. Come back later."

"If I don't see you now, I can't authorize your check for this month."

A heavy muttering and then the door locks clicked. A pale, suspicious eye peered out at her. Sour breath. Mrs. Mellison had old-fashioned rollers in her gray hair, covered by a hairnet, and wore a frayed, faded purple bathrobe. "So? See me."

"I have to ask you some questions."

"What questions? Doris never asked questions."

"Just a few routine things for our records. Do you have any legal documentation?"

"Like what?"

"A driver's license?"

"Are you crazy? You think I have a car? A nice shiny Rolls-Royce, maybe?"

Suzanne understood the old woman's reflexive hostility and felt sad that she had to be that way. "A legal I.D., then."

"How about my social security card?"

"That would be fine."

"Maybe I can find it."

After some shuffling around, Mrs. Mellison produced her dog-eared card. Suzanne ran through her standard series of questions: Are you eating regularly? Making rent payments? Do you have any boarders? Any outside sources of income?

Satisfied that Mrs. Mellison was status quo, she wished her a nice day, ignored her grouchy mumblings, and moved on to Apartment 9-G, Mary Jones.

The doorbell wasn't working. Suzanne saw a notation by Doris that the doorbell hadn't worked for nine months. She rapped on the door.

No answer.

She rapped harder.

There was the long silence of a truly empty place. Mary Jones didn't appear to be home. And since she wasn't expecting anybody, why should she be there? Suzanne moved on to 12-G, Carmen Sanchez. Of Carmen Sanchez, Doris had written, "Thinks she's a *bruja*. A witch. Has epilepsy, frequent seizures."

Suzanne felt tears fill her eyes at the thought of Mrs. Sanchez, pluckily battling her physical disability.

The answer to her ring was quick. A middle-aged Latino woman in a sequinned jeans jumpsuit, squarely built, her long black hair pulled back in a bun, stared at her suspiciously across the chained threshold.

Suzanne launched into Spanish, explaining that she was temporarily taking Doris' place.

In smooth, nonaccented English, Carmen Sanchez replied. "So now I see you to get my check?"

"Yes."

She shrugged and unchained the door. "Come in."

The room was lit by flickering candles, and the sharp scent of incense thickened the air. Suzanne noticed a yellow chalked pattern on the floor: it appeared to be a star of some sort, with strange symbols incorporated into each of its six points.

Mrs. Sanchez was an easy visit: chatty, friendly, full of gossip and advice. Was Suzanne married? No? Why not? There was never any need to be single. She, herself, had had three husbands and was now looking for a fourth. How many sisters and brothers did Suzanne have? Would she like to attend a seance?

Suzanne methodically fit her official questions in between the chatter, inspected Mrs. Sanchez's I.D., and finally made her escape, but not before accepting a jar of Mrs. Sanchez's love potion, guaranteed to solve her woeful single condition.

There was one other agency client in this building, wasn't there? She scanned the notes that Doris had left her. Ah, yes. Here it was: Female tenant in 4-G requires psychiatric evaluation. May be delusional. May be using drugs.

Suzanne studied the nameplate on the door. D. W. Smith, it read, in faded letters. She suspected that D. W. Smith was long gone, or, perhaps, merely one name in a series of sublets. All of these apartments were being endlessly sublet. She pressed the doorbell.

The sound of footsteps, light and steady.

The door opened.

"Yes?" A sweet voice, high, bell-like, serene.

The woman in Apartment 4-G was short. Really short. About the height of a nine-year-old child, in fact, but perfectly proportioned, and, startlingly, with the face of an adult—of an old woman, in fact.

Suzanne was nearly overwhelmed with sympathy for her: What must it be like to go through life with such a disadvantage? What a terrible chore it must be for her just to reach a light switch. She must be brave, very brave indeed.

She wore a neat green tunic and velvet leggings and soft shoes that matched her bright green eyes. She reminded Suzanne of a porcelain doll she had once seen advertised in a catalog: Granny Jones, flawlessly painted, amazingly lifelike. Will dress up any room.

"I'm here to make a preliminary evaluation for the ATDF," she said.

The woman regarded her blankly.

Suzanne prompted her. "The Federal Aid-to-Dependent-Families service?"

Now the miniature woman was frowning, casting a net of fine wrinkles over her parchment cheeks. "I told the one before you," she said. "I don't need an evaluation. I don't need your help. I just need peace and quiet so I can do my work." Such a clear, bell-like voice. Suzanne thought it would be pleasant to listen to a voice like that just before falling asleep.

"Please," Suzanne said, almost pleading. "There's no reason to be embarrassed. I can fit you in right after I see Mrs. Mellison in 6-G."

She was accustomed to some client resistance, had been trained to expect it. A social worker is never exactly welcome in the client's home. Her presence is, after all, a tacit admission of failure.

Her training manual had been quite explicit: "Take care to maintain a professional demeanor and treat the client with respect. Make the voice slow and inquisitive, not intrusive or interrogating. Approach the client in a nonjudgmental, nonconfrontational manner. This will facilitate information-gathering."

Suzanne stared at the woman, then flicked an eye at the stained, peeling wallpaper in the hallway, the splintering wood in the doorframe, the flickering ceiling light. "How long have you lived here?"

The small woman shrugged. "Not very long."

"How do you pay your bills?"

"Oh, I get by."

"You mentioned work?"

"I'm here to collect musical sounds."

Collecting sounds? Suzanne tried to imagine what that meant. She admired artistic tendencies—so many clients had them. And artists had such a difficult time in this society. All the more reason for this tiny woman to receive aid. But first she had to find out her work status. "Do you have a job?"

"I do a little of this and a little of that."

In other words, Suzanne thought, she could barely make ends meet. She was probably desperate, struggling, but too proud to admit it, the little dear.

"What's your name?"

"Lorelei."

"What a pretty name. And your surname?"

"Just Lorelei." The woman stared up at Suzanne, and a patronizing smile appeared on her face. In a crisp straight-forward tone she said, almost aggressively, "Look, you might as well understand me. I'm an elf. I'm here for a brief time only. And I don't need your help."

An elf. Right.

Suzanne prided herself on her composure. Her only outward response was a gentle nod. It was all beginning to fit together. Doris had been right: The poor woman was delusional—or perhaps even on drugs. In either case she required testing and consultation.

Using her softest, kindest voice, she said, "Okay, Lorelei. I understand completely." She dug into her purse, pulled out her business card, made a notation, and thrust it at the little woman. "Now, just for my own peace of mind, I've made an appointment for you at our clinic for next Monday. I'll bet you haven't had a physical in a really long time, have you? Well, I think it might be a good idea for you to come on down to our clinic and get checked out. I've written the address out for you. It's at the corner of Montgomery and Rawlston. Three o'clock. Really, we want to help. You don't have to be afraid."

The woman sighed, took the card, shook her head, and shut the door. Suzanne could hear the lock click. Twice.

A pity, such negativism. A real pity. Some people refused to get the help they needed. But she would follow up on this one. Her supervisor didn't call her "Suzy Steamroller" for nothing.

The rest of the week sped by. Suzanne made lasagna on Tuesday night and remembered to bring in a healthy portion for Gus, the homeless man who slept in the agency's doorway. Every lunchtime she spent listening to inspirational tapes on her Walkman. Saturday belonged to the SPCA and all those darling dogs and cats. Sunday, she caught up with housework, did her food shopping, and checked on the well-being of the old ladies in her building.

Monday and Tuesday she split between casework and paperwork. On Wednesday she was deep in a particularly complicated file when she remembered Lorelei and decided to review her test results. She dialed the clinic. "Phyllis Kuman, please."

"Kuman." The clinic's head nurse answered the phone in her rich, vibrant contralto. Behind her could be heard the sounds of people talking, a baby wailing, and doctors being paged.

"Phyl? It's Suzanne Samuelson. How are you?"

"As usual, Suzy-girl, just dealing with bedlam. What can I do for you?"

"I'd like to know the results on case 745-B. She would have come in Monday afternoon. I asked for the whole shebang. Drug testing. Mental/emotional evaluation."

"That's nice. Me, I'd just like a nice expenses-paid trip to Hawaii. We all want something we can't have. Your gal never showed."

"Damn." Suzanne ran her hand through her hair.

"I second that emotion. Now excuse me while I attend to those who, unfortunately, did show up today."

Frustrated and worried, Suzanne hung up the buzzing receiver. She hoped that Lorelei was all right. What if something had happened to her? Suzanne decided to see for herself.

The apartment hallway was just as dim, just as airless, and filled with the same stale cooking odors as before. Suzanne felt such sorrow for anyone who was forced to live this way.

She pressed the buzzer for 4-G.

Lorelei answered on the second ring. She was wearing the same green tunic and leggings. "You, again? What do you want now?"

"You didn't show up for the appointment I made for you at the clinic," Suzanne said. "Are you all right? I thought I should check on you."

Lorelei gave her a look of pure confusion. "I never said that I would go to your clinic, did I?"

Suzanne forced a smile. Resistance was something that had to be overcome with understanding and patience.

"Don't despair," she said. "I know it's not always easy to face a problem. But you don't have to feel like you're alone. You're not. Please, let me help you."

"But—"

"I'll reschedule your appointment."

"Please don't bother."

"Oh, Lorelei, don't give up. Please. I just want to help you. I'm here to tell you that it's possible to break the cycle of despair and self-destruction." Suzanne felt a lump born of selfless nobility building in her throat. "Please, please don't turn me away. I think I can help you. I *want* to help you. Let's work *together*."

"I told you, there's nothing I need help with."

"May I come in?"

"Absolutely not."

"I'd like to sit down with you for a while and just talk, woman-to-woman."

The tiny old woman studied her for a moment and Suzanne imagined that she was being x-rayed by those green eyes.

"I think you suffer from an excess of compassion," Lorelei said. "And you're certainly making me suffer from it. Allow me to lighten both of our burdens." She winked.

Suzanne felt an odd sensation, much like an electrical current, rush swiftly through her body. Her scalp, her feet—and everything in between—tingled for an instant. Then the feeling subsided.

She stared at the little woman. A surge of impatience— anger, even—arose in her. Why was she wasting her time here? If this Lorelei had no interest in helping herself, then she, Suzanne, wouldn't expend an ounce more of her energy either.

"All right, ma'am, suit yourself," she said sharply. "I've got other clients to see here."

Lorelei smiled a mysterious smile and shut her door.

Mary Jones in 9-G answered her door. She was an overweight, middle-aged black woman with tired eyes. Suzanne swept imperiously past her into the apartment.

The place was a pigsty, clothing scattered all over, dirty plates sitting on the kitchen table where they had obviously been since breakfast—or, perhaps, dinner the night before. A layer of dust coated everything. Typical welfare-recipient slovenliness, Suzanne thought. "Don't you believe in cleaning?" she said.

"Pardon?" Miss Jones gave her a confused glance.

"I mean, really, how can you live this way?" Suzanne demanded. She felt buoyed up by waves of righteous disgust. "Just because you're getting government assistance doesn't mean you've got a license to live like a slob."

Miss Jones seemed bewildered by the onslaught. She stared, wide-eyed, and then she burst into tears. Suzanne watched her coldly. People like her never had a tissue around when they needed it, did they? They simply didn't know how to plan ahead.

She paused, astonished to realize that she didn't feel a thing, not one bit of remorse.

A bit flustered, she left Miss Jones to her weeping and went to see Mrs. Mellison.

Mrs. Mellison greeted her with a loud complaint. "I think somebody stole my check."

"So?" Suzanne snapped. "What do you expect, living in a place like this?"

"Mrs. Mellison gaped at her, blinking rapidly. "What did you say?"

What did this woman want from her? "It's too bad your check was stolen," she continued. "Of course, I have no way of knowing if you're telling me the truth, do I? You might have already cashed it and hidden the money. You could be trying to gouge the government for another one. It's happened before. Oh, stop playing innocent. You know what I'm talking about, don't you, Mrs. Mellison?"

Wait a minute, Suzanne thought. That didn't sound like me at all.

All the response the older woman made was an odd stuttering.

"Come to think of it, a quick inventory might prove what I'm saying." Suzanne strode into the kitchen and began opening cabinets, peering inside.

Mrs. Mellison scuttled in after her. "Hey, miss. What are you doing?"

"I see two boxes of sugar here, Mrs. Mellison. That's hoarding, isn't it? And why do you need three onions? Two more in the bread box. Two sets of dishes. How could you afford two sets of dishes?" A small voice in Suzanne's head cried out in dismay over what she was saying. But she ignored it.

Mrs. Mellison's lower lip quivered.

Suzanne sighed. She was probably going to begin sniveling. Where were the tissues?

But the older woman's face worked itself around into a grimace of anger. She took a step toward Suzanne and, snarling, said, "I knew that phony-baloney nice-girl routine of yours was just an act. All you government people are the same. Bastards, every single one of you. You give us barely enough to live on and then blame us for surviving."

"I don't—"

"Get out. Get out of my apartment before I call the cops!"

Suzanne decided that Mrs. Mellison's actions were deeply paranoid and made a note to bring in a field evaluator. If Mrs. Mellison was a welfare cheat, she would put an end to it right away.

Mrs. Mellison slammed the door behind her. She hurried on to Carmen Sanchez's door.

Mrs. Sanchez greeted her with a wide grin. "Ah, Miss Samuelson. Come in."

In the darkened living room Suzanne gazed at the flickering candles, took a deep nauseating breath of the thick incense, and frowned. "Are you aware that you're probably in defiance of fire codes here?"

"I beg your pardon?"

"These candles are a terrible fire hazard. And that incense. How can you breathe in here? I'm surprised your neighbors haven't complained before this."

Mrs. Sanchez's dark eyes probed her. "Miss Samuelson, is anything wrong?"

Suzanne paused. She did feel a little odd. Not really herself. The interview with Mrs. Mellison hadn't gone well at all. But Mrs. Mellison was really not the most cooperative of women. She would worry about it later. "Fine."

"You seem, I don't know, different. Angry or something."

Angry? With a client? The thought caught Suzanne off-balance. How ridiculous. She was there to help these poor God-forsaken people. "I don't know what you're talking about," she said. "I don't have time to sit here gabbing. Do something about those candles." She nodded and saw herself to the door.

Back at the office, she sat down at her desk and began to review her notes.

She was shaken to discover what a soft-headed fool she had been about these people. Constantly making excuses for their shiftless laziness.

Not soft-headed, said her inner voice. Soft-hearted.

A knock at the door brought her nose up out of her files. It was Dale, her supervisor, looking rushed and hassled as usual. His dark hair was slicked down with sweat and he was chewing on one of a series of ever-present pencils in a perpetual attempt to stop smoking. "Staff meeting in ten minutes."

"Right." Suzanne usually enjoyed getting together with her fellow caseworkers to compare stories and plot strategies. She gathered up her files, got a bitter cup of coffee at the machine in the hallway, and, balancing it carefully, made her way to the conference room.

Lou Brawley, Anne Taylor, and Curtis Smith were already seated, chatting and sipping the bitter brew.

Dale bustled in. "Okay, troops, let's make our reports." He turned to Suzanne and his dark eyes twinkled. "So how did your attempts go at saving society this month, Suzy?"

"Save society? Don't be idiotic. It's really hopeless, isn't it?" Suzanne said. "All this pouring out of dollars. Not to mention time and energy. I mean, this is just a holding action to keep the masses of the poor pacified. You know that as well as I do."

You could hear a pin drop in that room. Four pairs of eyes were trained upon her, wide, unmoving.

"I think the whole thing's self-defeating, really," Suzanne added. She felt uncomfortable with the way everybody was looking at her but she forced herself to go on. "Welfare doesn't help anybody. If anything, it makes things worse. Why don't these people have jobs? We encourage laziness and dependency."

Dale cleared his throat. "Uh, Suzy? Do you feel all right?"

"I'm fine. Why do you ask?" Everybody was staring at her. She must have said something wrong.

"Let's skip the ideology, shall we? Do you have anything specific to report?" Dale was suddenly all business.

"I think we should get a field investigator to check out Case 494-C, a Mrs. Arthur Mellison."

"You think she's cheating?"

"She might be." Suzanne felt righteousness buoying her upward. "She's the sort who would."

There was another moment of strained silence.

"Anything else?"

"Ah—I'd like to know how the state can keep on finding the money we waste on all of this."

Somebody snickered. Curtis Smith's smile was openly malicious while Anne Taylor made quick circles around one ear with her forefinger.

Dale flipped the cover down on his folder. "Suzanne? I'd like to see you in my office. Right now." The supervisor stood up. "Meeting tabled until further notice."

Safely behind a closed door, Dale spun on her and said, "Just what in hell is bugging you?"

Suzanne backed against the door. "I—I don't know what you mean."

"Oh, get off it, Suzanne. Of all my caseworkers, you're usually the one with the biggest heart, the softest touch. What's gotten into you? Spewing all this weird rhetoric. You sound positively . . . Republican or something!" He patted his jacket, reached into the lapel pocket, brought out a cigarette, and quickly lit it, waving the match out and dropping it on the floor.

"Don't be silly." Suzanne wondered if he could be right.

He took a long drag, exhaled a cloud of smoke, and said, "Where's the gal who cared about flowers dying? Miss Compassion? I've never heard you talk like this before. You sound downright surly. Mean."

An odd stabbing fear caught Suzanne in her gut. Mean? Her? That was a new one. She had certainly been startled by the things coming out of her mouth. And yet—they were right, weren't they? "Dale, I'm the same person I ever was."

Her supervisor stared at her and took another drag. "Maybe it's fatigue. Burnout."

"I just had a vacation."

"Then I want you to get checked out by a shrink. I don't have time for this."

"Are you kidding?"

"Do it." Dale used the tone of voice reserved for the most recalcitrant clients.

Sighing, Suzanne said, "If you insist, I'll stop by the clinic on the way home."

"Not one of our shrinks. A real one." He flipped through his card file, made a notation, and handed it to Suzanne. "Here. Dr. George at the Gramercy Psychiatric Group. My sister was his patient. Insurance will cover this—it's job-related."

Suzanne made one last appeal. "But I tell you, I feel fine."

Frown lines appeared between Dale's eyes. "You don't sound fine, not to me. And I've known you for four years."

"But—"

"Suzanne, I'll put you on medical leave if I don't get a report from Dr. George within a week."

"You're the boss." Privately, Suzanne was relieved. At least now she could explain her confusions in private to a professional. With mingled relief and fear she took the referral from her supervisor.

Suzanne sat in Dr. Marvin George's waiting room, cooling her heels. An aquarium whose only inhabitant was some tired seaweed bubbled quietly in the corner. Dog-eared copies of magazines were strewn across the round coffee table near the couch. The entire place was upholstered in restful, calming beige.

Damned waste of time, Suzanne thought. But why don't I feel anything?

An inner door cracked open and a voice said: "Miss Samuelson?"

She stood and followed the voice through the door and into a plush inner sanctum of warm wood, muted paintings, and padded chairs. Even the tissue box coordinated with the blue-and-green upholstery of the couch. She sat down, feeling the sofa cushion give gently beneath her.

Dr. George was a thin bald man with a beak of a nose and sharp brown eyes that didn't seem to miss a thing.

"What brings you here?" he said.

"My supervisor."

"And how long have you had problems with authority?"

"I don't have problems with authority."

"I thought you said—"

"My supervisor thinks I'm having problems, problems with compassion. He indicated that it's not a desirable trait in a social worker."

Dr. George leaned back in his padded leather chair, nodding. "I see. And how do these problems manifest?"

"I'm not sure. I just told him what I think about the welfare system and he went ballistic."

"And what do you think?"

Suzanne couldn't help herself, she just blurted it out. "That it's mostly a waste of time. That it breeds dependency and laziness. That it's a pernicious influence on the lives of the poor, and if not linked to a work-for-assistance program, should be terminated in all but the most desperate cases of need."

He looked at her strangely. "You're a social worker, you say?"

"Yes, Department of Human Resources, Family Services division."

"Hmmm. Tell me more, Miss Samuelson."

There was a cold unhappy feeling in the pit of her stomach. But she couldn't stop herself, it was like a dam bursting. "And the people who get welfare, they're nothing but whining leeches. Constantly complaining, as if I owe them something."

Dr. George grunted. "Go on."

"Why, half of them are just cheats anyway. The rest take the entire check and blow it on a drunken binge. What good does it do them? What good does it do us to throw our hard-earned money at them? I'm so tired of listening to their complaints. 'My check is late. Somebody stole it. Why can't I get more money?' "

The psychiatrist seemed galvanized by her statements. "Fascinating," he said. "Suzanne—may I call you Suzanne?—I haven't heard talk like this in a long, long time. At least, not from someone who says she's a social worker."

So there WAS something wrong with her after all. Suzanne cringed inwardly, waiting for the blow to fall.

"A long, long time indeed," the doctor continued. "All I can say is that you're a credit to your profession. It amazes me to hear one of you mealy-mouthed socialists actually speaking sense for a change. If we had more social workers like you, we'd soon have fewer welfare cases to drag upon our country's precious resources." He stood up. "I can see no reason for you to return here. However, I'd advise you to be careful if you want to keep your job. Work from within to reform the system, it's the only way. Use tact, diplomacy, cunning. Whatever it takes." He gave her a chilly smile. "I'd like to shake your hand."

Reluctantly Suzanne pumped his hand. Dr. George didn't think there was anything wrong with her. Maybe she had imagined the whole problem. "But, Doctor," Suzanne said. "What about the compassion problem? I really don't feel a thing."

He shook his head, tragic wisdom gleaming in his eyes. "Not to worry. I agree with your iconoclasm. And I'll see to it that you keep your job. Work from within. There's no change unless it comes from within, right?" And, with a wave, he dismissed her.

Suzanne left the office, her head spinning.

* * *

Dale read the report of Suzanne's visit to Dr. George
and lit up the first of a series of cigarettes. Angrily
exhaling smoke through his nose, he said, "All I can say
is, watch your attitude. I just got our budget for next year
and it looks like I'm going to have to make cuts in staff."
His eyes drilled into her. "Do you understand me?"

Shaken, Suzanne nodded. Her job was on the line.

She did her best over the next two weeks—at least she
thought she did. The old woman who claimed she had
stolen a cab from her was just too slow in a fast-moving
city. And, despite what everybody else said, she DID
NOT cut into line at the bank. There was an opening
there, but nobody else saw it. And if the people at work
couldn't understand how they were contributing to the
demise of society as they knew it, well, she couldn't help
pointing it out, could she?

At the end of two weeks the SPCA told her that her vol-
unteer services were no longer required. Not a single
person in the office would speak to her. Even Gus, the
homeless man who slept in the doorway at work, turned
away when she approached. Suzanne knew she was in big
trouble. She would lose her job for sure, then her apartment, and probably end up fighting with Gus for space in
that very doorway.

Miserably she wondered if she were having a nervous
breakdown. Perhaps if she called Dr. George and begged
for another appointment he would see her. But that would
have to wait until after she had made her rounds for the
day: Mrs. Mellison, Jones, and Sanchez. And this was
another opportunity for her to try and get a fix on that
Lorelei character.

A small voice in her head told her that she was kidding
herself, ignoring the obvious, turning into just another
soulless cog in the welfare machine.

It's my job, she thought. For as long as I have it.

She buzzed at 6-G. When Mrs. Mellison opened the
door and saw her, fire lit in her eyes. "You have a hell of a
nerve," she said. "Showing your face around here after
the way you talked to me last time."

"But—"

"I want another caseworker. I've already complained to

your office. Good-bye and good riddance." She closed the door, not gently.

Miss Jones slammed the door in her face.

Only Mrs. Sanchez seemed willing to see her. But her radiant smile and welcoming manner were gone, and she maintained a dignified silence, merely answering yes or no to Suzanne's list of questions.

Suzanne noticed that she hadn't removed any of her candles: The air was thick with their waxy smoke. She forced herself not to say anything. She couldn't afford to alienate Mrs. Sanchez, too.

"Please," she said desperately. "Can you tell me anything about Lorelei?"

"What's to tell? She's little. She wears green, and she listens to rap music."

Suzanne made a face and said disgustedly, "Rap music?"

"Yeah. She's forever visiting Leroy in 5-G. He's teaching her how to rap. She's not bad." Mrs. Sanchez shrugged. "And, by the way, you'd better be nice to her. She's an elf."

"Are you crazy? You believe that b.s.?" Suzanne couldn't help herself. It just slipped out.

Mrs. Sanchez gave her a sharp look. "Why not? Professional courtesy, after all. And it costs nothing."

Reeling, Suzanne realized what had happened. If Mrs. Sanchez were right, if Lorelei were indeed some supernatural creature—an elf, for God's sake—then she had made a serious mistake with her. That damned elf must have hexed her and stolen every vestige of compassion she had. On the verge of tears, she explained her predicament to Mrs. Sanchez, how Lorelei had warned her off but she had ignored it. And now she was in deep, deep trouble.

The *bruja* nodded wisely. "I thought so. You got off on the wrong foot with her, didn't you? Well, you'd better make amends, pronto."

Suzanne wailed, "But how?"

"Propitiate her. Bring her a gift. Apologize for bothering her."

"A gift? What in hell am I supposed to get her? What kind of gift would an elf want?"

"I don't know. She likes music, doesn't she?"

Music. Suzanne thought wildly. A conductor's baton? No, too small. A tuba? Too big, especially for an elf. Then she knew. Yes, yes, yes, the very thing! A hand-held tape recorder and supply of tapes. Better throw in extra batteries, too, just to be safe. It would cost her a small fortune. But what choice did she have?

"A gift. Right." She hurried out of the candlelit apartment without even stopping to thank Mrs. Sanchez.

The next morning, Suzanne called in sick. The tone of relief in Dale's voice was unmistakable.

"Maybe you should take off the rest of the week," he said.

"I'll be in tomorrow." Suzanne said, and thought, or I'll be floating in the river.

She picked up her parcel, nicely gift-wrapped in green paper and ribbon—she had specified the color—and made her way to Lorelei's door. Her heart was pounding as she pressed the buzzer.

The elf answered quickly. When she saw Suzanne, she said, "Not you again."

"Please, may I come in?"

"Not if it's to bother me further about some stupid tests."

Suzanne wanted to tell her that the tests weren't stupid but she restrained herself. "No. I understand now, really. I want to apologize."

"I don't believe you."

"Really, I promise I won't bother you again." Suzanne was about to say something tart about small elves who hexed well-meaning humans who were only trying to help them, but somehow she held herself back. "And look, this is for you." Suzanne thrust her gift at the tiny woman. "To help you with your work."

"Nice wrapping paper." Lorelei carefully opened her gift. When she saw the tape recorder her face creased into a deep, wrinkled smile. "How thoughtful! I was going to get one of these." She looked up, stared at

Suzanne thoughtfully, and said, "I guess you are sincere."
She winked twice. "There."

A flood of conflicting feelings swept through Suzanne:
mirth, relief, disbelief, joy, and above all, wonder. "Are
you really an elf?" she said shyly.

"Yes," Lorelei replied. She pushed back her hair
and Suzanne saw to her amazement a gracefully fluted,
distinctly pointed ear. "Thank you again for this gift.
Good-bye."

As Suzanne walked toward the stairwell she noticed
that the overhead light was out. She would have to talk to
the landlord about it before somebody got hurt.

A tape was siting on her desk when she arrived at work
the next morning. At lunch, Suzanne popped it into her
Walkman and switched it on. After a few moments she
heard a driving, scratchy double beat, and above it, a
clear, bell-like voice chanting in steady rhythm:

"Yo, chill out and gather round,
Put an ear to what I'm puttin' down:
I'm short of leg and long of wit,
A rappin' elf, that's the gist of it,
I came up-world to catch the beat,
I've got it now, short and sweet,
I'll bring it back to my underhill homies,
The sprites, the elves, maybe even some gnomies,
But not the trolls, that's understood—
When it comes to rhythm they're just no good.
But when it comes to rhythm, I'm the queen of stealth.
I'm a rappin' elf, I can't help myself."

There was nothing else on the tape. It was enough.

Suzanne smiled. When she rang the bell at apartment
4-G on her next visit, there was no answer. She hadn't
expected any, really.

Carmen Sanchez was waiting for her, smiling. "She's
gone," said the *bruja*. "Do you feel better?"

Suzanne felt a flood of gratitude for the woman's
advice. "Yes." She grinned. "I do. Feel. Better."

"I suppose that's good," Mrs. Sanchez said. "Of course, in your business, it might be a drawback."

"No," Suzanne said. "Don't ever think that." She took a deep breath. She felt refreshed, revivified, ready to take on the wrongs of the world and right them. She gazed into the woman's apartment with its flickering candles, and smiled. "By the way, did I ever tell you that I like your incense?"

BY THE OAKS

by Janni Lee Simner

Janni Lee Simner grew up amid the oaks and maples of
New York and has been making her way west ever since.
She currently lives amid the palo verdes and mesquites
of the Arizona desert. She's sold stories to nearly two
dozen anthologies and magazines, including *Realms of
Fantasy* and *Sisters in Fantasy II*. Her first three books,
Ghost Horse, *The Haunted Trail*, and *Ghost Vision*, have
been published by Scholastic.

Kristy always suspected she'd been born into the wrong
world. She suspected it each morning as she waited under
dawning skies for the rickety yellow school bus. She suspected it in the classroom, where her teacher rambled on
about fractions and the causes of the Civil War. And she
especially suspected it as she stood alone on the schoolyard, while by the swingset the other girls giggled about
new colors of nail polish and braided each others' hair.

Leaning against the schoolyard fence, she would look
out to where two oak trees bent toward each other, imagining that the arch they formed was not an arch at all, but
a special kind of gate. If she walked around the trees she
would see only a hill, sloping down into the town. But if
she walked between them—and between from the higher
side—maybe she'd wind up in some other world, one
where nail polish and fractions took a back seat to more
important matters.

Still, she was startled when, leaving school one day,
she looked back at the arch and saw something stir
beneath its branches. She waited, tugging at a wisp of
brown hair that had flown free of her ponytail, for the
other children to leave before investigating. Then she

approached the trees slowly—from the nonmagical side. She had never actually walked through from the magical side, for fear that the trees would turn out to be only trees, after all.

The boy on the ground was real, though, curled in a tight ball and moaning softly. Kristy walked up and tapped him on the shoulder. The boy jumped, letting out a startled yelp, and ran to the far side of the tree.

"Wait," Kristy said, shoving her hands into her jacket pockets, "I won't hurt you."

The boy peered at her cautiously. He was shorter than Kristy, with long pants that dragged the ground and a large, loose shirt. His clothes were all the same shade of green, and Kristy wondered how she'd seen him against the dark grass. From his slight frame, she would have thought he was in one of the lower grades, but looking at his face, his eyes, she suspected he was quite a bit older than she.

"Hi," Kristy said, extending a hand. The stranger backed away, whimpering, and she followed him. At last he looked up at her. His eyes were the same green as his clothes, but had no pupils and seemed unfocused.

"You're—you're one of those awful humans, aren't you?" He spoke in a high, tinny voice.

"Not really," Kristy said. She was wondering how to explain that she'd been born into the wrong world when she remembered the gate and she said in a rush, "You came through the trees, didn't you? Please, take me back with you!"

The boy coughed and looked at her through slitted eyes. "Who told you about the gate?" he demanded. "What do you know of elven lands?"

"Then there really is another land through the trees?" Kristy had pulled the ponytail holder from her hair, but she was trembling so much it flew from her fingers. "And you're an elf? A real elf?"

"No, I'm a fake elf," the boy said dryly. "By the oaks, girl, my ears aren't round, are they?"

Kristy looked at his shiny black hair. The ears peeking out from beneath it were, in fact, slightly pointed.

"Now you have to take me with you!" she cried,

throwing her arms around his neck—whether to hug him or keep him from leaving she wasn't quite sure. The elf squirmed out of her embrace and tried to run away, but fell into a fit of coughing and collapsed upon the ground instead.

"My lady," he rasped, "have mercy."

"I'm sorry," Kristy said, kneeling by his side. "But you will take me back with you, won't you?"

"I wouldn't take you to my home if I were on my deathbed," the elf snapped. "And I am."

"Oh." Kristy's voice turned softer. "I'm sorry."

"Well, so I am," muttered the elf, brushing dirt off his clothes.

Kristy pulled up a clump of grass and twisted it between her fingers. "What are you dying of?" she asked, her voice still low.

"Well," he said, with a certain satisfaction, "strange liquids are forever leaking from my eyes and nose, and very soon I shall be drained dry. I can tell, because I'm forever weary, and no longer have the strength for even the spring dances. That's when the others finally cast me out. Until then they'd put up with me, hoped I'd get better."

Kristy looked at the growing pile of torn grass at her feet. "They kicked you out just because you were tired?"

"Just tired!" The elf jumped to his feet. "An elf who cannot dance in the spring is no elf at all. Besides, I'm not just tired. I'm dying."

The elf was overcome by a fit of sneezing. He wiped his nose on his sleeve and shoved the sleeve in front of Kristy.

"You're dying of a runny nose?"

"You speak as if it were a common illness, and not the rare and strange affliction it is."

"But it is common," Kristy said. "At least here it is." She tugged up a fresh clump of grass, but when the elf scowled, threw it back to the ground. He looked toward the trees, and afraid he would leave without her, Kristy stood.

"Listen," she said, "want to come home with me? I'm sure Mom and Dad wouldn't mind."

The elf sneezed again, and looked up at Kristy with a

gaze so pitiful she didn't know whether to laugh or cry. "Why not?" he said. "If I'm dying already, I can hardly lower myself further by associating with humans, can I?"

Kristy didn't answer. She turned to lead the way home; she'd already missed the bus. The elf followed, dragging his feet along the ground and coughing every now and then. He told Kristy that his name was Ryn, but little else.

Except, of course, that he was dying.

Kristy's mother stood by the door, alternately looking at her watch and the driveway. When Kristy finally climbed the steps, her mother's worried look quickly turned angry.

"Where were you?"

"Sorry, Mom." Kristy glanced down at her shoes. "I had to stay after for help with math. I forgot to call."

"Well, all right, then. But next time—"

Kristy cut her off. "Mom, this is Ryn. Can he stay for dinner?"

"Sure," her mother said, forgetting to finish the lecture. "Your Dad's cooking now. Why don't you—"

Before her mother could continue with "set the table," Kristy broke in, "Ryn, want me to show you around?" Ryn didn't answer—he seemed about to sneeze again—so Kristy grabbed his arm and dragged him toward her room.

Halfway up, Ryn collapsed, wheezing and coughing. "Surely the end can't be far now," he said, breathing hard. As Kristy sat beside him, he looked down at the living room, then at the banister.

"My lady," he cried without warning, "you've built your house out of wood!"

"Well, yeah," Kristy said. A large orange cat came slinking up the stairs and jumped into her lap. She petted it absently.

"Humans," Ryn muttered, still staring at the banister, "primitives all." He let out a long sigh that turned into another fit of coughing.

Kristy almost told Ryn that humans weren't primitives, at least not all of them, but she remembered that she didn't understand them too well herself. She jumped up, dumping the cat onto the staircase, and continued toward her room. Still wheezing, Ryn followed.

He stopped short at the top of the stairs. Off to one side, a tiny oak tree stood in a large ceramic pot. "What," he demanded, "is that?"

"Oh, I grew that myself," Kristy said lightly. "From an acorn, a few summers ago."

"Indoors? In a pot?" Ryn's voice rose.

"Yeah." Kristy tugged at the hem of her jacket.

Ryn whirled around to face her. "Are all humans such barbarians?" he demanded.

"We're not barbarians," Kristy said. She'd meant to say, "I'm not a barbarian, whatever the others are," but it hadn't come out that way.

"Then how," Ryn demanded, struggling to lower his voice, "do you explain this?"

"Explain what?"

"Your house, built out of dead trees. The only living tree within it," Ryn's voice cracked, "confined indoors, to a tiny pot. It's cruel. It's—"

Kristy thought he was going to say inhuman, but realized that wasn't quite appropriate. Was unelfish a word?

"Awful," the elf declared.

"It is not," Kristy said, almost yelling herself. "Everyone builds out of wood. And I water the tree nearly every day."

"You're only human. You wouldn't understand."

Kristy glowered down at Ryn. Even if she didn't like humans very much, she didn't like hearing Ryn insult them, either. "At least humans don't get thrown out of their homes every time they get a cold," she said.

"I already told you. I don't just have a cold, whatever that is. I'm dying." The elf shook his head wearily and knelt by the oak. "Poor little thing," he said, stroking its leaves. Then he burst into a fit of coughing so bad he couldn't speak for several minutes.

And watching him, hunched shaking over the plant, Kristy suddenly knew his rare and strange illness for what it really was.

"Step away from the tree," she said.

"Why? So you can torture it?"

"Just step away."

Ryn whispered something into the soil, started sneezing, and stepped back.

"Follow me."

The elf looked hesitantly at the tree, then at Kristy.

"No one's going to hurt it while you're gone," she said.

Ryn followed her. Once they were both in her room, Kristy shut the door and sat down on the bed. Sprawled out on a pillow, the cat regarded her with one eye, then curled into a ball and went to sleep.

"How do you feel?" Kristy asked.

"I already told you—"

"No. How do you feel now?"

"My nose still drips. And my eyes water."

Kristy opened the door. "Go back to the tree."

Ryn knelt by the pot, whispering something Kristy couldn't hear. Then he started coughing and wheezing all over again, and crying as well. "Oh, let the end come soon," he begged.

"Now back into the room," Kristy said without pity.

Ryn followed Kristy and stood by her dresser, breathing hard.

"Now how do you feel?"

"Tired. Ill. Like I'm dying," Ryn snapped. "Are you happy?"

"But you're not coughing, and you're not sneezing."

"Well, it does come and go."

"Go back to the tree."

Ryn trudged back out, and Kristy could hear him coughing. When he returned, he looked not only tired and sick, but also very worried.

"Oh, no," he said.

"You're not sick, and you're definitely not dying. You're just allergic to trees."

"Just allergic to trees?" Ryn cried weakly. "How can I go home now, even if they would accept me there?"

"You can't," Kristy said, reaching out to pet the cat. "Unless they have allergy doctors."

"I fear they do not," Ryn said.

"Well, you could probably see mine," Kristy said. "I'm allergic to cats—and all sorts of other stuff, too—but every week I get a shot and they don't bother me much at all."

"You expect me to see a human doctor? With the way you treat your trees, I tremble to see how you treat your people."

Kristy shrugged. "There are places without any trees. You could go to one of those."

Ryn shuddered. "What are these strange lands called?"

"New York City's one," Kristy said. "There are others."

Ryn looked at her, and Kristy thought he was about to cry. She almost felt sorry for him, and was searching for something comforting to say when her father called from downstairs, "Kristy, dinner in fifteen minutes."

Kristy stuck her head out the door and shouted, "Okay, Dad." Looking down the stairs, she suspected that her parents would never kick her out, no matter how sick she got or how few friends she had or how bad her math grades were.

Maybe she'd been born into the right world after all.

She returned to Ryn, who looked at her bravely and said, "I will see one of your doctors. If I need to, I will go to the treeless place." But then he bit his lip, and Kristy realized he was still fighting tears. "How can I survive in your world?" he asked. "There's so much I need to know. Where should I begin?"

Kristy ran her fingers through her hair, thinking. Then she grinned, sat down beside Ryn on the edge of the bed, and began to explain about fractions.

ALL THAT GLITTERS
by C. J. Henderson

C.J. Henderson is a fixture in the comic book field, writing for series such as *Lady Justice*. Other fiction of his appears in *100 Dastardly Little Detective Stories, 100 Crooked Little Crime Stories,* and *365 Scary Stories.*

While the candy blue light specific to televised special effects played in the background, the first of the evening's dictionary definitions scrolled across the screen while a throaty female voice read it aloud for the show's less literate viewers.

"Elves," she intoned with authority, "one of a class of imaginary beings, especially from mountainous regions, with magical powers, given to capricious interference in human affairs. Usually imagined to be a diminutive being in human form. A sprite, a fairy, a dwarf, a small child or a small, mischievous person."

"Elves," came another voice—this one male. "What do we really know about them?"

As the blue effect faded, the speaker moved from the shadows created by a pair of faux Greek columns, walking straight for the camera. His hands correctly placed to evoke trust from the audience, he lowered his voice a notch, continuing with the opening pitch for that week's supernatural exposé.

"For centuries they have inhabited our literature and our imaginations, but many of us have been forced to ask time and again—are those the *only* regions they inhabit? What of Professor Margaret Murray, the British Egyptologist and her theory that what we now call witchcraft all started with a diminutive race of pagan worshipers spread across Europe and the British isles? As she wrote earlier this century, 'The dwarf race which at one time inhabited Europe has left *few* concrete remains but *has* survived in innumerable stories of fairies and elves.' Was she correct? Was there at one time a people of small stature, highly gifted in the arts and primitive magicks? Were they a race that felt so alienated from the rest of humanity that they actually considered themselves outsiders to the human race?"

The man had hit his mark with his customary professional grace. Staring into the camera with soulful honesty, he said, "British folklorist Katharine Briggs preferred to describe fairy folk with a line dating from the seventeenth century, saying that they were 'of a middle nature, one between men and angels.' Was *she* correct? Was there a supernatural basis of origin for the creatures we know as elves? And, if they actually did walk the Earth at one time, is it possible that they are still with us today?"

The announcer paused to allow a moment of the Celtic music being laid down in the background to catch the audience's attention. Counting off the two full seconds the director had insisted upon, he watched for his cue light, and then allowed himself his customary opening look—soulful eyes combined with the upturning of one side of his mouth.

"I'm Marvin Richards," he told his viewers, his silver voice deepening to imply that there was something substantial and important about being Marvin Richards, "and this is *The Challenge of the Unknown.*"

While the former reporter turned "Ghost Shill"—as he was known by many at the network—worked his way toward the first commercial break, his studio guest sat in the Green Room, waiting for the time when he would tell his story. He was a relatively young man—perhaps a good fifteen years younger than he appeared. Whenever he was not staring mindlessly off into space, he shifted in his seat nervously, crossing and uncrossing his legs, running his fingers through his hair, craning his neck from side to side, and generally making the young woman who functioned as the show's guest handler more and more uncomfortable.

That point was noteworthy in itself.

Lora Dean was not used to people like Mr. Delroney. He was *too* worried, *too* panicked. The grand majority of the guests Dean usually chaperoned were anxious, but mainly because they were about to appear on television. On television—with their friends and loved ones watching.

Tuned in to see them on the tube, talking about being vampires, or witches—about living in haunted houses or having seen hairy hill people or a lake monster—about being abducted by aliens, probed by aliens, forced to have sex with aliens, or watched by aliens and men in black suits since they were very small children . . . Lora Dean had met them all.

The man with the Mothman photographs, people who were at Roswell, who had tales of the aliens in the freezer, the Flatwoods monster, and the Hopkinsville goblins.

Them *all.*

She had handled guests for the panels on the Jersey Devil, the creatures in Pascagoula, the Mad Gasser of Mattoon, and still more evidence on the Spring Heel Jack case.

Just, them *all.*

Until, that was, she met Mr. Delroney. Dean had seen every kind of out-and-out phony. She knew when the show's writers were cooking the books and laughing up their sleeves at the types of nonsense they could get away with shoveling out for the audience. She had also seen the people who *thought* they believed, the ones who had worked themselves up into such a lather over something that they knew—they just *knew*—had to be real.

There was a certain sadness in their fantasies, but she could always tell they were fantasies—the various fabrications they had taken to wearing in place of personalities. She could see it in the corners of their eyes, that distant blank spot at the very back of their field of vision—leakage from the one part of their brain that knew the truth and did its best to project what sanity it could from the sinking ship.

But Delroney did not project sanity. Not because he seemed dangerous, or not-in-control, or incapable of caring for himself. It was just that . . . if believing in lep-

rechauns was a mark of insanity, then Edward Delroney
was insane, because there was no doubt in Dean's mind
that the nervous man before her truly believed in leprechauns with all his heart and soul.

"You don't believe me," he asked her suddenly, shattering the wall of curiosity between then. "Do you?"

"What makes you say that?" countered the younger
woman.

"It doesn't matter," he answered. Lora Dean's job was
to make certain the guests were happy. It could sometimes
take hours to get a guest ready. They had to be as rational
and steady as possible before they were slipped under the
pressure of the lens. Since Marvin Richards' time was too
valuable to be used in such a manner, they had hired
someone else to do that job.

Trying to make certain that Delroney would be an "Up"
guest, and not a "Fidget" or a "Spacer—those were the
two kinds Richards hated the most, and the man in the
Green Room was both—Dean tried to draw him out . . .
get him talking, get him relaxed, earn her pay check.

You don't earn, the young woman reminded herself,
Mom and Dad don't eat.

"Of course it matters," she told the restless guest,
churning up enough sincerity to make him believe her.
Lora Dean was an attractive woman. She had been beautiful from birth and thus knew how to use the advantage
on a purely instinctive level. Filling her eyes with concern, she asked, "Why are you so upset? Camera shy?"
She did not believe the question, of course. It was merely
a tried and true method to get her charge talking. And,
after the customary moment of hesitation, Delroney
proved not unmoved by the young woman's charms.

Clearing his throat, he answered, "If only . . . oh, if . . ."
And then the far away look started to return. Cutting it off
before it could seize him, however, the man pulled himself back from the brink, asking at the same time, "I'm
not sure I should be here. I mean, it's such a gamble, such
a risk. What if I'm wrong? What if we're not ready . . .
as a race, I mean?" Then, his mind leaping to some
other place, he added, "Still, the chance to be done—
once everyone had heard, once everyone had been

challenged . . . I mean, once it spreads out to everyone, I'll be free. Won't I?"

Sure, Lora, why be a waitress? Take the TV job.

The memory flashed through the women's head. She and only she had talked herself into her current situation, she reminded herself. Now she had to make the best of it. Dean looked at Delroney with as much compassion as she could muster. He was a somewhat handsome man. His bio sheet said he was only three years older than her, but he looked to be twenty. Despite the weary age that some- thing had added to his face, she knew herself well enough to know that if they had met outside of their current cir- cumstance, she would have probably been interested in him immediately.

Yeah, she thought, *until he started talking about be- lieving in leprechauns.* Shoving her personal feelings aside, she admitted, "I'm not sure. What I mean is I'm not certain what it is exactly that you mean. But listen, they're not going to be ready for you for a good half hour. Why don't you tell me your story? You could think of it as a rehearsal for when you go on." She gave him less time than he needed to make up his mind, then urged, "I'd really like to hear what you're going to tell everyone." Her eyes filling with a calculated mischief, she told him in a conspiratory tone, "It would be like a sneak preview."

Delroney stared into the young woman's inviting blue eyes, then caught her off-guard by asking, "Well . . . are you a greedy person?"

Dean sputtered. She was at a loss for words. While her face gave away her surprise, the back of her mind raced over the facts, trying to help her assemble an answer.

Yes, she told herself, she had come to the city to exploit her looks for money. But that had a lot more to do with the desperate straits of her family than it did her own desires.

Do greedy people send half their pay home?

"No," she answered honestly, suddenly curious. "I don't think so."

Delroney weighed the feel of the woman's words against the gauge he had learned to form over the past six months. Feeling the odds were good here, he told her, "I believe you. I think you'd actually be okay."

"What do you mean?"

"I mean that selfless people who hear my story . . . well, it seems they just hear a story. I believe that it does help turn the tide, of course, but they aren't aware of it."

"Umm-humm," responded Dean. "And greedy people . . . ?"

"They die," answered Delroney without emotion. "More of them every time in . . . what did they call in back in school? Geometric proportion—no. Progression. Geometric *progression.*" As Dean looked on confused, the man explained, "The first time I told the story, I mean, just that person listening then died. But the next time, I was telling two people, and they both died. The next time it was four. Then sixteen. Then . . . well, I'm sure you understand."

Lora stared at the nervous young man. Rattling off death statistics actually seemed to be calming him. As she mentally checked to make certain her automatic smile was firmly in place, he said, "You see, as best I can figure it, whenever I guess wrong and tell my tale to a greedy person, the curse that kills them stretches out beyond them to the next greedy person it can find, and then the next, and the next, et cetera, until the math balances out."

Delroney looked up. Despite her best efforts, Dean's mask slipped a notch, letting her confusion show. In a way it was a good thing, for it helped cloud her growing fear from her charge.

Missing the worry starting to gnaw at the edges of the young woman's sanity, Delroney said, "I guess maybe I should start at the beginning. As you might know, I claim to have caught a leprechaun. It's true. I did. I was on a tour of Ireland with a group of friends from the school baseball team. It was a sort of graduation present to ourselves. Seeing how we won the state finals and all."

Dean listened with one ear as Delroney described his friends and their trip. When the tone of his voice announced that he was arriving at the meat of his story, however, her attention focused once more.

"Funny bunch—they were a funny bunch of guys. One

night they got me toasted in this town called Claremorris. When I passed out, they drove me about thirty miles out of town. Must have carried me for a couple more after that, because there were no roads where they dumped me." Delroney looked up, hoping to make Dean understand that he held no malice toward his friends.

"It was a joke—you know? A prank. I mean, if you think that was bad, I remember once . . ." So rapidly did the look on Delroney's face change to happiness that Dean was almost startled. The young man caught himself, however, and returned to the subject. Instantly his distracted, pained look returned as he said, "Well, anyway . . . it was my turn that night. They left me on the shores of some lake—figured I'd stumble around in the morning, find the road after a few hours, and then catch a ride back into Claremorris in the back of a sheep wagon. But that's not the way it worked. Something found me before I woke up." Dean's ears perked up at the mention of some*thing*.

"When I came to, I just couldn't open my eyes. I tried, but my head hurt too much even to groan. As I lay there, I began to realize I was on the ground—outside, I mean. I felt grass under my hands, my head, in my ears. I heard my own snoring and realized I was snoring so loud I'd woken myself up. Well, half-woken myself, anyway. Then . . . then I heard the voices."

How, wondered Dean, *how can he tell me this? How can he* believe *this?*

Delroney had not actually said anything unbelievable, but the look in his eyes showed where he was going, and the reflection of that destination somehow frightened the young woman.

"At first, I couldn't make any of it out at all. But, bit by bit, the more I listened, it all started to become clear. There were four or five different voices. They all belonged to tiny people who were . . . well, inspecting me. 'You saw them dump him,' one said. 'They left him. He's an offering. He's ours.' 'And who would want the great noisy beast?' asked another. 'The Talls don't make offerings to us anymore. They don't, they don't. He's just some poor fool what's been abandoned. We can take him if we want but he's not been bound over to us.'

"Well, I didn't know what all that meant then. But I did feel one of them climbing on my hand. I guess the way I was snoring, they all thought I was out cold. Anyway, being drunk and all, I didn't stop to think about the implications of what I was doing, I just grabbed. The next thing I knew, I had a handful of leprechaun."

"And that's how you caught a leprechaun?" asked Dean. relief flooding her voice. So simple, so easy—such a nothing little story. For a moment, she had the pleasure of believing that her growing apprehension had been silly. The moment passed, though, as Delroney told her,

"No. I mean, I didn't actually *catch* a leprechaun. I *killed* one." The young man swallowed hard, then continued, "You see, as soon as I grabbed the little guy, he bit me. Everyone that saw the wound said it was a squirrel bite—but, well ... anyway, the other ones disappeared instantly. The one that bit me, he took off straight for the lake behind them. But I was really mad—see? So, being a pitcher, it was just kinda natural for me to pick up a rock and throw it at him. I wasn't thinking, you see—I was just mad."

"And you hit him and killed him," filled in Dean. A dread she could not name oozing through her, she searched for a way to keep from having to believe the sincere storyteller. Seizing on a question she hoped would help shred his tale, she asked, "Then what happened to the body? Why didn't you bring it back with you?"

"Because," he answered, "before the little guy hit the ground the sky split. Lightning crashed all around me, the lake water boiled, and suddenly I was surrounded by hundreds, maybe thousands of the little guys. A lot of them were dressed in different shades of green, and some of them had red hair, but it wasn't like some cartoon—they came in all kinds of shapes and sizes—all still small, though, of course. Just a lot of pissed off little people all around me, that wanted my blood."

"So, what happened?"

" 'Come here, ye murderer,' " answered Delroney in dialect. "That was what their leader said to me. He called me forward and demanded I tell him where I learned of their secret meeting place. With a thousand little bows and spears pointed at me, I did what he said. I went forward. But I told him I didn't know where their secret place was, that I didn't even know where I was. Some of the other leprechauns backed me up, telling the head guy that I'd been dumped in the woods. He silenced them, though, saying that all Talls were treacherous, and that what my pals did could have been part of our plan to find their gold."

"Gold?" asked Dean—thoughts of her parents' desperate situation filling her head as they did whenever an image of wealth entered her brain. "You mean as in—at the end of the rainbow—a pot of gold?"

"Yes, exactly. The leader said that I had killed Bryan—that was the leprechaun I . . . hit—because I was after their treasure. Before I knew it, I was wearing chains woven out of grass. I know it sounds silly, but I couldn't break them. And so I stood trial for my crime in the moonlight. The leprechauns debated about me for what seemed like days. Then, finally, they decided it was time to release 'the challenge.' "

Delroney shook. He bit at his lip, palms of his hands pressed hard against his knees. Sitting in a sterile studio waiting room, far from any harm, Edward Delroney grasped desperately at control, fighting back the tears that always came eventually.

"I'll never forget that moment," he said, his voice straining against cracking. "The leader climbed up on my chest. Shaking his stick at me, he snarled, 'You Talls have had it your way too long. The stars is right now, and that makes it *our* turn.' Then, he touched my head and hissed, 'Go on! See the treasure you wanted. *See* it in your mind, you heathen bastard!'

"And I did. The image just appeared in my head. I saw a mighty cave with gold stacked to the ceiling. Gold in every form—coins and statues and jewelry. Ingots and scepters and crowns—barrels of it, mountains of it. So much I could barely comprehend it. But even though a part of me would have liked to have had it, I mean, of course, right? Most of me was still concerned about what I had done and what was going to happen and all. So . . .

well, the leprechauns said I was innocent. That I wasn't greedy, that I hadn't killed for their gold."

Dean marveled. Delroney's telling was so vivid, she could see the cave in her mind exactly as he described it. Down, she was sure, to the last strand of braided gold chain. And, she thought, that should have been the happy conclusion to the story, the part where everyone sat around and made friends. Even remembering what Delroney had already told her, Dean wished for calm, soothing words to come out of the old face on the tortured young man before her. She did not get them.

"Well, the head guy, he wasn't happy with the outcome. He started to rant about us Talls, and how we had taken so much without learning how to use it, driven the wee folk from their homes, and a lot of other stuff. Then, suddenly he whipped around, pointing his stick at me again. He cursed me, telling me that for the crime I had committed, I was sentenced to bring the challenge to mankind. I was to be forever compelled to tell the story of what happened to me that night . . . and that the consequences of each telling would be on my head. After that, they let me go—sent me along my way."

"And that's all there is to it?" asked Dean, knowing the answer already.

"No," admitted Delroney, turning his face away from the young woman. "I made my way back to Claremorris, got back to our rooms. My best friend, Danny Wrigley, he was the only one there. He asked me what all happened to me. And . . . and I told him."

Delroney went silent after that—his eyes lost in painful remembrance. Dean did not speak, not knowing what to say. She was lost in the hurt throbbing around the man before her, racking pain that came off him in waves. Without his speaking, she could tell the rest of his story. His friend had died—a heart attack, a stroke—something that would not seem out of the ordinary. The first to die. Then, Delroney's other two friends had returned, and he had told them everything, and they had died as well. The next pair.

"This challenge," asked Dean, holding her wavering voice steady. "What happens? I mean, you just told the

story to me. I'm still here. So, what happens? When does
it happen? When will I be safe? I mean . . ."

"Shhhhhhhhhhh," Delroney had put his finger to his
lips. "You're safe. I mean, you saw the gold, didn't you?"

And then Dean realized—the vision in her head of the
elven cave filled with lost treasure—had it really been the
power of the storyteller, or had it been the leprechaun
curse that had put the scene within her head? The young
woman gagged, trying to make words form within her
throat. She had so many questions—so many tangled bits
of thought crashing together in the center of her brain—
that she could not focus on anything.

And then suddenly, Mike Driscoll, the floor manager,
stuck his head in, saying, "Show time, Mr. Delroney. You
ready to tell the world about leprechauns?"

Delroney looked into Lora's blue eyes, felt lost in them
for an eternal second. Calm filling his tortured breast, he
nodded, saying, "Yes, I think so. Yes. Yes."

Lora stayed in her seat as Delroney stood. Her ability to
not desire the vision of gold had filled him with the confidence to move—now he could go out, confident that there
were more good people in the world than bad ones. That
he could give into the driving compulsion pressing
against his skull this one last time and prove once and for
all that humanity's place on the planet was justified.

As for Dean, she had done her job. There was nothing
more for her to do. As the door swung shut, cutting the
young woman off from anything but her current nine-by-
twelve reality, she suddenly felt compelled to go over
everything she had just heard. It crashed against her,
coming in repeated waves, a jumbled mix she simply
could not comprehend fast enough to catch hold of it.
Delroney's words flashed in and out of her head, stealing
her breath, paralyzing her.

*I'm not sure I should be here, I mean, it's such a
gamble, such a risk. What if I'm wrong? What if we're
not ready . . . as a race, I mean?*

　Selfless people who hear my story just hear a story
　It does help turn the tide, but they aren't aware of it
　And greedy people die
　More of them

Every time
In geometric progression
Two
Four
Then sixteen
Then . . .

Oh, God, thought Lora, her heart suddenly missing a beat. *Oh, God!*

Whenever I guess wrong and tell my tale to a greedy person, the curse that kills them stretches out beyond them to the next greedy person it can find

And then the next
And the next
Et cetera
Come here, ye murderer
Time to release the challenge
See the treasure you wanted. See it in your mind

And she had—all of it. A cavern that went on forever, stacked high with gold in every form— a world of gold, so much that a thousandth of it was beyond her comprehension.

Sentenced to bring the challenge to mankind
Forever compelled to tell the story of what happened that night
You're safe

Still, the chance to be done—once everyone had heard, once everyone had been challenged . . . I mean, once it spreads out to everyone, I'll be free. Won't I?

You saw the gold, didn't you?

And then, Lora realized the true scope of what was about to happen. Delroney, tortured by his curse— whether it was all just in his head or not, was about to go on live television and tell his tale to the world.

Lora leaped to her feet. She slipped in her haste, crashing down on one knee. As the pain shot through her, she dragged herself back to her feet. Limping painfully, different levels of her brain debated with her—

Just a nut
All in his head
Could it be real? Leprechauns? Mountains of gold?

Tears welled in Lora's eyes. The pain in her knee

throbbed, threatening to collapse her, spill her back across the floor.

Can't take this kind of stuff seriously
See people like him every week
But what if he's different? What if he's the one who's not crazy?

Desperately the young woman lunged for the door. She wanted to scream, but could not think of any words. What could she scream? What could she do—yell to everyone, Don't be greedy. Whatever you do, don't desire a mountain of gold.

Her fingers grabbed hold of the doorknob, seemingly as if in slow motion. She tore at it in desperation, frantic to reach the studio.

How long did I sit there? How far could he have gotten?

Far enough. Through the glass of the main telecast area, Lora could see that Richards had already turned his back on his guest, making his previously prepared comments to the camera. People turned to stare at Lora. The usually unflappable, beautiful young woman looked like a wild person. Her face flushed, hair disarrayed, eyes bulging.

Just another idiot, she thought, leaning against the wall to relieve the pressure on her knee. *Just another one of the usual crowd. God, you'd think I'd learn.*

And then, just as she began to smile, chuckling over what a fool she'd almost made of herself, Mike Driscoll— only a yard away from her—dropped his clipboard. As the falling piece of pressboard clattered against the studio floor, Lora screamed and Mike followed his roster, clutching at his chest. She saw Richards topple forward as well, slamming head first into the number two camera.

While, all around the world, glasses were dropped, planes fell from the sky, and babies went hungry.

And, near a distant lake, a mighty stone was rolled aside and little footsteps echoed, ready to reclaim a lost world.

JINGLES THE ELF

by *Richard Gilliam*

Richard Gilliam's stories have appeared in such diverse anthologies as Esther Friesner's tabloid magazine *Alien Pregnant by Elvis* and Fred Olen Ray's pulp magazine revival *Weird Menace*. His nonfiction writing includes the magazines *Sports Illustrated* and *Heavy Metal,* and the motion picture trivia section of a CD-ROM project for the Sci-Fi Channel. He has also edited such anthologies as *Tales from the Great Turtle* and *Phantoms of the Night*.

To say that the fine leather pack that Jingles found was the start of his difficulties or those of the wizard Mandor would be to unjustly place the blame upon the pack. Jingles, alas, was frequently the source of his own difficulties, while Mandor was a wizard who seldom made allowance for the inconveniences caused to him by the petty and the inconsiderate. No, I will say that it was Jingles with whom this tale begins, though I will also say that the pack was responsible for its own intemperate actions and that Mandor might well have found it in his best interest to help better prevent the unfortunateness that came to occur.

Had Jingles had an honest profession, he might not have been so bored as he was more mornings than not. Not that Jingles had not tried a profession. Indeed he had tried several, but it was not the nature of Jingles to tinker with things or to sit on a hill and tend the fairy sheep or to do any of the many other things that the wee folk do to make their lives and the lives of their kin easier. Fortunately for Jingles there are few of the magical peoples who are so generous as are elves of Eindhoven when it comes to sharing food and shelter with those who have none, and it should be said that Jingles himself was a pleasant enough fellow whose clever wit and roguish charm seldom failed to entertain those who invited him to the dinner table.

Mandor, as is the case with many persons learned in the arts of enchantment, was neither cruel nor compassionate, for cruelty and compassion are conditions for which a concern with the affairs of others is a prerequisite. Mandor's overdominant concern was Mandor. He cared not for the world except that it turned every day and provided him with a place where he could live in the manner most pleasing to himself. Moreover, he was careless in his magic, which is to say that while he was a skilled and precise conjurer, Mandor thought little more than about his efforts' most immediate effects.

A bored elf is a danger to all, particularly a well-fed bored elf, for at least there is a chance that a hungry elf will find some constructive endeavor rather than indulge in the mischief that has been the bane of elfdom for longer than any of the wee folk can remember. And thus it was that on a bright, sunny morning while the more industrious elves tended to their chores that Jingles came to be walking in the forest Glenallan. I will not take time to remind you of the long history of the wee folk and their adventures in the forest Glenallan, or of the enchantment placed there that granted life to all things not born directly from nature. Jingles knew better than to wander through the forest Glenallan. All elves know better than to wander through the forest Glenallan, but Jingles was a well-fed elf who was bored, and of the many things that can be said about the forest Glenallan, few have ever described their visits there as boring.

The new-risen sun had not yet reached more than a quarter of the way toward its midday zenith when Jingles heard a muffled giggle coming from a dense copse of small bushes at the western edge of the clearing where he had stopped to rest. The clearing was itself noteworthy, with many ancient stones some of which bore carved writing and others of which were shaped into the semblance of animals not seen in their living form by any person of the wee folk since long before the founding of Eindhoven.

Jingles took little interest in the stones. Indeed, if he had, his boredom would likely have been relieved by an altogether different adventure. Such arcane refuse might well have drawn the attention of some other elf more accustomed to effortful thinking, but such was not the way of Jingles, who was far more attracted to laughter than he was mindful of the forest's legends.

As Jingles approached the sound, he came to notice what he first thought to be yet another of the rocks which lay strewn throughout the area, but which on closer view appeared to be a container of some sorts, though the cloth which covered it was of a strength and smoothness unfamiliar to Jingles. Of Jingles' virtues, hasty curiosity was a frequent victor over caution and judgment, and thus it was scant moments before Jingles had crossed the meadow and began opening the strange find.

The metal clasp which held the straps of the carton startled Jingles, for not that Jingles' nimble fingers had any difficulty in opening the clasp, but that metal should be used for such a trivial need when strong string or well-cut leather would easily have sufficed. Inside was what Jingles estimated small treasure, four bottles of wine, some crackers and a large round of cheese. For an elf accustomed to living off the generosity of others, this was a significant moment and Jingles busily strapped the pack onto his shoulders, thinking of how pleased farmer Jones would be when he brought both cheese and wine to share at this night's meal. Jingles had thus far been careful not to show too much interest in Matilde, his host's daughter and only child, but now with items of value to display he could perhaps look for an opportunity to elevate himself from guest to suitor.

Despite bearing the additional weight of the pack, Jingles' journey out of the forest seemed much quicker than his journey inward, for such is the nature of time that it passes much faster for a bored elf after an activity of interest has been found. And what an activity it was, daydreaming and planning his rise to be a gentleman of property, first through the courting of Matilde, and then through the cultivation of the verdant acreage that Jingles was quite certain would be farmer Jones' wedding gift to his new son-in-law.

But Jingles, while well accustomed to daydreaming, was not so accustomed for having a potential means for implementing such a plan. He began to think of what embarrassment might occur on the fifth night that he arrived to court the fair Matilde, the night after the night when his fourth and final bottle of wine had been shared with farmer Jones. Jingles had observed that the elves from Gnisnal often came to Eindhoven to purchase wine, leaving him to believe that perhaps he could sell his wine at Gnisnal for a sufficient premium to allow him to purchase five or perhaps six bottles from the vats of Eindhoven. And so, as it is a trait of elves to be able to reckon directions from the positions of the skies, Jingles took the measure of the sun and headed westward toward Gnisnal.

Meanwhile, Mandor had left his island home, journeying forth on his twice annual purchasing trip for supplies. This was no simple market excursion, for worm's root could only be purchased in Gravensmore, and beetle dung was generally difficult to find outside of the marsh cities, not to mention that the quality of moldspore had been disappointing his last two trips, leading Mandor to believe it likely that he would have to travel as far as the lesser lakes to complete his needs. With the summer solstice but four weeks hence Mandor would need the smoothest of journeys. Otherwise, he would be unable to keep promises to his several clients, all of whom had prepaid for his services, and each of whose patronage was needed lest Mandor be forced by economic circumstance to become a town wizard, that lowest rank to which a member of the conjuring profession can descend.

Mandor had stopped in the village Elbe, unexpectedly finding a very fine badge of transcription and purchasing it most eagerly, though badges, even ones of such unusual capabilities, were not the purpose for this journey. The forest Glenallan lay between Mandor and his next stop, which was the marsh cities, and while Mandor certainly had the expertise to prepare sufficient wards to allow him to cross the forest safely, he nonetheless decided that it would be faster to take the Circle road that connected the cities separated by the dangerous woodland.

While it may seem ungainly that any wizard of significant repute would travel by cart and ox, such was the practice of Mandor, who had found that itinerant merchants were generally given the benefit of the haggle far more often than were adepts of the ninth realm. Prices were always higher around the time of a solstice, fresh ingredients being at a premium and magic being in high demand. No need to flaunt one's status—peers would recognize such a traveler no matter what garb the wizard wore, while the unsanctioned citizenry could potentially be a danger should they chance to learn too little about too much.

Gnisnal lay westernmost among the towns surrounding the forest Glenallan, its people somewhat rougher and hardier than their more genteel cousins to the east. Though in recent years trade with the frontier lands had greatly increased, the merchants guild of Gnisnal steadfastly had blocked all outsiders who attempted to profit from it, establishing a series of burdensome permit fees and foreign commerce taxes so as to make unprofitable any new business which attempted to open there. Mandor seldom stopped in Gnisnal during any of his travels—once to fix a broken wheel and another time to visit a client—but for the most part he found the people of Gnisnal unpleasant and their goods both inferior and overpriced.

Jingles, it should be said, was having not so good a go of it, at first not noticing the prickly underbrush that grew thicker as he traveled, nor paying much attention to the meepish "ouch" that occasionally could be heard from the vicinity of his person. He emerged from the brush into a deep cluster of tall trees whose many branches and leaves blocked his view of the sky altogether. Jingles was hungry, for though elves are small, unlike some of the large peoples, they must eat frequently since little food can be stored within their diminutive frames or in the interior of their narrow stomachs.

The round of cheese would easily have satisfied Jingles' hunger many times over, but he thought better than to nibble on it, lest it be spoiled for sale at market. Instead he decided upon the crackers, taking perhaps more than he should, but nonetheless leaving a sufficient number for eating during his journey back to Eindhoven.

The scrapes and scratches on Jingles' legs and arms were more annoying than painful. He was not willing to declare himself lost, but neither was he willing to go back into the thick underbrush that had preceded his entrance into the tall grove. Had Jingles been more inclined toward thinking, he might have noticed that the pack that he carried bore no scratches at all, though his shirt and his shoes had each sustained newly made marks of rending. There was little to do but travel forward, with forward being defined as toward the opposite from which Jingles had come.

Few elves have ever been so happy as to see the inner edges of the Circle road as was Jingles when he emerged from the tall grove and exited the forest Glenallan. He was a bit south of Gnisnal, he reckoned, looking at the sun which sat only slightly more westward than when he had last glimpsed it. There would still be time to finish his business in Gnisnal and travel back to Eindhoven before farmer Jones and his family began their evening meal, particularly since no farmer worthy of his land would ever stop work this time of year until well after the last of the day's light had fled from the skies.

The market of Gnisnal was at the center of town, with shops and booths lining either side of the Circle road. Many a traveler had complained of the congestion this causes, because like Mandor, the folk of the land much preferred to take their business to friendlier cities. Indeed, if it were not for trade with the frontier territories, Gnisnal would be just another foul-tempered town, long ago overtaken by ruffians and their ilk.

Having arrived in Gnisnal, Jingles was not quite sure to which person it would be best to sell his wine. He knew none of the elves of Gnisnal who frequented the wine merchants of Eindhoven. His best tack, he thought, might be to offer his find to one of the merchants here rather than waste the afternoon trying to squeeze a little more price, while at the same time adding to the risk that he would not be able to return to Eindhoven this evening in time to begin his plan.

Jingles had wandered to near the northern end of the commerce area when at last he spotted a merchant's stand that had Eindhoven bottles for sale.

"Good sir," said Jingles. "I am Jingles of Eindhoven and I have for sale four bottles of exceptional wine that I should rather not have to carry with me for my homeward return."

The merchant gave no sign of particular interest, but nodded which Jingles took as an indication to hand him the bottles.

"An unremarkable vintage," said the shopkeeper. "From North Callahan. I had hoped you had brought Eindhoven wine to sell."

Jingles was crestfallen, for never had he thought to consider that his wine might prove inferior to that which the people of Eindhoven were accustomed.

"I'll give you two bottles of Murg, or one of Eindhoven for the lot," said the shopkeeper, his face a studied exercise in disdain.

Jingles sighed and shook his head no, taking his bottles and replacing them in his pack. If he could not raise enough goods to court the fair Matilde, then at least he had four bottles of wine to comfort his disappointment. Waving the shopkeeper only the slightest acknowledgment of good-bye, he turned and stepped back toward the road.

"You crooked slob, you know these bottles are worth more than your entire shop combined! You should be forced to drink swamp bilge for a year and then see if both your honesty and your taste in wines improve."

The voice startled Jingles, for he had not spoken the words, but he had little time for pondering when the shopkeeper charged toward him, spiked club in hand. Jingles darted in front of a carriage, and then behind a handbarrow, tripping upon the latter and coming to rest just short of the wooden wheels of what he judged to be the most immense ox-cart he had encountered thus far in his young, and perhaps not destined to be lengthy, life.

"Whoa!" came the cry of the driver, as Jingles heard

the click of the brakestock struggling to immobilize
the axle. His pack, which had fallen from his back,
lay wedged and crushed beneath the wheel, his life having been saved only by its stopping of the wheel's
momentum.

Mandor cared little about the elf that was in his way,
and was far more interested in the vibrations he was
feeling from the item that rested under the left front wheel
of his cart. Stepping down from his seat, Mandor glared
toward the elf.

"That pack, I would have it," said Mandor, never one to
delay himself with the courtesies common to most people.
"Quick, the traffic behind us is blocked, and I would be
out of this town before we attract attention. Two gold
shirepieces and a silver quarter. That is a fortnight's
wages for most such as yourself."

Despite a feeling of general uncertainty, generated in
about equal parts by his near death experience and the
towering presence of Mandor, such economics were not
lost on Jingles. The silver quarter alone would purchase
six bottles of Eindhoven wine, with more than enough
coppers left over for cheese and crackers. Perhaps he
could still court Matilde, and purchase a new suit of
clothes to enhance the process.

"Done," said Jingles, thinking that he would have to be
careful on his homeward travels with such coin in his
pocket.

"You've made yourself a good buy there, wizard," said
the pack as Mandor loaded it into the cart."

"Yes, I know," he whispered, "but let's talk about that
after we're out of this town. These yokels could prove
inconvenient if they thought there was a profit to be made
by detaining us."

Jingles saw a tall man dressed in blue approaching at a
rapid pace. He did not like the size of the club in his hand,
or the sneer on his face, but neither did he think himself
likely to be able to successfully run away.

"Unlicensed trading," said the man, his club held just
in front of Jingles' face. "Luckily the wine merchant
you insulted alerted us to your illegal activities. The fine
for that is five gold shirepieces. Or if you don't have

that, we'll confiscate your property and banish you from the town.

Mandor grumbled, but quickly handed the constable the fine, climbing back into the cart and proceeding out of town before more trouble could occur.

"Still a bargain," chuckled the pack, the lurch of the wheels covering the sound so that only Mandor could hear the comment. "The elf didn't seem like such a bad sort, but wow is he in for a surprise when he heads home."

Mandor looked to the rear and saw that the elf and his newfound money had been quickly separated. The pack was a most fortuitous find, and there was ample time before reaching the marsh cities to begin learning its secrets.

Jingles, to his credit, did not cry, though he was exceedingly forlorn as he began his journey north. He now had less than he had begun the morning with, his clothes so tattered that he would be humiliated to be seen by Matilde or any of the other maidens of Eindhoven.

"It's your fault we're so torn," said the shirt, startling Jingles out of what little composure he had remaining.

"Yeah," said his shoes. "First you take us into the forest, and then you mistreat us as soon as we become aware enough to understand that you don't have enough sense to avoid a scratchberry patch."

"If you want Matilde so much, you might think about asking her father if you could help with his chores," said the pants, barely attempting to disguise the contempt in his voice. "This rip in my seat makes me drafty, and since you got no more clothes in this world, you might as well get used to having company. . . ."

IMAGES OF SMOKE

by John Goodnow

John Goodnow lives in Iowa City, Iowa where he writes his own style of strong, quirky fiction. He is a competitive fencer, an inveterate gamer, and known as "the Father of Shurikendo." This is his first fiction sale.

"Is it the gods who put this fire in our minds, or is it that each man's relentless longing becomes a god to him?"

—Virgil

"Halloween is a safety valve for the psyche," the lay psychologist in the cheesy devil suit said to the clown. "Or it used to be. Nowadays, instead of giving our dark side a little room to breathe, people send their children out dressed as E.T. or Big Bird to collect candy. The kids don't even get to play tricks anymore. Society has sanitized the holiday."

"Oh, come on, Nick," retorted the clown. "The kids have a good time; it's all fun and games for them, and they are too young to worry about their 'dark side.'"

"If it's all fun and games," Nick answered, "then why do the parents have to check all the candy to keep someone from poisoning the children?"

The clown was caught without a ready reply, and Robert O'Keefe left them to refill his drink. He made his way through the costumed crowd to where the host presided over a steaming cauldron of mulled cider. He mouthed some pleasantries to the valkyrie who served him, then sauntered outside, where a large bonfire presided over the festivities like a palsied priest. A group of partygoers had linked hands and were dancing widdershins around the fire, which was moving to a tune of its own choosing.

For a moment, Robert felt like joining the dancers. Then he remembered that they were like all the other people at the party: people whose dreams were vague, amorphous shadows, whose goals were unfinished paintings, and whose spirits burned with the feeble glow of cigarettes, giving off more smoke than light.

He walked around the bonfire at a distance, watching the dancers, who imitated the ancient celebration of Samhain without knowing how or why, and he considered how his own life was a dance performed to music no one else heard. Not for the first time did he wish with a quiet yearning that he could find just one person to share his dance, or even to acknowledge the music.

A breeze scuttled out from the murky trees; the bonfire gestured wildly and poured smoke onto the dancers, who ran away with tear-blinded eyes. One woman ran straight at Robert, who had watched with a detached amusement and now stood frozen in the grasp of some ineffable emotion, waiting for the imminent collision. At the last possible moment (or perhaps beyond it), the woman stopped, and rubbed her eyes vigorously with her palms, as if banishing a long and dream-troubled sleep. Then she lowered her hands and looked at him, and Robert knew that she was one whose spirit burned with all the brilliance of the bonfire.

They stood thus for a dozen heartbeats, which, given Robert's emotional state, was barely long enough for him to notice that the woman's costume consisted solely of a long green summer dress and soft silver-green slippers. She smiled, a quivering, shy smile, yet even so it was clear her long, fine-featured face had been created to smile, to express the joys of life.

"Who are you?" she asked. Her voice held the shadow of some accent Robert could not recognize, but which made his scalp tingle.

He smiled at her, drew his black rune-patterned cloak more closely about him, and stated very severely, "I am the archimage O'Keefe; I command the powers of wind and water." He flourished a wooden wand. "What would

you have me do? Open the fairy mounds so we can pay
our respects to the elves?"

No sooner had he spoken than the young woman
blanched; she shivered as if a snake had slithered over her
feet, and the tentative smile fled her face, replaced by an
expression of helpless fear. Her reaction took him by surprise. He wanted to apologize for whatever it was that
now gave her the appearance of one haunted, hunted by a
fate that killed all hope of happiness. He felt a sudden
urge to do something, anything, that would cause her to
forget her fear, bring the strength of joy again to her.

The awkward tableau was shattered by the elements.
Winds roared around them; spectral shadows flew from
darkness to deeper darkness; rains fell from a suddenly
overcast sky. Robert took the woman by the hand, and
they ran to his car, which was much closer than the house.
He had driven a half-mile toward town before it occurred
to him that she might have had her own car, or been with
someone else. He stopped the car, as he realized that it
would have been more logical to have gone back to the
house, where the party was still going strong. He felt as
though some instinctive impulse had taken over, forcing
him to leave the scene of the party, as though fleeing
some unseen terror. A quick glance showed him the
woman was still shivering; she appeared to be in a state of
shock.

"Uhm . . . do you live around here?" Robert inquired,
trying to draw her out of her strained silence. She shook
her head, brushed wet hair from her face.

"Are you staying with friends?" This received the same
reply as his initial attempt. O'Keefe looked at the woman,
whose rain-straightened auburn hair dripped water onto
the car seat. He sighed and wondering why he bothered,
("You know why," a little voice whispered), tried one
more time.

"Would you like to go back to the party?"

The woman jumped as if he had stuck her with a
cattle prod.

"No!" she shouted; then, finally showing an awareness
of her surroundings, she smiled nervously and smoothed
back her wet hair with both hands.

"I'm sorry," she said. "I didn't mean to shout. It's just that, well . . . I, uh, I would rather not go back there now."

The sky seemed slightly brighter. The windshield wipers squealed across the now-dry windshield. Robert turned them off.

"That was a very strange storm," he remarked, noticing that his fingers tingled and his forehead was cold. They stared at each other, and Robert tried to think of some way to say what was on his mind without making it sound like a common pickup. She saved him the trouble.

"Look," she said, "could we go someplace where we can dry off?" Robert smiled, nodded, and quickly drove her to his apartment.

They warmed themselves before the old stone fireplace in the living room of Robert's second-story apartment, and while the fire dispeled the chill, Robert discovered that his guest's name was Leslie, (she skated like Peggy Fleming around the question of a last name), and that she looked great in jeans and an old flannel shirt.

"Men's clothes are so comfortable; I could wear them all the time," Leslie said. "Even though they don't flatter me."

O'Keefe smiled wryly. "I was just thinking how good you look in men's clothes."

They both laughed, a little nervously, and to fill the ensuing silence Robert poured more brandy.

"What do you do for a living?" Leslie asked.

O'Keefe looked at his guest, wishing, first that she was more than a guest and, second, that he could give as an answer some exciting, romantic, impressive occupation.

"I'm a research assistant with the University News Service."

"That sounds like a very interesting job." Leslie tucked her legs up on the couch and began curling a strand of hair around her finger. "What sort of research do you do?"

Leslie was an expert in the fine art of listening, and despite the fact that his curiosity burned to find out more about her, she managed, with timely questions and the magic in her lustrous brown eyes, to keep him talking about himself for what seemed like hours. She took him on a trip back across the years, back to a time when dreams had life, before he had relegated them to the back pages of insignificant periodicals.

When she excused herself to go to the bathroom, Robert was burning with shame that he had lost so much of himself, that Time had peeled away his character like layers of an onion, until he was left with a core that was barely recognizable, even to himself. At the same time, he felt hope stir within, awakening ravenous from an unnaturally long hibernation.

He glanced at his watch as Leslie returned to her seat by the fire; it was almost midnight, and he was suddenly afraid. *Don't leave me,* he thought desperately. All the magic he had ever sought in life was encompassed in her slight frame.

He wanted to tell her that, but Time's scour had eroded his confidence to believe in magic, and he hesitated.

"Well, now that you've been subjected to the life story of Robert O'Keefe, how about reciprocating?"

Leslie smiled, with a warmth that matched the fire. "I'd like to, but it's a very long story." Robert was about to encourage her when she put a hand to her mouth to stifle a yawn.

"I don't think I could get through it tonight." She put her glass down and looked at Robert; the firelight danced in her hair and shadows caressed her face. A sudden chill crept along Robert's neck, and he felt that if only he could find the right words (or the courage to say them, his little voice whispered), he might finally grasp what had always slipped through his fingers like smoke. After a moment, Leslie dropped her eyes.

"Robert, I, uhm . . . I don't have a place to stay tonight." Her lovely voice, with its uncanny accent, wavered a little.

Robert reached out, put his hand on hers. His fingers tingled.

"Yes, you do." Embarrassed by the catch in his voice, he stood abruptly, and took the empty brandy glasses to the kitchen.

"You can take the bed," he called from the kitchen. "I'll sleep on the couch." She protested strongly, but he took some extra blankets back to the sofa and pulled off his boots.

"Go on, take the bed. It's not often I'm so gallant," he lied.

It was not much later that the melodies of tiny silver bells stirred him from one of the half-dreams, half-visions that periodically preceded his sleep. Fingers, reaching softly through darkness, brushed his shoulder, slid down to rest on his hand. Their hands clasped tightly, as though daring anyone to part them, then she came into his arms. Later, just as he was drifting off to sleep, she whispered, "I heard you calling for me."

Something woke him. It wasn't the sunlight streaming through the south windows, nor the birds singing with unseasonable vigor. It was the realization that his body's time clock was telling him it was past time to punch in. Groaning, he sat up and blinked his eyes, focusing on the ashes in the fireplace. Memory of the night pounced like a playful kitten, pushing aside all thoughts of work. The bedroom door was ajar; he walked over and looked inside.

There was no one in the bedroom, nor in the bathroom. There was no sign of Leslie at all. Robert sat down on the bed, wearily wondering if he had dreamed it all. Rejection of that thought came immediately, not only because he wanted so much for it to be real. but also because he was an intensely pragmatic person who believed in the reality of his perceptions.

A quick search revealed Leslie's dress hanging in his closet. It was made of some thin, satiny material, and looked so fragile in the morning light he was afraid to touch it. He shook his head and wondered dully where she had gone, why she had left so silently. The nine o'clock whistle shook him out of his reverie, and he hurriedly got ready for work. On his way out, he wrote a note for Leslie, giving his phone number at the office, and left it taped to his door.

O'Keefe had never been a clock-watcher, but on this day his eyes darted anxiously between the wall clock and his telephone. The echoes of the five o'clock whistle had not died when he was out of the office and sprinting for his car. All the way back to his apartment his little voice kept whispering "She's not going to be there," but his heart was pounding as he parked and ran up the steps to his rooms.

No Leslie. No note, not a sign that she had returned. O'Keefe ran down the steps and knocked on the door to the first floor apartment.

"Hi, Rita," he greeted the short brunette who opened the door.

"Hi, Bob." She wiped pastel chalk from her hands. "Come on in. Joe just stepped out for some pizza."

"Thanks, but I'm in a hurry. I was just wondering if you'd seen a young woman around the house today. She's about medium height, with long auburn hair."

Rita shook her head; strands of hair fell from the red bandanna that held it in place.

"No, I haven't seen anyone here. But I was gone this morning teaching. Joe was around then, but he was out taking pictures part of the time. Why don't you wait and ask him?"

"No, uh, thanks, but I've got to go. I'll check back later with him." Feeling very awkward, O'Keefe left quickly, before Rita could ask any questions.

He drove out to see Steve and Val, who had hosted the annual Halloween party and always knew everyone by name. Surely they could tell him about Leslie. ("Are you sure you really want to know?" his little voice asked him.) But something deeper than that little voice drove him, urging him to hurry, before . . . what? O'Keefe did not know.

"Well, hello Robert." Val, the red-headed valkyrie of the night before, greeted O'Keefe.

"The mulled cider's all gone, but I've got tea in the pot. Come on in and have some."

O'Keefe gratefully accepted the offer, and before he knew it, he was pouring out his story while he sat with Steve and Val at the kitchen table.

"No, I don't know anyone named Leslie. The description doesn't ring any bells." Val glanced at Steve; he shrugged.

"What costume did you say she wore?" Steve asked.

"A light green summer dress. It was very soft, silky. Not really a costume, I guess. It's still at my apartment."

"Robert!" Val exclaimed. "You devil!" She smiled wickedly. O'Keefe blushed, and hated himself for it.

"Look," he said after a moment. "It just doesn't seem right. She left her dress at my place, took my clothes and left without a word. Why would she do that?" He looked from one to the other beseechingly. "I want to find her." O'Keefe, frustrated, stopped and looked down at his steaming mug.

"We'll help if we can, Bob," Steve said. "You know, strange things have been known to happen around here on Halloween," he added, smiling impishly. Val gave him a withering look.

"Well, it's true," Steve persisted gamely. "Val, you remember last Halloween. That big black cat ran out from the cemetery in back of our place, raced around the bonfire three times and jumped right in it. Needless to say, there was no trace of it afterward."

Val clucked her tongue at her husband. "In the first place, you don't know that the cat came from the cemetery. I remember it as being black and white, and in all likelihood the cat ran off into the darkness unseen. A cat would not jump into a fire."

Steve just shrugged. "That's the way I remember it. Anyway, what would you expect when we have a cemetery on one side and a witch on the other side?"

"A witch?"

"Sally Reardon is not a witch," Val countered. "She is a lovely lady who likes to tell stories and read the cards."

"Say," Steve snapped his fingers. "Didn't she have someone visiting: a niece, or granddaughter?"

"Her niece. Well, I suppose . . . hell, let's go see."

Sally Reardon's house was a quaint little cottage built of stone. The stones looked as though they had been stacked together in a slapdash fashion that would tumble to the ground if you leaned on them. While the outside did look like a witch's dwelling, the inside was reassuringly mundane. Bricabrac-lined shelves, lace tablecloth, bentwood rocker, the interior reminded Robert of his grandmother's apartment.

And Sally Reardon reminded him of . . . he wasn't sure. She was dressed in a bulky knit sweater and jeans, and her reddish-gray hair was tied back in a scarf. She seemed to fit right in with the house's interior, but there was a certain half-hidden pixy light in her gray eyes that hinted at things far from mundane.

After introductions had been made, and they were all seated in the tiny living room, Sally winked at Val and turned to Steve.

"So, you've brought around another one of your friends to see the witch."

Steve grinned sheepishly, but countered, "You bring it on yourself, Sally, with all your talk of your fey Irish blood, and your tales of the 'little people' as though they really existed."

"That does not make me a witch, young man; only exceptionally wise." She grinned as if at some private joke. "Now, then, what might I help you with?"

"We're trying to find someone," Val answered, "and we wondered if it might be your niece. Did she by chance visit our party last night?"

"Susie? No, she left yesterday morning. Why did you think it was her?"

Robert told her what had happened, and found that although she was noted as a storyteller, Sally Reardon was an excellent listener. Her youthful eyes were intent on him throughout his rendition of the events leading to his visit to her home.

When he finished, Sally sat very quietly for a moment, still staring at O'Keefe.

"Let's try something," she stated, then stood and walked over to the cupboard and took out a small box.

"Come, sit down at the table." She opened the ornately carved box when they were seated and took out a deck of cards. They looked like tarot cards, but were hand-painted in an antique style that was soothing to the eye.

"Pick the card that most reminds you of Leslie," Sally instructed, handing the deck to Robert. He sorted through the strange cards, and finally chose one.

"Hmm," Sally studied the card, which depicted a young woman dressed in a long white gown, seated on a grassy knoll, with a book in her lap.

"It doesn't really look like her," Robert explained. "But I had a certain feeling when I saw the card." He shrugged. "It just felt right."

"That's the way it should be," Sally answered. "Now, we shall see what we will see." She placed the card on the table, then shuffled the rest of the cards and rapidly dealt them in a pattern around the first card.

She studied the cards for what seemed to Robert a long time. O'Keefe glanced at the cards, but staring at them made his head spin. Briefly he saw a crescent moon, swords, a rustic tower surrounded by marshy woods, a knight, and something his mind refused to picture. Then the woman scooped up the cards and carefully deposited them in their box.

Afterimages from the cards flickered through Robert's mind for a few seconds, then he heard Sally say, "Those minxsome spirits must still be celebrating. The atmosphere is uncertain; I couldn't read anything in the cards." She smiled easily, but Robert sensed a tension coiled like a snake between them.

Sally offered them tea, but they politely declined and left. Steve and Val apologized for being unable to help Robert, and reminded him of their next party.

O'Keefe drove home, disgusted with himself for getting carried away by some whimsical emotion and letting himself be embarrassed by some loony old lady who deluded herself with supernatural garbage. His little voice was painfully (or blessedly) silent. He vowed he would never again get involved with weirdos like Sally Reardon.

Two days later he recanted his vow. November had made its entrances with excessive bluster, and the work had piled up on O'Keefe's desk like an early blizzard, mostly news clippings and releases dealing with leftover Halloween oddities. When he got home that evening, Robert was exhausted and full of the bitter dregs of bottled-up emotions he tried to ignore. He had just thrown off his jacket and collapsed on the couch when the phone rang.

Robert jumped off the couch, then cursing himself, he answered the phone.

"Bob. This is Joe. I have some pictures down here I want you to see."

Robert was about to beg off when Joe added, "Rita told me about your visitor the other night. I really think you should see these pictures."

Almost against his will, Robert hurried down the steps and rapped on their door. Joe opened it and let him in, looking pale and a little afraid.

"What's wrong, Joe?" His friend steered him to a chair in the living room, next to a table where Joe had placed a pile of photos.

"Look at the pictures. Then you tell me."

Robert sat down and shuffled through the pictures. They were all scenes from the neighborhood, many from just outside the house. Although he marveled again at the way Joe managed to take sights one saw everyday and create works of art, Robert saw nothing strange in any of the shots. He looked questioningly at Joe.

"Look at them again, the ones taken outside the house. I'll get you a beer."

When he returned, Robert had set aside all but three of the pictures.

"These show a kind of fuzzy area, like a patch of fog, in the backyard." Joe nodded emphatically. "But there wasn't any fog that day, was there?"

"No, there wasn't," Joe replied a little too quickly. He was sitting on the edge of his chair, nearly shivering with nervous energy.

"But there was a man standing there."

"Huh? I don't see any man. Is it some kind of optical illusion?"

"Huh-uh. And it's no malfunction, nor faulty film or processing. I double-checked everything."

"Well, then, what the hell is it? Where is the man?"

"He's right there." Joe jabbed his finger at the three photos. "He just didn't show up on the film."

O'Keefe's weariness and bitterness, welled up too long, bubbled over at this.

"Go to hell, Joe. If this is some kind of joke, it is not funny."

Joe looked shocked. He wasn't expecting such a response from his friend.

"This is no joke, Bob. Look, I don't know what to make of this. I don't know if it has anything to do with your mysterious friend or not. But I thought you'd like to see it." He looked pained. "To be honest, I wanted to show you so you could reassure me that I'm not losing it."

O'Keefe took a deep breath, let it out slowly.

"I'm sorry, Joe. I've been in a lousy mood. If I could believe I haven't 'lost it,' maybe I could reassure you."

They sat quietly for awhile, drinking their beers.

"I'd like to see if I can find out anything about this," Robert said. "Could I take one of the pictures with me?"

"Sure. Take all three. I have the negatives in a safe place."

"Thanks. If I find out anything, I'll let you know."

Later that night, O'Keefe sat staring into the fire, pictures on his lap, phone by his elbow. His little voice was whispering to him, reminding him of all the things he had let go in his life, all the opportunities he had let slip through his fingers, the women who had slipped through his life like smoky wraiths, leaving behind no trace of their presence. Finally, he reached over and picked up the phone.

"Hello, Ms. Reardon? This is Robert O'Keefe. Could I come out and talk to you? Good. I'll be there in thirty minutes."

Sally Reardon stared at the pictures and listened to Robert's story. Then she turned her eerie gray eyes to his face, and asked calmly, "What would you like me to do?" Her expression was unreadable. Robert felt his neck getting warm.

"I want you to explain this to me. I'm sure it has something to do with Leslie's disappearance."

"Even supposing I could explain it to you, I doubt you'd believe. Besides, what makes you think I know anything?"

"Because you lied about your cards. You saw something

there; there is something you're trying to keep from me. Why?"

Sally sighed. "Because you're not one who would believe in what I would have to tell. And yet . . ." She took his chin in her strong, weathered hand and looked into his eyes. "And yet, the cards did point to you." She shook her head, the madonna smile returning to her face.

"Well, then, I should tell you what I know. Then it's up to you to believe in it."

She fetched her cards and returned to the table, beckoning him to join her.

"Listen to me carefully," she said, shuffling the cards absently in her hands. "Seven years ago, your Leslie stumbled onto something better left alone. She found one of the doors to the realm of the Sidh and she crossed over."

"What are the Sidh?"

"It's an old name for the fairies. Don't scoff, they are all around us. Just because you have never seen them doesn't mean they aren't there. Anyway, whether she did so out of loneliness, or boredom, or caprice, I cannot say. But when she entered their world, she disappeared from this world."

"Then why did she come back?" (His little voice might have told him, but he was listening to Sally.)

"Perhaps she was lonely, or bored. The Sidh offer no sure cure for those afflictions. I do know she should have reason to fear."

"To fear what?"

The wise woman muttered a blessing, then said, "The Dark Man. She heard his call seven years ago and went to him at Samhain: Halloween. But, like most self-indulgent young folk, she went looking for an ideal, "only to be confronted by what really is there."

"But if she was afraid of this creature, why did she wait seven years before leaving him?"

Sally Reardon laughed, bitterly, as if remembering a thing she would as soon forget.

"Like as not, she deluded herself with the image that the Dark Man was what she wanted. Such fey beings do have their charms. She let herself be blinded to the dangers."

"For seven years?"

"Time passes differently in that realm; you'd do well to remember that," Sally admonished.

"Well, what can I do?" Robert felt frustrated, unable to believe and unwilling to let go. He felt like a hound that had locked its jaws on something that held no known shape. "I mean, she did go back to him, didn't she? Or . . ." The reality began to creep upon him.

"He took her back? Against her will?"

Sally Reardon just nodded. She had dealt the cards and was reading them.

"Look." Her voice was commanding. She took hold of his hand. O'Keefe stared at the cards. They still made his head spin, but this time he didn't look away. There was an icy tingling inside his head, and he saw what had happened.

He saw, with some second sight, the Dark Man's approach. He seemed made of moonbeams and shadows, and he moved like quicksilver. Music moved with him: the glittering strains of some ghostly harp flowed around him, through him and into the house. It was the music that woke Leslie. Robert saw the look on her face as she became aware of her lover's presence. Fear, yearning, hope, fought with and fell to the obsessive resignation that moved her slowly to the door. As she passed the couch where O'Keefe lay asleep, she hesitated, torn between reality and the dream born of a rain-swept night, then, drawn on by the seduction of the harp, she left.

O'Keefe's vision blurred, but the music echoed maddeningly in his head, until his fists pounded the table and he cried, "Stop!" He opened his eyes, looked at his hands, still trembling with rage.

"You hypnotized me," he accused, not daring to look at Sally. "None of this is real. It's all a monstrous dream you're using to peddle your damned fortune telling."

Sally Reardon picked up her cards and calmly replied, "You know, in your heart, that's not true. I can help if you let me."

O'Keefe stood up so quickly the chair fell over. His

sight was clear now, but he still did not look directly at his host.

"I'll bet. For a few hundred bucks I'm sure you could foretell an eventful future for me. Well, I'm not buying. Good bye." He started for the door.

"Wait!" Sally cried out. "Listen, Mr. O'Keefe. When you decide what is real, what you truly want, I'm still willing to help. But remember this: Leslie's last chance to be freed is on the night of the winter solstice. If you can't release her from the Dark Man then, the doorway to our world will be closed to her forever. She'll be his for eternity." O'Keefe stormed out of her house, and drove home at reckless speed.

He walked through his darkened apartment to the kitchen, took the bottle of Scotch out of the cabinet and sat looking out the window. He tried not to think about Leslie and the Dark Man, but that seductive music kept returning, whispering to some thing buried in the crawl-spaces of his unconscious, inviting his anger.

After an hour or so, the Scotch silenced the music and smothered the rage, leaving him with an all-to-familiar loneliness.

The next morning he woke on the couch, and for a minute, in the muzziness of a hangover, it seemed that everything had been a dream. He might even have convinced himself of the deception, except for his little voice.

"Go check your closet," it whispered. He told himself, and his little voice, that there was a reasonable explanation for what had happened, and he said it with such vehemence that he deafened himself to the other thing the little voice was trying to say.

The next few weeks passed in a haze for Robert. Life went its round in a blur of shadows for him. He had searched all the old news files for any mention of a Leslie disappearing seven years ago, but he found nothing. After that attempt, his spare time was spent draining glasses of Scotch and wondering what had drained all the color out of his world. Even his little voice was silent.

His nights were filled with dark dreams. Time, and time, and time again, he would run through impossible mazes like a drugged rat, or fall into dank wells where the only one who could help him out was one he dared not call. Men and women of terrific aspect stalked misty forests, the stars whispered to him, he stood on moonlit promontories searching the horizons and waiting without hope. The dreams were confusing, depressing, disturbing, but they overshadowed his days.

One night in December, less than a week from Christmas, the deathly colorlessness and seasonal loneliness drove Robert to a drab little bar a short distance from the campus. He sat at the end of the bar and ordered his usual Scotch. The dreadful sameness of the place weighed on him. A slow look around the bar reinforced his melancholy. The fire he had always felt, that had marked him from within, seemed to be smoldering in a bed of ashes. He felt no different from those around him, who seemed to enjoy the drab atmosphere, but he felt no closer to them.

He stared into his drink, as if it held within its amber depths the key to his future, and anger stirred at his casual acceptance of the dreary way his life was taking. He was on the verge of some logical decision when he thought he heard someone call his name. Turning, he chanced to look in the mirror at the back of the bar. The man who looked back at him wore his face, but was dressed as the knight in Sally Reardon's card. Shaken, Robert forgot whatever decision he was about to make, drained his glass, and went home.

Later that night, just as he was on the edge of sleep, he heard faint music coming from Joe and Rita's apartment. It was one of their Celtic records, and it had a soothing effect. It eased Robert into sleep, but as he passed into that realm, the music changed, shifted to the strains of a harp that stirred the fury he had been running from in all those dreams. It sprang on him suddenly, and he changed. He was a ravening wolf, intent on destroying all the shadowy forms oppressing him.

Robert woke late that Saturday morning; dark clouds had done their best to hide the sun which usually woke him, but he woke quickly, as if from a dream that had just ended. He sat up and felt as if a valve had opened, releasing all the fears and inhibitions that had hounded him these past weeks. A new vitality poured forth, and he recalled the dream.

He was threatened by shadowy forms, their shapes vague but their evil very clear. They had captured others and were now after him. A great rage filled him, shaped him and moved him. He was a wolf, and his foes feared him. O'Keefe remembered stalking his prey, but no matter how hard he tried, he could not recall what came of the battle. Yet he felt the power inside, ready to be unleashed. There was another force he felt, and he knew that, regardless of logic and intellect, he wanted to find Leslie, and he knew only one way. He got dressed and drove out to see Sally Reardon.

The winter solstice was ushered in by the sounds of distant thunder, and found Robert O'Keefe sitting with his back against a headstone near the far end of the cemetery, watching a certain spot in the marsh very carefully. It was unseasonably warm, but rain had been falling steadily for an hour, and O'Keefe was chilled to the bone.

He should have felt miserable, for sitting in a graveyard in the middle of a soul-freezing rain, and for an inability to rationalize in any way what he was doing there. But he was warmed by the satisfaction of doing something that needs no intellectual justification, with which his little voice concurred.

A gust of wind blew the rain into his face, but the stuff Sally had put on his eyelids seemed to protect his eyes. She had told him, as she applied it, that it would allow him to see in the realm of the Sidh. He just hoped the rain wouldn't wash it off. The ring Sally had given him felt like ice on his finger. Protection, she had said, protection and control. He blinked his eyes, and then he saw it. A circle flickered into existence at the edge of the marsh, about five feet in diameter and marked by a greenish phosphorescence. He ran down the hill and without hesitation stepped into it. His vision blurred and immediately cleared, and the first thing he noticed was the tower. A cylinder of mottled grayish stone capped by a cone of thatch, it rose from the marsh, seeming to thrive on the decay.

As O'Keefe moved toward the strange causeway that linked the tower to dry ground he realized that the rain had stopped. Looking up, he saw a hazy twilight sky that he somehow knew was perpetual in this realm. He felt his sense of time sliding out from under him, threatening to leave him adrift, and it scared him and thrilled him. The tower beckoned to him; his yearning swept him along like a leaf on a stream, and he wasn't sure if this relentless longing was for love of Leslie or for something he could never find in his world.

Then the music began. The notes of the unseen harp reached out and enveloped him in their crystalline beauty, drawing him forward. O'Keefe stepped onto the path through the marsh, the music swirling around him, and his anger burned within him. Another step, and another, and he felt his rage like a wild thing struggling for freedom. The ring grew even colder, the chill spreading through his body, and he seemed to hear Sally's voice whispering, "Control." Just then, there arose in front of him a living wall of mud and branches, of the essence of the marsh, shaped somewhat like a gargantuan grizzly bear. It reached out for him. Robert took a deep breath and raised his arms, the ring seeming to be helping him on an unconscious level. He opened himself to everything around him, and shouted, "I am the archimage O'Keefe; I command the powers of wind and water." The icy sensations seemed to concentrate between his eyes, and a wild wind whipped into the marsh being, followed by torrents of water. The creature was swept away by the elemental forces, and the path was again clear.

Robert ran up the stairs, opened the tower door, and stepped across the threshold. The interior was very dim, lit only by flickering lights like will-o-the-wisps. The room was empty, with a stairway that led upward. Robert went up the steps as fast as he could, feeling the press of time. On the next level, he found Leslie, and the Dark Man. He was tall and thin, fair of hair and pale-skinned, with pointed ears and short curved horns sprouting from his forehead. Despite his appearance, Robert looked into eyes that glowed like coals and saw the darkness within, and he knew somehow that the Dark Man feared him. The

Dark Man stepped between Robert and Leslie, and laughing hideously, raised his arms and gestured with his fingers in some arcane motion. Fire roared, surrounding Robert, and panic and rage clutched at his heart. The flames drew closer, and the rage within burned to match the fire.

No words were spoken, but Robert could feel the Dark Man calling to him, telling him to let go, relinquish control, to become the power that the Dark Man feared. O'Keefe feared the loss of control almost as much as he feared the Dark Man's power over Leslie.

The flames burned hotter, closer, and just as Robert felt all self-control slipping away, his little voice whispered, "Follow the ring. The ring will show the way."

Just as the heat and the fury turned him inside out, releasing the wolf within, the ring turned impossibly hot, burning him to his very soul with some unbelievable energy. He became the wolf, but the uncontrollable rage that he had feared had turned to ice. The flames died as he stepped through them. He stalked slowly toward the Dark Man. The wolf, which had been dark in his dreams, now seemed to glow with some inner light. The brilliance caused the Dark Man to flinch, and he backed away from the wolf, who moved relentlessly toward him. The eyes of the wolf glowed like lanterns, and the light lanced into the Dark Man, who fell to the floor mewling in pain. The wolf stood over the Dark Man, and with a single bite snapped his neck.

Robert found himself standing before Leslie, and he put his arms around her. They embraced silently for a moment. Then Leslie was crying softly, whispering, "I didn't think you'd come," over and over. Robert cupped her face in his hands, looked into her eyes, and said, "I heard you calling for me."

Robert led the way back to the cemetery. Behind them, in the marsh, an owl hooted. They looked back, but the tower had vanished as if it had never been. They looked at each other, and Robert smiled.

"Do you live around here?" he asked with a gleam in his eyes, as the color returned to his world.

"Not anymore." Leslie answered his smile. Somewhere

a harp was playing the music that Robert had been following all his life, and the happiness he felt was in finally having someone to share it with.

"Let's go home."

MERCENARY OF DREAMS

by Lawrence C. Connolly

Lawrence C. Connolly's fiction has appeared in *Border-lands 3* and *4*, *Castle Fantastic*, *New Amazons*, *Twilight Zone Magazine*, *The Splendor Falls*, *Year's Best Horror Stories*, and *365 Scary Stories*. He lives in Pennsylvania.

"Tell me again," said Cara, looking back at the human boy as she pointed to a double-bladed ax in the center of the table. "Who is that?"

The human gave an awkward, half-faced smile. His metal tooth-straighteners flashed in the firelight. "Who?" he muttered. He gave his head a bemused shake.

His name was Jason. He was twelve in human years, which gave him an intelligence roughly equal to that of a paring knife. Still, he had the qualities that Cara needed. He was small. His body and hands were the right size for elven armor and weapons. But more importantly, the blood in his veins was human and could be spilled without upsetting the clan elders.

"It's weird," said Jason. He waved a slender hand over the weapons that lay in neat rows across the top of the table. "I can't get used to you talking about these things like they're people." He picked up the doubled-bladed ax. Cara watched the sinewy tendons bulge in his slender arms as his shoulders adjusted to the weapon's balance. "You should ask me *what* this is, not *who*."

"Look," said Cara. "You either show me that you know this stuff, or I'll find someone else to kill the dragon."

Jason shrugged. His face clenched with an expression that showed he was willing to play along, and then he said, "All right. *Who* is it? It's Trom-tua, the heavy ax."

"Show me how she fights."

Jason gripped the polished handle as he stepped away from the table.

"Remember," said Cara. "Hold the stock tightly, but relax your arms. Let Trom-tua do the work."

"All right," said Jason.

Trom-tua hissed right and then left, moving so swiftly that the double blades on her polished head were little more than a glowing mist. Then, as quickly as she flew into motion, Trom-tua stopped and came to rest, standing straight and tall in Jason's white-knuckled grip. "That was cool!" he said. He set the ax back on the table. "You could cut a lot of trees with that!" he said.

"You could," said Cara. "But you won't." She leaned back across the table. "Now tell me," she said, pointing to a hooked dagger. "Who is that?"

Jason picked up the dagger. He studied the blade. Filaments of reinforcing iron spiraled down the length of the curved shaft, giving the weapon a cruel, serrated edge. "It's Olc-fiacail," said Jason.

"Show me what she does."

His arms blurred as the dagger cut the air.

"All right," said Cara. "Now tell me who you're going to wear."

He turned, looking back at the armored suit that hung behind him. The suit was made of leather and reinforcing plates of iron. "Cogadh-garda," said Jason. "The war guard. The iron skin."

Cara and Jason left the burrow and stepped out into the green light of evening. Jason walked ahead of her as he moved toward the ravaged land on the mountain's east slope. Trom-tua, the two-headed ax, hung from a leather sheath between his shoulders. Olc-fiacail, the hooked dagger, hung from his belt. All around him, Cogadh-garda, the massive suit of skin and iron, clattered and creaked. She noticed the confident swiftness of his gait, and she knew that he had given himself over to the suit's will, just as moments before he had given his arms to Trom-tua and Olc-fiacail. He walked like an elven warrior.

The forest opened before them as they reached the end

of the trail, and suddenly they were standing on a barren
slope. The ground was parched and brittle. A few hundred
feet down, a dirt road snaked around a pile of uprooted
trees. Beside the road stood a row of partially constructed
homes. Between the homes lay skids of cinder blocks,
bricks, plastic-wrapped wallboard, and a numbing assort-
ment of prefabricated wooden frames. Farther down, a
herd of earth-moving vehicles slept in the leafy shadows
at the clearing's edge.

"Where's the dragon?" asked Jason.

"Be here soon," said Cara.

Jason sat on the edge of a felled tree. His eyes scanned
the slope. "It's weird," he said.

She expected him to go on. But instead he fell into a
pensive silence. When she glanced at him, he looked
almost thoughtful, sitting with an elbow on a leather-clad
knee and his fist clenched beneath his chin. The weapons
and the armor had begun to change him. He looked almost
heroic.

"What's weird?" she asked.

"That a dragon would get pissed about a few mountain-
side homes."

"Not so weird," said Cara. "The dragon's not the only
one who's . . . what's that word again?"

"What word? Pissed?"

"Yes," said Cara. "The dragon's not the only one who's
pissed."

The clan elders had sent for Cara the moment human
surveyors began staking off portions of the east slope of
their forest.

"We can't abandon another forest!" said Teanga, the
speaker for the clan. "We can't continue to flee the
moment humans arrive!"

"But it's not just the humans," said Saoi; he was one of
the oldest and wisest of the clan. His eyes were smooth
and shiny, like stones in an ancient stream. "The dragon
has complicated things."

"Pah!" said Madra. He had the temper and build of a
ferret—all spit and sinew. "When we first came to these
woods, you said the dragon would sleep forever."

"The humans roused it," said Saoi. "It was their machines—all that digging and blasting."

"But of course," said Teanga, "the dragon won't reveal itself to the humans."

"But now that it's beginning to stir," said Saoi, "it will certainly cause trouble for us."

"So," said Cara. "You've got a double problem."

"That's why we sent for you," said Teanga. "The Sidhe spoke well of you. They said you were a problem solver."

"I try," said Cara.

"Can you get rid of the human dwellings and the dragon without causing trouble?" asked Saoi.

"Without trouble?" said Cara. "No."

"What Saoi means," said Teanga, "is can you get rid of them without spilling elven blood?"

"That's very important," said Saoi. "Our clan can't live where elves have bled."

"I can take care of those things," said Cara. "Everything will be as you've requested."

"And your fee?" asked Teanga.

"The usual," said Cara. "Payable when you're satisfied that I've done what you've asked."

"In the meantime," said Saoi, "we'll supply you with anything you need. Although," he cast a smooth glance toward the satchel of weapons and armor that Cara had brought with her, "it seems you came prepared."

"Nevertheless," said Cara, "there is one thing I didn't bring. If you could supply it, I'd be grateful."

"Name it," said Madra.

"If it's not asking too much," said Cara. "I should like to be supplied with a human boy."

As Jason stared at the slope's partially built homes, Cara gave voice to the spell that would draw the dragon from its lair. It was a simple song, sung in a high pitch that the boy could not hear. The song assured the dragon that the humans were nowhere in sight. The song goaded the dragon by claiming that the new structures being built on the mountains were intended to mock the dragon's clan. The song challenged the dragon to come destroy the human mockery before the humans took over the mountain.

She sang the song twice. And then she flattened her toes and felt the earth for dragon tremors.

At her side, Jason continued to stare down at the row of partially built homes.

"That's going to be our house," he said, pointing to a cinder block foundation near the edge of the road. "I was down there with my dad when your friends found me." His voice trailed off.

Cara got the impression that the boy was having trouble remembering what had happened . . . how it was that he had been with his father one moment and with Madra and Teanga the next. Again, he muttered, "It's weird." Then he looked up at Cara. "Are you really elves?"

Cara nodded. "That's one of our names."

"Where're you from?"

"From a time when the whole world was forest," said Cara.

"When was that?"

"Long ago," said Cara. "Far away. In another part of the dream."

"What dream?"

"The dream called earth."

"Earth isn't a dream."

"It is," said Cara. "It's many dreams. Human dreams, elf dreams, dragon dreams—all competing for control." The earth begin to shiver in the grip of her toes. "Get ready," she said. "The dragon's coming."

Jason stood. He reached behind him and pulled Tromtua from the harness between his shoulders. Holding the double-headed ax in front of him, he stepped away from the fallen tree. Then he turned in place, scanning the darkening air for signs of the dragon. "Where is it?" he asked.

"Close," said Cara. She stroked the ground with her toes. "I can feel it."

Jason continued to turn in place. "Why can't I see it?" he asked.

"Because you're looking the wrong way?"

He stopped turning. He looked at Cara. "The wrong

way?" he said. His voice cracked. "I'm looking everywhere!"

"Look there!" she said.

She pointed. He followed the line of her index finger. His breath hitched in his throat as he realized where she was pointing. He glanced up at her, giving her a look that seemed to say, "You're kidding, right?"

She was pointing at the ground . . . less than twenty feet from the scuffed toes of his armored boots.

"There's nothing there!" he said.

The tremors in the ground were unmistakable. "It's a big one," she said. "Bigger than I thought." She reached for Jason. "We'd better get back." She tugged his arm, pulling him toward the woods as the slope exploded.

The force of the blast threw them into the trees as a black-veined fireball billowed from the shattered ground. And within the flame, looking like the twitching wick of a living candle, the dragon's neck unfurled.

This was the moment that would tell all. Either the spells and the weapons and the glamour of the armor would transform the boy into a warrior . . . or all would be lost.

She turned to look at the boy, but it was too late. He was gone. Already the iron will of Cogadh-garda had taken control, and the boy's leather-clad legs were hurtling him back toward the slope. She saw him silhouetted against the dissipating fireball. Arms rising, ax swinging, voice cutting the air with the shrill cry of battle—the child lunged forward to face the dragon.

Flaming ash spewed from the shattered slope as the dragon splayed its talons upon the ground. Then, with a motion that was surprisingly lithe for a creature of its size, the beast pulled its ropy body free of the crevasse. With its forked tail cracking like a whip, the monster turned, unfurled its wings, and soared down toward the base of the slope.

Cara looked for signs of the boy as she stumbled through the ashy air. But now all that she could see was the distant silhouette of the dragon. It had alighted atop one of the earthmovers near the bottom of the slope, and it was spewing flames over a row of partially constructed homes. The beast's head turned slowly as it panned its flaming breath . . . and it was then, as the skeletal homes exploded into balls of flame, that Cara saw the boy. . . .

He was climbing the dragon's neck, using the sharp spines of its dorsal fins as if they were the rungs of a jagged ladder. He had returned the double-faced ax to the leather sheath, and the heavy weapon twitched against his back as he inched toward the creature's head. Cara watched him, and even though she knew that the iron skin was doing the climbing . . . even though she knew that the spells she had worked were giving him courage . . . and even though she knew that when he wielded the ax, it would be the weapon and not his arms that would guide the blow, she could not help feeling admiration for the human boy.

He perched atop the beast's head, straddled the peaked ridge in the center of its skull, pulled the ax from the harness, and brought the blade down between the beast's eyes. Cara heard the blade clang deep into the scaly head, and she winced at the muffled crack of bone. The monster screamed. It arched its neck, throwing its head back until Jason, still clinging to the polished stock of the double-bladed ax, fell and slammed against the creature's body. . . .

And then, slowly—so slowly that Cara was certain that her eyes were tricking her—Jason floated down along the monster's side. It was not until she saw the waves of molten blood surging from the serpent's flanks that she realize what she was seeing. Trom-tua had plunged her double-bladed head deep into the monster's thoracic cavity. The beast stood, frozen in a moment of mortal shock, while the ax, pulled by Jason's weight and the weight of the armor, cleaved the creature's side. . . .

By the time Jason reached the ground, the leather of his armor was aflame with the heat of the dragon's blood. Cara ran to him, pulled the barbed dagger from his belt, and slashed the stays that bound the front of his smoldering armor.

The iron skin fell away. Sooty, bleeding, and nearly

naked, Jason emerged from the burning heap of leather and iron. Cara grabbed his arm and pulled him up the slope. They scrambled around the shattered mouth of the dragon's lair, and then, as she was pulling the boy into the woods, a thundering roar exploded behind her.

She turned. The dragon had regained its senses and was shooting toward them. Its jaws gaped, expanding until they seemed ready to swallow the entire world. . . .

She grabbed the boy's head and covered his eyes. And then, with a terrible crash, the creature dipped its shattered head and plunged into its burrow.

There was a moment of silence.

And then, deep beneath the mountain, the dragon threw its flanks against the walls of its lair. It thrashed and writhed until the east slope imploded, and the work of the humans—the skids of wood, the stone-lined foundations, the skeletal homes, and even the earthmovers—all vanished beneath an avalanche of collapsing rock and clay.

The boy was dazed. His eyes stared inward as the elven healers attended him in the burrow of the elders.

"What do we do with him?" asked Teanga.

"Put him back where you found him," said Cara.

"Pah!" said Madra. "We found him by the foundation of his home. That's a place that doesn't exist anymore. The quake swallowed it!" He sounded delighted. It had not yet occurred to him that, although he had gotten what he had asked for, his troubles were far from over. . . .

The burrow's door swung wide. Rith, the clan's runner, raced in. He skidded to a stop in the center of the room, whirled about, and said, "The boy's father has returned." Rith's lean cheeks reddened with the pressure of his broad smile. "The human troopers stopped him at the base of the slope. The poor man was dazed. The spells were leaving his mind, and he was babbling like a madman. I heard him telling the troopers that he had driven away without his son. He kept apologizing, as if the troopers cared. He kept saying, 'How could I forget my boy? What was I thinking?' "

"So there are troopers in the forest?" asked Teanga.

"Yes!" said Rith. "Troopers, land developers, gawkers—all kinds of people, and they all want to know what happened!"

"They'll leave soon," said Saoi. "They'll see the destruction, and they'll leave." He beamed at Cara with his smooth, stone-like eyes.

Cara turned away. She picked up her satchel of weapons, collected her pay, and then took the dazed boy by his arm. "I'll return him to his father," she said, guiding him toward the leafy door. Then she turned, glanced back at the elders, and said, "May your glamour be strong."

They seemed not to notice the hollow ring of her words.

She put her lips to the boy's ear and whispered the poem of forgetfulness. Then she released him and watched from the shadows as he stumbled toward his father.

"Dad!"

The father turned, ran forward, and embraced the boy. The boy wept in his father's broad arms.

Watching the scene, Cara caught a precognitive flash of the future. She saw the boy emerging into brooding adolescence. She saw the father perplexed by his son's fascination with knives, blades, leather, and flames. She saw the summer home finally being built on another slope a mile away—a slope that the land developers insisted was safe, but that the boy sensed was teetering on the edge of something half remembered.

The boy would never feel secure on the slope. Within three years, the father would sell to another family. By then, the slope would be teeming with homes, and half the forest would be under development. . . .

Eventually, all of the world's old-growth forests would be gone, and lands that had always been in the stewardship of nature and elves would vanish beneath asphalt, concrete, single-grass lawns, mulched gardens, and monocrop farms. . . .

But all of that lay in the future. For now, Cara watched as the father led the boy away through the flashing lights, and from the forest behind her came the slow, brittle chirps of the first crickets of August.

Cara held her breath and listened to the crickets.

It was a painful sound—like the slow, inexorable shattering of an ancient dream.

THE LEGEND OF SLEWFOOT

by Mark A. Garland and Lawrence Schimel

Mark A. Garland is the author of several novels, including *Dorella*, *Demon Blade*, and *The Sword of the Prophets*. His short fiction has appeared in *Xanadu III*, *Monster Brigade 3000*, and various other publications.

Lawrence Schimel is the co-editor of *Tarot Fantastic* and *The Fortune Teller*, among other projects. His stories appear in *Dragon Fantastic*, *Cat Fantastic III*, *Weird Tales from Shakespeare*, *Phantoms of the Night*, *Return to Avalon*, the *Sword & Sorceress* series, and many other anthologies. Twenty-four years old, he lives in New York City, where he writes and edits full-time.

"You're hopeless!" Tina cried. She was going easy on Lee by stopping at that. She could be a lot crueler, and he knew it.

Still, Lee felt like someone had punched him in the chest. He wasn't sure he'd feel any better if he changed his mind and went along, and he was pretty sure he had already ruined his chances of impressing Tina.

"Not entirely," Lee said. He wanted to say something, something just right, but he didn't know what. Instead he turned and started to go, kicking at the dry autumn leaves on the roadside as he went.

"You're just scared," Tina called after him, sounding annoyed.

"It's getting late," Lee argued, pausing. Tina tended to like the dynamic types: sports nuts, tough guys, loud mouths. Lee wasn't any of those, but he didn't want to act completely pathetic, either. "None of us are supposed to be out in Spirit Woods after dark. Just because you want to get grounded for the next ten years doesn't mean I have to."

"Scared!" Tina taunted. "And hopeless!"

Or just a fool, Lee thought. He felt even worse, seeing all of his careful plans starting to fall apart. This was the first time Tina had asked him to do anything with her, which was something he had been wanting for a while now. She was one of the cutest, most popular girls in the ninth grade, and one of the most interesting, an irresistible combination as far as Lee was concerned. They rode the same bus to school, and Lee had managed to improve his seating little by little, until he wound up in the seat right behind her. She'd actually started to talk to him. Then he'd gotten the nerve to ask her if he could stop over after school, and she had said yes!

Now his best efforts were going to waste. And he was doing it to himself.

"You never said anything about Spirit Woods," Lee said, still trying for what was surely a hopeless save. "I could have told my parents, and they would have let me go. I just have to keep them informed."

Which was half-true. Lee did have to keep them informed, but they wouldn't have let him go into Spirit Woods after dark if he'd told them a month ago. Nobody really knew what was behind the old legends, and Lee's parents were among the many who didn't want their children finding out.

"Why do you think I asked you to bring a video camera?" Tina said. "So you could take pictures of us?"

That was exactly what Lee had imagined. He didn't say so.

"I thought boys were supposed to be the brave ones," Tina scoffed. "Obviously, not all of them."

Lee nodded in silence. She was right, after all. He couldn't imagine what it must be like to be as bold and confident as Tina was—all the time! That was part of what fascinated him about her. Lee couldn't help being practical and methodical, he was just made that way. It had made him an honor student, but it hadn't helped his love life any. "Why do you want to find Slewfoot so badly, anyway?" he asked, doing his best to eye her suspiciously.

"Because I'm bored, of course. I go to school, I watch TV, I hang out with my friends, and that's it. I wish I was sixteen so I could get my license, but I've got a full year to go. I have to find something to do in the meantime."

"Like being attacked by some creature in a forest?" Lee asked.

"No, like being the first person ever to get actual pictures of that beastie. Haven't you ever wanted to be famous? Or rich? Or both? I bet a video like that would be worth something."

Lee hadn't ever really wanted to be famous. Being rich, though, had a certain appeal. Still. . . .

"Can you at least loan me the video camera?" Tina asked, sounding a little less hostile.

Lee shook his head. It was a great camera, brand new, a handycam with a 24X zoom lens, auto steadying, auto light sensors, and one of those flip-out color view finders that let you watch what you were taping. A very expensive camera. "I can't. It's my mother's. She doesn't even know I took it. If I don't bring it back with me—"

"How am I going to get any film of Slewfoot without a camera?" Tina said, rolling her eyes. She folded her arms and looked at him a bit sideways. The weather was warm for late September, warm enough for shorts and t-shirts. Lee couldn't help noticing how great she looked.

"Well?"

"What?" Lee sputtered, snapping out of his daze.

"Think of it this way. If your mother's camera is the first to take a genuine picture of Slewfoot, she'll be famous, too."

Somehow, Lee didn't think that would wash. Getting her camera back with a video of some great monster swallowing her son whole probably wouldn't please his mother one bit. And he wouldn't be too happy about it either.

Slewfoot had lived in Spirit Woods, just past the northern edge of the Hollydale suburb, for at least a couple of hundred years. Everyone knew that, because everyone's great-grandparents said they knew people who had actually seen him. And the stories of disappearances were too numerous to count—people, dogs, cats, farm animals—they went back to when Hollydale was just corn fields and pastures.

Some said Slewfoot was an old monster grizzly bear. Some said he was a giant ogre that lurked under the train bridge—when no one was around. Or a kind of extra-large, triple EEE Bigfoot. But everyone knew Slewfoot was there to guard something in Spirit Woods, and that's where the stories grew wild. Lee had heard that the woods were a sacred place for some kind of ancient occult group, a hiding place for escaped convicts, a refuge for a pack of wolves, an unmarked graveyard filled with the bones of warriors killed in a massacre, even a landing site for UFOs.

Nobody really knew, though, because no one still alive had ever seen Slewfoot, let alone discovered what he was guarding. Over time that beast had gotten smarter, they said, so you just couldn't find him so easily anymore. But he could find you.

"Come here for a minute," Tina said, suddenly smiling, wiggling one finger at Lee. "I have to tell you something. No tricks. Just come here."

Lee was suspicious, but he took three giant steps, which brought the two of them almost nose-to-nose.

"The truth is," Tina whispered, acting a little shy all of a sudden, "I kind of like you, you know . . . but you're acting like an idiot."

Lee swallowed hard enough to hurt. His heart was pounding like crazy, and he wasn't used to it getting so much exercise while he was standing still.

"Okay, okay, I'll go," he said. "But I don't want to be out too late."

He'd have to try telling his mother a story, which was something he ordinarily didn't like to do, but this was clearly an extraordinary situation.

"Great!" Tina said. "Come on. We're going monster hunting!"

Lee had been in Spirit Woods before, a few years ago, but it had been bright daylight and he'd been with several friends, all of them toting cap guns and Super Soakers, and even then they hadn't gone very deep. Just as far as the pond, and the little stream that ran in one end and out the other. Beyond that lay a bank of hills, and the end of the world, as far as Lee was concerned. As they reached the stream, he stood beside Tina and peered into the gloomy shadows of dusk already enveloping the underbrush. A bullfrog croaked nearby. Lee was sure it was trying to tell him something. He tried not to think about it.

Tina headed straight for a spot where a tree had fallen across the water, spanning the twelve feet or so between the banks. "You gonna stand there all day?" she called, as she climbed on the rough tree trunk and started across, hands out for balance.

Yes, Lee thought, but he climbed up and went after her.

No path led the way through this part of Spirit Woods, so they made their own, and for the first time Tina actually slowed down. The underbrush was hard to navigate, and sharp twigs bothered her legs and arms.

"You go first," she said after a while, noting that he at least had pants on. So Lee took up the lead, making his way ducking and turning through the trees and tangles.

"What exactly are we supposed to look for?" he asked her, as he tried to figure out the easiest way through the brush.

"Ouch!" Tina slapped at a mosquito that had bitten her arm. "I'm not sure," she said, sounding a little frustrated. "What I mean is, I don't think we're supposed to be looking for anything. I'd planned to let Slewfoot notice us."

Lee stopped short and Tina, who'd been staring at the ground in order to avoid letting the worst of the brambles scratch her legs, crashed into him.

"What?" they both cried, simultaneously.

"You startled me," Tina said.

"This is crazy!" Lee shouted, feeling slightly frantic now. It was getting pretty dark, and all the trees were beginning to look the same. "I thought we were going to sneak up on Slewfoot, get him on tape, and get going before he noticed us. You're telling me your plan was to hope the monster found us! Were you going to ask *him* if he wanted to be famous and rich, too?"

"Well, maybe he *does* want to be a famous monster, instead of just a local legend. Hey! Where are you going?"

"Home." He glanced to one side, then the other. "As soon as I figure out which way that is."

Lee looked back the way they'd just come, and noticed that the brambles there looked just as impenetrable as the rest, even though they'd just come through them. There wasn't any path at all. Lee couldn't even see any of the branches they'd broken to clear the way.

They stood facing one another in the deepening twilight. Her fear was beginning to show in her face, and she looked vulnerable for the first time he could ever remember. But at the same time, she seemed no less resolute in her determination to find the monster and take that photo. She knew there was danger, but she was still trying to accept that.

There was something about that underlying courage that excited and inspired Lee, and he thought it made Tina seem even sexier, especially right then, with the light just so, and a leaf caught in a strand of her hair. He felt suddenly short of breath. He had an urge to lean forward and kiss her, and he had the crazy idea that maybe she was feeling the same way, that there was something pulling them toward each other, inevitably. He was almost willing to believe it . . .

He wanted to say something again, something just right, but he didn't know what.

Suddenly Tina grabbed his arm. "What was that?" she whispered.

"What?" Lee asked, wondering what sort of utterly insensitive creature had managed to mess things up so badly.

Then he heard it, too, a loud cracking sound that came from much too close behind them. Next, he heard the roar.

"That!" Tina said, staring into Lee's eyes. Lee thought he saw a hint of regret in her eyes, but whether it was for their lost kiss, or their impending doom, he couldn't tell.

"You have to get us out of here," Tina whispered hoarsely.

It was your brilliant idea to come here in the first place, Lee thought, but he didn't say it. The roar sounded again, and sounded even closer.

"Run!" Lee shouted.

He grabbed for her hand as they started through the underbrush, not caring when the thorns and branches scratched their limbs and caught at their clothes. Sometimes Tina was a step ahead of him, pulling him onward, and sometimes it was Lee in the lead. They had no idea where they were going, all they knew was that they were running away from Slewfoot, who was still right behind them.

There was another roar, so close that they couldn't help but look over their shoulders. Something enormous was crashing through the brush, about to emerge. Lee opened his mouth to scream, only to have the breath knocked out of him as the earth dropped away. He held tight to Tina's hand as they both fell through sudden darkness, to land sprawled on a hard stone floor.

Tina caught her breath first. "Oh, that landing hurt," she said, rubbing at her backside.

"At least we seem to have lost Slewfoot."

They both looked upward, searching for the open sky to show where they'd fallen from, but there was only cave wall above them, glowing softly with its own unearthly light.

"Where *are* we?" Lee asked, breathless with wonder and fear, as they both took in their surroundings.

"Maybe we fell through the rabbit hole into Wonderland," Tina said. "Like Alice."

"I don't know about white rabbits," Lee moaned, "but I can already see my mother running around crying, 'He's late, he's late.' "

They stood up, listening to the silence.

"Now what?" Lee asked.

"Now, we explore," Tina said, sounding a bit too excited for Lee's taste. "Hand me the video camera," she added. "It wasn't broken in the fall, was it?" The camera had fallen on top of Lee, and he was sure he'd have a bruise to prove it. Still, he checked to make sure that his mother's expensive camera wasn't damaged, and then slowly handed it to Tina.

"Shouldn't we be trying to get out of here?" he asked.

"That's what I said," Tina quipped.

"You're not going anywhere," a new voice said, dark with menace. Both Tina and Lee turned, expecting to find that Slewfoot had caught them at last.

Instead, they found themselves staring at a two-foot-high man who looked to be at least a hundred and eighty years old. His gray beard was almost half as long as he was tall, and he had a pointy nose and chin. He was dressed in what looked like a skinny pair of liederhosen; he wore no shoes, but had a bright red cap on his head.

"Who are you?" Tina asked.

"I'm the one to be asking that question," the little man said, his voice still sounding deep as a tuba and full of implied threat, "since you're the ones who are trespassing on our faerie mound, and nearly clobbered me to death you two did, dropping through the roof like that with nary a warning or a by your leave."

"We're sorry," Lee said, "it was all an accident. We didn't see that hole and—"

"Yes, yes, well, well," the little man said, "as long as you're here, you may as well make yourself useful. Help me carry these logs to my house." Tina and Lee hadn't noticed the pile of logs he was standing on, much more wood than he could've carried by himself.

"Where did that come from?" Tina wondered aloud.

But the little man had already climbed down, picked up a single stick, and started walking away. "Maybe it fell through the roof, like we did," Lee said, picking up an armful of branches.

"I think he's an elf," Tina said, sounding breathless.

"Yeah, I'd kinda thought he was an elf. What else would he be? Especially in that outfit."

"Do you realize what this means?"

"Maybe he'll show us the way out if we help him?"

"I doubt that. Elves aren't to be trusted. Didn't you ever read the Brothers Grimm?"

"Of course I did, and that's why I know that elves will

never do anything for free. If you help them, they'll some-times help you in return, although you've got to be very careful what you ask for. Right now, I'm just grateful not to have been eaten by Slewfoot. Besides, wouldn't you at least want to ask him if he'd like to be a famous elf, and take his picture?"

Lee hefted his bundle of kindling and dashed towards the arch where the elf had disappeared. Behind him, he could hear Tina muttering to herself as she picked up some kindling. Lee looked over his shoulder at her, then ducked through the archway.

The place they were in seemed to be a network of caves and passageways made from that strange glowing stone. As they walked, following after the little man, plants and bushes seemed to spring up, and suddenly they noticed that the walls and cave roof had dropped away. The night had grown cold, and they could see stars above the trees. Soon they came to a small cottage beside a stream, and followed the elf inside.

"Put the kindling down here," the elf told them, pointing to the rack near the fireplace, and Lee and Tina did. They then sat down on the bench in front of the fire, while the elf busied himself about the cottage.

"I bet you're expecting me to feed you now, too," the elf said, grudgingly.

"Not at all," Lee said. "We'd just like to go home."

"Don't worry about that," the little man said, "You're never going to leave here."

"I was hoping he wouldn't say that," Lee moaned.

"I think we will," Tina said. "There's always a test, isn't there? Or three wishes, or something like that?"

The elf got a curious look on his face; Lee decided it was amusement. "Three tests, actually," the little man said.

"I knew it!" Tina yelled triumphantly. "And we're sure to win them."

"Perhaps. But in the meantime, you should be glad you carried the wood. It is cold, and now you'll have some-thing to keep you warm through the night."

I can't stay here all night, Lee thought to himself, my

parents will murder me! If, he reflected, I live long enough to get home.

"It is cold," Tina said, rubbing at the gooseflesh on her arms.

"Then put another log on the fire," the little elf replied.

As Lee stood up to do so he felt a sudden need to be extra cautious, though he wasn't sure why. He stood still for a moment, staring into the flames."

"What's the matter?" Tina asked.

"I feel like something's wrong."

"Of course you do."

"This is different," Lee said, frowning. He turned to found the elf regarding him closely. Tina seemed to notice it, too.

"Maybe you're right," she said, tugging thoughtfully at her hair. Abruptly she stood up with him, and put her hands out. "There's no heat!" she announced, as if she'd discovered gold. Lee realized immediately that she was right. The trouble was, he felt like an idiot.

"I'd put another log on the fire," he hurriedly told the little man, "if there was a real fire to put it on."

"Suit yourself," the elf snarled, and climbed up the ladder into the loft.

Tina and Lee kept waiting for him to return, both of them silent as they stared at the ladder and each other and the fire that did not warm them. At last Tina said, "I think he must have gone to sleep."

"I wouldn't be so sure," Lee said, "but it certainly feels like he's not even up there."

"I wonder if he'd try to stop us from leaving?" Tina said, though Lee wasn't sure she was asking him.

"If the fire's not real, then how will we know what is real and what isn't?" Lee cautioned, thinking again. "What if he doesn't have to do anything to us? We could accidentally kill ourselves."

"So what do you suggest we do?" Tina asked tersely.

"Wait. Maybe he'll lose his powers with the morning."

"That's vampires."

"Even so, I don't think I'd want to be roaming about Spirit Woods this late at night, with Slewfoot already having caught a whiff of our scent. I'd say my mother is going to skin me alive when I get home anyway. I'd rather be alive when she does."

"Maybe," Tina said.

As Lee looked at her, it occurred to him that for now there were just the two of them, together in a secluded cottage, sitting in front of a crackling fire—even if it wasn't real. "At least I'm here with you," he added softly.

Tina smiled at him, and lay her head on his shoulder. When he'd gotten over the initial shock, he gently put his arm around her.

"I'll have to give this some thought," she said, without further explanation. They held each other for a long time, and must've fallen asleep, because they awoke to the morning light in their eyes. They were sitting on a stone not two feet away from the edge of a cliff. As Lee stood and rubbed the sleep from his eyes, he realized with alarm that if he'd gone and put a log on the fire last night, he'd have stepped right off the cliff! He stared over the lip of the precipice, which dropped away for over a hundred feet.

"That was close," he said, sitting back down on the rock next to Tina.

"Yeah," she said. "But we still have to figure a way out of here, wherever 'here' is. There're no cliffs in Spirit Woods, nothing this high off the ground."

Lee looked around and realized she was right. Again. If this cliff were in Spirit Woods, they'd be able to see it from town, certainly, and for that matter they should be able to see town from the higher vantage of the cliff. But all he could see was woods and wilderness surrounding them on all sides. That, and the path. They were standing at its edge, a wide, well-trodden dirt path that disappeared around the back of the low, tree-covered hillside behind them.

"That's gotta lead somewhere," Lee said, trying to sound assertive, trying to take the lead. "Let's go."

"No, this way," Tina said, and with that she turned, dashed back a few yards, and started climbing the little hill behind them. "This is the way that old elf went. I'm going where he went." She smiled. "Besides, he owes me a photo op."

For a moment Lee just watched her go, telling himself she was as crazy as he'd suspected, but as she disappeared over the top he gave in and scrambled up after her. He found her several yards away, standing on the far side of the hillock, looking down. Lee leaned over, following her gaze to what was the next section of the path, where it curled around the hill's backside.

"See that dark place?" Tina asked.

He could see what looked like a pool of shadow directly below, crossing the path, a place much darker than even the other shadows nearby.

"Watch this," Tina said. She kicked at the loose dirt and stones beneath her toes, sending a small shower down the incline. When the stones touched the darkness, they vanished in a brief, bright flash. Lee just stood there, unable to speak as he imagined what would have happened, had they gone that way as he'd wanted. He felt his stomach harden.

"Come on," Tina said, tugging at him. "Let's go."

He followed numbly, wondering of himself how the world could have made such a big mistake. They hadn't gone more than a few hundred yards when they came to a clearing full of monsters. Thirteen monsters, in fact, all standing in a neat row in the middle of the glade. Slewfoot, Lee decided, every one of them. They were enormous, each one at least a dozen feet tall with massive fur-covered chests and arms, and bear-like claws that raked the air. Their heads were bear-like too, but they didn't seem to have any ears, and where their snouts should have been there was only a gaping mouth full of shark's teeth.

"Gimme the camera," Tina hissed, sticking out her hand. Lee pulled the strap off his shoulder and flipped the view finder out, then handed it over. She aimed the camera, adjusted the zoom so all the monsters would fit into the picture, then pressed record.

"They're all the same little old elf," Lee noted grimly.

"Yes, but only one of us is me," the elves all said in chorus. "The rest are only illusions. But both must find the right me, if either is to go free. Fail, and you'll be together, in the caves of the faerie mound, forever."

"Simple as that," Tina said, her voice a little shaky, though she kept holding the camera steady.

"It has to be the one in the middle," Lee whispered in Tina's ear.

"Or the one on either end," Tina whispered back.

Lee let out a sigh. "There's no way to tell."

"Yeah," Tina said. She let go of the record button and lowered the camera. "We're in a lot of trouble, I think." Lee suddenly realized he was next to tears. He wanted nothing more than to hold her in his arms, but he wasn't sure he ought to, and he didn't feel like he'd earned the right. Not yet. First, he had to think of a way. . . .

"Give me the camera," he said, snatching it away before Tina had her hand completely free. He flipped open the camera's little control panel, pressed rewind, and held it for a few seconds. Then he held the camera so that both of them could see the color view screen, and he pressed play. The image of the field before them came into focus, and on the far right, there stood a single little old elf.

"Get him!" Tina howled, but Lee was already lunging. They raced through the tall grasses, covering the distance in seconds as the elf's eyes and mouth all opened wide.

Suddenly he turned to run, but Lee was already in the air, leaping, falling. He tackled the elf hard, then he felt Tina land on top of him, knocking the wind out of his lungs. Lee gasped as Tina rolled off him. He couldn't feel the elf underneath him anymore. He looked around, and discovered that the two of them were lying on the bank of the pond, by the little stream, in exactly the spot they'd been in when they had entered Spirit Woods.

"That was incredible!" Tina said, grinning wildly, tears streaking her cheeks. She helped him get to a sitting position. "Really incredible!" she said again. "What made you think of that?"

He gasped again, tried to get his voice working. "Just," he huffed, "my turn," he finished.

"Yes," Tina smiled, "it certainly is." She put both arms around him, and pulled him to her. Lee wanted to say something, something just right, but he didn't say a word.

THE GIRL WHO WAS TAKEN INTO THE HILL

by *Diana L. Paxson*

Diana L. Paxson's novels include her *Chronicles of Westria* series, and her more recent *Wodan's Children* series. Her short fiction can be found in the anthologies *Ancient Enchantresses*, *Grails: Quests of the Dawn*, *Return to Avalon*, and *The Book of Kings*.

There was man named Halvor who lived over by Midsaetr Hill who had a very beautiful daughter called Sigrid. Except for that, he was not a lucky man, for his sons had died young and his land was poor. But he looked to his daughter to make a good marriage and repair the family fortunes, and it seemed that his hopes would be well rewarded, for she caught the eye of Lavrans Kristensson, who had a prosperous farm down in the valley. And if his relations thought the match a poor one, no one could say him nay, for his father had died when he was young and he was the head of his family. And so they were betrothed, and the wedding feast was set for the following autumn, after the harvest.

That summer, as the custom was, Sigrid went up to the saetr with the other unmarried girls to keep the cattle in the mountain pastures. In the morning and the evening they would milk them, but once the cheese was setting and the butter churned, there was time to sew on her wedding clothes. Lavrans had a sister called Borghild who was up on the hill with them that summer. She had a sharp tongue, and Sigrid was determined that she should have no cause to dislike the match her brother had made. The other girls teased Sigrid for being so industrious, but not too unkindly, for though they might envy her beauty and her good fortune, her manner to all was the same after she had been betrothed to a rich man's son as it had been before.

In truth, Sigrid did not think too much about her betrothed. Lavrans was a pleasing young man, well-thought of by all the dale, and she meant to make him a good wife, but she had accepted him less from love than for the help he might give her family. Still, she knew that his people thought her beneath him, and if she could not match his wealth, she was his equal in birth and pride. She had no gold thread with which to adorn her wedding garments, but her needlework could stand with any in the land, and so she sewed.

And thus is went until the middle of the Haying Moon. Sigrid sat on a stone at the edge of the stretch of hill they called Alf Moor, finishing a seam. Some of the cows had gone dry already, so that the milking did not take so long as before, and the other girls had gone down the hill. The long northern twilight was just fading into dusk, a time that is neither night nor day, and she could still hear the tinkle of the lead cow's bell. The quiet was very welcome, and Sigrid sighed as she bit off the thread, reluctant to leave it.

But she had never yet failed to do what was expected of her, and the other girls would worry if she did not come soon. She smoothed out the linen and began to fold it neatly.

"What are you sewing?"

Sigrid whirled. She had seen no one on the path, and besides, this voice, though light and clear, was male. Near the stone, the pines marched close to the meadow, and it was very dark beneath the trees. She peered into the shadows, remembering the tales the old women told to keep girls from wandering off alone.

Sigrid let out her breath carefully. "Who is there?"

"Many days have I watched you, working and working while the other girls lay gossiping on the grass." Her invisible companion spoke once more.

Afterward, she told herself that he had simply been hidden in the shadows. But in that moment it seemed as if a figure were shaping itself from mist and darkness. She saw a glimmer of pale skin, a glint of hair fairer even than her own. Then he emerged from the forest and stood before her on the grass.

"I am Erl the son of Alvis. My lands lie to the east of this dale. And you are Sigrid, and you are very fair."

East of the sun or west of the moon? she wondered, staring. He was as tall as she, and slender as a young pine, and the blue depths of the night sky filled his eyes. *It is you, man of the Hill, who are fair.*

Her hand went to the little golden cross she wore, but though the Christ might repel unholy wights from Midgard by day, at dawn and dusk the ways between the worlds lay open, and Erl had as much right to walk here as she.

"Maiden, I will not harm you," he said gently. "It seems to me that a woman so skilled would make a good wife for me."

"I am betrothed to Lavrans Kristensson of Kvistad," she answered him.

"But not married. And if his lands are good, mine are better, for I am a king in my own country, and my wife would go decked in fine linen and gold."

"My sisters at home are dowerless, and Lavrans has sworn to provide for them," she said.

"Wed with me, and for your morning gift I will show you a mound where treasure is buried, enough to provide for all your kin." He held out his hand to her.

Sigrid tried to remember Lavrans' blunt, pleasant features, but she could see nothing but the man before her.

"I have given my troth—" She closed her eyes. She felt, like a breath of wind, a movement near her. His kiss was white fire. Then someone called her name, and he was gone.

"Sigrid, Sigrid!" Borghild hurried toward her across the moor with two of the other girls behind her. "Someone was with you—I saw him! Where has he gone?"

She shook her head. "Who could be here on the moor at such an hour?"

"An alf!" exclaimed one of the others, laughing, but she crossed herself all the same. "Were we not warned to be careful?"

"Did you see his back?" asked the second girl. "Was he rough like pine bark, or did he have a tail?"

Sigrid shook her head, but Borghild peered into the forest.

"I saw something," she repeated. "I will mix up some tysbast and orchis and woody nightshade with pine sap for you to smear on your braids—" She grimaced as Sigrid's hand went protectively to her fine hair. "Unholy wights cannot stand to be near it, you know."

"You saw a shadow," Sigrid answered more sharply than she had intended. "And even if it had been other, if one's will is unbroken, the Invisible have no power."

"Do you think so? Well, for the sake of my brother's honor I will make you a charm just the same." Borghild replied.

"Never mind that—" said the younger of the other girls. "Now that we have found Sigrid, let us be on our way, or we will all be lost in the dark!"

In the days that followed, Sigrid often found herself looking up from her sewing to gaze across the treetops to Midsaetr Hill. Its bald stone slopes rose like the walls of a fortress from the dark fringing of pine trees, and in the hard light of noonday, she could tell herself that her encounter with the alf prince had been no more than a dream. But at day's ending, when the last rays of the sun flushed the sky with rose and mist began to rise among the trees, the granite hillside became a curtain of shifting light and shadow, and it seemed to her that if she could only look at it in the right way she would see through it to the lands within.

But even if Sigrid had wished to delay, Borghild made sure that she walked back to the saetr with the others, and after a time she ceased to look behind her when they passed the stone. But sometimes her skin prickled as if someone were watching her, and in the mornings she would wake smiling, though she could not remember her dreams.

At the end of the summer the men came up from the farmsteads to drive the cattle to the home pastures and the girls rode back on the wagons with the butter and cheeses they had made. As Midsaetr Hill disappeared behind the trees, Sigrid braced her shoulders and stared down the road to the valley where Lavrans was waiting. At Midwinter she would be married, and her new household would keep her too busy to dream.

Sigrid's wedding was to take place just after Santa Lucia's Day. There were some that whispered it was courting ill-luck to marry during the Yules, when the barriers between the worlds went down and all manner of unholy wights were free to range the land. But Lavrans had wished his godfather, a merchant who spent the good weather at sea, to be present. What better time for a wedding, said Lars, than this holy season when folk were accustomed to gather for feasting and merriment.

"Do you fear nothing?" Sigrid asked one evening when Lavrans had ridden over to sit with her by the fire.

"I fear winter storms and summer lightning," said Lavrans, "and when I served in the King's army and saw the enemy running toward us, I was afraid. But I have no fear of things I cannot see."

Sigrid sighed, remembering the elven man. Lavrans was a good man. Surely his steady strength would protect her against that other suitor who still haunted her nights. But it was not fear she felt when she thought of Erl, or if so, her fear was not of him but of that last little part of her spirit that was not yet willing to give up dreams.

"And I fear sometimes that I do not deserve you. You are as good as you are fair, and I am only an ordinary man." Lavrans put his arm across her shoulders and she leaned against him.

"You have managed your farm and supported all your kinfolk since you were sixteen. That is not ordinary," she said softly. "Your lands are more prosperous now than when you inherited them. You courted me for my handsome face, but what you need is a housewife who will tend your house as industriously as you tend your land. And that I will do, and prove to your family that you were not bewitched when you pledged to marry me."

Lavrans laughed a little and his arm tightened around

her. When she lay in his bed, Sigrid thought then, she
need not fear to be tempted by any elven sorceries.

Sigrid sat beside her new husband in the high seat of
the long hall, dizzied by the heat and noise of so many
people crammed into the room. The toasts had been going
on for some time, and everyone was merry. Lavrans Kristensson had brought his bride home from church in a
sleigh, jingling with bells. They had agreed that the feast
should be held at Kristenstead, for Halvor's house was
too small, and since most of the guests were friends or
relations of the groom, they were staying there already. It
was just as well, thought Sigrid as she watched them
drinking, that a short journey to one of the other buildings
was as far as most of them would have to go.

She would have to go out herself soon, after drinking so
much ale, but as she stirred, Lavrans laid his big, blunt-
fingered hand over hers and squeezed. They were strong
fingers, callused with work, for Lavrans was not a man to
let his people labor while he sat at ease. *No more am I,*
she thought then, for though her own hands seemed pale
beside his, they were deft with a needle, and had enough
strength to milk a cow. *We are well matched, whatever
his kin may say. . . .*

Lavrans' family sat at the table to the right of the long
hearth, the figured silks of the women's headdresses bob-
bing as they talked, like the plumage of fantastic birds.
Both men and women wore bright colors; their garments
glittered with pins and chains of fine gold. Her own
people, on the left, seemed drab as wrens beside them, but
they held their heads high, and made up in handsome features for what they lacked in gear.

Sigrid smoothed the blue skirts of her own gown
proudly. A high-born bride would have gone in silk, but
though Sigrid wore wool, its bodice and the bands that
edged its hem were worked with an interlacing of flow-
ering branches worthy of a queen, and her linen smock
was edged in handworked lace. For ornaments she had
only a silver belt clasp and the paired brooches, linked by
a thin chain, but her hair lay spread like a cloak of gold
across her shoulders, and Lavrans assured her that its liv-

ing gold outshone all jewels. But the silver-gilt wedding crown, that her family had somehow managed to retain through all its tribulations, was as splendid as any jewel in the hall.

Lavrans turned to speak to his uncle, who had the place of honor at his left, and the other man laughed. Sigrid took advantage of his distraction to slip from her seat and make her way outside.

The crisp air was welcome after the heat indoors, and Sigrid felt her head begin to clear. When she emerged from the outhouse, instead of returning, she moved toward the gate, stepping carefully through the snow. Beyond the garth, white fields stretched away toward the birch wood. The early winter sunset was reddening the sky behind the winter-stripped lacework of branches, piling clouds promised more storms. She should get back to the hall before Lavrans came looking for her, but she felt unwilling to move. Her breath hung in the air in puffs of moisture as she leaned against the gate, gazing out across the quiet fields.

"Help me—"

Sigrid straightened, peering up the road. A woman was struggling through the snow, so swathed in shawls her features could hardly been seen.

"Please help—my son is back there—"

Sigrid had grown up doing for herself; it seemed foolish to call the men from the hall when she had two good arms. She opened the gate and stepped through.

The old woman grasped her arm—or was she old? Beneath the shawl her eyes seemed vividly bright and blue.

"Where is he?" Sigrid asked. "Is he hurt?"

"He is hurt to the heart, with a wound that only you can heal. . . ."

Her own heart pounding in sudden alarm, Sigrid tried to pull away, but the woman gripped her as a tree root grips rock.

"Let me go!" she cried, "In Jesu's name!"

The woman flinched, and Sigrid knew then that she was of the alf kind, but her grip did not ease.

"I shall not release you, for you have stepped outside the garth, and now, in this time between the old year and the new, neither your strength nor holy names can ward you. It is my own son who lies sick for love of you, and to his hall this night you must go."

"They will come looking for me—" Sigrid exclaimed.

"Let them look!" the alf woman drew from beneath her shawls a piece of elmwood, like a roughly carved children's doll. But when she cast it down it seemed to ripple and change. Before Sigrid could blink, a simulacrum of herself was lying there, with her golden hair spread bright against the snow.

The alf woman plucked the wedding crown from her head and cast it down beside the still form. Then her grip tightened. Sigrid tried to hold back, but the snow slipped away beneath her feet as her captor began to run. Barns and sheds disappeared behind them, the birch wood blurred past, so swiftly did the alf woman skim across the snow. Sigrid tried to break off branches to mark her trail, but they slipped through her grasp. Only the tears on her cheeks, frozen to crystals by the wind of their going, fell to the earth behind her, if any had had eyes to see.

Shape and color rippled and ran around her, and Sigrid knew they were leaving the world of humankind. Too soon, the gray slopes of Midsaetr Hill loomed up ahead, glowing as if lit from within. She tried to cry out, but the wind plucked the breath from her lips, and then, for a few moments, she knew nothing at all.

When Sigrid came to herself again, she was standing in a stone-built chamber with a closet-bed set into one wall. On the hearth in its center a fire flickered merrily, the smoke drawing away through some vent in the arched ceiling. Skins of the white bear warmed the floor, and hangings covered the walls. Like the curtains of the bed they were embroidered with a skill that moved Sigrid, for all her mastery of needlework, to awe. The wooden fittings of the bed and the chests and benches were carved in intricate interlacings of branch and flower, as was the framing of the door. In the flickering light they quivered as if a wind blew through the wood and stone.

I am dreaming . . . she told herself, but her hair lay tangled on her shoulders and her cheeks were still tingling from cold.

"You will want to wash now," said the alf woman behind her. She had taken off her shawls and mantles and stood now tall and fair with her pale hair braided around her head, wearing a green silk gown. She clapped her hands. As she turned back, she saw Sigrid staring.

"What are you looking at?"

Sigrid blushed. "All the old tales say that the folk of the hill are fair before but rough as tree-bark behind."

The alf woman laughed. "In your world that is so, for we were made from the birch and pine trees as you humans were formed from ash and elm, and we show our origins when we walk in Midgard, but here we are fair and whole."

Two maidens came through the doorway, rosy as apples with russet glimmers in their brown hair. Unresisting, Sigrid allowed them to undress her and escort her to another chamber where scented water steamed in a pool hollowed out of the stone. Here the carvings on the walls waved like waterweed, flecked with colored crystal that glistened in the lamplight like living jewels. Soaking in that warm water, Sigrid felt a sweet lassitude stealing the strength from her limbs.

But presently her attendants assisted her to emerge and took her back to her chamber. While she was bathing, the two maidens had brought in a blue silk gown whose workmanship was finer even than her own, and ornaments of gold.

"You must wear this as well," said one when she was ready. Sigrid turned, and saw the other girl holding what looked like her own wedding crown.

"What is this doing here?"

"Where else should it be? Is this not your wedding day?" Smiling, the girl set it on her hair.

As they led her along the passageway Sigrid blinked in confusion. She remembered being married to Lavrans Kristensson, but perhaps that was a dream, and she would wake to find it her wedding morning, and the church bells ringing. Indeed, if she listened carefully, it seemed to her she could hear the church bells now. Then they came to a wooden door whose weight was belied by the delicacy of the carvings that covered it.

It opened on a lofty hall and a great company sitting at long tables set with dishes of silver and gold. At the high table sat a young man. When he saw her he rose to his feet and held out his hand, and she recognized the lover who had come to her on Alf Moor. Erl had seemed handsome in the shadows of a northern twilight. Now, in the light of the torches, he was as beautiful as day.

"She is come!" Sigrid has come, who shall be my bride and my queen! Welcome her!"

Sigrid would have held back then, but the maidens were pushing her forward, and all that shining company were rising and lifting their drinking horns and hailing her as fairest of the daughters of men.

"Here is my kingdom—" said Erl, helping her to sit down beside him. "Is it not more splendid than your mortal lover's farm?"

"Whether it is or it is not makes no difference," said Sigrid, "since it is to Lavrans Kristensson that I was married this morn."

"By the rites of the new god. . . ." Erl broke bread onto a golden plate and offered it.

Sigrid shook her head. She knew better than to eat or drink in Alfheim.

"Why do you refuse me?"

"Because I am pledged to another man, and to have two husbands living is a shame I will not bear."

Three harpers were playing at the other end of the room, golden harpstrings flickering in the firelight, sweet notes cascading through the air like silver rain. In the space between the fires the alfar danced.

"He is not your husband." Erl took her hand. "You have shared a feast with him, but not a bed. You have fulfilled your oath to wed him by your customs, but the union has not been completed, either by your rites or by ours."

Sigrid could only stare at him. Lars had the homely grace of earth, but Erl was so beautiful it dizzied her to look on him. His eyes seemed the same shade as his tunic,

the color of the moonlit midnight sky. If she gazed into
them too long, she would float away.

"You are neither maid nor wife, as this night is neither
the new year nor the old. Why do you think I have waited
to claim you? Only at this moment could you come to me
without being forsworn!" He was sitting very close to her
now, and the sweetness of his touch was like strong mead.

"You have a choice, Sigrid," he whispered. "Now, neither your oaths nor your family's wishes need constrain
you. I will provide for them as I promised, and you will
no longer roughen your white hands with labor, for you
shall want for nothing, living as my queen."

"What should I do, doing nothing? I was not brought up
to be a queen," she whispered brokenly. "It is ill-done, my
people say, when high degree weds with low. Surely it
would be more unequal still for a mortal to mate with one
who cannot die."

"Oh—we can die. . . ." His lips twisted bitterly. "It is
only age that passes us by."

"*I* will grow old," she said then.

"Sigrid, my Sigrid . . ." he lifted her chin so that she
had no choice but to look into his eyes. "It is your bright
spirit as much as your fair face that I love. Our time
together may be short, my lady, but while it lasts, we will
have such joy!"

"No—" Sigrid whispered, but no one seemed to hear
her. Sight blurred, and for a moment she saw not the elven
harpers but old Einar the fiddler, and it was not the alfar
but the mortal wedding guests who danced. *Soon, I will
go out of this hall and find myself in the farmyard at Kristensstead,* she thought.

But there was no way out of Midsaetr Hill.

The company lifted their horns to toast the bride and
groom, and Erl's mother and the two maidens led Sigrid
back to her chamber, escorted by alf women so fair she
could not imagine why Erl would even look at her.

"I have not consented to this," she said as they drew the
silken nightrobe over her head. "I am not his wife."

"If you do not agree, bale and bann will cling to you
forever, therefore be wise, and consent," said the alf
woman sternly. Then she left Sigrid alone.

* * *

She was still sitting on the bench beside the fire, looking into the flames, when Erl came in.

"Why do you torment me?" she said, looking up at him. "You can possess my body, for I am sure that you are far stronger, as you are more beautiful, than any mortal man. But would you have me hate you for what remains of my life, and all of yours?"

"All of mine?" Erl laughed bitterly. "You do not understand. My folk love rarely, but when such a passion comes to us, it is more dear than life itself. We fear it, for an alf who makes such a bond with a mortal shares her doom."

"Then leave me, for your own sake as well as mine!"

"And we desire it . . ." he added, as if he had not heard, "for we believe that in doing so, he may gain a soul. . . ."

For a few moments there was no sound but the whisper of the fire, lamenting the deaths of trees. Then Erl knelt before her.

"Sigrid, will you not pity me? Can you not love me at all?"

"Love you?" she echoed. "How could I not love you, who have come walking out of my dreams? But all my life I have had no treasure but my honor, and that requires me to be a wife to Lavrans Kristensson, no matter what I may dream."

"Is honor the light that shines through you?" he whispered, eyes wide. "Is that the fire that has kindled my own? I will not force you, Sigrid, for that would be to kill the thing I love, and then I would lose both life and soul." He rose, crossed to the table that stood by the wall and poured a pale sparkling mead from the flagon that was set there into two silver cups.

"But drink to me once only, my Sigrid, before we part—"

Erl's gaze held hers, as deep as midnight; she could not look away. Sigrid felt the cold smooth curve of the silver in her hand, felt like a little shock the impact as his cup clinked against hers. She saw him lift it to his lips, and without thinking, drank from her own.

The taste of the mead was fire and starlight, sweet on

the tongue, burning in the belly, exploding in a shower of sparks that reft her senses away. Sigrid swayed, and the cup fell from her hand. In another moment Erl was beside her. She felt him lift her to the bed. His face was very close to hers, and he, too, seemed made of starlight, but love and sorrow glimmered in his eyes.

"You *do* have a soul . . ." she whispered, gazing up at him. For a moment his face twisted with a very human pain. Then he bent to kiss her, and though grief filled her heart, she did not push him away.

Sleeping in the arms of her elven lover, Sigrid dreamed that she was at Kristensstead. She looked down and saw her own body lying in what should have been her marriage bed. Its posts were still twined with Yuletide greenery, but Lavrans knelt beside it instead of lying next to her. He held one of her hands clasped between his own, and his cheeks were streaked with tears. *Am I dead?* she wondered. Surely she would have been lying in a coffin instead of Lavrans' bed if that had been so. But though she wanted to wake and comfort him, she could not make those still limbs stir.

When Sigrid opened her eyes, it was to the stranger reality of the stone chamber. Erl lay beside her, the tension that had strung his body released at last. He must have lived for centuries, but his sleeping face was as innocent as that of a child. She reached out to touch, once more, that smooth brow, that shining hair, but drew back her hand.

She could feel, already, the beginning of heartache as she slipped out of the bed and began to put on her own woolen clothes, that looked so crude and ugly next to the elven gown. She must have made some sound then, for he stirred.

"What are you doing?"

"I am trying to become Sigrid Halvorsdaughter once more. . . ." She saw the peace in Erl's face disintegrate, and in its place the first shadow of mortality. "You said you would not force me, and I do not accuse you. But if honor is what you love in me, then you must let me go."

"It is the doom of men to lose what they love," he said

softly. "I see now that this is true. But I never thought it would be so soon. Is there no way I can persuade you to stay with me?"

"One way you know—but if you take it, we will both lose our souls. By the joy we shared, I beg you to set me free."

Sigrid thought she heard him groan, then he spoke again.

"You speak truth, and I cannot deny you. I ask only this, that the first son you bear be named after me."

"It is ill-omened to name a child after a living man," said she.

"I shall not be living," Erl answered her. "I told you how it is when love comes to our kind." She looked at him, and saw that it was true. "But perhaps, in the child, I will come again."

Erl's mother wept as she led Sigrid through stony passages to the gateway of the Hill. The great door opened; the elf woman gripped Sigrid's hand, and drew her into whirling darkness.

Very gradually, she became aware of the flicker of firelight and a murmur of voices. The wall she glimpsed through the bed curtains was of planked wood, and she could see a spot where the cloth had been mended. Confused, she looked about her. To one newly come from an elven hall, the workmanship seemed shoddy, and everything showed signs of wear and fading—of mortality.

But at the end, she had seen mortality in the face of the alf king, and known herself the cause. *What have I done, condemning a man who loved me, for nothing more than my sworn word? Condemning myself to this ugly human world?* Remembering, her eyes filled with tears.

The bed curtain was pulled back and Lavrans, with his earthbrown hair and muscled shoulders seeming, in that moment, as ugly and mishapen as a troll's, gazed down at her. As he realized she was awake, the same look of wondering joy that Erl had worn when she lay in his arms shone in his eyes. Sigrid knew then that no choice could have saved both of the men who loved her. But if she had been untrue to herself, she would have betrayed both of them.

"You've come back to me—" he babbled, sitting on the edge of the bed and taking her hand, carefully, as if it were a bird that might fly away. "Nine nights you lay like one dead. Some said you *were* dead, but I could feel that your heart beat still. Borghild said the alfar had taken you, and we rang the church bells to call you back—"

"I heard them," she whispered as he paused for breath. "Your sister spoke truly, but to me it seemed only nine hours that I spent in Midsaetr Hill."

He stared at her, not understanding. There was no magic in the touch of Lavrans' fingers, but they were strong. Did he love her enough to accept what she must tell him? If honor was all that was left to her, she could not begin their marriage with a lie.

Slowly, for she felt as weak as if she had indeed lain for nine nights in enchanted sleep, Sigrid told her husband what had passed in the alf lord's hall.

"I tried so hard to remain faithful—" she whispered at last, "but though my heart wept, when I drank the elven mead I could not rule my body, and so he lay with me."

"Your body was here," said Lavrans. "No one can be blamed for what happens in a dream."

"What lay here was an illusion, and if I had chosen to stay in Alfheim, it would have faded away."

"Believe that if you wish, but no one will question your honor, for all saw you lying senseless in the snow."

"Do *you* believe me?" she asked. "Will you still want me as your wife when I prove my words by digging treasure from the alf mound Erl showed me, and when I bear his child?"

"Whether I believe you or whether I do not . . ." Lavrans' callused finger touched her cheek, "what I know is that you chose to return to me. For that I will forever honor you. And as soon as you are stronger, we will complete our marriage, and whatever child you bear I will claim as my own."

Nine months after her wedding, Sigrid Halvorsdaughter was brought to bed of a fine boy. Some were surprised when they christened him Erl, a name that was customary neither in Lavrans' family nor her own. But neither kindred, rejoicing in the contents of the money mound that Lavrans and Sigrid had found in the forest, were inclined to protest anything they might choose to do.

Erl Larransson grew strong and fair, and folk nodded wisely and said he had inherited his mother's beauty. But Sigrid never quite regained her health after his birth, and though she lived to see him grown, she bore no other child. Lavrans loved the boy with a father's fierce passion, and in time Erl succeeded to all his lands, which had increased, by this time, to include not only Halvor's farm, but the fields and forests all the way up to Midsaetr Hill.

But some folk noted that although Sigrid was a kind mother, when she gazed upon her fair son there was always a touch of sorrow in her eyes.

CHANGELING

by *Mickey Zucker Reichert*

Mickey Zucker Reichert is a pediatrician whose twelve science fiction and fantasy novels include *The Legend of Nightfall, The Unknown Soldier,* and *The Renshai Trilogy.* Her most recent release from DAW Books is *Prince of Demons,* the second in *The Renshai Chronicles* trilogy. Her short fiction has appeared in numerous anthologies. Her claims to fame: she *has* performed brain surgery, and her parents *really are* rocket scientists.

The elevator lurched to a stop on the fourth floor of the Royal Oaks apartment complex. Valerie Roberts shook glitter from her dark hair in the familiar, lengthy pause before the door rattled open. Balancing her purse against her arm, she dug through tissues, wallet, and bric-a-brac. She continued walking as she did so, the occasional need to rest the bottom of the purse against her thigh turning her gait into a clumsy shuffle. Her keys jostled free, and she paused before her door to zip the purse closed.

Valerie ran her fingers through her short, feathered locks, dislodging more of the tiny, multicolored squares of glitter. She smoothed her sweater over ample breasts and a stomach with just enough bulge to make every sweet a guilty pleasure, including the Rice Crispies bar her colleagues had forced down her in honor of her twenty-fifth birthday. An angry cardiologist's outburst over a three-day-old dictation had cut short the forty-five minute break her fellow typists had taken for her celebration. Valerie's dictaphone had then called up four in a row of Dr. Morton "Mumble Mouth" Dunwoven's recordings, his rambling, garbled words and frequent corrections seeming even more prominent than usual. Her last letter had been drafted by a cocky resident who launched past twenty syllable, Latin diagnoses, then stopped dead to spell "range of motion."

Ordinarily, Valerie did not worry about her appearance after a frustrating and tedious day of medical transcription. But today she felt certain her roommate, Annette Weaverton, had planned something for her birthday. The notable absence of a cheery welcome in the morning and the equally glaring presences of Jeffrey's Nova and David's Buick in the parking lot made her certain a "surprise" awaited her on the other side of the apartment door. Valerie rubbed at her violet eyes, hoping they did not appear too bleary, and plastered a happy smile on her features. Inserting the key, she twisted. The lock clicked. She pushed the door open into a dark apartment.

"Nettie?" Valerie called, shoving the door closed. "Are you home?" She flicked the hall switch. Light flared from the electric chandelier, bathing off-white walls and a blue-and-green-speckled carpet.

A flash of movement from the living room followed, then a jerky, non-unison shout. "Surprise! Happy quarter century, Val!"

Only three voices. Thank God. Valerie broadened her grin. "Thanks, guys." She headed past the kitchen entryway, the aroma of her favorite take-out pizza wafting from it. Entering the living room, she tossed her purse and keys onto an end table. Jeffrey sat on the center cushion of the couch, a thick arm draped across Annette's shoulders. David hovered near the archway, the thin, plaid shirt she had bought him for his twenty-fifth tucked into a pair of black corduroys. Blue eyes sparkled over a happy grin, and his wavy, honey-colored hair lay neatly combed over his brow. As Valerie approached, he caught her into lanky arms. She sank into his embrace, enjoying the mingled scents of laundry detergent and aftershave.

From first glance, Valerie had believed David the handsomest man she had ever seen, with his lean 6'4" frame, prominent triangular nose, and sturdy chin. Later, she realized, her friends and colleagues did not share the physical attraction that had first drawn her to him and allowed her to later discover the gentle character and intelligence that accompanied those perfect features. The situation first surprised and, later, pleased her. She could enjoy his looks without worrying for his ego, nor for jealousy and competition.

Valerie retreated, and David released everything but her hand. Choosing one of the two upholstered chairs, he pulled her down onto his lap. "How was your day?"

"Typical," Valerie replied, glancing around accustomed furnishings. A shelf above the television supported Annette's collection of jade, onyx, and china elephants. The rectangular table between the couch and chairs held a double layer cake with vanilla icing and so many candles it resembled a porcupine. A knife and a stack of plates perched beside it, along with three presents. Annette's careful ribbons made a striking contrast to Jeffrey's over-taped, unsymmetrical paper. Striped with a store logo, the third and largest had obviously been professionally wrapped. "And your day, Dave?"

"Anything but typical." David snugged an arm across Valerie's lap, supplying a brief rundown of a pharmacy technician's life. "Mr. Fannsta finally admitted he didn't need his placebos. Ms. Harrie confined her complaints to three body systems. And Jack didn't yell even once."

Before Valerie could comment on any of these small miracles, Annette leaped from the couch, tossed back her cascade of mouse-brown hair, and broke in, "Enough small talk. Presents and pizza."

Jeffrey shrugged an apology for his girlfriend's boundless energy, his eyes as darkly brown and soulful as Annette's. Shiny black hair without a hint of curl and copper skin that tanned to a deep brown in summer revealed the mixed Hispanic/European heritage that his last name, Johnson, did not.

David smiled, patting Valerie's hand affectionately. "Open mine first." He slid from beneath her, dumping her into the chair.

Valerie settled amid the cushions as David snatched up the store-wrapped box and plopped it into her lap. Exhaustion pressed her, and she found herself struggling through a fog to find the proper gratitude. At times like this, she wished she shared Annette's perpetual cheerleader attitude. "Ooooh. Great wrapping job. Best I've seen you do."

"Funny." David perched on the edge of the table. "I found out something really neat. If you spend enough money, the store wraps it for you, and you don't wind up stuck to the floor with a mile of Scotch Tape."

Jeffrey glanced toward his own disheveled package. "But you can't beat the personal touch that showed you cared enough to wrap it yourself."

David followed Jeffrey's gaze. "Or to crumple it into an ugly glob as the case may be." He returned his attention to Valerie. "Open it. Open it."

"All right." Valerie pulled up a corner, carefully unfolding each edge.

Jeffrey moaned. "She opens like a girl."

"More like my grandmother." David gave Valerie a look of mock sternness. "You're not planning to reuse that, are you, Grammy?"

"I *am* a girl," Valerie reminded, finishing the process in the tidy, polite fashion trained into her since adolescence. "But definitely *not* your Grammy." The paper fell away, leaving only a few bits clinging with tape to a white clothing box. She tugged at the lid, hand slipping beneath an edge. Silken material glided across her palm. Then, the cover slid free to reveal a chocolate-colored fur peppered with snowy white spots.

Startled, Valerie leaped to her feet. The box tumbled, spilling the fur in a heap on the floor. "Oh, my God. Oh, my God." She found herself incapable of other words. An animal lover since preschool, she despised the bare thought of slaughtering for pelts. *And now I own one.* Hot tears burned her eyes, and she hopped around the gift now unceremoniously discarded on the floor. "You know how I feel. David, how could you? How dare you!"

David's smile wilted, and he stammered. "I—I wanted to get you something nice. I didn't want . . . I didn't mean to . . ."

Jeffrey tried to help. "Val, it's not like you're a vegan or anything."

It was an old argument Valerie had fought since high school. "Humans are omnivores. We're supposed to eat meat. It's natural. Slaughtering helpless creatures for their fur is different." She rounded on David. "Did you eat the minks that supplied this?" Rage slammed her in a sudden rush that left no room for argument. Eyes streaming, she rushed for the door.

David's voice chased her. "Val, honey, it's not mink. It's that new mynax. Synthetic."

The words only fueled Valerie's anger as she charged from the apartment back out into the hallway. *Synthetic, my ass.* One touch had told her differently. Nothing that perfect could be manmade. She sprinted to the stairwell, charging down the steps before anyone could follow. She needed some time alone. *I thought he was different. I thought he listened. I thought he understood.* The certainty of a break-up brought a fresh round of tears. Deep inside, she knew she was overreacting, that the need to return a gift did not mean an end to an otherwise wonderful relationship. But the fire burning her insides told another story. For the moment, she could see nothing past hurt and wrath. Her relationship with David had ended.

Valerie charged down the concrete steps, an arm shielding her face so that no one she passed might see her crying. Whether to friend or compassionate stranger, she did not wish to explain. But she passed no one in her flight to the second floor. Her roommate and friends would expect her to head out into the evening air; she often used walks in the cool night to calm herself in unhappy times. Instead, she trotted off the second landing, through the corridor, to the laundry room.

At dinner time, Valerie found the room deserted: lights off, one of the four dryer doors ajar, the six washers still and silent. She closed the entry door, hinges shrieking in protest. Finding a dark, quiet corner behind a washstand, she huddled against the cold, painted cinderblock and howled out her pain. She knew no one would hear her; the thick walls and heavy door contained sound better than any others in the building.

You're making too much of this, Valerie told herself, but the words refused to register. She could not help imagining terrified minks crammed in a cage, dodging a human's groping hand. One by one, the butchers seized

them, flaying them alive and chucking the bleeding
bodies in fly-infested, rancid piles. Her stomach lurched,
and she tasted bile. She had had a hand in this, if only
because of a stupid boyfriend blinded to the bigger picture
of what he had done. *Maybe it is synthetic.* The thought
did not soothe. The feel of the fur belied his claim. *Even if
it is, it makes me look the hypocrite. And if its beauty
drives even one woman to want a fur, or one man to buy
one, I've contributed to the horror.*

A gentle hand touched Valerie's shoulder.

She stiffened, hating David for following too soon, for
not understanding her need to work things through before
they could heal the rift. She jerked her head up suddenly,
unable to stifle her wrath. "Go away!"

A stranger retreated from her shout, visible only as a
distinct, male shadow in the darkness.

Valerie screamed.

"No, no," the other spoke with an unrecognizable,
musical accent. "I won't hurt you, Valerie Roberts. I
promise."

Valerie watched his every movement, heart pounding,
anger forgotten. "Turn on the light," she demanded.

As he turned to obey, relief flooded Valerie. She
watched him trot toward the door with a grace that made
David seem gawky in comparison. He fumbled with the
switch far longer than such a simple action should war-
rant. The bare bulb in the ceiling snapped to life, momentarily blinding. Panic seized her in the instant she could
not see, and she struggled to locate the stranger through
the pear-shaped blotch of opacity that followed the brilliant flash against her retinas.

He stood near the door, also blinking away afterimages.
Red hair fell in shaggy layers to his shoulders, a style
more appropriate for seventies women, though it suited
him. Violet eyes, much like her own, loomed large in a
young, oval face. He wore a thin, hand-embroidered shirt
cut square at the neck and belted at the waist. Beneath the
hem peeked loose pants without zipper or snap, and
supple boots covered his calves. Though shorter than
David, he stood a few inches taller than her 5'8" frame,

though she suspected he weighed less than her. He looked as if he had stepped off the set of *Robin Hood*.

Valerie's suspicion turned gradually to curiosity. Her heart rate slowed, and concern for her safety faded. "Who are you?"

"My name is Ailonwenn." He smiled. "You can call me Al."

The Paul Simon song came instantly to Valerie's mind. She rose, rubbing away tears. "Do you live in the building?" She glanced at the door, still closed, and wondered how Ailonwenn had entered without inciting wild squeaks from the hinges, as she always did.

"No," he said, watching closely, as if to judge her reaction to his every word. "I'm not even of this world."

A lunatic. The pounding in Valerie's chest resumed, and she wished him anywhere except between her and the only exit. "Oh," she said, patronizing. "I see." *Watch what you say, Val, or you might goad him to attack.*

"And neither, originally, are you."

Valerie continued to indulge, circling the room in an attempt to encourage Ailonwenn to move as well. "None of us truly are, are we?"

Ailonwenn's eyes narrowed, his voice frighteningly sane. "You're talking nonsense, Valerie Roberts."

She gathered her courage. "And you?"

"Am speaking only truth." Ailonwenn leaned against the door, the gesture so casual that Valerie wondered whether he chose the position from accident or intent. "You're a changeling."

The word made no sense to Valerie, barely remembered from childhood fairy tales. "A what?"

"Have you never noticed that you little resemble your parents?"

The words hit close to home. It had often bothered Valerie that her brother looked so much like her mother while she inherited little recognizable. "I have my father's laugh. My mother's hair color." Only then oddities came to light. "How do you know my name? Or my family?"

Ailonwenn addressed Valerie's first comment. "If you search hard enough, you can find likenesses among anyone. But your eyes are unmistakable." He widened his own. "You're an elf, a changeling switched at birth. And I know you because I had a hand in that."

Understanding dawned, and Valerie laughed. "All right, David. Nettie. Jeffrey. Come on out. Joke's over."

Ailonwenn rolled his eyes, clearly impatient. "No joke, Valerie Roberts." He raised his hands, running his thumb along his fingers. The bulb flickered, then the room plunged into darkness. A moment later, the light returned, but Ailonwenn had disappeared.

"What . . . ?" High movement caught Valerie's attention, and she found him hovering several feet above his previous position. She grunted, unimpressed. "Wires. And anyone can throw a switch. I said, 'joke's over.' You got me. Take it too far, and it ceases to be funny."

"It's no joke," Ailonwenn repeated, drifting to the ground. "No wires."

"Then make me float, Al."

"I can't," Ailonwenn gave the answer Valerie knew he must, then added the unexpected, "Our magic doesn't work on elven changelings."

"Uh-huh." Valerie searched for a discarded object, finding an empty detergent bottle balanced on top of the garbage can. "Here." She seized it, running her hand over all sides. Satisfied no one had tampered with it, she placed it on one of the washers. "Make this float."

Ailonwenn shrugged, then raised one hand, thumb swiping his fingers again. The canister jumped, then abruptly lifted into the air.

Valerie back-stepped with a startled gasp.

The container dropped back to its place. "We need your help, Valerie Roberts. Will you give it?"

Valerie seized the plastic bottle, examining it further. She looked at Ailonwenn, again noticing the similarity between their oddly colored eyes. *Could it be?* "What do you need me to do?" she asked uncertainly.

"Return to Faery. Help us rescue the mynax."

Mynax? Valerie recalled that as the word David had used to describe the fur. *Mynax. Synthetic.* Yet she had known better. "You say I'm a changeling?"

Ailonwenn nodded.

"Switched at birth?"

Another nod.

A whole new world opened up for Valerie, frightening and undefinable. *My mother's not my mother. My father's not my father. Switched at birth.* "Why?"

A ghost of a smile touched Ailonwenn's lips. "Elves have maintained contact with Man World forever. Changelings are the only way to keep the channels open. Without them, our worlds would become parallel and unreachable."

This is crazy. Logic deemed it so, yet the elf's magic convinced her the situation went far beyond the grasp of common sense. "So elves live among us?"

Ailonwenn shook his head. "It's been centuries since we've done anything more than maintain enough contact to keep language and gestures current. But if something happened to our world or, more likely, to yours, the endangered ones could cross to safety."

"Are you . . . we . . . really immortal?" Valerie attempted a glimpse between the layers of hair for pointed ears, or some proof she faced a creature other than a man.

Ailonwenn grew noticeably calmer as Valerie's questions turned from doubt to interest. "Elves are somewhat healthier and live a bit longer. How much of that is lack of pollutants, smoking, and drinking, I don't know. Reaching a hundred is common, even among the changelings." He scraped a spot of dirt from his pants with a fingernail. "Time passes slower on Faery. We have five years to each of yours, so came the stories of our immortality. I'm 22 there; I'd be 110 on this world."

"More likely dead."

Ailonwenn shrugged. "More likely."

Valerie found the details impossible to believe. "I'm a changeling." Understanding refused to penetrate. "If I lived on Faery I'd be . . ."

". . . exactly five," Ailonwenn finished.

"Wow." Valerie still found herself looking at the situation in an oddly detached manner. To do otherwise meant denying the only reality she knew. "Why do you need me?"

"I'd rather explain there. It'll make more sense."

Ailonwenn turned his violet gaze directly on Valerie. "And I won't have to keep fielding your disbelief."

Valerie did not know which question to ask first. "I can come back?"

"Whenever you wish."

"It won't do anything to me?"

Ailonwenn hesitated. "Nothing physical. I don't know how you handle emotional shocks. Then, of course, if you stay too long, there's the time difference to consider."

"Time difference," Valerie repeated, thoughts far beyond her own questions. "I'll get to see my real mother and father?"

Ailonwenn's face lapsed into crinkles of raw confusion. "Your *real* mother and father raised you."

The words baffled Valerie, "I thought I was a changeling."

"You are."

"So I'm not my parents' natural child."

Ailonwenn blinked very slowly. "So you're unnatural? You mean, like plastic?"

"No," Valerie could not believe the elf so dense. "Our relationship is just unnatural. Not blood-related."

"You're talking nonsense again, Valerie Roberts." Ailonwenn's look turned stern. "If blood was the only way to determine family, marriage would be incest. There's nothing "unnatural" or "unreal" about Paul and Nancy Roberts, nor the way they loved and raised you." He changed the subject abruptly. "Will you help?"

Valerie refused to commit herself to something as yet undefined. "I'll come with you, and I'll listen." She added emphatically, "*If* I get to meet my parents."

Ailonwenn's shrug conveyed that he still did not agree with the phraseology or understand Valerie's interest. "As you wish."

"How do we get there?"

"Sit, Valerie Roberts."

Valerie complied, cross-legged on the floor.

"Now close your eye and concentrate. Visualize an opening, and I'll guide you to the route.

Valerie clamped her lids tight, only then noticing the dry stinging of her eyes and the puffy rims around them.

She pictured a black hole, like that of a burrowing animal, surprised at how easily the image came. It widened without need to concentrate, and a current of shimmering colors draped it like a veil. Startled by its appearance, she jerked backward, opening her lids. The washroom flooded back into view.

Ailonwenn toppled from a washer, a sideways movement all that saved him from landing in her lap. "What did you do that for?"

"What?" Valerie asked, scurrying away from the elf as he regained his feet and returned to the washer, rubbing his left wrist.

"That was the opening. Next time, don't run from it. Go through it."

Go through it? The suggestion seemed madness. *How do I go through something in my head?* Valerie did not ask aloud. It seemed fruitless. Again, she took a position on the floor, head low and eyes screwed shut. Concentration brought the hole back into view, and the multicolored curtain followed, fluttering in an invisible breeze. A dizzy sensation of change overtook Valerie. Her body seemed to spin and pull. Then, a moment later, she stood in front of the opening; and it felt as normal as breathing. Ailonwenn stood beside her.

"How . . . ?" she started, and her vision became an unfocused swirl.

"Don't question!" he shouted. "You'll lose it. Just go!"

Valerie dropped all thought, and the opening reappeared. Ailonwenn dashed through, and she chased him into a spiraling tunnel that stole all sense of time and place, upending her into a wild sensation of falling. She gasped, flailing through ripples of wind and slashes of color. Then, light appeared in front of her. She staggered toward it, disoriented, wondering if she had discovered the passage described by so many after near-death experiences. She emerged a moment later to a sea of violet eyes.

Ailonwenn said something Valerie could not understand, and the press of elves retreated far enough for her to emerge. She stumbled forward, only then realizing that the tunnel had disappeared and she need not have bothered to move at all. She glanced behind her, seeking any

sign of the passage and finding only an immense stretch
of purple wildflowers speckled with elves and ending in a
vast, towering forest. Between the trunks, she caught
glimpses of distant mountains. Though autumn at home,
here the beaming sun and gentle breeze riffling the
flowers suggested spring or early summer. Perspiration
gathered beneath her sweater, direct contrast to the thin
tunics and shifts the elves wore.

Valerie turned Ailonwenn an accusing glance, containing panic. "You said I could get back."

"Whenever you wish," Ailonwenn repeated. "You control the portal."

"Oh." Once spoken, it seemed obvious. *Did I think
there was a permanent door to Faery in the Royal Oaks
laundry room?* The question sobered. *Or inside me.*
Valerie could no longer dismiss Ailonwenn's claims as
madness. *I'm a changeling. I'm standing in Faery with a
bunch of elves.* Her mind still refused to process the
details. *Not a joke, so it has to be a dream.* She studied
the array of colors and the playful breeze that sent her
short locks dancing, certain of their existence. Many of
the elves looked as human as Ailonwenn, but others
sported angular features, odd proportions, and slitted, cat-
like pupils. Hair colors ranged from white to inky black,
though the former seemed no more common on elders
than young ones, and red predominated the way it never
did at home. Despite the variety of facial features and hair
colors, everything else about the elves seemed less
diverse than humans. Each sported the violet eyes that she
had grown used to seeing in the mirror but nowhere else.
None appeared to weigh more than a slender human;
some looked positively skeletal.

An elder with eyes recessed into wrinkles and hands
like parchment gestured Ailonwenn aside. A monkey
perched on his shoulder, one small hand clutching his
neck and the other still at its side. Violet eyes, like the
elves', stared out from a flat-nosed, thin-lipped face with
less hair than most of its ilk. Sleek brown fur coated its
body, spotted like a newborn fawn's, aside from its head
where lengthy locks spilled from its crown, more human
than animal. The tail curled around the elder's arm.

Valerie recognized that fur instantly. *Mynax! So, I was right.* A chill swept her. She could not stop herself from imagining the adorable little creature screeching while humans hacked away its skin to make the coat or stole, she had not noticed which, that lay on her apartment floor.

Ailonwenn and the elder conversed in private for several moments while elves and human examined one another. Valerie fought the shame of her thought and another burst of anger. *David, how could you?* Her brows lowered as she considered. *Mynax don't exist on our world. Where did David get that fur? Is he a changeling, too?* No answers came yet, but she trusted Ailonwenn to explain.

Shortly, the young elf came to her side. "Valerie Roberts, would you please accompany us to the village?"

Valerie nodded. "But please, just Val will do." She fell into step beside him, as did several of the elves, and they headed toward the forest on a narrow path hemmed by flowers. "Is that a mynax?" She inclined her head toward the monkey.

Ailonwenn did not bother to follow Valerie's gesture. "Yes. He's called Yendin. Would you like to meet him?"

Valerie smiled. "Very much."

Ailonwenn made a high gesture. Something thumped against his back with a suddenness that sent Valerie into a startled crouch. The mynax clung to Ailonwenn like a backpack, then skittered to his shoulder. It reached out its hands to Valerie.

"Ohhh, may I hold him?" Valerie scarcely dared to hope, accustomed to pet shops and zoos where such actions were usually forbidden. She held out her hands to the animal, and he snuggled into her arms. She cradled the mynax like a baby, his fur remarkably dense and soft as liquid. Her hands sank to the warm body beneath it.

Ailonwenn did not bother to answer with words, but his grin spoke volumes.

The creature made a sound that more resembled speech than the chattering of a monkey.

Ailonwenn translated. "He said, 'hello.' "

"Really?" They reached the edge of the woods, then

plunged into the trees without changing pace. The path became broader and better defined, branches neatly trimmed and weeds folded from the trail. Valerie mentally berated her herself, *Yeah, right. The animal talked to you, Stupid.*

"Ralka." Ailonwenn repeated the sound the mynax had made. "It means 'hello'."

Valerie froze in her tracks, and the elf behind her had to swerve into the brush to keep from running into her. Those ahead stopped and turned. "He can actually talk?"

"All mynax can." Ailonwenn jerked his head in the direction they had been traveling, a clear gesture to continue. "The adults function at about the level of a two-year-old child, with as much variation."

Valerie started to walk again, stroking the mynax in her arms more carefully. The enormity of the responsibility of carrying it trebled the instant Ailonwenn compared it to a toddler. Her long love of animals had always held an edge of reality. She understood that eating meat fulfilled necessary cycles of nature and that research on them rescued a thousand times as many human lives, yet she despised gratuitous slaughter, unnecessary testing, or killing to satisfy the inexplicable human vanity of wearing a coat that had once belonged to another living being.

Valerie crooned to the mynax as she might to a human youngling, feeling silly. "Hello, Sweetie. You are a cute one. And so soft."

The mynax nestled deeper into her arms, his smile containing an echo of humanity. He made a comfortable sound.

Ailonwenn laughed. "He doesn't understand a word you're saying, of course. Not English. But he's sure enjoying the attention." He switched to a musical language with smooth, crisply enunciated syllables, clearly directed at Yendin. The other elves remained respectfully silent throughout the walk, occasionally stopping to gather berries or roots.

Glimpses of buildings appeared between the trees at intervals and, after a few more paces, movement occasionally caught Valerie's eye. "How old is he?"

"Yendin?"

Valerie nodded.

"Twenty-six."

"Gracious." Valerie studied facial contours gently rounded by fur. "You're older than me."

"Older than me, too," Ailonwenn added. "But still young. Their lifespan's about the same as ours. Aside from elves, mynax are the only naturally occurring animals on Faery."

"Really?" Valerie looked around, now realizing the only noises came from the elves trooping around them. Large numbers of people kept woodland creatures scarce on Man's World, too; but she would have still enjoyed birdsong. A lizard, snake, or salamander might wriggle beneath a rock, or she might hear something larger retreating into the brush. Most notably, no flies or mosquitoes buzzed around them despite the damp warmth of the forest. Only after she registered that observation did she grasp onto the rest of Ailonwenn's statement. She used his own phrasing, "No others natural? So there're plastic animals in Faery?"

Ailonwenn smiled tolerably. "I didn't say natural, I said naturally occurring. Decades ago by our reckoning, centuries by yours, we accepted a few ponies through a channel. They fit our lives well, without damaging the cycles. We also have a penned area, much like your zoos, where we keep some of the creatures that were disappearing from your world. Like the dodo. And the unicorn. Sometimes we try to reintroduce them, though we haven't had a lot of success."

"Some successes," a slight, alien-faced female added, joining the conversation."

"A few," Ailonwenn admitted.

Unicorn? Valerie wondered if the elves accounted for the occasional "rediscoveries" of species believed extinct. Or for sightings of Loch Ness monsters and Sasquatch. She tickled Yendin under the chin, and he threw back his head for more. "Berala," he said, a word she took to mean "good" or, perhaps, "more."

"We can't handle all your vanishing animals," Ailonwenn went on. "Carnivores, for example. Our world's not made to handle them. We don't have mice, rabbits, or small birds, and bringing even two might upset the entire balance."

Now, Valerie noticed that Ailonwenn had no canine teeth. *Like me.* The dentist had noted the lapse when she was a child, shrugging it off as an insignificant oddity. *I really am a changeling. An elf.* Finally, the idea penetrated. *I'm an elf. This is my world. My Faery.* She glanced around at the unfamiliar, exotic faces. *My people.*

The trees thinned, the forest breaking into a clearing. Cottages filled the area, with small patches of grassland between them. Constructed of stone, thatch, and sticks, they remembered her of nothing so much as mingled scenes from *The Three Little Pigs.* Beyond the first several rows, fields stretched as far as her vision, the tiny dots of pony-drawn plows interrupting the landscape at irregular intervals. Children raced, giggling, through packed-earth streets; and a group of adults wrestled with a pull rope, placing posts for some new construction. Paddocks filled with sheep, goats, and pigs seemed conspicuously absent, and Valerie kept expecting chickens and dogs to dodge amid the children.

Yendin clambered from Valerie's arms to perch upon her shoulder, tail wrapped delicately around her neck. His fur drifted like a light touch of velvet across her cheek.

Many of the elves looked up as Ailonwenn and Valerie approached, their greetings exuberant, so unlike the stiff aloofness of most humans. *My people.* Valerie beamed, seeking the opposite of every unpleasantness humanity embodied. She glanced at the elves sweating and struggling with the pull rope. "Al, if you've kept close enough contact to learn human languages, why not their technology? It sure makes life easier."

"Partly different resources. Partly choice." Ailonwenn touched Valerie's back to usher her toward a common house at the farther edge of town. "Our fossils don't make good fuel, perhaps because it's all vegetation. We choose a lifestyle that's peaceful and simple compared to yours."

"So why maintain contact at all?"

"It's harmless. Our interference has helped mankind from time to time, and the knowledge we gain from them, scientific and historical, has proven invaluable. If all the channels closed, we could not reestablish any more. Our worlds would become forever separated."

"You mean our world and their world."

Ailonwenn gave Valerie a measuring look, then shrugged. "As you wish."

"I'm an elf," Valerie asserted.

"You're a changeling."

A flash of defensive anger followed. "Do you discriminate against changelings here? Are they looked down upon by other elves?"

Ailonwenn's eyes widened, his expression unchanged. "We look down upon no one here. Changelings have been an accepted fact of life for longer than any of us have lived. Every six years, thirty to your reckoning, we open a channel. We switch the babies. No one's harmed."

"No one's harmed!" Valerie could scarcely believe her ears. "Children are stolen from their parents and given to others to raise."

"Traded," Ailonwenn reminded. "No one loses anything."

"How can you say that?" Valerie's shout rose above the soft exchanges of the elves. "I lost the chance to grow up here. In my world."

"And grew up in another, better in some ways and worse in others." Ailonwenn stopped in front of the building, waiting to resolve the conversation before entering. "Imagine, Val, that you had a beloved daughter. One day, you discover the nurses in the hospital had confused her with another baby girl at birth. Would you love her any less?"

"I'd want *my* daughter back. My *real* daughter."

"You'd switch back?"

"Darn right."

Ailonwenn sighed, grumbling beneath his breath. "I'll never understand humans."

I'm not human! Valerie nearly screamed; but, seeing that her previous shouting had driven Yendin to slide toward Ailonwenn and raise his hands plaintively, she kept the thought to herself.

High-pitched squeals of joy rose over the silence that followed Valerie's complaints. On a broad stretch of

grass, a grinning man played an animated tickling game
with a young girl, his pride in her evident. Blonde curls
tumbled along her shoulders, mixing with grasses and
wild flowers. *Father and daughter, no doubt. Born to one
another.* Valerie sighed. The sight raised memories of her
own childhood leaping into the leaves her father raked
while he laughed, eventually joining her, though it meant
repeating the morning's work. Anger retreated behind a
grudging smile.

Yendin settled against Valerie's ear.

Ailonwenn held open the common house door. "If you
please."

Valerie entered an enormous room, mostly filled with
a long table. A half-dozen elves sat at an end, the head
seat and the one to its left open. Sweet spices perfumed
the room, resembling allspice, ginger, and cinnamon
together.

Ailonwenn walked Valerie to the head seat. "These are
some of our wisest, all Speakers. That means they know
human languages. All of these speak English."

Three male and three female elves nodded a greeting
that Valerie returned before sitting. All could pass for
human, perhaps why they had been chosen to visit Man's
World and learn human languages. Ailonwenn took the
other empty chair.

The farthest, a skinny female with straight, brown hair
spoke first. "Did Ailonwenn tell you why we asked you
here, Valerie Roberts?"

"Val, please," Valerie corrected. "And, no. I've kept
him busy with questions about this world and about
changelings."

Ailonwenn nodded vigorously, conveying his frustra-
tion as well as the truth of her words.

The dark-haired male directly to Valerie's left got
straight to the point. "Then you know we currently have
two channels."

Valerie glanced at her guide. "Actually, no. We didn't
get to that."

Ailonwenn elaborated. "We usually have two to four.
Rarely, one. If either of the change-partners dies, their
channel permanently closes. Because of the time differen-

tial, that's always the partner on man's world. Lenore Stephens died last year, your time. She was eighty-four."

Valerie performed the math swiftly. "I'm twenty-five. That means five years till the next changeling. So, that would leave me . . . and someone who just turned fifty-five."

"Thomas Toddwell-Hillary," Ailonwenn supplied.

Several of the elves hissed their displeasure. Yendin loosed a high-pitched noise followed by a single word.

All of the pieces fell together in that moment. Valerie voiced her understanding. "This Thomas Something-Hillary is hunting the mynax and selling their fur on Man's World." She gave David the benefit of her doubts. "And calling it a new synthetic to expand his market."

Somber nods met Valerie's revelation.

"But why do you need me?"

Two rows of violet eyes shifted to Ailonwenn, and he complied with the explanation. "We've tried talking to him, without success. We can't oust him with violence. It's not only against all our laws, it's completely foreign to our nature."

Valerie interrupted, "I don't know anything about fighting either. Can't you just use magic?" Memory answered her own question. In the laundry room, Ailonwenn had admitted his spells didn't work on elven changelings. "I'm sure there're people more competent than me who can help you. Ex-military. Heck, the cops would probably be glad to help. Illegal fur trade. I'm sure he'd do plenty of jail time."

The elves exchanged knowing glances, and several shook their heads. "You don't understand," inserted a white-haired male who appeared middle-aged. "Elves can travel back and forth through the channels, but humans have no magic. We can haul them from Man's World to here, with the help of the changelings who control the channels. But we've never been able to get them back."

Guessing Valerie's next concern, Ailonwenn added, "Elven changelings can travel freely through the channels. That's Thomas Toddwell-Hillary and you."

Valerie lowered her head, barraged by emotions. These same elves had stolen her life and now only she could help them. *By facing off with an illegal fur trader who's surely armed.* She considered the poachers in Africa so driven by money they thought nothing of murdering lawmen. Fear trembled through her. *There's nothing I can do here. Nothing at all.* "I'm sorry," she said. "But I can't—"

Yendin skipped from her shoulders to the tabletop, babbling in the elves' singsong language. The repetitive syllables were meaningless to Valerie, yet the terror and need in the violet eyes told more.

"He's the only one left among us," a young female said softly. "The others hide in the trees, but the changeling lures them out with promises and food. They're smart enough to understand the danger but not to avoid it. And they have trouble differentiating him from us."

The mynax went still, but his eyes locked with Valerie's, a silent plea.

"All right," Valerie said before she could stop herself. Her fingers on the tabletop trembled, and she found it impossible to still them. Her bargaining skills returned before she committed herself irrevocably and without personal reward to drive her. Mind's eye still filled with the loving exchange between father and daughter outside the conference room, yearning for that closeness, she haggled. "I'll talk with him. And if I rescue the mynax, I get to stay here as long as I want. And to meet my parents."

The elves around the table exchanged startled glances, except for Ailonwenn who rolled his eyes and shrugged with obvious resignation.

The female who had spoken first addressed Val again. "You may stay as you wish. We can arrange to send your change-partner to Man's World if you seek permanence here. But your parents are there—"

Ailonwenn interrupted. "Don't bother. It's wasted breath." He glanced at Valerie, his expression rife with judgment. "Valerie Roberts, you leave us no choice. You have a deal."

A winding walk through woodlands brought Valerie and her continuously growing escort to a vast sapphire grassland. In the distance, tree-lined stone hills broke a view that otherwise seemed endless. A hundred or more elves of varying ages hovered a safe distance from the rocky cliffs, as if trapped behind an invisible barrier. An elder met the approaching Speakers, glancing at Valerie several moments before politely looking away. He said something in their native tongue.

Valerie stopped. Yendin seized a handful of her hair to steady himself as he shifted from her left to her right shoulder, nearer the conversation. After a brief exchange, the elder squatted, finger parting a circle in the grass. He waved his hand over the figure he had drawn. The grass melted like stained glass, swirling into colored patterns than gradually resolving to a dark image interrupted by regular silver stripes.

Elves gathered around him, blocking Valerie's view of the magic, peering over the shoulders of the elder and the Speakers. Ailonwenn's brisk gesture sent them scattering. He beckoned to Valerie.

Valerie came, elves watching her every move with cautious curiosity. Staring into the etched circle, she saw cages stacked against stone, each stuffed with a mynax who barely fit its confines. Most huddled, shivering miserably. A few lay still on their sides, only an occasional twitch of ear, paw, or tail revealing life. A terrified youngling opened and closed its mouth in tiny cries that the magic rendered silent. A pile of spotted fur lay in a corner. No sound of any kind accompanied the picture, only the outraged or sympathetic whispers of the elves surrounding Valerie.

Yendin loosed an animal howl that cut Valerie to the heart. She reached up and ran her fingers through the hair cascading from his head, raking tangles from the silken locks. A male elf approaching his teens cried unabashedly while a woman, surely his mother, tried vainly to comfort him.

A shadow passed along the edge of the magically conjured image as it faded and the elder rose. Ailonwenn explained in English. "That's a view inside the second cave." He pointed toward the hills. "Thomas

Toddwell-Hillary is there, the presence you may have
glimpsed toward the end."

Valerie realized every eye had turned to her. The time
had come to act, and she had no idea how to proceed.

Yendin clung to her head the way a shy child hides
behind his mother's leg.

"It's probably best if you stay here," Valerie suggested,
reaching for him.

The mynax dodged her questing hand, though whether
because he did not understand her or chose not to leave
for other reasons, she could not guess. The elves' tension
heightened visibly, their milling turning to quiet rigidity
or fidgeting.

Valerie headed toward the hills. *Here goes nothing.* She
doubted even the most unreasonable man would slaughter
a young, unarmed woman without a clear warning.

The grass parted around Valerie's dress shoes and, not
for the first time, she appreciated that she had chosen
comfort over heels. Blades tickled against the nylon covering her ankles. She glanced at the sun sliding toward the
rocky cliffs, then back toward the caves. In that moment,
a blocky, male figure appeared against brush and stone.
He clutched a rifle, leveled in her direction.

Valerie gasped, scrambling for boldness. He had not
shot her yet. Surely that meant he would give her a chance
to talk. "Mr. Hillary?"

"Toddwell-Hillary." The gun remained in place. "Back
off, elf. How many of you do I have to kill before you
realize I'm not kidding?"

Valerie froze. The gruff voice held no hint of bluff, and
she felt certain he had left more than one elven corpse
since he started butchering mynax. It certainly explained
why the elves kept their distance. "I'm not an elf."
Valerie's own reply startled her. "At least no more so than
you. My name is Valerie. I'm the other changeling."

A brief pause followed during which the man did not
move. Yendin's fingers gouged Valerie's face, clearly
unconsciously, and she suddenly wished she had been
more insistent about leaving him. Rather than convince
Toddwell-Hillary of the folly of his actions, Yendin

would more likely draw his fire. *Toward my head,* Valerie lamented.

"Prove it," Toddwell-Hillary growled.

Valerie cleared her throat, instinctively reaching for the purse she had left in her apartment. She hesitated, searching for other identification. Sudden realization of the danger posed by his weapon stole logic, and she rattled off Man's World details in an express-train patter: "Arch Deluxe is a plain old Quarter Pounder with dijon mustard. New Coke tasted like Pepsi. Razzles is a candy, not a gum. Forest Gump's mother said, 'Life is like—' "

"Enough!" the poacher roared. "Any elf could pick up trivia. Come where I can see you."

Valerie's feet seemed rooted. "Promise you won't shoot me." Though she tried for stalwart courage, her voice emerged as a squeak.

"I'm not promising nothing." Toddwell-Hillary deliberately worked the bolt, sending four definitive clicks rolling across the valley.

Fear trembled through Valerie, but she managed to shuffle forward. "Yendin," she whispered. "Go back."

The mynax only tightened his hold.

"Yendin, please."

The mynax made a deep noise. He lowered his face over Valerie's head to meet her gaze, upside-down violet eyes wide and confident. His expression conveyed a trust so complete it revitalized her. *I can do this.* The payment she had extracted from the council lost significance when it came to motivating action. *For Yendin, I can do this.*

Raising her head, Valerie strode toward the waiting killer.

Toddwell-Hillary remained beneath the cave's overhang, watching Valerie approach, the gun still raised. As she reached the edge of the scraggly tree line that scarcely hid the hills, Yendin grasped a dangling branch and skittered into the confluence of leaves above their heads. The rifle followed the movement.

"No!" Valerie shouted, desperately charging the other changeling.

The rifle's muzzle swung back to Valerie, stopping her mid-rush. The man cursed. "You let it get away," he accused. "You cost me a couple hundred. For that alone I should shoot you." She saw him clearly now, a paunchy man past middle-age, a caricature of the weekend hunter. A polo shirt hung loosely over broad shoulders, tucked into a pair of grimy jeans. Stubbly, sandy hair with a hint of red poked up from his scalp, without recession or sign of balding. Wide, violet eyes, a small nose, and high cheekbones softened his otherwise coarse features.

Faint, echoing whimpering emerged from deeper in the cave, sharp as a puppy's first night howls.

Cut to the quick, Valerie accused, "How could you? How can you murder those beautiful, defenseless creatures? How do you live with yourself?"

Toddwell-Hillary's eyes narrowed to slits. The rifle remained steadily trained on Valerie. "I only kill elves when they threaten me."

Though the more significant crime, Valerie let that go for the moment. "I mean the mynax."

"The monkeys?"

"Yes."

Toddwell-Hillary studied Valerie as if she had turned into an insect before his eyes. "They're animals, Valerie. I'm not doing anything that doesn't happen on our world every day."

Valerie took some solace from an accomplishment she doubted she could achieve moments before: she had gotten him talking. "Mynax aren't minks." She abandoned her deeper convictions for the moment. The food versus fur argument would never sway a poacher whose livelihood depended on the latter. "They're intelligent animals."

"So are pigs," Toddwell-Hillary returned. "But it doesn't stop anyone from eating bacon."

"There's no comparison." A rustling overhead stole Valerie's attention momentarily, and the poacher cocked his head toward the sound as well. She continued hurriedly and loudly, trying to cover Yendin's noise and keep him safe a few moments longer. *Run, Yendin. Get away!* She wished she could broadcast her thoughts, though the language barrier would remain. "The mynax are intelligent like human children. They can talk."

Toddwell-Hillary spat, his sputum dark from tobacco. "I've trapped and captured fifty or so. Not one's ever said nothing to me. If begging for life don't get one to talk, nothing will."

"They don't speak *English*," Valerie asserted.

The man dismissed Valerie with an impatient wave. "And dogs speak bark language. And cats speak in meow-voice." He gestured with the gun. "You're an idiot. And you got ten seconds to get out of my sight."

An anguished shout rang across the meadow. Valerie jerked her head toward the elves. The boy she had seen crying darted toward them, wailing elven syllables she should not have understood. Yet intonation spoke louder than words. Without comprehending how, she knew he took responsibility onto his own tiny shoulders, believed himself the reason for the deaths of elves and mynax alike.

The rifle swung toward him.

"No!" Valerie shrieked, too late. The rifle boomed, shattering her hearing. The elfling jerked backward, then crumpled into a heap on the grasslands.

"Kahl, kahl, kahl!" The female who had been comforting the child rushed to his side, a male diving between her and the fallen boy, clearly to protect her from the same fate.

"Please don't hurt them," Valerie sobbed in desperate helplessness, ears ringing and throat aching. "They're just trying to help the . . ."

But Toddwell-Hillary did not aim his gun at the child's weeping parents. He staggered backward, eyes growing round as coins. "No," he whispered. "Oh, no." His words degenerated into nearly incoherent cursing.

Seizing a chance at control, Valerie forced her own grief aside. "Do you see what money has driven you to? You shot a helpless child."

The poacher toddled unsteadily, then regained his balance. "Damn." He glanced at Valerie as she drew dangerously close. The gun jerked back into position, a spare foot separating its barrel from her chest. "Freeze."

Valerie halted, tears blurring her vision. "You shot a child."

"I killed an elf." Deeper in the cave's shadows, Toddwell-Hillary gained a dark sheen that added to his aura of menace. "An animal."

"You don't believe that." Valerie kept her voice steady with effort, needing to believe the boy was only wounded. "You're a changeling. An elf yourself."

Toddwell-Hillary growled.

Valerie continued while she had him on the defensive. "And I saw that look on your face. You regretted what you did."

"I did." The poacher took a threatening step toward her, narrowing the gap. "Not because I killed an animal, you moron. Because I killed the *wrong* animal."

The hovering threat of death muddled Valerie's thoughts. It took inordinately long for her to recognize the man's point, the age of the one he had shot supplying the final clue. *Five years to one. And he's fifty-five.* She glanced at the child, now as certain of his death as Toddwell-Hillary and of his very deliberate sacrifice. Memory returned, in Ailonwenn's voice: "*If either of the change-partners dies, their channel permanently closes.*" Despite the waste of a young and precious life, Valerie forced a smile. "He trapped you here, didn't he?"

Toddwell-Hillary's grin out-eviled Valerie's, though a lopsided tilt revealed worry he otherwise hid. "Not if you let me through your channel."

My channel. Valerie finally had a bargaining tool and she clung to it, holding thoughts of the dead child, the caged mynax, and despondent elves from her mind. Allowing any of those through might destroy her ability to think, let alone bargain, with a madman. "Why would I do that?"

"Because I have a gun."

"Good strategy." Valerie forced herself to meet Toddwell-Hillary's eyes, hiding her hands and their incessant trembling. "Fix it so you can never leave."

Toddwell-Hillary pursed his lips. "If you refuse to let me through, the effect is the same." He worked the bolt, loading another round into the chamber. "But I get the satisfaction of slaughtering you *and* assuring no elves ever reach our world again."

Valerie found the perfect solution. "I'll tell you what. I'll let you through. And you never return."

"Agreed," Toddwell-Hillary said, to Valerie's surprise. "But I take my haul with me."

Valerie said methodically and without emotion, "You go empty-handed."

"I have the gun."

"I," Valerie said as emphatically, "have the channel."

Toddwell-Hillary's eyes turned ugly. "I take every captured monkey with me, or I shoot you in some nonfatal part. Then I do it again. Eventually, you'll agree to the terms. Might as well be before I start."

"You can't," Valerie sputtered, wishing herself further, the elves closer, that she had never come or agreed to speak to Thomas Toddwell-Hillary. Panic stabbed through her, paralyzing, and she realized a dilemma that went far beyond torture. Using similar threats, he might find a way to force her to shuttle him back and forth for eternity. No policeman would believe a story of changelings and channels. A worse thought followed: In another five years, another changeling. *Would he dare exploit a newborn baby?* She glanced over her shoulder toward the dead child in the field, his parents wailing over his body, and knew the answer. *No wonder he agreed so easily.*

Toddwell-Hillary seemed to have grown in the moments of Valerie's indecision. "You have ten seconds to decide." He started counting immediately, "One . . . two . . ."

"Wait!" Valerie shouted. "Give me a moment to think." Tears nearly blinded her, and terror drove her to run even as it rooted her in place. Her body heaved, locked into uncontrollable tremors that resembled seizures. *Get control. Control. Think!*

". . . three . . . four . . . five . . ."

Valerie's mind replayed the boy's brave rush in an endless loop. *He surrendered his life for the mynax.* For her to give in now meant allowing a child to spend his life in vain. *I don't want to die.* A survival instinct rose, crushed by a morality that blazed suddenly into bonfire.

". . . seven . . . eight . . ." Rage entered Toddwell-Hillary's tone. He would revel in her torment.

"Do it," Valerie managed, bracing for a pain she hoped would steal her consciousness as well. "I won't work for you."

". . . nine!" The number emerged beneath another's high-pitched scream. A spotted, brown blur flew from the branches, landing atop the poacher's head.

Yendin! Valerie's eyes scarcely had a chance to focus before she leapt to assist. Her fingers closed over the gun barrel even as it jerked skyward, tearing her palms along the sight. She clung as if to a lifeline, wrenched awkwardly like a marionette as Toddwell-Hillary clenched tighter and slapped at the mynax simultaneously.

Even one-handed, the man proved stronger than Valerie. She could not rip the rifle from his grip, and the barrel swung widely as they grappled for control.

Toddwell-Hillary hissed, the sound scarcely audible beneath Yendin's animal howls of rage. Blood dribbled from the poacher's scalp, joining a line of sweat along his nose.

Get him, Yendin. The gun tipped sideways, the sight slitting the edge of Valerie's left hand. She lost that hold, winching the other tighter in savage desperation.

Toddwell-Hillary's hand closed around Yendin's head, and he hurled the mynax fiercely to the ground.

"Yendin," Valerie sobbed as the animal crashed, bounced, and rolled limply. A flash of rage lent her the strength to shove the rifle toward him. Its tip volleyed erratically, then glided beneath the hem of Toddwell-Hillary's shirt.

The man cursed harshly, blood streaking his face, and turned his attention fully to Valerie. She read murder in eyes designed for eternal peace. Pain screamed through her left hand, and the muscles in her right arm throbbed a sympathetic chorus of agony. A weight slammed onto her left forearm, and she startled backward before her mind identified Yendin.

The mynax looped a paw through the trigger, even as a violent twist by Toddwell-Hillary finally broke Valerie's grip. His foot shot behind her, and she tumbled to the ground, cringing as she anticipated the first bullet.

The gunshot exploded in her ears, and she curled fetally

against certain anguish. The pain proved less than she expected; she could not even tell where the bullet had hit. *Am I dead?* The ground quaked, unaccompanied by sound; her aching ears would not admit any. She fought muscles tightened to inflexibility unable to move, though she did manage to raise her eyes.

Toddwell-Hillary lay still on the ground, the tiny entrance hole in his chin belying the splattered gore scattered beyond his ruined head. Yendin squatted between her and the corpse, sucking on an awkwardly dangling paw. The gun lay on the ground nearby. The elves moved toward them cautiously, all except for the parents of the sacrifice who remained in place, rocking the body of the boy and crooning as if pacifying an infant with a lullaby.

Valerie lay still, terror draining from her in a rabid burst of tears. She felt like an infant herself, desperate for the security of her mother's arms and the succor that only her father's mild voice could bring. She wanted David, too, hating herself for the worry she had inflicted upon him. He had clearly believed the fur synthetic, had picked a special present because he loved her. She owed him an apology.

Elves funneled into the caves to attend the captured mynax, animated conversation reverberating through the confines. Ailonwenn remained behind with two other elves, one of them the man Valerie had seen playing so joyfully with his young daughter. *My change-partner.* Valerie shook her head at the irony. *He knew from her first day that she shared none of his blood, yet he is no less her father. They are no less a family.* Suddenly, so many of her beliefs seemed shallow and unjust.

"Your so-called parents," Ailonwenn said. "Toracillius and Rebtarin. As promised."

Valerie glanced at the strangers at his side, their expressions polite but grim. The female bore hair the same dark brown as her own, worn in the shaggy, elven style. Here, Valerie found her own small nose and high-set ears. The male was a blond, his mildly slanted eyes and long, slender fingers the source of her own. Valerie next glanced at the mourning parents at the farthest edge of the meadow, watched them grieve for their real son while their blood child lay, despised, near the cave that had housed his immorality. She returned her attention to the closer elves, nodding to each in turn. "Thank you for giving me life. Now that I almost lost it, it's a gift I've learned to treasure. The best birthday present anyone has ever received—though most don't appreciate it."

"You're welcome," Toracillius said, the words inadequate but all that seemed possible.

"But," Valerie added. "My parents are back on Man's World." She trained a steady gaze on Ailonwenn. "And so is my life."

Ailonwenn's grin seemed to encompass his entire face, though something took away from the happiness he should embrace wholeheartedly, if not from her decision than from winning a tired argument. She attributed his reticence to the death of one of their own. Or, perhaps, he could even feel sorry for Thomas Toddwell-Hillary.

Rebtarin glanced toward the meadow's edge, not wholly able to hide her relief. Surely, she had worried for losing her child, the one she had raised since birth. Valerie could scarcely believe she had once considered tearing a five-year-old from the only parents she had ever known.

Ailonwenn took Valerie's bleeding hand. "I wish I could heal you, but . . ."

Valerie finished for him. ". . . your magic doesn't work on elven changelings."

"I'm sorry." Ailonwenn clamped a cloth over the injury.

"It'll heal." Valerie looked at Yendin. The mynax raised sad eyes to her, voicing tiny grunts of sorrow. He still clenched his paw, wrenched or broken when it wedged in the trigger guard. "You can help Yendin, though."

Ailonwenn frowned. "I shouldn't, but I will for you." He reached down to the mynax, and Yendin held out his arms for comforting. Ailonwenn did not heft the animal, however, only touched the injury as if doing so might burn him.

Irritated by Ailonwenn's lack of sympathy, Valerie

cradled the mynax, and Yendin snuggled into her arms. Ailonwenn muttered a few words, stroking the injured appendage without affection. It quivered, seeming to straighten even as Valerie watched. "Good-bye, Yendin," she whispered. "I'll come back and visit. I promise."

Yendin nestled his head against her chin and chuckled deep in his throat, a sad sound.

"Is he all right?"

Ailonwenn refused to look at the mynax. "I'm afraid he no longer exists. He broke the law, and now he's outcast."

Shocked, Valerie's mouth fell open. "But he saved—"

"He killed. We can't allow him among us any longer."

Valerie argued Yendin's case as the mynax could not. "It was an accident. He didn't mean to kill anyone. Did you, Yendin?"

Ailonwenn said something in elven.

Yendin lowered his head and responded with a single word.

Ailonwenn's eyes blazed. "He says no accident. He deliberately pulled that trigger, and he understood the result."

"But he's a hero," Valerie started, then stopped. She cuddled the satiny body and dared to hope. "Could I . . . may I . . . take him with me? Killing's against our morality, too, but we allow it in self-defence." She did not bother to add that human law did not extend to animals.

Yendin clung.

Ailonwenn's brows shot up. "Why not? Just one can't upset the balance of nature." He muttered, "More than mankind already has." Finally, he smiled. "Good-bye, Valerie Roberts." A catch at the end suggested he wished he could bid the best to the mynax as well. But he said nothing more.

"Good-bye, Ailonwenn." Valerie hugged Yendin, knowing young children learned languages quickly. She had watched a three-year-old adopted from Russia learn to speak fluent English in weeks. Only then, she recalled the joy and pride in the eyes of that girl's new parents. *Real parents, not plastic.* Valerie felt certain Yendin would learn to communicate as well in his new world as his old.

Cradling her new charge, Valerie lowered her head, imagining the rainbow cave that would take her back to familiar reality. To her real and natural parents. And to David.

Don't Miss These Exciting DAW Anthologies

SWORD AND SORCERESS
Marion Zimmer Bradley, editor
☐ Book XIV   UE2741—$5.99

OTHER ORIGINAL ANTHOLOGIES
Mercedes Lackey, editor
☐ SWORD OF ICE: And Other Tales of Valdemar   UE2720—$5.99

Martin H. Greenberg, editor
☐ CELEBRITY VAMPIRES   UE2667—$4.99
☐ VAMPIRE DETECTIVES   UE2626—$4.99
☐ WEREWOLVES   UE2654—$5.50
☐ WHITE HOUSE HORRORS   UE2659—$5.99
☐ ELF FANTASTIC   UE2736—$5.99

Martin H. Greenberg & Lawrence Schimel, editors
☐ TAROT FANTASTIC   UE2729—$5.99
☐ THE FORTUNE TELLER   UE2748—$5.99

Mike Resnick & Martin Greenberg, editors
☐ RETURN OF THE DINOSAURS   UE2753—$5.99
☐ SHERLOCK HOLMES IN ORBIT   UE2636—$5.50

Richard Gilliam & Martin H. Greenberg, editors
☐ PHANTOMS OF THE NIGHT   UE2696—$5.99

Norman Partridge & Martin H. Greenberg, editors
☐ IT CAME FROM THE DRIVE-IN   UE2680—$5.50

Buy them at your local bookstore or use this convenient coupon for ordering.

PENGUIN USA P.O. Box 999—Dep. #17109, Bergenfield, New Jersey 07621

Please send me the DAW BOOKS I have checked above, for which I am enclosing
$_____ (please add $2.00 to cover postage and handling). Send check or money
order (no cash or C.O.D.'s) or charge by Mastercard or VISA (with a $15.00 minimum). Prices and
numbers are subject to change without notice.

Card #_____ Exp. Date _____
Signature_____
Name_____
Address_____
City _____ State _____ Zip Code _____

For faster service when ordering by credit card call **1-800-253-6476**

Allow a minimum of 4-6 weeks for delivery. This offer is subject to change without notice.